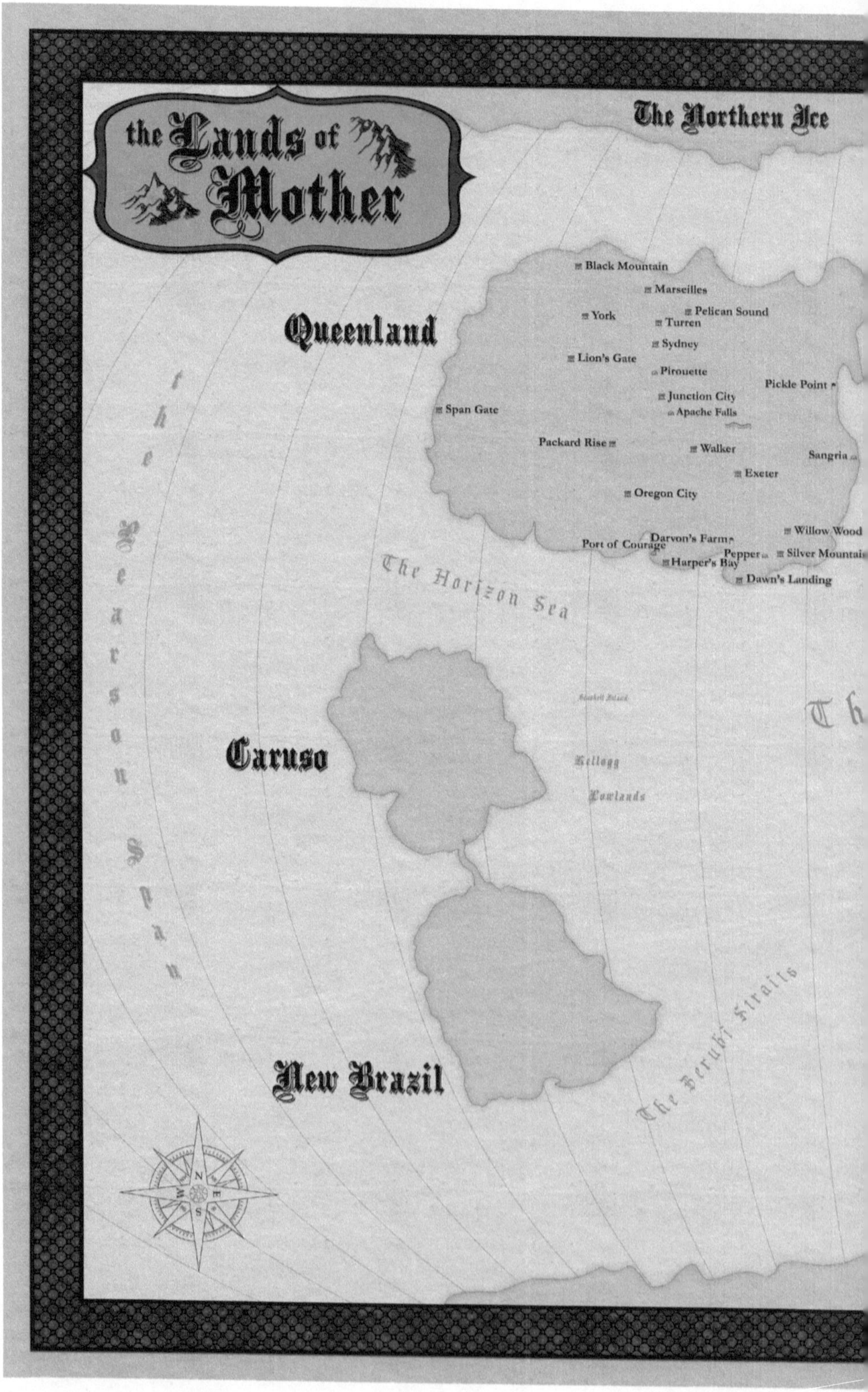

the Lands of Mother
The Northern Ice
Queenland
Black Mountain
Marseilles
York
Pelican Sound
Turren
Sydney
Lion's Gate
Pirouette
Pickle Point
Junction City
Span Gate
Apache Falls
Packard Rise
Walker
Sangria
Exeter
Oregon City
Willow Wood
Darvon's Farm
Port of Courage
Pepper
Silver Mountain
Harper's Bay
Dawn's Landing
The Horizon Sea
the Pearson Span
Caruso
Kellogg
Lowlands
New Brazil
The Berubi Straits
N E S W

Dakota
Great Sea
the Pearson Span
The Emerald Ocean
Eagle Islands
New Texas
Sea of Storms
The Southern Ice
Legend
Village
Larger City
Capital
Battlefield
Point of Interest
Road
River
Mountains
Hills
Forests
Sites & Features to Be Found Within the Lands of Mother

Lands of Mother

Jon Latham

DEDICATION

FOR TRISTON

Acknowledgements

A huge thanks to my friends Nancy Einertson and Cindy Shaw for their diligence in making it through the draft, providing input and still calling me friend.

To Dan Dunklee for believing in the project and the hard edit.

To Steven Hammond for the wood burning and cover artwork.

To Joshua Muster and Chris Estep for putting the map together.

Mother

June 28th, 531
Queenland
Landing Road

The King had not particularly cared for this ride. He could not remember a more troubled one. Even the Own were somber, knowing what he was about to do. He had left his wife and son at the breakfast table in tears, as even they knew. Now, as it drew upon sup, he was finally approaching Dawn's Landing. The parchment from His Holiness had arrived last evening with the Sisterhood's verdict and the sentence His Holiness had pronounced.

He had grown up in a small village, the eldest of two children. His parents were good and honest people, and they instilled into him the need for honor and integrity. Most of the punishment he and his sister received from their parents was related to their character. If the two broke something, neither his mom nor dad made a big deal of it, but if what they broke was their word, or they made a decision that hurt another, or if they lied, the punishment would last for weeks at a time.

Neither parent ever raised a hand in anger, nor did they as much as scold. Punishment consisted of denying them things that they liked. Certain desserts were forbidden, or playing with their best friend, or family game night. They both knew they were wrong, so they took their punishment in a way they knew their parents would approve of, with honesty and integrity, never trying to avoid the punishment.

He had tried to be the parent to his son that his parents had been to him, and had criticized himself on occasion for not handling things in a way that would make his parents proud. Four words were forbidden when he was growing up, and he had made sure he had never uttered them to his son. His parents had never said the words 'Because I said so' to him or his sister. They never even implied it. When he or Sandra would ask a question, they would answer with truth on every occasion and then they would deal with whatever pain or confusion that truth caused. He didn't ever remember hearing 'Because I'm the parent', or 'For your own good' either.

Sir Kevin of the King's Own, his personal guard, rode on his left side and his niece on his right. She must have looked over at him more than a hundred times during the ride wanting to say something reassuring, but knowing as well, there really was nothing to be said.

As they approached the gate, he turned to his niece, "I must ask a favor of you, Marie."

"Uncle?"

"On the new day I would like you to ride with the train and express my apologies to Darvon. We are supposed to hunt this weekend, but this will bind me to the Landing for at least a week."

"It will be done, Uncle. I'm sorry this came to be."

"It is distasteful, but she brought it upon herself. It must be done. His Holiness has pronounced her sentence."

While the rest of his command began setting up camp inside the Beast wall the King and the Own entered the gate and rode directly to the stables, where their horses were tended to by the stable master, himself. They picked up bicycles and began the ride to the carpenters to pick up the block.

With the block tied to the back of Kevin's bike, they began the last leg of their journey, the ride to the sisterhood. When they arrived, the Own placed the block over the grate leading to the city sewers while the King walked up the marble walkway. Many of the sisters looked upon him with sadness as he passed, some would touch his arm, but he didn't acknowledge any of them. He was about to do something that had never been done in the history of Mother and he was not inclined to be social.

He climbed the stairs to the apartments of the Holiness, went to his knee and knocked on the door. The door opened almost immediately, "My King, it is good to see you well. Please rise. Allow me to get my robe."

The King watched as the Holiness donned his blue robe that was significant to his confronting a criminal with the verdict and sentence. The two of them left the apartments together and began descending the stairs. At the main floor they were joined by High Sister Tillie and descended again to the prison level. The King had never been in the prison level of any sisterhood and was more than surprised at what he saw.

The prison guards were sisters, and not muscular bulky sisters but normal sisters, most of which were rather young. He knew that the prisoners were allowed out of the cells to the exercise room. He couldn't imagine it being difficult to get past these tiny women. But, he also knew there had never been a reported escape in the history of the sisterhood.

"Sister Delaney, we are here to retrieve Pamela Canton and impose her sentence," Sister Tillie told the petite Sister at the desk.

"Yes, High Sister. Right this way," Sister Delaney responded.

The Sister led the way down the hallway, past the cells containing those responsible of various crimes to the last cell on the left and opened the door. The sister walked in and announced the King, His Holiness, and the High Sister. The prisoner stayed in the bed and looked over at them.

"I am going to burn you all when I get out of here," she said, "And make no mistake, I will get out of here. I will burn your families and every friend you have ever had."

"I announced His Holiness, please show him the respect he deserves," Sister Delaney said to the woman.

"I am the Queen of Mother, you stupid slut. Get on your knees when you talk to me," the prisoner responded.

Tiny little Sister Delaney walked over to the bed, causing the prisoner to jump up and go right away to her knees. Sister Delaney stood next to the prisoner and faced His Holiness.

"Pamela Canton," began the Holiness, "You have been found guilty of seventeen counts of murder and three counts of murder on a mass scale, and I hereby sentence you to death by means of beheading, to be carried out immediately."

"I am the Queen, dumb shit! You won't even be able to survive without me."

"Perhaps not, but over three thousand people didn't survive with you," The Holiness responded.

The High Sister and his Holiness led the way up the staircase to the front of the sisterhood, followed by the prisoner and her guard, and the

King brought up the rear. Before they walked outside, the procession stopped and waited for two sisters coming down the hall with hand and foot wraps. The prisoner saw them and attempted to bolt, but Sister Delaney caught her with one hand under the left arm, swung her and with her right hand, pinched the prisoner's neck causing her to crumble in pain. The two sisters hurriedly wrapped her feet and hands, leaving her head and neck free.

"Please, Brent," cried the prisoner, "Help me. Slay these horrible people and free me. I will make it worth your while. You lust for me; I know you do. Help me and I'm yours."

The two sisters lifted the prisoner and carried her through the door to the block. The Holiness and the High Sister followed, the King came last.

The prisoner's rants and raves were drawing onlookers and soon a crowd was gathering. The sisters dragged her kicking and screaming and draped her head over the block. The King walked up to the prisoner and drew his long sword. *Please, Mother. Make my stroke true.*

"Brent, please. You know me. These charges aren't. . . "

The King hung his head as he watched his Queen's head tumble and roll. He felt suddenly filthy and in need of a shower. His blade was covered with blood and he tried to think of the means to clean it in an attempt to get his stomach not to heave at what he had just done.

"May Mother have mercy on us," he said to all.

The onlookers were not pleased at being there. Many were retching and heaving, some were becoming doomsayers, warning of Mother's revenge. Most were just sobbing and hugging each other. The Holiness had walked out to the bench which sat in the only patch of grass left at the sisterhood, removed his sandals and stared at the city. The High Sister was instructing the other sisters to take the body to the grievers. She picked up the head and followed them. The Own washed off the block and the marble walkway as best they could, and then attached the block to the back of one of the bikes and one of them rode off with it toward the carpenters.

The King just stood there with his head hung. His captain took his sword from him silently and walked to one of the granite benches and sat and began to clean it. The King's niece was beside him looking at his eyes.

"It had to be you, Uncle," she said, "It is high treason for another to do. I will walk with you to the Mansion, so that you may clean the splatter."

Marie slipped her arm through his and they made their way to the Queen's Mansion. They didn't talk, so Marie tried to decide how this would affect life on Mother. Droughts would surely be a problem with no Queen to power the flow of the rivers and streams. Wilders and outlaws would run rampant. How long would the people's need last? Would it be Pamela's normal lifespan before Mother would grace them with another Queen?

They reached the mansion and the entire staff was downstairs waiting for word. At the sight of the King, Pierre and Fred took a knee where they had been standing near the table, Margaret and Yanina sobbed in each other's arms, Theresa's head buried itself in the shoulder of Arnold. Kristen knelt at the foot of the stairs, emotionless.

"My King needs a shower," Marie said to Kristen.

"Right away, Princess," Kristen answered and ran up the stairs.

Marie led the King up the steps, toward his room and when they entered, the King went to one knee in silent prayer to Mother.

"See to his needs," she said to Kristen as she made her way back downstairs. When she got to the table, she removed her head gear and asked if there was coffee. Theresa brought her a cup and asked what His Majesty would have for sup. Marie asked her to prepare something light in the way of fish or fowl. She wrote out a note and asked Fred to deliver it to the Commander of the City Watch. She looked at Pierre and asked him to box up the Queen's belongings and have Fred take them to the sisterhood.

Margaret approached and informed her that she could no longer work at the Mansion, citing nightmares and sadness. Marie assured her she understood and asked her to let the sisterhood know so that they could locate a replacement.

Marie wasn't sure where to go from here or what, if anything, could be said to calm the populace. One week is the longest period of time Mother had been without a queen and then only because Queen Patricia had landed in the plains of New Texas. It took that week to find her.

The Kings of the Lands had a rough time with looting, as well as outlaws and wilders during that period and she didn't anticipate it would be any different this time. Queen Pamela was the only queen Marie had ever served. She was too young during Queen Shirley's reign to even know what a queen was or what she did, but every one she talked to throughout her life had assured her the former Queens of Mother were not to be compared to Pamela, all having been good and powerful women.

His Holiness waited in Sister Tillie's office for her to return from the grievers. Mother had given him good news indeed. The fear of having to wait the entire natural lifespan of Pamela for the arrival of a new Queen was now gone. Mother had provided him with the name of the new Queen. The water would continue along its normal path. The clinics would not run out of Queenstone. Everything would return to normal and hopefully, he and the King would be able to put some fail-safes in place before she became fully to power. Preventing another Pamela.

He would have Sister Tillie notify the road sisters to pass the word, and the King himself was at the Queen's Mansion, so it would be easy to get him the word. It would be so kind of Mother to sweep the new Queens right into the sisterhood, but of course that never happens. He chuckled to himself. He had finished the parchments, so he summoned Sister Cindy to run upstairs and fetch his seal. Once his seal was attached, the parchments would be shipped to the other five kingdoms, in the event the Queen landed there.

While he was waiting for Sister Cindy to return, Sister Tillie arrived. She was more than overjoyed at the news and couldn't wait to spread the word, so he allowed her to run to the mansion and notify the King, but that she needed to get right back to help him with the notices being sent to other sisterhoods within Queenland.

Marie and the King sat on the patio, each with their own piece of the newspaper and a glass of tea trying to decide which theater to attend as a distraction.

"Another thing we must do before we head back to Silver Mountain," the King began, "Is run over and see your parents. She was a thorn in my side when we were growing up, but I miss her. You will not repeat that."

"You two are ridiculous, Uncle. Each time I see her, she asks how you are and then tells me not to tell you she asked."

Both of their heads turned at the sounds of the screams coming from within the house and everyone was hugging each other, jumping up and down and clapping like a bunch of school kids. Marie noticed Sister Tillie in the midst of them, trying to free herself from the hugging and make her way to the patio.

"His Holiness has given us good news, My King. We have a new Queen,"

Caruso
Kingston, Dock Terminal One

Brittany Stone was the self-made Queen of Mother. She held more power than any ten wilders and could bend others to her will, including most of the Earth animals. The animals of Mother presented a problem, but they would eventually come around. She would not be recognized by the people, but that would change. They would soon not have a choice; his death would prevent him from naming another queen. Eventually, Pamela would mis-step one too many times, leaving Mother with no one. Brittany would step up to fill the void.

Thomas, King of Caruso, had been hounding her incessantly for the last year, and needed to be disposed of. He was making it very hard to build an army. She had built one though. Ten thousand men, sixty wilders and three hundred cats. It would be a simple matter to lure him away from the Kingston Sisterhood. Once he was deep enough in the Plains of Conga, her forces would wipe him out.

She had left instructions with her generals. King Thomas should be dead by sunset.

Earth

May 18th, 2125
Phoenix, Arizona

Melanie Thurss sat at her desk computer entering the last of the week's bills. She glanced over her shoulder and saw Matty still flustered, trying to do his homework without her help. It was the way she had always taught him. Do his best by himself and then she would sit with him and they would go over it together, helping him through the difficult parts.

Melanie wasn't an independent woman. She depended on Dan and was perfectly happy with her life and his place as the bread winner. The only job she had ever held was at The Burger Hut to pay for her car and insurance as a teen-ager. That's where she met Dan. His idea of a good meal was a 'Double B' Burger' on the way home from work. They would laugh each time he came in at his lack of desire to cook. He said it was a time thing. He was just too busy. He even worked when he got home. Dan was an architect.

She was only nineteen when they married and within a year, Brie was born. Any hope of furthering her education went out the door, but Dan made more money than they needed anyway, so she settled into the routine of a stay at home mom. Todd and Matthew came along and she stopped thinking of anything other than being a mother and a wife.

She kept herself in the best shape she could for Dan. She didn't want to be one of those wives that stopped caring about their bodies after they landed a husband. She loved him. He was more than just her husband, and she thought it her responsibility to be attractive for him.

She wasn't skinny by any means, but her legs were long and spindly, not very shapely, and her breasts? They were nothing more than ordinary. She didn't think she was attractive at all, but she still got attention when out and about. She was a fair-skinned redhead with high cheek bones and big eyes. She thought her nose to be enormous, but apparently it was just her that felt that way.

She was thirty-five and still found her life exciting. Dan kept her entertained on his days off with hikes or camping or simple walks in the park and she seemed to still excite him too, even after sixteen years of marriage. All in all, her life was good.

The kids were always laughing and having a good time as well. She loved her family.

She finished the bills and made her way in to clean up the dinner dishes. It was just her and Matt here, right now. Depending on how long Dan was going to be with Todd, and how long it would take for Matty's homework, she may actually have a few minutes to crack her book. She finished loading the dishwasher and wiped her hands. Dropping the towel on the floor, she grabbed the counter to steady herself. She was very dizzy. She looked at Matty and he was looking at her with a frightened stare. Why does he look blurry? What is happening? She tried to run to Matty, but fell to the floor.

Mother

Queenland
Darvon's Farm

"Not this year, little one," Darvon said to his son, "You are not of age, yet. Besides, who other than you can take care of your mother while I'm away?"

"Papa, she has magic. She doesn't need me. I can hunt. I've been practicing."

"No arguments," Darvon said sternly. He watched as his son pouted away. He was a good boy, but way too young to be traipsing around Queenland with a bow and quiver. He had told himself he would take Bobby out one day on a play hunt for rabbits or squirrels, but one thing had led to another and it never took place. This year when the harvest was done he would put everything else aside and take him.

He picked up the paper that had come on the last day's train and sat in his favorite chair, kicked up his feet and read the headline.

Queen Pamela Guilty!!

Good, what an evil woman the Queen had become. She had no respect for life. She flooded three villages and killed thousands for no reason. He was just about to start the story when his wife called from the kitchen.

"Breakfast is ready, honey. Will you fetch Bobby, please?"

Darvon sat the paper down and walked to Bobby's room. He found the boy making his bed and helped him finish, and the two went to the dining table and found waffles awaiting them. Bobby ran to the kitchen and grabbed the maple syrup, but didn't make it even two steps before his mother switched the jug with the peach topping. The poor boy was having a horrible morning.

Desiree sat next to Bobby, across from Darvon and asked, "What chores have you today, honey?"

"We are harvesting the fruit on the North Forty, today. I have a buyer in Oregon City that wants three bushels. I hope to have them ready by the time the train arrives," He looked at her, then at Bobby, then back at her. As silently as possible, he said to her, "Guilty."

Desiree's heart skipped a beat. What would they do without a Queen? How would the people of Mother even survive? The Queenstone at the clinics draw from her. Most of the rivers and streams that feed the wells would dry up. There were too many things that happened on Mother that drew their power from her.

"Has she been sentenced?"

"I have not read the story yet. Bobby and I will leave right after breakfast for the North Forty. The paper is on my chair."

The rest of breakfast was quiet, with each of them contemplating what would happen. Bobby, being seven, was not yet subject to the worries of the world, his biggest concern was trying to eat around the chunky parts of the topping.

SWEPT

Queenland
Darvon's Farm

The day was warm. There was a gentle rustling of the leaves as the summer breeze made its way through the treetops, providing a peaceful clicking sound. The sky was cloudless and the birds were resting in the branches and on the ground, pecking at this bug or that seed.

A few squirrels busied themselves chasing each other or feeding from the droppings of the trees and collecting for later. The birds would take flight when they approached, not wanting to challenge the larger aggressor. On occasion, one of the birds would get brave and drop to the ground near a squirrel, causing it to leap in fright, but then the bird would fly back off to light on an overhead branch. A deer entered the clearing, causing all to scramble, but the deer stopped short of grazing, staring at the figure on the ground.

All, in fact, stayed clear of the woman lying in the middle of the clearing. Humans after all, could not be trusted and were always trying to chase them or catch them. They could feel the heat from her body, so they knew she wasn't dead, so the best course was to stay clear. They all scattered or flew off at the signs of movement.

Melanie awoke face down as if she had fallen. Fright took over immediately as she had no idea where she was. The last thing she remembered, she had just finished doing the dinner dishes and was on her way to the table to help Matt with his homework when she got dizzy. Her face was tingling as well as her hands and forearms as if she had been lying here for a long period and they had fallen asleep. She rubbed her hands together and patted her face as she stood up and surveyed her surroundings. She was smelling something sweet, a strange aroma that she hadn't smelled before. There was also a whirring sound that made her think a helicopter was nearby. The blades weren't thundering rapidly, however. More like it hadn't taken off yet or had just landed.

She wasn't near Phoenix, it was 105 in Phoenix today, and it couldn't be more than 75 or 80 here. "Hello," she said loudly, but no response came. *Okay, calm down. Think. Did someone drug me? How did this happen?* She looked herself over. She was still wearing the shorts she was wearing at home, the same white blouse, the same socks and shoes. She still had her wedding ring, which would have been the most valuable possession, so this wasn't a robbery. She checked her right rear pocket and pulled out the receipt for the milk she had bought earlier at the gas station.

"Matty," She screamed out.

"Matthew," She repeated when no response came the first time.

She was obviously deep in some very thickly wooded area, everything was green high and brown low. Surprisingly there was very little underbrush and no paths. She looked under the trees all the way around and saw nothing and no one. She stood quietly and listened. All she heard was the helicopter, a few chirps and the breeze blowing through the trees. She looked where she had fallen. The only footprints were hers. She looked up. The trees were so thick she couldn't have been brought down through them, or she would have a scratch or two. There were no broken branches or leaves around and there were no broken bones, so she wasn't dropped through.

Realizing how unsure she was how she came to this place, screaming was probably not the best idea she had. She headed the direction of the helicopter, weaving her way between the trees. She knew she needed to get free of these trees. Despite her confusion, she was not as frightened as she had been a few moments ago. She felt she was supposed to be here, she just wasn't sure how she knew that, or where here was exactly.

The Beasts were finishing their meal and became uneasy and agitated. They were large cumbersome animals with brownish hair and a stub for a tail. Each paw had three, twelve inch claws protruding from them, to hold the prey in place, as they ripped the meat free. The underbelly was hairless for the most part, as their legs were so short in proportion to the rest of the body that the stomach dragged the ground more often than not. The head of the Beasts bore a snout full of sharp, yellowed teeth. They used those teeth to fulfill their function in life, which was to kill and eat. Their capacity for thought was minimal, but then they didn't need thought. They knew how to eat and they knew how to drink. Nothing else was important. The uneasiness and agitation came from their sense of the intruder. The vile little thing that will deny them even more.

This little thing kept them from getting to the other little things. Always changing the land so that they couldn't get around easily. Always making the ground raised so that they couldn't climb. The little things tasted good, but the Beasts couldn't get to them anymore. They were either staying up high or behind those walls, but the Beasts remembered the taste. This little thing isn't behind a wall. Killing her will be easy and it will end the walls and the high lairs if they can get her before she hides.

Melanie had walked for some time. She was getting closer to the helicopter, but because of the thickness of the trees, couldn't even see the sun. She kept the sound to her front, and made her way around and through the trees. She was feeling a sensation on her skin. It was creepy. It felt like the air was passing through her very skin. From the inside out. She was getting thirsty as well, which made her wonder how long she had been lying there before she awoke. All she had to do was get into the open to get her bearings. The initial fright was gone, but she remained somewhat confused. It was time to take her mind off of it so she began thinking of what Dan must be going through, fretting and wondering what had happened to her. What were the kids thinking? Are they thinking their mom ran away? Matt had been looking at her and saw what was happening to her. Either that or it was happening to him, too. The look of fear on his face was not something she was going to forget. He must have told his dad. He knows I didn't run out on him, I know he does.

Brie was out with her friends, and she was a very curious girl anyway, so when she got home she would have asked where her mom was over a hundred times. Thankfully, Dan was on his way home with Todd, so Matt wouldn't have been alone long if, and it's a big if, he wasn't around here, too.

She looked down at her hand and saw that she had been eating something. It looked to be some sort of fruit and was positively thirst quenching. *Where did I get this? How did I know it was edible?* She looked at the trees and realized she was now in what appeared to be an orchard.

The area had a definite familiarity, she must have been here or somewhere near here before. In any event, she could see that the orchard was ending, opening to a meadow of sorts and she heard a child's laughter. She moved off the path and began inching her way towards the sounds. When she got where she could see, she went down on her belly to watch and listen. There is that tingling again and the sensation that she was supposed to be here. Was she dreaming? Was that other life a dream?

The whirring was very close, but she now had doubts that it was a helicopter. The child, appeared to be a boy of ten or so with a bowl haircut and he was tossing fruit to a man, who was catching them in a basket. Must be his father. Would he know how I got here? She was beginning to be unsure if anything had been done to her. She didn't feel beaten, she definitely hadn't been raped, her arms weren't sore as they would have been had she been dragged and she was beginning to doubt drugs, as she woke alert. The only thing she really felt was confusion.

Staying here on her belly was not going to work. The feelings and thoughts passing through her were just confusing her more, so she came to the decision she would need to confront the man. As she began to rise she felt warm breath on her back, even penetrating her shirt. She turned and came face to snout with the largest dog or wolf she had ever seen. The dog was shoulder high to her, and she was five and a half feet tall. It was huge and frightening. The animal just panted and looked at her. Fear surrounded her. She was frozen in place and couldn't even run. She just stared at the animal as it stared back at her. Then the boy was there petting it and as he did, the dog or wolf calmed and sat.

The boy said nothing, just looked at her and at the man who was looming over her, and back at her. Both the man and the boy were in very colorful outfits that looked like they had been patched together without any noticeable pattern. Much to her surprise and concern, neither looked particularly surprised to see her. They looked at her as if she was their neighbor, but she had no idea why.

She decided to do away with formalities, "Why am I here? Did you bring me here?"

The man responded with an unfamiliar accent, "Things are not as you see them. Come."

It was a command not a request, and she felt she should be upset at the tone but had no idea why. She knew she wouldn't get anywhere out here by herself so she followed the man and the boy. The boy led the way and the man followed her with the dog thing. As they climbed the knoll she looked out on where she had been and it was endless trees behind them. There were hills, knolls and meadows in the direction they were walking and a stream weaving its way towards a small lake in the flat lands to her right. It looked like something out of a jigsaw puzzle. No city or town visible. Then she saw it. The whirring was coming from the largest windmill she had ever seen. It seemed twenty stories high.

"May I use your cell?" She asked the man.

The man kept walking without answering. *Guess not.* As they walked, more dog things showed up, appearing out of the woods. Many of them.

"What breed of dog are these and why do you have so many?" She asked.

"Not dogs," the man answered.

She thought about pursuing it, but realistically she didn't care what he called them. She did care about one thing, though. She wanted to know what had happened to her and where her husband and kids were.

"Please. I miss my family; can you please take me home? If you tell me where I am, I can direct you there. I will pay you when we get there."

"No! No home," the man said.

"What? What do you mean by that? You're never taking me home? Can you call me a cab, at least?"

"Home is gone."

She was getting nowhere with this buffoon and he was quite obviously not the brains of the outfit. She decided to wait and try to plead her case with whomever was in charge.

As they reached the top of a hill she saw a small house that was surrounded on all four sides by a canopy about two feet off the ground.

The house was more a hut, with mud and straw being used as plaster or mortar holding the wood beams together. The roof was made of what looked like thatch and bark and more mud and straw. It appeared to be pushed into a hill that flattened on top like a mesa. There was a barn of sorts and hundreds of baskets. There were assorted pens that had a few cows, some pigs and chickens. There were also many solar panels on the slopes of the hills. She thought the combination to be a little funny looking.

There were many horses, tied to posts in front of the house. The boy took off running, followed by a few of the dogs. Most stayed with her.

There was a dirt road that ran in front of the house extending into the hills on the left and along the stream and lake to her right. There didn't appear to be any intersections. There was also what looked like a beach or sandbox next to the lake.

From the left came an endless train of horse drawn wagons and her first thought was that this was an Amish community. Until she saw the men and women on horseback wearing what appeared to be some sort of uniform and appeared to be some kind of authority. In her present situation, that was just what the doctor ordered. The wagons would pass the house by the time they reached it. She decided to go for it and took off running towards them, yelling for help.

As she looked over her shoulder to see if the man was closing on her, she was surprised to see that not only was he not chasing her, he didn't seem to be the least bit concerned that she was running. He kept his head faced toward the house and continued to walk at the same pace he had been. She was being chased, no paced, by several of the non-dogs. They could have dropped her in seconds, but they just loped along with her, not more than five feet away, with their heads turning every direction as if they were looking for commands.

She decided it would be prudent not to antagonize the man or the dogs, so she stopped. The animals stopped, as well, continuing to watch all around. She glanced toward the wagons and saw that several of the uniforms were making their way toward her, at a quick pace. She had a sudden feeling of safety, as if nothing bad could happen to her now. She had no idea what prompted the feeling, but for the first time since she had awakened she felt totally at ease.

As the uniforms approached, she got her first look at the actual clothing. The torso and the rest of the body were covered with a leathery type of material, with occasional bulges where it appeared something had been stitched into it. *This is body armor.* The stitched areas covered the pelvic area, chest, outer sides of the arms and legs. The shoes or boots were made of the same material as was the helmet. Each of them had a bowie knife strapped to their leg, a sword at their belt, and a longer sword strapped on their back. One had a crossbow attached to the saddle. *That one was a female.* She had the strangest feeling she had stumbled upon a renaissance festival of sorts. Yet, she felt she knew these people. *What in the world was wrong with her? How could she possibly know them?*

She didn't feel threatened, but at the same time she came upon the realization that it was not them that made her feel at ease. It was the animals; the dogs. She didn't know why, but she felt they were there to protect her.

One of the males was darker skinned, "Are you harmed, my lady?"

"I am not, but I have been kidnapped and I would like to file charges. Are you the local police?"

The look of bewilderment on the man was obvious. The woman, who looked more like a child, kept her eyes focused on Melanie, saying nothing. The light skinned man clapped his hands twice and pointed towards the house and the dogs immediately took off in that direction.

The spokesman continued, "I am Jeremy Slater of Road Safety, this is Thomas Peron of my company as well, and this is Princess Marie of the King's Own. We are none of us familiar with the police you mentioned or claim you make. Might we have your name and origin?"

Oh my God, are you kidding me? Where the hell am I? "I am Melanie Thurss, and I'm from Phoenix, Arizona. Is there someone else. . .?"

Before she could finish the question the female climbed down off her horse, pulled the sword from her back, drove it into the ground, going to one knee, she began rambling about honor and devotion. The two men looked at the Princess with the same stupefied look that Melanie must have had. That didn't last long however, because they both seemed to come upon the same mental disorder as the Princess, and followed suit, both dismounting and kneeling.

The Princess spoke, "May I escort you to the sisters, Majesty?"

"Melanie! Not Majesty, will the sisters help me get home?"

"No, Majesty. No one can help with that," came the girl's reply.

"What will you have us do, Princess?" asked Thomas, looking back and forth between the princess and Melanie.

"Ride with haste, inform the sisters that our Queen has settled," The Princess responded.

With that, Jeremy and Thomas mounted and rode hard at the wagons. Princess Marie let out a blood curdling whistle that caused Melanie to wince and cover her ears. She caught movement out of the corner of her eye and saw the animals returning and quickly. The princess raised her hand and twirled it in a circular motion and the animals began fanning out and circling the two of them. It came to her then that the animals weren't looking for commands earlier, they were looking for threats.

"I don't mind saying, I am a little frightened right now," Melanie said, "Am I in danger?"

"Danger is everywhere Majesty, but I give you my word of honor. No harm will come to you this day, while I and the Protectors live."

"That's a little dramatic. Who are the Protectors?"

"Darvon's pack, Majesty," She pointed at the dog things.

"Why did you say no one could help me get home? Can't we call someone?"

"I have called the sisters, Majesty. They are better equipped to answer your questions."

"Quit calling me that, damn it. I don't like it. My name is Melanie."

"I cannot, Majesty. It would be disrespectful. You are Queen Melanie. Only the King himself may address you otherwise."

Queen......Queen Melanie?

As much as she was liking the sound of that, Melanie was also filled with trepidation. Specifically, what kind of relationship does she supposedly have with this King, and why is everyone so vague about getting her home? Had she herself suffered from something? This girl seemed to know her. Melanie did feel as if she belonged here and the feeling was stronger as each minute passed, but she did have a family. She knew she did. It couldn't have been a dream. Or is she dreaming now? If the Princess was right, her questions were about to be answered as the wagon was approaching.

Jeremy and Thomas dismounted as well as the wagon driver, and all repeated the previous kneeling ceremony. The driver was just a girl that couldn't have been more than fourteen or fifteen. She was wearing shorts and a pullover, both of a brown hue. Pale skinned with very dark brown, not quite black hair. She had gone to both knees and cupped her hands in her lap, bowing her head. *How is she going to be able to answer my questions? What the hell kind of sister is this?*

"You must tell them to rise Majesty, lest they grow old and wither." That came from a woman that emerged from under the covering of the wagon, a woman of about thirty, who wore a very plain gray potato sack of a dress and a white headband.

"Rise," she said, eager to end this charade.

"I will be very glad to answer every question you have Majesty, and I will do my best to put your mind at ease, or at least as much as is possible considering what has happened to you. First, if you will be generous enough to release Jeremy and Thomas that they may return to their duties, and the Princess that she may ride to inform the King of your arrival."

"How do I do that?" asked Melanie as she scratched at her arms and the creepy feeling.

"You say, 'Return to your duties.'"

Doh!!!

"Please return to your duties, and thank you. Princess, please inform the King of my arrival."

What? Why did I say that? Why is this coming so easy to me?

Jeremy and Thomas bowed, mounted and were off, but the Princess didn't move. She looked at the sister and the sister looked back and frowned, "Did you give your oath to the Queen, Princess?"

"I did, Sister Ann. My apologies. The Queen looked confused and vulnerable."

"Naught can be done for it now. Find Sargent Dirk please, and ask him to send someone to notify the King and return to us." She looked back at Melanie, "If it pleases you, Majesty." With that the Princess turned to Melanie. For reason's she couldn't imagine, Melanie nodded and the Princess was off.

"My Queen, I am honored to welcome you to Mother in the name of Supreme High Sister Kai Ming and the Sisterhood," Sister Ann said and then turned to the wagon driver, "Help the Queen into the wagon, Bethany."

"I'm not getting into that wagon," Melanie said, "I'm not doing shit until someone tells me what's going on and why I can't go home."

Bethany pulled steps from under the carriage and placed them so Melanie could easily climb into the wagon. The sister clapped her hands twice and all the Protectors turned to look. She did the circular thing and patted her shoulder and they adjusted to encompass the wagon and laid down, facing away in all directions.

"Please," Sister Ann said, "You need to be sitting to hear this anyway. If you will come inside, I will begin explaining what happened to you. Once you know, we will take any advice you can give us on getting you home."

Sister Ann opened the drape to the covering and Melanie after several seconds of thought, stepped up and through. There were four other 'Sisters' inside. One was writing and three were reading. Sister Ann read the thoughts in Melanie's eyes and explained.

"One of the many duties of the Sisters is keeping the 'Chronicles of Time', as they were named by King David. They are a history of everything that has happened in our land for the last five hundred years. Longer to be precise, by thirty-one. The Sisterhood was started five hundred and twenty-three years ago by Queen Emily. For the eight years prior to that they were just called scribes. Sister Frances here is a scribe," as she pointed at the writer. "She is writing the things you say and that will become the history for the Sisters and Queens of the future.

"The other three sisters you see before you are reading past histories of former Queens, with which they will teach you. We can discuss this more as time goes by. You have more pressing questions I am sure, so please ask."

"Why can't I go back home to my family?" Melanie asked the first question on her mind.

"The home that you remember no longer exists as far as we know. Certainly the people do not. All living creatures were swept from Earth and are randomly settling here. It would appear Man has been given a second chance. The Earth was dying, that seemed to be widely known. What we have learned is that where you were on Earth, at the time, meant nothing as to where and when you settled here. There are documented instances where a man mowing his front yard appeared here fifty years after a woman who was inside cooking his dinner. Yet every settler remembers the exact same date on Earth. May 18, 2125."

Okay, this woman is obviously off her rocker, Melanie thought. She knows something, though. She knows the date I fainted.

"There are also instances where a father at work twenty miles from where his daughter was attending school, settled here three feet from his daughter. There was and is no pattern to the appearances, we have been instructed to quit trying to create one. The only constant is people that were touching at the time, appear at the same time and place here. To give you scope. All the people were swept off Earth at the same instant. The first settler arrived here over 500 years ago. They are still arriving."

Wacko! Gone!

"A good deal of our population have been born here, but we are still getting new settlers. Just before we left Dawn's Landing, a boy was in my chambers that I had never seen before. It turned out he was a new settler as well. Where they show up we cannot pinpoint, nor when."

This is too much. Is there no one that will help me? ...but what if she tells it true?

The tears would not stop, despite her attempts. The thought that she would never see her family again was just too much.

"Can you find out what happened to my family?" She asked the sister.

"Only the King can command our deviance from our normal duties, Majesty. I am sure he will allow us to do this for his Queen, if she were to ask him. The sisters have many duties not just chronicles, and there are not nearly enough of us. If I may Majesty, the sun has left us and I would like to be inside Darvon's Keep soon. The Princess has returned and can handle the Protectors, and I can teach you the etiquette of being a Queen on the way, if it pleases you."

"Very well, but I am no queen and I still have many questions."

"As you wish," Sister Ann nodded to Bethany, and the wagon jerked into motion.

Sister Ann continued, "When you get to the Keep, all will kneel to you. You must wait until they are settled before you give them leave to rise. The first on their knee will look unfavorably on you if slower men do not have to respect you as they have.

"Once formalities are over many will flock to you, wanting to be favored with your protection. You will need twelve men or women for the Queen's Own. I would suggest setting something up with the Princess as a code to tell you who is worthy and who is not. The Princess is wise for her youth and knows a drunkard from a good man. The Princess can pick the guard herself if you will name her your captain."

"Can I do that? I thought she was the King's Guard or whatchamacallit."

"She is. However, Sir Kevin will be happy for her and for himself to be rid of The King's niece. You will need to knight her first. Only knights may be captains. You must ask for her sword, ask her to kneel, place the sword on her shoulder, and ask her this question: Do you Princess Marie, give your oath to the Queen of Mother and no other? When she says yes, however she says it, you need to say I now name you a Knight of Queenland and Captain of the Queen's Own," With that Sister Frances handed her the same words in written form, with instructions to memorize them.

"One more thing Your Majesty, as we are almost there. When we are walking in, some may be without. They will take a knee. It is not necessary to give them leave to rise. They will rise once you pass." She tapped the paper, and Melanie began memorizing the words.

When they arrived, Melanie climbed down with the help of the Princess and immediately asked her for her sword. Princess Marie's eyes got the size of half dollars, but she drew her sword and handed it hilt first to Melanie. It was amazingly light, but she could tell it was also very sturdy and sharp. She hoped she didn't cut the poor girl's ear off.

"To your knee, Princess." Melanie placed the sword on the princess's shoulder and asked, "Do you, Princess Marie, give your oath to the Queen of Mother and no other?"

"With my last breath, I so vow, My Queen."

"I now name you a Knight of Queenland and Captain of the Queen's Own."

"I will not fail you, Majesty. What is your command?" Marie asked eagerly.

"You will choose the Queen's Own and see me safely to Dawn's Landing. You will choose only the best for the Own, whether they be here or elsewhere." *What? Why did I say that?*

"As my Queen commands."

Several people standing outside had witnessed the knighting and began to rib the Princess, which brought a smile to her face, as she turned to lead the procession into the home. She returned the jibes as they were beginning to kneel.

It happened as Sister Ann said it would upon their arrival, with all the kneeling and pleas to get her favor as one of the Queen's Own. Knowing that some would be looking unfavorably on Marie if they were not chosen, she made her first proclamation.

"I have knighted Princess Marie and named her my Captain. I have assigned her the task of selecting the Queen's Own with my wishes for whom will serve. She will make these selections based on those wishes. It will not be a reflection on who you are if you are not selected."

Why am I talking like this?

With that the attention switched to Marie, Melanie and the sisters proceeded into the keep. Melanie was surprised at the size of the keep. From the outside it looked like a shack of a home, but once inside it bore deep into the hills.

The sisters took Melanie into a side room that contained a table and chairs. They placed all their books on the table, and directed Melanie to the head. Sister Ann had a short conversation with a man standing outside the room, and seated herself as well.

"What would you know first, Majesty?" Sister Ann started.

"How soon will I see this King? I need to know about my family."

Sister Cindy replied, "Nothing is more important to the Lands than the Queen, Majesty. As soon as the rider reaches the King, he will take to saddle immediately. We will in all probability meet him on the road on the new day."

Not nearly fast enough, but what could be done? "What is expected of me? Are he and I to be married? Am I to be ' matched ' and bear his children? Because I won't."

One of the sisters whose name she did not yet know, burst out in laughter that prompted a stern look and fist to the table by Sister Ann, "I apologize for Sister Kate, Majesty. She has not been a Sister, but months."

Sister Cindy answered the question, "Majesty, here the King and Queen do not couple. Seldom do they even cross paths unless they summon one another. The Queen resides at Dawn's Landing, but the King's home is miles beyond. Queen Pamela and King Brent met only twice. You have no relationship with the King other than he is your King. You must try to do as he bids and he must do as you bid, but he is wed."

The relief from that bit of information was exhilarating. "Why me? Why am I the Queen?"

"Your name was given us by His Holiness," Sister Ann answered, "He does not share with us how he knows. We believe he also possesses a certain magic or ability that provides him with knowledge that the rest of us don't share."

"Magic? You're shitting me, right? What do you mean, also? There are others that have these abilities?"

"Everyone, Majesty! Everyone here has stronger abilities than they or their ancestors had on Earth. As an example, Darvon's ancestors were wheat farmers in Spain, I believe it was called," she looked to Cindy for confirmation and got a nod. "The man could sprout an apple tree from a stone."

"Many of the doctors believe," Sister Ann continued, "that here on Mother we actually use a larger portion of our brain capacity, allowing us to be wiser and better at what we do than were we on Earth. They also believe not all are using the same portion of the brain. Doctors are firm that there is no such thing as magic. It is their belief that the powers you have, and others don't, comes from the fact that you are using up to twenty percent more of your brain capacity. We sisters don't share that belief. Their theory doesn't explain the wilder."

Marie Mercer, Princess of Queenland, and newly appointed Captain of the Queen's Own sat at the Garcia's kitchen table with two members of Road Safety. The only two she felt acceptable for the Own. Being a member of the Own differed greatly from Road Safety or even the King's forces. She had personally witnessed the two in action in battles with outlaws and on one occasion a wilder. Both were fearless and would not be intimidated by others.

"I must be certain," Marie began, "That you understand what you are accepting when you agree to be a member of the Own. Life as you knew it is over. If the Queen dies and you live, you will be dishonored for the remainder of your days. People, citizens will look upon you with disfavor, your fellow soldiers will view you with scorn and disgust. You will be cast out, ridiculed as a coward and a failure. Your family name will be synonymous with contempt. Yes, it is the ultimate honor to be the Queen's protector, but you must know. . . failure is not conceivable."

Both men sat silently listening to their potential captain, careful not to interrupt, absorbing her words and gaining a certain amount of pride, with each statement. When he was certain the captain was finished, one of the men spoke.

"I can't speak for Will, Highness. As for me? Your words do not frighten me. If the Queen dies and I live, I will have deserved all you have said. There is no chance of that happening, however."

The other man pointed at the speaker, "What he said."

"Raise your left hand and place your right over your heart," Marie said to the first man and he immediately complied.

"My life and my blade belong to the Queen of Mother. I shall not fail her," Marie said. Each of the men in turn repeated the captains words. The Queen's Own now consisted of Captain Marie Mercer, Mitchell Stanton and Willard Hartaugh. The Own were three, and immediately put to the test.

The howl came from the edge of the northern orchards. Marie had come to the Garcia farm enough to know that was a warning from the Protectors.

Two Beasts burst through the tree line, headed right at the farm. Marie pushed Mrs. Garcia and her son toward the keep. "Where might we hide the Queen?" she asked.

"All the way down the right tunnel, last room on the left," Mrs. Garcia pointed, "In here Bobby, now," she said to her son, pushing him into the laundry room. Marie thought that to be curious, but it left her mind as quickly as it entered as she, Willard and Mitchell charged toward Pamela.

Before Melanie could ask her next question, Princess Marie came bursting through the door and ran right at Melanie followed by two uniforms. Melanie flinched in fright and threw up her arms in defense. She was lifted from the chair easily.

"With me," Marie said to the sisters. She took Melanie's arm and tugged her out of the room with the help of one of the uniforms. Melanie found herself running between the two to keep from being pulled down. The sisters were running behind clutching their papers. The other uniform was in the rear and would have run into anyone that stopped or slowed since he spent more time looking where he had been, instead of where he was going. They had run for what seemed like hours, but was probably just minutes. Melanie was so out of breath she was near collapse and her legs seemed to be losing their feeling. The only thing keeping her up was Marie and the uniform, neither of which seemed to even be breathing hard.

The Princess and the uniform shoved her through an opening and she was followed immediately by the sisters. The Princess slammed the door shut leaving them alone, but Melanie could hear her outside the door shouting commands at the other two. Surprisingly, when she looked at the sisters, only one of them looked the least bit frightened. That being Sister Kate whose head was buried in Sister Cindy's shoulder as Cindy was patting it and whispering soothing words. Sister Ann looked at Melanie and asked her if she was ready to continue the briefing.

"Are you nuts? What the hell is going on? Why were we running?" Melanie asked, with a little more volume than she intended.

"The Queen's Own will tell you what prompted their haste when they are ready, Majesty. The Queen's Own will always act in the best interest of Your Majesty. Of that you can be certain. They are however, not to be questioned. Queen Emily made the proclamation that soon became law that the Queen's Own and King's Own were to be the highest authority in the land and were to do no kneeling. Not even to His Holiness, who even the King and Queen must kneel to.

"Sister Nancy, what were Queen Emily's words?"

Another of the sisters that must have been Sister Nancy replied, "A lot of things can happen while the Own are on their knees checking to see if my shoes are tied," With that they all started laughing, including Sister Kate.

What in the world is wrong with these people? Something is obviously wrong and they're all laughing. I have awakened in an insane asylum.

Hours went by with more questions and answers, and Melanie had to admit that the sisters knew their history. Every time Melanie asked a question or made a statement, Sister Frances was scribbling and when the question required a longer answer, she would rub her wrists, so Melanie would spend a few minutes absorbing the answer before asking the next question, in an attempt to give the sister a break.

Melanie learned why some things were coming easy to her. She was part of the planet and as time passed would develop and learn her abilities. Apparently the Queen possessed the strongest abilities. She could even form rivers and mountains with no more than thoughts.

The name of the planet was Mother, the name being given by one of the first 'Settlers', a woman named Stephanie that had become friends with Queen Emily. There was no electronic technology of any kind, except medical, as it had been banned by the first King. Kings came and went and were appointed by the Queen, who held the position for life. The previous Queen had died, slain by King Brent on the orders of His Holiness, who was apparently God himself the way he was revered by the Sisters.

Some crimes were punished by him after a trial by Sisters. Queen Pamela used her abilities to commit mass murder, wiping out several villages with a flood. She was judged, 'The worst form of evil,' and sentenced to beheading by the King's hand. The King had no issue with the sentence as he had told His Holiness for years that she was no fit Queen. King Brent had been appointed by a prior Queen, and on the first meeting, Brent and Pamela got along, and she saw no reason to make a change. Pamela was fine for her first couple of years, but then she 'lost herself' as the Sisters put it, but when they described Queen Pamela's actions, Melanie would have chosen different words.

After several hours, the Princess opened the door and several cots were carried in by some of the uniforms. There was a cot for all five sisters and Melanie. Melanie couldn't help but feel a Queen should have a little better bedding than this when the Princess explained, "My apologies, Majesty and ladies, we will need to depart at first light and you must be rested. We were taken by surprise by the Beasts and we will need to get to Dawn's Landing with all haste."

"What kind of beast?" Melanie asked.

"I will answer all your questions on the new day, Majesty. Sleep is needed most. The journey will be hard and fast."

One of the sisters tapped Melanie's arm and shook her head, and Melanie took it to mean shut up. She wasn't sure how she was going to sleep but knew the sisters must need rest, so she laid down and tried to think out this bizarre day, as the uniforms and the Princess departed.

"Wake up, Majesty," Someone was shaking her shoulder and when she pried her eyes apart, she saw the Princess had come back into the room for some reason. "What is it?" she asked.

"We must be off, Majesty. Daylight is upon us and I would like to make Dawn's Landing by nightfall."

What? Already? I just laid down. "I'm up. Is the coffee ready?"

"You will need to drink that on the trip, Majesty. We must be going."

Melanie noticed she and the Princess were the only ones in the room. Even the other cots were gone. She felt suddenly like a lazy bones and tried her best to be perky as she, the Princess, and the two uniforms made their way back. They walked forever, so she was not far off with her thoughts on how far they had run last night. Melanie was introduced to Mitchell Stanton and Willard Hartaugh as new members of her Own, and she was getting a briefing on last night's attack, but it didn't prepare her for what she saw when she reached the outside.

It was a good thing she had eaten nothing but a fruit since her arrival because she could not stop retching. There was blood everywhere and not just blood, but what looked like intestines, boots with the feet still in them, parts of uniforms and other things so grotesque looking she couldn't even place them. There were also two very large creatures at least six times the size of elephants, one of which was being cut upon. She had defiled this poor woman's porch. Marie helped her out to the bloody ground and held her up, but bent over, and she continued to purge.

Are they butchering it?

Bethany had placed the steps to the wagon, but Melanie was not ready yet to have her stomach bounced around and told the Princess as much.

"Do you know how to ride a horse, Majesty? We really must be gone from here. We lost eleven soldiers last night and three of Darvon's Protectors. His wife is more than eager to have us gone. If you need to be sick you can do so atop the horse."

"Or you can take your shoes off, Majesty," said Sister Ann from the wagon, "Stand barefoot upon the ground."

Melanie was ready to try anything that would keep her from embarrassing herself more, so she found a small spot that wasn't covered with yuck and took off her shoes and socks and stood in the dirt. Her feet began to tingle, the same tingle she had felt when she had awakened in the woods and it worked its way up her legs. With the tingle she noticed a slight vibration, as well. *Holy moon over Miami. What the hell is this?* Power was surging into her. Energy like she had never known before. Her legs felt light. She knew she had control of them, but it was almost like they weren't there.

As it worked its way into her thighs and then her hips she realized it was also providing a feeling of wellness. When the tingling reached her stomach, the sick feeling went away. It continued up to and past her chest and into her neck. Her whole body was feeling exhilarated. She was excited and her pulse was racing. As the tingling was working its way up, her lips tingled and she realized she no longer had a desire for coffee or any sustenance. Past the nose she could smell the blood and carnage, but the flowers and trees as well. She could smell the Beasts. Gross! Her vision was blurring and then clearing. She realized she could see everywhere at once, even behind her. No, that's not sight. She didn't see behind her, she felt. The area was bustling with activity. Casket like boxes were being loaded in wagons, horses tied to the back of the wagons. Everyone was moving quickly. Supplies were being transferred to make room for the caskets. Four people were staring at her. Sister Ann, the Princess, Bethany and a young blond woman from the side of Darvon's house.

When the tingling ended at the top of her head, everything became clear to her. She knew who she was, how powerful she was, how powerful the planet was. She knew things there was no way she should and it continued to pour in. She felt a draw of some sort. She was extremely powerful, but some of that power was being pulled from her. Water, the pull was because of water flowing underground. Springs were everywhere underground and she was altering their flow just by being merged into Mother. Not direction, but quantity. She saw the Beasts sprawled upon the dirt and knew they came here looking for her. To kill her. She was an intruder. They knew the other little things could not survive if she were dead. The plants that grew their food would die. The water would leave the mountains. The little things and the animals they ate would have to come down. All the animals would be theirs to eat.

They were not the worst of it. They were as deadly as they were large, but there were other creatures, much faster and quicker to kill. There were women like her. She could feel them connected to Mother, but they had anger and rage built up inside them, and they didn't care for the Queen at all. They connected to Mother as she did, but they weren't as strong, even though some never disconnected. Contact with soil, rocks and trees, all would connect them with Mother.

She walked toward Darvon's house and saw the blond woman begin to show signs of discomfort as she approached. The woman went to her knees. Her bare knees. Melanie could feel her. Fear surged through the woman. Her thoughts were of having displeased the Queen. She was certain Melanie was going to have her killed. She was shaking, trembling so much Melanie could hear the teeth clatter.

"What is your name?"

"D-D-Desiree, Highness. I am Darvon's w-wife."

"Rise, calm down and have no fear. The Beasts will not return, and I am not Queen Pamela. I am Melanie, and I will not have you harmed. I am very grateful for your hospitality last night. Is there anything I might do for you to repay your kindness?"

"I would never presume to be that important to my Queen, Highness. I only fear for my husband and child, I didn't mean that you were not welcome."

"I will keep you in my thoughts, Desiree. If something comes up that you need, send word to me at Dawn's Landing."

"Thank you, Majesty, but I am unworthy of such kindness."

Melanie's exasperation with the woman's humbling nature was interrupted by the feeling of horses approaching, and quickly. Coming from the same direction the wagons had come from the previous day.

Melanie turned toward the woods and searched with her mind. She searched left, then right, then found what she was looking for about two miles out. Six Beasts, all that was left of their herd. She continued out with her thoughts running along the ground and found the perfect place. Just beyond the woods was the mouth of a canyon. Inside the canyon on the far end was a waterfall. At the base of the waterfall many animals were drinking from the lake.

She returned to the Beasts and positioned her thoughts just this side of the herd. With her mind, she dove into the planet. Down and down, until she found an underground pool. She found she could move the very soil. She created a thin tube like opening leading up to the surface and moved rocks, shale, and whatever else she could find that would suit her needs into the pool. A little of this and a little of that. She began vibrating everything rapidly, until the pool heated and began to boil. The pressure mounted and mounted until it was ready. She opened the tube and a geyser erupted that she could hear from where she stood. All heads turned toward the sound. The noise so frightened the herd they took off lumbering toward and into the canyon. She knew they wouldn't be able to climb back up this direction. They were simply too cumbersome. There would be plenty of food where they were going.

She suddenly realized Sister Ann and the Princess were staring at her, "Majesty, might I ask what you have done?" asked the sister.

"I sent the Beasts to a new place with plenty of food and water, far from here so they can no longer threaten Darvon and his family. I should also tell you that many horses are coming from the same direction you did. Would that be the King?"

"With luck, Majesty," said the Princess.

The sister looked at her with a sad face, "Majesty, please put your shoes back on. You will find you have overdone. You cannot exert that much at first. You must adapt."

"It didn't seem all that difficult, kinda fun, actually."

"Please, Majesty," Sister Ann said, handing her the shoes. She sat and put her left sock on then her right. . .

When she woke, Desiree was holding a cold wet cloth to her forehead while Sister Ann, the Princess and one of the uniforms she had not seen before were standing over her.

"Takes a little getting used to, I hear," The uniform or soldier, as the Princess had called them, was grinning from ear to ear.

"I'm glad I could provide you with some humor," Melanie returned, "Don't you have something you should be doing?"

"Indeed, but I came to see you instead."

Oh, shit!

"I take it you're the King?" She asked, sheepishly.

"Pleases me to meet you, Highness. King Brent at your service. Please call me Brent. Majesty gets boring after a time."

"Tell me about it. I am Melanie, Mel for short."

"Well, Mel. If you feel up to it I would like you to meet my troops, so they can do their kneeling and set up camp. Then we can chat, if it pleases the sisters and the Princess, who now has a head ten times its proper size since you have seen fit to knight her."

"Uncle!" The Princess screeched at him.

The King laughed and Melanie couldn't help but chuckle herself.

Melanie stood and what must have been two or three thousand soldiers went immediately to their knee, with the exception of the few surrounding the King. Melanie could only hope those to the rear would be able to hear her.

"Rise." Thankfully they began to stand.

Melanie took a minute to really look over the wagons for the first time, and they were a sight to see. Last night's talk with the sisters had alerted her to certain differences between Earth and Mother, to include travel. These wagons were diverse and looked complicated. A couple looked like the wagons out of the old west, including the rounded canvas tops, but the majority were considerably different. The wagons being pulled by the oxen were longer by more than half.

There were two that looked to be made of a metal of some sort, which she learned were 'Ice wagons' and carried refrigerated items packed in dry ice. Some were obviously transports of a sort as they had many window slots in the side. There were buggy looking wagons that had only one horse pulling them, one of which had a picture of an envelope on the side. The wagon the sisters were in was painted white and the canvas over the top was elevated in the center, but squared instead of round and was a sky blue.

The driver bench on almost every wagon was cushioned, and there were more levers and pedals than she had seen on any car on Earth. The wheels were different sized as well, the only common factor being they seemed to be made of the same rubber as Earth's, narrower and larger in circumference for sure, but the same material. Some of the wagons were low to the ground and some sat higher.

The King turned to one of the men beside him, "Sir Kevin, would you be so kind as to tell the men to set up camp, we will stay the night. Mel, do you feel up to a walk?"

"I would love to, but may I ask? I would be very grateful if you would allow the sisters to locate my family. I miss them horribly."

"These sisters won't be able to help you. They carry nothing with them other than the words of past Kings and Queens. It would take twenty wagons to haul all the parchment they keep in those libraries. I can't see why they can't spare a couple sisters to do the Queen's bidding, once we return to Dawn's Landing. The rest can take up the slack."

"Thank you Brent. Are you native to this land?"

"I am. My mom was the settler. It took her a couple of years to finally accept that her life had started anew, but eventually she fell in love with my dad. They had two children. Myself and my sister Sandra. Marie's mom. That's your captain in the event she never introduced herself."

"She did, and I am very grateful for the help and compassion she has shown me."

"Don't tell her I said this, but I am very proud of her. Anyway, Sandra married a mine worker, and Marie is the eldest of their three offspring. Jason and Justin are twins of twelve. The four of them live in a small village about six miles or so from Dawn's Landing."

"How did it come upon that name if I may ask?"

"Many years past, one of the few youngsters that made the transition without difficulty from Earth to settler, found herself awakened on the shore of the Horizon Sea. The story reads that she worked her way up the shore to a grassy knoll. Although she did struggle at first, she built a little shelter with leaves and broken tree branches.

"She found a way to start a fire using stones and dead grass. She fed herself by catching fish bare handed. She would travel to Simmons creek almost a mile away, and haul water back to her shelter in a makeshift bucket of fish skin and bark. She lived on fish and water for weeks.

"By chance, on one trip to the creek, she came upon an elder that had come to the creek to teach his grandson how to fish. The elder was from that very village that Marie is from, Empire is its name. The old man tried to get her to return with him to Empire, but she refused. She didn't want to impose and wanted to wait there for her parents. I know this doesn't seem all that impressive, but I personally would have been honored to even gaze upon her. Dawn was eleven. Eleven! A remarkable young lady.

"The old man left her his horse, directions, and all the supplies he could spare and he and his grandson rode back to Empire on his son's plow horse. When he got there he told the story of this remarkable little girl. Different men and women of Empire would ride out to her every day and bring her things. Carpenters built her a proper shelter, farmers planted some crops and tailors made her clothes.

"On one trip through the countryside, the sisters stopped at Empire and were told the story. They changed their course and went to visit Dawn. The sisters and Dawn took an immediate liking to each other. Two of the sisters stayed to visit, while the train went to notify the King. As it turned out the King was not at Harper's Bay when they arrived, so they told the story to Queen Celise.

"Much to the dismay of the Queen's Own, the Queen had to meet this young lady and so she was off. She became so enamored with Dawn and the beauty of the land that she asked Dawn permission to live there with her. She told the sisters to document the entire beach and the meadows from tree line to tree line as Dawn's Landing.

"Dawn joined the Sisterhood and lived out her life without ever setting foot outside Dawn's Landing. She watched her little twig shelter grow from a population of one to hundreds of thousands just in her lifetime. Today a million, maybe two. She never found her parents."

Melanie's eyes were wet with pride at the story of this young lady and she felt a sudden urge to mount up and be off to see the city, but she remembered Marie saying it would take dawn to dusk to reach it and it was already near midday. "Why did you say one of the few youngsters that made the transition?"

"The youth of the Earth relied heavily on electronic toys and other such things and have too much trouble adjusting to life without it and they kill themselves frequently."

The shock of that statement ignited the fury in Melanie, "And you do nothing! You just accept that? You don't quarantine them or get them help to adjust?" She realized she was screaming and touched the

King's arm. "I'm so sorry, I didn't mean you personally."

"My apologies for angering my Queen. It is not that we do nothing, Mel. If someone wants to end it, I mean really wants to, my entire army couldn't find a way to stop them. We continue to search for ways to help them in their transition. Just yesterday a rider arrived from Silver Mountain with a sister's parchment about a woman of seventeen that has nearly ended suicide in the city and surrounding villages of the mountain through her counseling of others her age, and introducing each to a sponsor of their own. Although I live there, I don't spend as much time there as I should and I was not even aware. I was on my way there when your rider arrived."

"What is this girl's name? I would like to go with you."

The King turned to Sir Kevin. "Kev, have someone fetch the rider from Silver Mountain, the Queen would speak with him."

"As you command," Sir Kevin motioned to one of the Own and the man began running back to the house. It was then that Melanie realized how far they had walked. She wondered if the planet was somehow interfering with her recognition of distance. It must be two football fields back to the house.

She also noticed for the first time that Marie had been talking to various soldiers of the King's Own and couldn't help but wonder if she was raiding the King's Own to fill the Queen's Own. As if having read her thoughts, Sir Kevin spoke.

"The Princess has asked to speak to the King's Own to provide them with the opportunity to take up residence at Dawn's Landing, Highness. It is a much smaller city than Silver Mountain. It will provide no challenge to replace them. There are many capable men, and my King almost never gets into dangerous situations." The last was followed by a lot of laughter including from the King, but Melanie guessed she would get the joke later.

"Thank you, Sir," Melanie said to him, "You are too kind for helping." Sir Kevin bowed his thanks.

When they reached the summit of the hills, Melanie's breath was taken away by the beauty she beheld. There were green trees, red trees and even yellow trees surrounding grassy meadows and knolls, a mountain was in the background and there were buildings of all shapes and sizes stretching from the base of the mountain up into the mountain itself and as far in both directions as the eye could see. It was huge. To the right was a smaller mountain that capped in a deep green mesa. There appeared to be a few structures there as well. There were also many wind turbines atop the mountain's slopes, more modern than the windmill here. There was a very large river twisting through the valley with the occasional stream branching off. On the left side of the larger mountain she could barely see the edges of what must have been a huge waterfall judging by the mist that was visible. A lake could be seen as well but it didn't seem to be attached to the waterfall or the river, causing her to speculate how it became a lake.

"Is that Silver Mountain?" She asked the King.

"No, Mel. That is Emily River. The river and lake were formed by Queen Emily as a means to quench the thirst of the animals and to give settlers bearing on their arrival. The city and villages that you see came after."

"This is by far the most beautiful land I have seen in some time," Melanie realized she was gawking and smiled at the King. "I'm sure you have seen better, but I'm a city girl and don't get out much, or at least I didn't. I'm sure I will be out more now."

"Not so, Mel. You will find yourself at odds with the Own if you desire to stray from the Landing. Many here would see you harmed, not just the Beasts. There are outlaws about, who also would feel better if you were not here to cause them trouble. They prey on small villages and country homes such as Darvon's. The fuzzy little creatures were not the only ones from Earth to settle here, either. Lions and tigers came as well, and some of those tree swingers of yours are mean little creatures.

"I do what I can to keep the outlaws in check, but they are elusive and sometimes escape. The ones I do catch, the sisters try to convert instead of sending them off to the prisons. They act the part and when freed, are right back to the old ways."

Melanie pondered this, "I would feel them coming. Wouldn't I? I knew you were coming when I was in touch with Mother."

The King flushed with what Melanie thought was embarrassment but as it turned out he was angered. "You must not! Too long with Mother corrupts, even when seasoned. Queen Pamela thought she could stay in touch with Mother at all times. Five hours only had passed before Sister Tillie found her and instructed the Own to lift her from the ground. Evil consumed her that day. She was never the same after."

The runner was returning with several horses and another man, plainly dressed, which must have been the rider from Silver Mountain. The soldier spoke, "Mrs. Garcia calls for sup, Majesty." He was looking at the King.

"Very good, I am famished," said the King. Melanie felt a little hungry herself, but she didn't know if she was up to eating one of those Beasts, so she decided to ask.

"Do they taste good, these Beasts?"

Sir Kevin responded, "They taste like your socks would after you had worn them for months and then walked through a pit of tar, Majesty! … and they chew about the same."

"I don't understand; they were being cut up. I thought they were being prepared for a meal."

No one spoke at first, finally the Princess enlightened her. "We must retrieve the bodies, Majesty. Their families will want their remains for a proper service."

No wonder no one spoke, they didn't want to see me retch again. Mind over matter! Mind over matter.

Melanie was back in control of her stomach and headed for one of the horses. The Silver Mountain man was on his knees as she approached. "Rise sir, what is your name?"

"Jerrod, Majesty. Jerrod Millstone."

"Who is this woman you spoke of? Do you know what she does that we might alert other cities and villages?"

"I don't know her name, Majesty. They just call her Breathers. She has large sessions with all under 20 years that will attend. She just talks. Never an evil word. Everyone likes who they are when they leave her."

"Thank you. Will you be returning to Silver Mountain, soon? I would like you to give this young lady my thanks and my blessing."

"I will be back there in two days, Majesty. Maybe three. The Landing tomorrow and then if fortune is with me, Silver Mountain by nightfall on the next day, else the morning after. I will gladly express your wishes."

"Thank you."

She looked at the horse and noticed the strangest saddle she had ever seen. No stirrups, just what looked like leg braces or some such things. She wasn't sure how she would get mounted. She decided to grab the pommel and hoist herself up, hoping not to embarrass herself by falling.

"It is a warhorse, Mel. I can lift you up if you like or I can have Kevin kneel here and you can use his back to step up."

"I am not stepping on......eek." As she was hoisted into the saddle like a bag of dry leaves, she gave the King a reproachful look and simply said, "Show off!"

With Marie on one side and the King on the other, she began the ride back to Darvon's Keep. She asked where the wagons were headed before last eve's incident and Marie answered.

"These are not the same wagons that you saw on your arrival, Highness. Those continued their journey to Oregon City, shortly after the attack. These are the wagons that left Oregon City, destined for the Landing. They arrived in time for Road Safety to be doubled against the Beasts. The only wagon that is the same is that of the sisters. Those that arrived with the Oregon City train went back with the other train, so that you could stay with sisters you were familiar with."

That makes sense.

Her thoughts strayed to this young lady called Breathers. If she could somehow have her travel village to village and teach someone there to do what she does, she could effectively end the problem. How to convince her to set her family and friends aside would be a different matter. Her own daughter would like her. She. . .

"How old did you say this woman was?" she asked the rider.

"Seventeen years, Majesty."

"How long has she been with you?"

"She came to us as a settler two years ago."

Oh my God! Oh my God!

"Brent, you must take me to Silver Mountain, right away. Breathers might be what they call her, or it might be her name. Brie Thurss. She might be my daughter."

"I am happy to hear you may have already found a family member, Mel. I will be very happy to check and if so fetch her to the Landing as soon as I know you are safely there, but the Own will not let you travel at this early stage."

"What?" Infuriated, she turned to the Princess, "Princess?" The Princess who was still talking with the men of the King's Own turned and came towards Melanie.

"Majesty?"

"Please tell the King he can take me to Silver Mountain, my daughter might be there."

"I will not do that, Majesty. We simply are not ready. The Own are not staffed and the Queen still has much to learn of our history and her limitations. I will ask you to see the reasoning. It would be better to ask the King to bring her to you, and safer."

"You have my word, My Queen," the King said, "I will bring your daughter to you safely. If you were to travel at this time, many things can happen, few of which would be pleasant."

Grr! Apparently the Queen is a glorified prisoner. "I don't have an overwhelming sense of freedom, right now. I feel like a hostage. I thought I was the most powerful person on the planet."

The King answered, "You are, Mel. Before we unleash that power on the populace, however. We would like to know that you can practice constraint."

How long are they going to be shoving Pamela down my throat?

"If I might remind you, as well," the King continued, "What a good idea containing your teens for their own good was a couple hours back."

Terrific, and he's using my own words against me.

Mel gave the King her most dangerous look that Dan called skank-eye, "Very well, your royal meany, I will take your word."

"Hahaha." There was that laugh again, "Will you sit with me at sup, that we may continue our talk?"

"I would be honored," She answered.

When they arrived back at Darvon's, the soldiers were working on the second Beast. She turned away and tried not to think of all those soldiers that had died for her. She had the feeling of not being worthy of that kind of sacrifice, and if not for the fact that she had tried to make believe that the Beasts would have threatened regardless whether she was there or not, she probably would be walking back in the woods by now.

When they entered the house, the King went right to Darvon and they began a conversation. Marie and Kevin were in a corner continuing with theirs, so Melanie began looking around. She came upon a chair and was trying to figure out how it was crafted. The legs were round, not square. The seat was padded. It would appear the locals haven't denied themselves everything. It was even sturdy. Melanie tried to get it to wobble and it wouldn't. Very well crafted.

Something smelled very, very good and she realized she was hungrier than she originally thought. She turned toward the smell and noticed the little boy on his knee in front of her.

"Well, hello there young man, please stand up so that I might see your face."

The boy stood and faced her.

"You are a strapping young fellow, what is your name?" she asked.

"Bobby," the boy said.

"Bobby, how old are you?"

"Seven."

"Seven, Majesty!" The female voice came from behind her. She turned to find Desiree on her knees.

"Okay, you know what. This isn't going to work for me. You already went to your knees once today. You don't get to do it again. Stand up." She noticed one of the Own looking her way and summoned him. She was very embarrassed but she forgot whether it was Mitchell or Willard, not yet able to associate the name with the face.

"Highness?"

"You are, again? I'm so sorry."

"Mitchell Stanton, Majesty. How may I serve?"

"Find me a sister. Any sister. No. Sister Frances," Mitchell was off with a bow.

"You have a very handsome son, Desiree. He caught me admiring the workmanship of your chair."

"You are too kind, Majesty. I think he is handsome, also." She rubbed his hair, "As for the chair, it is just a plain chair, not to compare with your Majesty's to be sure, but it serves our needs."

"Considering the lack of technology, the workmanship is remarkable."

"Oh, you misunderstood someone, Majesty. We have the same skills as those on Earth, but some things have just been forbidden. You won't find any cell phones, gasoline transports, guns, gas lines, or nuclear generators here for example, but we have working toilets, stoves and other such necessities, and craftsmanship is better here than it was on Earth."

Melanie's jaw must have fallen through the floor, because Desiree's smile turned to laughter.

"I am a settler, Majesty, some ten years past. I awoke in Darvon's arms in his kitchen. After my original shock was over I realized he hadn't hurt me or kidnapped me. He tried to explain what had happened to me, but he butchered it badly and I stayed confused until the sisters came. Perhaps we can talk more at sup, I must prepare the table."

"I am already promised to the King's side," Melanie answered.

"Majesty, as you can see," Desiree pointed at the King who was still talking to Darvon, "The King will not mind. He and Darvon are hunting pals since their youth, and they don't see each other much anymore."

"I will speak with him; I would love to hear more of your story. In the meantime, may I help you in some way with the food?"

Sister Frances arrived, "Majesty?"

"Write this down. The same person should not be allowed to kneel twice to the same monarch on the same visit."

"I will share this with the King and His Holiness, Majesty!" With that she was off to the King.

"Majesty," Desiree continued the conversation, "Thank you so much for the offer, but I would be thought less of, if you were found in my kitchen."

"Okay, I will respect that. Will you direct me to your powder room?" Melanie had to see this.

Desiree giggled and pointed the proper hallway.

Melanie went in the direction instructed and came upon the toilet. It was a regular toilet, the seat wasn't white, it was a smoothed wood. There was a constant flow through the bowl and when she looked closer she saw a hole in the back of the bowl where the water was coming from. The water angled in a circular motion through the bowl which was backed against the stone wall. There was also a shower and a wash basin backed against the wall. She couldn't wait to hear how this was done. She leaned against the stone wall to see if she could see any tubes behind the sink and right away her hand began to tingle. The tingle was making its way up her arm when Mitchell, watching her from the doorway said, "You shouldn't merge without the sisters being with you, My Queen."

"I didn't realize I was merging. Thank you for reminding me though. I was just curious how it worked. Would you shut the door please? I need to test it." She smiled at the Own and the door was shut. It hadn't come to her until then that she really needed a change of clothes, especially underwear, but her shorts had grass stains as well. *What exactly does the Queen wear?*

After she was as cleaned up as she was going to be, Melanie and Mitchell went back out to where the dinner guests were and found the King still talking with Darvon. Kevin and Marie were still discussing the Queen's Own, and Desiree setting up the table, with the help of two soldiers. She was beginning to feel like a fifth wheel when she almost ran into Sister Kate. Melanie couldn't remember seeing Sister Ann in some time.

"What happened to Sister Ann, Sister?" She asked.

"She is asking Mother's forgiveness, Majesty," came Sister Kate's reply.

"For what? What did she do, if I might ask?"

"Sister Ann feels it was wrong of her to suggest you take off your shoes to quell your stomach, Majesty. She feels you weren't ready for Mother, yet."

"Please go tell her I am fine, no harm done."

"I will pass your message to her, Majesty."

Melanie headed for the King and companion, causing Darvon to immediately take a knee.

"Please rise, Darvon," Melanie said, "I am so embarrassed of what I was thinking when I first arrived. Please accept my apology."

"I was not offended, Highness. You are not the first settler to land at Darvon's. Mine own wife came to me here."

"Desiree is a very lucky woman sir, and thank you none the less," she looked at the King, "Brent, might I beg off our conversation for later? I would like to finish a talk I was having with Desiree."

"I'm not sure I find that flattering, I was looking. . . "

Melanie put on her best 'whatever' look, crossing her arms, "Oh please, you haven't left Darvon's side since you've been here."

The King flushed and glanced at Darvon, "You have found me out, Mel. I will concede to your wishes. We can talk more on the way to Dawn's Landing."

There were only seven place settings at the table, and her curiosity was quelled when the sisters proceeded into the keep and the soldiers including the Own went outside. Darvon and family, the two captains, Brent and Melanie were the only ones at the table.

The place settings were just like on Earth. There was a knife, a fork on either side of a stoneware plate. There were cups as well and she could smell the aroma of the coffee. The main dish appeared to be pork, but there were vegetables and fruit as well, and potatoes and rolls. Melanie remembered the earlier talk of everyone having enhanced abilities here. The same skills, just better. Melanie came to the conclusion Desiree must have been a cook on Earth, because just the smell made her mouth water.

Marie pulled out a chair next to Desiree, and Melanie sat. Once everyone was seated, Melanie noticed everyone bowing their heads so she bowed hers as well. No words were spoken however, so she wasn't sure if she was expected to say Grace. To her surprise, the King raised his head and began dishing the vegetables onto his plate.

How totally rude is that?

Then Bobby asked the King for help with the fruit and the King dished pork onto his plate instead and got a hurtful look for his trouble. He noticed Melanie looking at him and said, "Dish up Mel, you are at the table of the best cook in the land. May I pass you something?"

One by one the others began raising their heads and dishing food, talking, laughing and Melanie decided they were saying a silent Grace.

Kevin was giving Marie advice and talking about a soldier at Willow Wood that would make a good Second. Brent and Darvon were boasting about the elk hunt they had undertaken in their youth and Bobby was trying unsuccessfully to steal a fruit as first Darvon and then the King would move the bowl without missing a beat in their talk. Melanie was trying to absorb as much as possible while eating. The King had the right of it, this was the best she had tasted in some time. Even the coffee was delicious. Ten minutes or so into the meal, Desiree finally raised her head and began dishing her food.

"My word!" Melanie said as she glanced at Desiree.

"I apologize, Majesty, I have a lot to be thankful for. Also I asked Mother to guide you well. You are the first Queen I have met and you make us feel safe and hopeful."

Melanie was aghast and felt the flush in her cheeks. "Desiree, those are kind words and I hope I can live up to your expectations."

"I didn't mean to cause you discomfort, Highness. We just came off an unpopular Queen and the populace is starving for contentment to replace the fear."

The conversation continued throughout dinner and Melanie actually learned more from her talk with Desiree than she had with the previous talks with the King and the sisters combined. There were many dangers. The Beasts were not the only inhabitants of Mother when the settlers started arriving. There were other "Fearsome things" as well. There were also wilders, which seemed to frighten Desiree the most, as they could also tap into Mother even though they could not draw the power that Melanie could. Some believe there were people here as well, though Desiree chose not to join that belief since none had actually been seen. Certain technology was banned, but not all. Telephones, cars, electronics and such were a big no-no, but the comfort things such as plumbing, furniture, etc. was okay. Melanie had been wrong in her belief that there was no electricity. There was no nuclear energy, but the land relied on boosted solar and wind energy to provide power. (Man will find a way! She remembered reading somewhere.)

Previous Queens had reshaped mountains and made them habitable with springs and waterfalls, but cities and townships being built in the valleys where the Beasts and other animals lived was taboo because the Queens would not allow the "Natural balance" to be tampered with.

There were other lands far away and across the seas that had identical laws. The laws seemed to be the same everywhere, but she admitted being unsure why since the cultures were so different.

"Do these lands have their own Queens?" She had asked when this topic came up.

"There is only one Queen, Majesty, and one Holiness, but they each have their own King. Kings are like rulers of the land such as the President was in ours."

"What about the Queen, and His Holiness?"

"There was no person on Earth that would equate to the Queen, but His Holiness would be similar to The Pope."

There's a scary thought. I've never even seen the Vatican. "You say there are other cultures, do they have their own religion as well?"

"Brace yourself for this, Majesty! Every land speaks the same language we do, though the sentence structure may be different, and every culture worships Mother. You will have to speak to His Holiness about why. Even the sisters don't know."

"What do you mean the sentence structure may be different?" Melanie asked.

"Not all sentences translate exact," Desiree explained, "You and I may say something like 'The breeze is cool', but in another language it might translate to 'Cool is the breeze'. You will understand, but it will seem like you need to correct someone's grammar, on occasion," Desiree giggled, "Mother allows all to speak like words, but not necessarily sentences."

'Pleases me to meet you.' Melanie remembered the King's statement.

"Okay," Melanie continued, "You say there are turbines and solar panels for electricity that are boosted. There wouldn't be enough room on the planet for the solar panels and turbines to furnish cities with enough energy, so boosted by what?"

"That is above my knowledge, Majesty. Perhaps the sisters can explain."

History and Geography were the main topics in the schools. No shock there, but the other topics were on-hand farming, food processing, plumbing and carpentry which was a little bit of a shock. Math and spelling were to be taught at home before the student got to school which was only five years long. The student would start at age eleven and go until his sixteenth year. There was no summer break, and school was ten hours a day. There was no college, only apprenticeships. Neither Desiree, nor Melanie were fond of this arrangement. Farmers went without their children for five years as schools were only in villages and cities, so settlement and farm children stayed at the Sisterhoods, and took the caravans home on the weekends. The children would miss their families, but they had other children to play with. It was the parents that suffered the most. Melanie stored this information for later.

The conversations began to wind down and Marie was after her to get some sleep, as they needed to make the Landing by nightfall on the new day. They would be leaving early. Melanie had to admit she was beginning to tire. Desiree walked with her to the room where she would sleep. When they entered, Melanie thought, now this is more like it. No cot tonight, woohoo.

The walls were a light paneling, there was a nightstand next to the wall with a light globe above it and a book on the stand. The bed had a light tan spread and two pillows. Melanie tested the bed which was so soft she felt like she was falling through. Desiree had it right, there was no lack of comfort here.

Desiree opened a chest at the foot of the bed and provided pajamas. "I'm sure these will be too big for you highness, but they will provide you some modesty."

What a sweetheart. She can tell just like I, that we are close in size. "Desiree, I don't know how to ask this, but I didn't exactly bring a suitcase. Is there any way you can spare me something to wear tomorrow? I promise I will have them cleaned and returned, once I reach Dawn's Landing."

"Majesty, you honor me I will put something together."

Desiree left the room and Melanie slipped into the pajamas, cracked the book and began to read. It was a novel. It was good to let her mind rest from reality.

When Marie walked in, Melanie was asleep with the book on her chest. "Wake up, Majesty. We must be gone from here."

"It can wait until I shower," Melanie answered groggily, happy to be awake and free of the horrible nightmare she was having about the Beasts.

Melanie found the shower room again with the help of Marie and found a washcloth, towel, a bar of soap and a knee length dress, a pair of panties and some socks on the basin, along with a small bottle marked "Lustra", which apparently was a shampoo. The shower had no way to regulate the heat that she could tell, so lukewarm was the best she could do, but at least she felt clean. Once she had washed everything she could reach, she stepped out and dried herself off. The dress fit her like a glove. A blue floral design that she had to admit looked pretty good. She looked everywhere for a brush, but couldn't find one. Oh, well the girl can't be expected to think of everything.

She opened the door and nearly yelped. There were those Own

again. *Have they never heard of privacy?* Desiree was there with a hairbrush, as well. Melanie smiled at her and reached for the brush and Desiree pulled it back, grasping it with both hands.

"Please, Majesty. May I?"

Melanie remembered back to last night's sup talk and remembered how much 'honor' went with doing for her, so they walked back to the room Melanie had slept in, and Desiree began brushing out her Queen's reddish tangles.

While her hair was being brushed Melanie listened to Desiree say after several months at the Landing she came to realize that Mother had placed her in Darvon's arms for a reason, so she took the next caravan headed his direction and told him how she felt and that she was supposed to be with him. He had wanted to know what had taken her so long to see that. Melanie had it right, she had been a short order cook on Earth and had been deposited in his arms in his kitchen. The sisters had married them on the spot. The rest was history.

The brushing was finished and she felt wonderful. "Desiree, thank you so much for the clothes and the brushing. Are you by chance in need of any friends? I seem to be a little short in that category."

Desiree looked like she had seen a horror movie, her eyes were so big Melanie couldn't see the eyelids. "You honor me, Highness. It would be wonderful to be considered so."

"Very well, then. Rule number one: Hereafter, you will call me Mel."

"I cannot, Majesty. It would be... Highness, I would feel as if I were disrespecting... I will do my best, Majesty... I mean Mel."

On arriving at the table she saw just one place setting and guessed everyone else had already eaten. She glanced outside, it was just beginning to show a semblance of light.

"Would your… you like eggs or pancakes... Mel?" Listening to Desiree stammer was humorous, but she controlled it.

"Surprise me, Desiree. I am going to stick my head outside."

Before she took two steps, Mitchell darted past her out the door and was craning his head in both directions. Oh, brother! She saw that the soldiers had almost finished breaking their camp. One of the wagons was being emptied under the supervision of Sister Ann, but she couldn't see the King. The Beasts were gone which peaked her interest. She would have to ask about that. The blood was still visible but all the other signs of the carnage had been cleaned up. "Mitchell, do you know, is that wagon for me?"

"Yes Majesty. You, His Highness, Sister Frances, Willard and myself."

"Good, I wouldn't want to try to ride a horse in a dress."

She went back inside and laughed at the two eggs sitting on top of two pancakes. It was delicious as she knew it would be. That coffee, though. She had never tasted the like. "Des, are there any containers that I might take some of this coffee with me? I hate to keep asking you for things."

"The sisters already have some coffee as well as sandwiches, Highness. The King said this would be your only sit down meal today. . . I mean, Mel. . . sorry, and he wanted me to make sure you ate plenty. Do you need more?"

"I am fine. The King doesn't need to be fattening me up. It is delicious."

"You are too. . . thank you, Mel. . . and oh, my! Thank you, Mother."

Melanie followed Desiree's eyes and saw that it was raining out. *If it rains long enough that should clean up the blood. Now, if I can figure out how to get to the wagon without getting Desiree's dress all muddy.*

"Des, what happened to the Beasts?"

"The soldiers dragged them to the sand pit while we were sleeping. Sometimes it seems like those men and women never sleep."

"Sand Pit?"

"Some of our refuse goes into the Pit. It is pulled down into Mother and she makes it into fertilizer or other things. The sisters know more than I about the Pits."

Marie Mercer was beside the Queen's wagon, interviewing Gary Umber of the King's Own and Phillip Stems of the King's force, making sure they knew what would be expected of them. Gary already knew, having been a member of the King's Own for the last ten years, and Phillip didn't bat an eye at the prospect of forfeiting his life if it came to it.

They each raised their left hand and covered their heart with the right and said the oath and the Queen's Own was at five.

The King, Kevin and Marie came up the steps and the King spoke, "Would My Queen like me to carry her to the wagon or is she waiting for the rain to stop?"

"There are three of you, can't you just carry the wagon over here?"

"Hahaha!"

Wow I love that laugh.

Marie introduced the two newest members of the Own and Melanie knew she wouldn't be able to remember the names with everything going through her head, but she was polite and smiling at them as she accepted the oaths.

"Be with me. Evil comes."

Melanie turned around and looked at Desiree, "What do you mean by that?"

Desiree looked stunned at being addressed, "By what? Majesty, I said nothing."

Melanie looked at the King, at Kevin, at Marie and back at Desiree. They were all looking at her waiting for an explanation, so she blew it off as hearing things.

Melanie gave Desiree a hug, lifted her dress to mid-thigh as if that would matter, and began dodging her way around puddles. About half way to the wagon the skies opened up and the rain became torrential. So much for the 'do! She sped up, dodged more puddles and made it to the wagon. Marie placed the steps and Melanie climbed up and in and found sister Frances already writing. The King followed her in and the two Own sat on the bench with Mitchell taking the reins. The thundering on the top of the wagon was deafening and she reduced the urge to cover her ears. She had already shown too many signs of weakness; she couldn't chance everyone thinking her a wimp. Melanie looked at Sister Frances and pointed to her tablet. Frances, with pen in hand, prepared to write and gave the Queen her most solemn look. Guessing Sister Frances was ready, Melanie made her proclamation speaking in a raised voice, "It's loud in here." Sister Frances cocked her head and smiled but wrote nothing. *Oh my goodness, she* got *me.*

Mitchell, Willard, Gary, Phillip, Mitchell, Willard, Gary, Phillip. She went over the names of the Own, hoping not to embarrass herself again, and she was pleasantly surprised at how comfy the ride was. There was the occasional rut similar to potholes on Earth, but mostly it was very smooth.

Landing Road

Melanie and the King talked for several hours about life on Mother, the different 'Kingdoms', technologies, bans, laws, peoples, the High Holiness, the Sisters and the judicial system, herself, the animals and when discussing these animals Melanie was certain she would never forget the conversation. Brent wanted to do away with the Beasts, but he had met with resistance from her predecessors.

"They serve no purpose. They eat. They shit. Nothing more. Just one of those evil creatures could, unchecked, feast on an entire village, Mel. They need to be done for. I will not press this issue or ask for your agreement now, but once you are settled it is a topic we need speak of."

"I don't need to be settled, Brent. I know the Beasts are dangerous, but I need to agree with the former Queens. You simply cannot eradicate an entire species."

Well, that went over well!

The King had gone silent and stayed that way for what must have been an hour. He would occasionally stare at her angrily and she met that stare with her own and the King would always be the one to break the eye contact. "We will talk of this again, My Queen, once you are settled."

"I will always look forward to our talks, My King, but the result of this topic will not bend to your view."

After another hour of silence and stare downs, the conversation continued along different lines and Mel was becoming the better for it. She was surprised to learn that Darvon's home was considered a Kingdom landmark. Antiquated, in a fashion, and neither Darvon nor the King wanted it modernized. This topic was a pleasant one and both she and the King were engaged and talking from the hearts.

"Wilder!" Came the scream from somewhere outside. "Wilder to the west."

The wagon jerked forward and then right as she flew across the wagon square into the stomach of the King, who let out an uff and then placed her face down on the floor of the wagon. "Down, Sister," he screamed at Frances and down she went, joining Melanie on the floor of the wagon. The King went to the back of the wagon and peered out.

Mitchell was cracking a whip and screaming at the horses. Melanie raised her head to see where they were going and saw that they were approaching a tree line. She felt a hand on the back of her head and her face was shoved into the floorboards. "Ow!"

"Apologies, Highness," Sister Frances said, "My hand slipped."

Melanie was trying to remember what she knew about wilders. But she had entirely too much information crawling through her brain. The wagon pulled up just short of the tree line and the King jumped out, mounted and sped off in the direction they had come. Other wagons had been charging towards the trees as well and pulled up next to Melanie's wagon. Melanie began to rise to get a look, but Frances laid across her holding her down. Melanie spouted, "Don't tell me. Let me guess. You're whole body slipped, right?"

"You must stay down until the Own say different, Majesty."

Right on cue, the back of the wagon opened up and The Princess, and two more of the Own were inside with Mitchell and Willard still seated out front. The Princess had Melanie and Frances get up and sit on the tree line side of the wagon while two of the Own sat on the road side facing them. The Princess went outside and stood watching the direction they had come.

"Get your hand off the ground, soldier," Marie screamed at someone.

Melanie remembered now about wilders. They merge with Mother as well. She should talk to the woman and see if she can get her to disconnect, but she would never get past Marie. "I should talk to her, Captain. Maybe I can get her to see reason."

"That's not going to happen, Highness. She has passed the ability to reason."

"How do you know for sure? I am the Queen, I think. . . "

"Gary, if she moves knock her out," Marie said.

"Aye, Captain!"

Gasp! Melanie could not believe what she just heard. The sweet little Princess fully intended to render her unconscious. Being a Queen sucks right now.

This is accidental, it is not possible she knew we had the Queen with us. The King was about to reach the front line. Five hundred or so of his best, were lined between the road and the wilder, most of which were archers with their arrows ready, but not aimed at the wilder. Good, good, don't provoke her. As he rode up, Sir Bryce was calmly talking to the line, "Stay calm, hold the line, don't be afraid, and stay focused."

"Where did she come from, did anyone see?" the King asked as he arrived.

"The scout said she looked more shocked to see him than he was her, Grace. She came out of the trees and probably just wanted to cross the road. If she would have given us a better look I would have had her taken down, but with our situation I didn't want to chance a miss."

"Thank you Bryce, I don't know how I would have overcome losing a third, especially with the feeling I get from this one. We will wait her out for a time, we have been making good time and are more than half way there. We may be forced to initiate something though; we need to be at the Landing by nightfall. Stay alert."

"She is a beautiful woman, this one. Such a shame," Sir Bryce shared.

"Only on the outside, Bryce. Inside she is as black as night," The King said as he began walking the line telling the archers to stay strong.

The wilder watched and waited.

What do they want? Why are they just sitting there? They have to know I am not exposing myself to their arrows. Why did they move those wagons away? What do they contain that I would want? There are too many of them for me to throw fire at, they would shoot those arrows and kill me.

There, at the wagons, someone has touched the ground. Fear surges through him. . . but not for himself. He fears. . . gone. Did he fear for someone else? Is his wife in one of those wagons? Why don't they leave, they must know I'm not going to take this many on.

Those two in the middle of the archers. They don't have arrows. They must be uppity-ups. I could throw fire at them. No, I would have to step out and the arrows would take me. What's in those wagons?

"What happened to her?" The King wanted to know after several minutes of not seeing movement.

"She just left, Highness. Walked back into the woods," Bryce answered.

"Stand your ground, I'm going to get the wagons moving. Once they are back under way keep yourself between them and this wood."

The King rode up and told the Princess to put the wagon third in line. The Princess, Gary and Phillip departed the wagon and the King climbed back in. Shortly, they were back under way. The King sat in the back and watched. He tried to be jolly even though she could feel his stress. "Well, that was pretty uneventful," he said.

"I don't care for the way the Princess acted in your stead, Brent. One of the Own was told to knock me out if I moved."

"She has one job, Mel. One. Don't deny her that. She will do what she needs to do to keep you alive one more day."

There was more conversation as they moved along, but they didn't look at each other as the King continued to stare out the back. The talk was of dangers, specifically wilders, which Brent called a bunch of little Pamela's. She was beginning to think about that coffee when the King jerked and she saw it, too.

"Wilder! Wilder to the North!" came the shout too late.

A ball of fire came out of nowhere and hit one of the wagons behind them. The wagon exploded as flames engulfed it. The driver was blown off, but the contents were gone as the wagon disintegrated in seconds. She hoped none of the contents of the wagon were people. The concussion blew her against the back of the bed, and the King jumped from the wagon screaming "Loose! Loose!"

Hundreds of arrows flew in the direction the ball had come from, but there was nothing there to hit. Riders charged, more arrows flew over their heads toward where the wilder had been. The King saw her at the same time Melanie did.

"There," he screamed and pointed, "To the right, loose!"

Riders turned and arrows flew, but she fired again and ducked back into the trees. The fireball went through one of the riders, and struck another wagon. Same result, except this time the driver was not quite so lucky.

How is she doing that? I can move rocks, water, roots. How can she throw flame?

Magma!!

Off went the shoes and socks.

"NOOOO!" screamed Frances who jumped and tackled her before she could get out the back. Melanie twisted herself and stuck her hand in Frances' face and pushed as hard as she could. Mitchell and Willard bolted off the seat and darted right at her, but she was too fast and out the back she went, jumping to the ground. The power entered her feet even with her running, and was surging upward but she wasn't there yet. Come on, come on! Four horses were charging after her, but she darted first on one side of the wagons and then the other. Shouting and screaming was everywhere. More wagons were on fire, five, and then six. Thrum, thrum went the arrows.

Mother was in her. She was running fast. Very fast. Faster than the horses. Holy cow! The power surged through her. She was running so fast, she questioned if she was touching the ground.

She headed straight for the trees that were hiding the wilder. She could hear everything and see everywhere. Dead soldiers. Too many. Too many.

The wilder felt the power surge coming from the wagons. I knew it, I knew it! I feel her! They were hiding something in those wagons from me. It's that bitch Queen.

Melanie was just about at the tree line when she was seen by the wilder. Flame erupted from the hand of the wilder and headed right at her. Barricade! The earth exploded in front of her but the flame passed right through and barely missed her. She felt her face on fire at the closeness of it. She darted in the trees with the horses close behind. Her body kept running, but her mind went down, down, down. Through rocks, streams, dirt, shale and she found it. The wilder's source. Join. She felt the fire. She felt the surge of power. She was not alone. The wilder was here. Coming right at her, mind chasing mind. Up she went, as fast as she could. The wilder was chasing but losing ground. Desiree was right, Melanie was stronger.

She was up and headed out of the tree line. Their eyes connected, and Melanie could sense the hatred in the woman. *Her eyes are yellow. Is that what mine look like? Is that why my vision blurs?* The wilder fired again. This one would not miss. Just as the ball was about to hit her she was knocked to the ground. She jumped back up, firing with both hands as fast as she could, but she was untrained and the balls were flying past the wilder left and right. She was throwing everything she could, fire, rocks, dirt, but she was no match for this woman, the wilder had been joining Mother for too long and had the advantage. She had to take cover and get closer.

Marie was close to the wilder, and noticed she was focused on the Queen.

With the power in her, the Queen is too fast for us. The horses can't catch her and she can change direction too fast. I must end this.

With that, Marie charged the wilder. Freeing her crossbow, she loaded a shaft and fired. The shaft struck true, into and through the shoulder. The wilder fell to her knees. Marie twisted free of her right leg brace and slid to the side, using the warhorse as a shield. A fireball flew past where she had been. She loaded, took careful aim and fired again, this one striking the right breast and sinking deep into the chest. She tossed the crossbow and bolted off the horse without bothering to rein up. She landed on her feet but fell forward into a somersault. She drew her long sword and charged at the woman.

"I'm sorry," she heard the woman whimper through the pain. With all of her strength and the inertia of her charge, Marie shoved the long sword into and through the chest. She twisted left, then right and the woman screamed. Marie pulled the sword free and drew it back eying the neckline.

"May the Riggers feast on your evil heart!" she said and swung with every bit of strength she had.

Melanie heard the wilder scream and saw the head fly off the shoulders, but she didn't look away and she didn't retch. There was no feeling at all as far as a queasy stomach. Nothing. She didn't care for the violence. She had never been in a violent situation before and this was a strong indication that she didn't care to again. She didn't even know this woman. What had filled her so full of hatred? She was being lifted and she felt Mother leaving her. This time there was dizziness, but no fainting. She saw she was in the arms of Willard and one of the other soldiers was wrapping her feet with a strange fabric. She remembered her shoes were in the wagon.

When Willard set her down, she found Mitchell lying dead at her feet. He had pushed her down and taken the fireball instead of her. It had burned him through and through. Near the wagons the King was kneeling over a soldier with his head hung. Frances was running toward her carrying her shoes, sobbing wildly. *Why is she crying?* Marie was on her back next to the dead wilder, breathing heavily. The other two of the Own standing over her. Melanie had made a mess of this. *So many dead. Too many. Because of her. Why couldn't she listen?*

She sat on the ground and cradled Mitchell's head in her lap. *Please, Mother, let him not have children.*

"He died in honor, Highness. The Own would each gladly give our lives to keep you safe."

Small words, Willard. Small words. The tears finally came.

BREATHERS

Silver Mountain Sisterhood

"Why do I have to wait so long to join the Sisterhood?"

Sister Grend was admiring the laughter of the children and couldn't help but smile at the fun they were having just chasing each other. Interesting sport, this 'tag'. She couldn't remember that far back as much as she wanted to. She wondered if she was ever "It". She was 80 years now, today being her day of birth. She was slower, more stooped and her old bones ached horribly.

"You must be of twenty years to join the Sisterhood, Brie. We have discussed this many times. In three years, you will probably change your mind as many times," Sister Grend answered.

"I will never change my mind, Sister." Brie countered, "Every profession on Mother has apprenticeships. Why not the Sisterhood?"

"When you become a sister you will know why. I am proud of you Brie, and Mother knows we could sure use your talents with today's youth, but sister Kai is firm about this and will not waver. I will speak no more of it. I am tired and need my rest. Help me up the steps child, and then see to your chores."

"Yes, Sister. Thank you for walking with me."

"You saw me walking towards the plaza and were afraid I would fall down and hurt myself is why you came running to ask if I would walk with you. Do not think I don't know that."

Brie giggled and helped Sister 'Grandma' up the steps.

The Sister apartments were pretty modest compared to most homes in Silver Mountain, at least the actual rooms were. They didn't really have anything more than a bed, a nightstand and a small closet, with a 4 drawer chest in it. They didn't need more. They never wore anything other than the tater sacks as Brie called them. That and their headband. Brie wanted to be a sister in the worst way. The Sisterhood is where those new to Mother would call home until they could adapt.

All swept children lived here until a family could be accepted as temporary parents. With the skills the sisters had, it was usually a quick process. The older children were less desirable. Brie thought that to be mostly because the accepted families didn't want the extra headache of breaking bad habits.

The compounds were set up more as a commune than anything else. They took up three times the space of her high school on Earth, parking lot and all. The second and third floors were all apartments for the swept, and assorted small rooms for the sisters. The third floor had a room on the gate side that was never used and Brie and others were never allowed in it, not even as part of their chores. Brie had asked once, but Sister Helen had scolded her for even asking. The first floor was all offices, dining and game rooms, libraries, studies, conference and many others. There was a lower floor as well, but it was only used as a jail. There were never any soldiers going in and out and she didn't understand what kept the prisoners from just walking out. When she asked, she was once again scolded. None of the chores assigned to the children ever went there either.

Brie led Sister Grend to her room and helped her lay down. Then she went to the social room and checked through the library to see if there were any new books she hadn't already read five times. She found none so she walked to the kitchen and saw Sister Ellen making cupcakes.

"Ooh, may I have one?" She asked.

"Sit."

Brie pulled up a chair to a table and Sister Ellen placed a lemon cupcake in front of her, looked her over and said, "You don't have your usual ear to ear grin today, Brie. Do you need to talk?"

"I'm worried about Sister Grandma. Each day she looks weaker and weaker. She seems to get annoyed at me when she finds me doing her chores, and today before I laid her down for her nap she told me do my chores. She was with me this morning when I did them. She used to know my chores were always done early so that I could go to the meetings."

"You are not alone, child. We are all worried about her, but she is eighty today. She has had a long life."

Great! Even the sisters are giving up on her, Brie thought.

"Don't look at me that way child. We have no intention of folding our arms and letting her die. We will continue to work hard on the doctors about their lack of motivation."

"Thank you, Sister. I don't know what I'll do when she passes."

"What you've always done, you will just be a little sad when you do it."

As Brie was eating her cupcake and thinking on Sister Grandma, she was also thinking about tonight's meeting and a particularly troubled boy that was thinking of her in the wrong way. He was a nice enough boy, but Brie had her mind set on being a sister. Being a sister didn't give you much time for boys. She had picked tonight as the night to pull him aside and tell him true.

Brie thanked Sister Ellen and walked the hall to see if anyone was in the game room. She found Frankie and Henrietta playing cards and sat down to watch. Frankie was seventeen and Henrietta had just turned seventeen. They lived here, as Brie did, as all children settlers do until a family could be found. *So many people think we kill ourselves because we have trouble adapting to life without electronics, when I'm sure it is because we have such a feeling of not being wanted.*

Brie was swept when she was fifteen and many attempts were made to find her a new family but no one really wanted a fifteen-year-old girl, citing hormones of all things. Once she turned sixteen, the choice became hers. Brie decided she had liked being with the sisters and stopped trying to match with a family.

She laughed at Frankie when he tried to lay a jack on a nine and both Frankie and Henrietta laughed with her. She talked to them while they were playing and it looked like they were happy. Frankie had found out today that a family on Miller Street might accept him. Legal adoption was not allowed because technically the kids still had parents. If the sisters found both parents were proven dead then legal adoption was authorized. The problem was that it took a long time to find out and took a King's decree to start the process. Sister Zia had been checking another boy's vital statistics, vital statistics, what a dumb name, and had noticed when she was working, that Brie's dad was one of the very first settlers here and had died almost five hundred years ago. As hard as it was for Brie to hear, she couldn't imagine how hard it must have been for Sister Zia to tell her.

Brie wanted to be a sister more for knowledge than anything. She loved learning about the animals especially. She didn't particularly like the Beasts, the Riggers, or those Bangors, but most of the animals of Mother were almost cuddly. The Abedi creature that more resembled a squirrel would walk right up to you. Brie, when she was outside with some spare time would feed them corn. They loved corn and would sit on the bench with her and eat it. As cuddly as they were, the Beasts feared them. A hunter some years back had an Abedi pet and he was cornered by two Beasts. When they saw the Abedi, one turned and ran. Well, they apparently can't run so it loped off, but the other dropped dead of fright right where it stood. The sisters still shake their head about this one, but the Queen was very upset.

Brie's hero was the King, even though she had never met him. Everyone, including the sisters spoke proudly of him. Not even His Holiness had that unanimous of a record. Hardly anyone liked the Queen. The Queen liked the Beasts, and she apparently killed people for no reason. The sisters never mention the Queen but she overheard two of them talking that she was on trial for murder. That was months ago, and Brie was curious what happened but if she were to ask, the sisters would know she was eavesdropping. She had not yet figured out how to bring up the subject of the Queen.

It was getting dark outside so she said her goodbyes to Frankie and Henrietta and made her way to High Sister Heather's office. She found the sister at her desk, as usual, with her head down trying to decide which task was more important. Sister Heather was the High Sister and made the decisions as to which sisters were going where and which were doing what. Sister Grandma had been scratched from her lists years ago, but Brie hoped that one day she would be on them. Brie was unsure whether to knock or clear her throat.

"Come in, Brie," Sister Heather said, without looking up.

How does she do that?

Brie went in and sat down. Sister Heather looked up, "Leaving early, tonight?" She asked Brie, with a smile.

"I have to talk to a boy tonight, High Sister. I'm not looking forward to it, but he thinks of me in ways he shouldn't."

"Touchy! Have you decided what you are going to say?"

"Mostly. The rest will come as we talk."

"Well it looks like I will be here awhile, so if your meeting is not too long tonight, perhaps I will be here when you get back. Would love to know how it goes."

"You look busier than normal. May I help? I want to be a sister really bad, High Sister. I will do anything you need."

Sister Heather smiled at her, "Brie honey," *Uh oh, that's never good.* "I am proud of this desire you have to join the Sisterhood, but you are simply too young. We don't want you to make a life decision at this age. It is just not practical. I have submitted your name to Sister Kai. Thank you for the offer, but I have this. Now be off so that I might get to it."

Sister Heather put her eyes back down to her papers and then said, "Henrietta, quit hiding behind the corner, please."

Henrietta poked her head out. "I would like to go to the meeting with Brie, High Sister."

"Very well, but Brie has something to do and you will leave her to it and not be listening to things you are not invited to. You have lost your game room privileges for tomorrow."

Henrietta hung her head, "Yes, High Sister."

Brie rose and walked out the door and punched Henrietta's arm as she passed, giving her a stern look. The two of them walked the hall and out the front door of the Sisterhood, toward the bike stalls. Brie had been blessed with the same bike since her arrival and had suffered only one chain break. She was very attached to her bike and had detailed it herself with stripes and other decals. She also had painted her name on the basket rack. She unlocked it and waited for Henrietta.

High Sister Heather had lifted her head from her work as Brie was walking out. She watched the girl and thought on this boy, trying to decide if it was going to be a stalking problem. Brie was not dressed in a provocative way and never had. She was a beautiful young woman. That much was certain, but the Sister had never noticed Brie flirting or teasing boys or doing anything that she would consider to be un-ladylike. In fact, Brie conducted herself professionally at all times. Sister Heather blew the problem off; certain Brie was mistaken.

Dawn's Landing, front gate

Melanie sat in the wagon with Sister Frances as they closed in on the city. The Princess rode the rest of the way with her, the King and Frances. The King and The Princess had talked almost the entire rest of the trip, but Melanie could remember none of it. Her thoughts were elsewhere. Too many dead.

Mitchell Stanton, husband and father of two-year-old twins. A veteran of Road Safety and the first to be accepted to the Queen's Own. Took a fireball through the chest that was destined for her, her very first hero and savior on Mother, and hopefully the last. I refuse to pass the buck on expressing my sorrow to the wife and children.

Sister Ann, unwed and tremendously devoted to the Sisterhood, the very first sister she had met, doing no more than riding in the wrong wagon. So devoted to Mother as well, but no more. Thanks to me.

Sister Kate. So young. Married less than a year ago. Just barely joined the sisterhood. Just in time to die. Because of me.

Sister Nancy, another whose life was the sisterhood. Loved being a traveling sister because of her love for meeting new people and the hopes of finding the swept. Dead.

Sister Cindy, so helpful and knowledgeable, widow and mother of two with a grandchild on the way. It will never see its grandmother, because of me.

Jeremy Slater, the first soldier she had met, dying in the belly of the Beast, fighting to protect his Queen. The first at the throat of the Beast.

Sir Bryce Cannon, the King's best commander, taking a fireball through the heart while charging the wilder.

All because of me!

The names would not be forgotten. The faces flashed before her with each name thought of. Fifty-three men and women in the two attacks.

Dead!

Over 100 injured. For me? She wasn't worth the least of them. She would go to every service. Every one. Not just those she knew. Fifty-three times she will weep. She will go to the clinics to visit the wounded, each of them. She will feel no better afterward than she does today.

The remainder of the trip all she and Frances did was bawl. She had decided then she would never remove her shoes again. She will miss the feeling of being merged with Mother but this was just too much.

When they arrived at Dawn's Landing the crying didn't stop, but she was in awe nonetheless. The King had the right of it. Darvon's Keep was antiquated. The buildings here were just like those of Earth. Three and four story structures. There were markets, carpentry shops, schools, baseball fields, stadiums, offices, housing areas, parks and motels that were apparently called lodges here. It was just like home, almost. There were no skyscrapers, and there were turbines, solar panels and bicycles everywhere, and paved roads. It was an absolutely huge city and the buildings were massive in girth.

As they wheeled into town, the wagons would leave the train, taking this road or that road. With her eyes and her heart she followed the wagons containing the dead as they diverted off and headed to an area that looked more commercial than residential. Except at the crossroads, the wagons and horses stayed on the shoulder.

On the way to wherever her wagon was going, Willard didn't seem to know but the Princess was directing him, she noticed some street performers entertaining the masses of a park. There must have been hundreds, but without television or radio this was in all likelihood the only entertainment around.

A thought occurred to her so she asked Sister Frances about finances. Everyone worked in one capacity or another depending on their abilities, and was paid for their services. The treasuries of the land were under control of the Queen. There were no pennies, nickels or dimes. There were "Silver quarters" and "Gold halves," neither of which had silver or gold in them. Just like Earth then. The currency consisted of ones, fives, tens, twenties and fifties. There were no two dollar bills or anything larger than a fifty. Trying to get a grasp on economy she asked how much a gallon of milk is because she knew that to be ten fifty in Phoenix.

"We don't have gallons, Majesty, Milk is delivered by ice cart in quarts only and they are two for a gold half."

One dollar for a gallon of milk?

"That seems pretty reasonable, are all dairies priced alike?" Melanie asked.

"All prices are set by the Sisterhood, Majesty. The merchants provide the sisterhood of proof of their costs and overhead, the Sisterhood figures in a proper profit for the merchant and those prices become set."

"What happens if the retailer wants to raise his prices?"

"He can't, Majesty. He can only charge a certain percentage above his cost. Greed is high crime. He would need to provide the Sisterhood with a cause."

"High crime? What are the other crimes?"

"Petty, middle, high, felony and capital."

"What is considered capital?"

"Treason, murder and violent crimes against children, the penalty for capital crime is beheading."

"Ugh. That grosses me out, but it must save a lot of prison space, what about rape?"

"Felony Majesty, which results in castration, life imprisonment and forfeiture of all funds to the victim."

Gasp! Castration? "With the forfeiture of all funds aren't you concerned the victim might be lying?"

"Lying is considered a petty crime, lying to a sister during a trial is high crime and you will be caught. It is one of our abilities. We just know."

"Am I going to be brought up to speed on the crimes and punishments?"

"It is part of your training, Majesty."

"Good, because I obviously have much to learn about many things. Do you know what it is that boosts those?" She asked, pointing at the turbines, "Because even though they seem to take up that whole peninsula and along with the solar panels, the whole mountainside, there's no way they can power a city this size."

"Queenstone Majesty, but don't be deceived. The turbines and solar collectors and panels have five hundred years of modifications. I can assure you, they put out some power."

"What are those towers over there?" Melanie asked, pointing near the shore line, a half mile east.

"Solar collectors, Majesty. It would not be a good place for an afternoon stroll. They get a little warm."

"Okay, I don't want to make myself dizzy, so I'll ask at training what Queenstone might be."

"It is considered a mineral Majesty, but I think they only classify it so because they have no idea. The previous Queens have been very outspoken about its use and handling. You will be very knowledgeable about it and quickly. It is called Queenstone for a reason. Like the underground springs, that constant seepage feeling you get is for the Queenstone, as well. It would dry up without you. None but the Sisterhood know that though. Queen Emily said no one but the Queen must merge with it. That is why the sisters ruled as they did on wilders."

When they arrived at their destination which Frances had called the Queen's residence, it was hardly the castle she was expecting but it wasn't a shack, either. It resembled a small mansion. She was at a loss as to why a Queen would need a house this big. She soon found that she was not the only resident. Visiting Kings and dignitaries having business with the Realm had guest quarters plus, there was a rather large staff.

"What rule is that?" She asked Sister Frances.

"The wilder are treasonous, Highness. No one but the Queen touches Mother. There are no exceptions."

When she got out of the wagon there were three people on their knees. She wiped her tears as best she could and they were introduced to her as Fred, who was her "Cabbie". His responsibility was to get her where she needed to be. Pierre, the head of house, was responsible for supervising staff and a very lovely young lady by the name of Kristen, who was identified as the Queen's Lady. She did basically whatever the Queen told her to. As it turned out, Kristen was the highest paid employee on staff, which included Pierre. Kristen looked about Brie's age, and apparently did not answer to Pierre, but only to the Queen.

When she was escorted into the house, Melanie found three women standing, not kneeling waiting to be introduced. She was stunned but curious as well. She whispered to Frances, "Why aren't they on their knee?"

It was Kristen that answered, "If we knelt inside the mansion My Queen, we would get nothing done. Queen Patricia ruled it so."

"I like Queen Patricia and I may never leave here," said Melanie. Kristen smiled at that.

Pierre introduced Yanina, the evening housekeeper. Ursula, the head of the Queen's finance, and Theresa, the Queen's chef. Yummy in my tummy please, a little hungry here.

"What is your most urgent need, My Queen?" Kristen asked.

"I'm hungry, I need a shower and some clean clothes."

Theresa spoke, "What would be your main dish, Highness?"

"Something beefy, please. I haven't eaten since this morning. There will be eight for sup."

The Princess looked the most confused. Theresa simply bowed and headed off. "Captain, I would be honored if the Own would join The King, Kevin, Frances and I for dinner."

"Me, Majesty?" Frances looked like she swallowed a wine cork, "I cannot dine with the Queen of Mother."

"This is my wish," Melanie said, ending the need for further conversation about the matter.

Everyone went to their knee except the Princess.

Oh! You have got to be kidding me, Melanie thought, having just been promised they wouldn't kneel to her inside the mansion.

"Really?" She asked them all.

"Rise," came the voice behind her. She turned and smiled as Brent had arrived.

The smile went away quickly, "My King, I don't know where to begin to express my sorrow for your losses."

"Death is a sad thing, Mel. It is unfortunately a part of life on Mother, as I'm sure it was on Earth."

Kristen spoke, "My Queen, I am so sorry about your journey. If I may interrupt you for a moment so that I might be off to purchase you some clothing. What size were you on Earth?"

"It depended on the maker. I am a woman's size medium shirt, size three or four jeans, mostly and I wear a seven and a half shoe. I have a pair of shorts that I was wearing when I was swept, in a sack somewhere."

"And your bra size, my Queen?"

Oh, my God, girl. Show me some privacy.

Melanie whispered the answer to Kristen, and Kristen took Ursula aside and they went off to what must have been the Queen's petty cash.

"Evil comes. Set them free."

Melanie whipped around, but no one was looking at her. "Who said that?" She asked.

Everyone looked her way and the King spoke, "Said what, Mel?"

She determined everyone's look of bewilderment was genuine and guessed she must have imagined it. Not wanting anyone to think she had lost it, she said the first thing that came into her mind, "Who said I was fat? The jeans were mostly three's." She smiled.

"I can assure you Mel," the King said laughingly, "There are none among you that don't enjoy breathing."

Silver Mountain, Main Street

Brie and Henrietta left and made their way down the street towards town hall. It was nice to have someone to talk to as she biked the two miles, but tonight she had planned on passing the time by going over what she was going to say to Isaac. She was only half into the conversation with Henrietta when she realized she had been asked a question.

"You were eavesdropping. That is rude, you know that. She was very fair."

They came upon an officer of city watch, waving them down with a huge smile, and braked their bikes to the side with several others. She guessed it to be the welfare check station for the day.

"Good evening, ladies. Routine whistle-check. Heading home?" He asked.

"No, officer. I'm Brie Thurss. I'm holding a meeting at Town hall tonight. Henrietta here, is also coming."

"Yes, I heard about you. I am proud to meet you. I am Martin Trist." He stuck his hand out and she shook it.

"Thank you, that is kind," she replied.

"Do you ladies have your whistles?" He asked.

Brie presented hers, but Henrietta had forgotten to bring one so the soldier pulled one from his pouch and handed it to her. They were once again off after the standard spiel directed at Henrietta for forgetting hers.

They arrived at the Town Hall and some had already started arriving. True to form, Isaac was sitting out front waiting for her.

Brie and Henrietta greeted Isaac and chatted for a few minutes and Henrietta went inside to meet with her friends. Brie and Isaac sat on the wall of the steps and Brie began.

"Isaac, you know I want to be a sister, right? I want it in the worst way."

"I know. You have said as much."

"I hope I'm not embarrassing myself here, or making you uncomfortable, but I have been sensing that you might be developing feelings for me beyond friendship?"

Isaac flushed and looked surprised, "I love you, Brie! I am so honored to even be in your presence. You are like a God here, but no. I'm not looking for that kind of friendship. The things you say, the things you do are uplifting to everyone. Not one person I know has ever said one bad thing about you. My friends think more of me when I tell them I know you. I know that's selfish but I am alone in the world and my friends are my life. Some watch you stop and talk to me before you go in."

Oops. Guess I misread this just a little bit.

"Well, I love you too Isaac, and I know how important friends are so if you want to stage a talk, you just say the word."

"You're too nice, Brie. I'm surprised you even talk to me, to be honest."

"Hey, let's go inside, okay?"

Brie and her groupie went inside and began to mingle. It was too early to start the meeting, as some were still trickling in. She got into several different chats. She had learned that Auburn's favorite thing to do was walk on the mountainside and listen to the birds chirping and try to see some bighorn sheep clinging to the mountain. Henrietta piped in that it sounded boring to her and Brie said that she thought it sounded great.

Mark and Brie talked at length about his desire to be a singer. "I can go from park to park and keep a notebook of how many people I can make smile."

Brie thought it might be a good idea for him to sing at her meetings, as an introductory type of thing. She said she would talk to the sisters and see if she could get him paid entertainer's wages.

On her way to see what Mattie and Phyllis were talking about, as people were beginning to gather around them, she was stopped by Dave Hanson. *Oh goody, God himself has arrived.*

"Oh, hi Dave. Are you here for the meeting?"

"I could give a rat's ass about your meeting, Breathers. I'm just here so the girls can see what they're missing. Have any of your friends asked about me yet?"

"Gee, not yet Dave, but I'm sure any day now. Excuse me."

She joined the conversation that Mattie and Phyllis were having and understood why so many were gathering.

"He chopped her head off," Mattie was saying, "Right there at Dawn's Landing for everyone to see."

"I'm telling you, Mattie," Phyllis rebuffed, "The King can't chop the Queen's head off. She's the Queen. When you're the Queen, you're the Queen for life."

"My dad was there with his boss, for two days now and he just got home before I left to come here," Mattie countered, "He said the Queen was found guilty of germicide and His Holiness sentenced her to death."

"Genocide?" corrected Billie, rolling her eyes.

"Whatever Billie, who cares? She's dead. We have no Queen," Mattie snapped at the correction.

"How long ago did this happen Mattie, did your dad say?" Brie wanted to know.

"He said that they got there about four in the afternoon, two days ago, and the King was just standing there with his sword all bloody and his head hanging down. Dad said he knew it was the Queen because she was all wrapped up, even her feet and hands. Queens can't be Queens without their hands and feet. Everyone knows that. He also said that last eve the King took off with all his men in a big hurry, heading west. Why would the King take to march at night? Only trouble. See, the Queen is dead and the King is already marching."

Brie figured it was time to start and end the meeting. She had to get back to the apartments and talk to Sister Heather. She climbed to the stage.

"Attention, please," she said in her highest voice. Slowly the crowd quieted.

"First of all, I want to tell you all that I love you very much. You are all very important to me so please don't stray outside the city and get eaten by any four legged critters." Laughter erupted. "Please help me see you again by always carrying your whistles," She glared at Henrietta, "If any harm comes to you, it comes to me, too, as well as the rest of your friends. So take care of yourselves and be kind to one another. I am going to ask for a couple of volunteers to stay here until seven to let any late-comers know I have called off the meeting." The crowd began to buzz.

"Please quiet down, you will know why in a minute. Volunteers?" Henrietta, Mark and Todd raised their hands. Good they all live at the apartments. Brie waited for the buzzing to end and then spoke.

"Most of you have heard the rumor that the Queen was on trial for murder. This has not, and I emphasize not been confirmed by the sisters, but I just learned from Mattie Reardon that the Queen was put to death two days ago by the King. Beheaded for Genocide."

She barely got the last part out before the assembly erupted in shouts and screams. Cries could be heard throughout the hall. Some knees were buckling, some were darting out the door, but the meeting was definitely over. Not even the people in front could hear her now.

Brie headed out the door and rode as fast as she could toward the apartments. The officer she had seen on her way to the meeting was still on patrol. "Slow down, girl. Are you okay?" he asked. She threw him a thumbs up and kept on riding, but slowed down to match the rest of the riders.

Dawn's Landing, Sisterhood

The man set down his book, and went to pour himself some water. He found a basket of fruit and helped himself to a summer apple. He loved summer apples and would make a steady diet of them, but they caused his bowels to seize if he ate them in excess. He walked to the patio door and peered out unto the city. He studied the architecture and admired the craftsmanship of the buildings.

Children were playing in the square, throwing a rubber ball at each other with the other trying not to get hit. There were a couple of teenage boys sitting on a bench talking. About teenage girls, he bet. A cart was being pushed along the sidewalk with bags of groceries and a young woman that he thought might be the Queen's Lady was riding quickly in the direction of the clothing markets.

Off in the distance he saw the never ending Horizon Sea, and a fishing boat doing its best to catch the ever elusive Spraig. He would have to ask for Spraig for sup tomorrow. As rare as it is, Arabella always seemed to find a way. He loved Spraig more than any other fish, but they were really hard to catch and soon became a delicacy.

He needed to get back to his walks. He missed his fresh air walks along the shore. He would have to talk to Sister Tillie and begin those walks again. He was about to sit back down with his book when there was a knock at his door. He walked to the door and looked down, because he knew whomever had knocked would be there. Annoying habit, this kneeling.

He opened the door. "Sister Tillie, please rise."

"She has arrived, Holiness!" Sister Tillie stated.

"Is she well?"

"No, Holiness. She is very distraught. There were two terrible battles getting her here. One with Beasts and one with a wilder. The King took heavy losses, and we. . . we. . ."

"How many?" The Holiness asked, understanding the stutter and already beginning to frown.

"Four, Holiness."

"Please give me their names, that I might ask Mother to keep them close," His Holiness said.

"Sister Ann, Sister Cindy, Sister Nancy, and . . . Sister Kate, Holiness."

Silence. . .

Sister Tillie's nerves were reacting to the stare she was receiving from him. She displayed a twitch in her lip first and then her eye. She began to tremble. She had not been looking forward to this meeting since she heard the news. This would cost her the High Sister rank, at the very least.

His Holiness finally spoke.

"You will give the Queen as much time as she needs to gather herself, before you even mention a meeting with me; and you will gather yourself as well, so that you might persuade me why you sent a married sister on the road."

The air from the door being slammed mussed Sister Tillie's hair. She began to cry, because she knew allowing Sister Kate to take the assignment was wrong when she did it. She wasn't sure why she agreed to it. There were other sisters she could have sent in the ill sister's place.

Queen's Mansion

Sup was beef bits of some sort cooked in a wine sauce, which was later turned into a thick gravy used to cover the best mashed potatoes she had ever tasted. There was a corn and bean mixture as the vegetable. The bread very much resembled the bread sticks that she bought all the time but bigger. The meal was served with a delicious red wine.

She looked at each of the Own, one at a time and asked them to share with her a little about themselves. "I am ashamed that I knew so little about Mitchell. I would like that not to happen again."

The captain started, "My name Highness, is Marie Mercer. You already know my relationship to the King. My mother is a miner's wife. I have two brothers, both of twelve. My father works long hours, but was good to us just the same. I have been with the King two years now."

"How old are you, Marie, if I may ask?"

"Twenty-two, Majesty."

My God! A twenty-two-year-old girl charged into that wilder? Marie may have been young, but she was in excellent physical condition. Even through the uniform, Melanie could tell there was some muscle there. She was a short woman and Melanie couldn't see the hair color, because it was apparently sinful to remove the headgear, even at table. They all looked like they were about to go into battle any second. She would need to work on that, since she was done with battles.

The Princess looked at another of the Own and he began, "My name is Phillip Stems, Majesty. I am twenty-five and widowed. My wife was taken young before bearing our children. I have one brother that lives across the Great Sea. My parents have passed as well."

"My name is Gary Umber, Grace. I am forty-seven years old. My wife is Samantha Umber of the King's staff. We have one son, Harold of the King's Own."

"My name is Willard Hartaugh, Majesty. I am twenty-nine, unwed, without family, and I would like to take this opportunity to express the condolences of the Own at your recent sadness. I pray you will honor this as truth. Had you not distracted the wilder woman, heavier damage would have occurred and our captain would be dead!"

"Hear! Hear!" was unanimously heard around the table and Sir Kevin raised his wine and said, "To Our Queen, who will go down in the histories as Queen Courageous, may she live forever." All lifted their glasses in tribute, including Frances. Melanie bowed her head, but had no intention of drinking to that.

The Queen waited until the toast was finished, and followed it with one of her own. "Here is to the most courageous men and women I have ever seen. To the men and women of the King, to the Own and the sisters. To all the innocent citizens of Dawn's Landing who perished on that battlefield. May I never be subject to such violence again?" All drank to the Queen's toast.

"If I might ask," the Queen went on, "Did anyone happen to notice the color of my eyes when I merge with Mother?"

Marie answered, "As blue as the sky at Darvon's Highness, but when you were in battle with the wilder, they were red."

That doesn't make any sense, my eyes are green. Red hair, green eyes. "The eyes of the wilder were yellow. Why is that?"

The King answered. "You will have to ask her, Mel. Oh wait, you can't."

Laughter erupted and for the rest of the meal conversations paired off, but Melanie did not stop thinking about those yellow eyes. Nor did she see the humor in the King's jest.

During the course of sup, Kristen had returned and carried her items upstairs. She had come down a few minutes later and sat patiently on a rather elaborate looking couch. Melanie, having finished eating, excused herself from the conversations and headed for the staircase. Kristen met her at the foot.

"I know you will be busy, Highness," Kristen said, "But perhaps later we could go to market and get you some proper clothing. I picked you up some pajamas and a couple of shirts and sets of socks and underwear, but I only got you a single pair of casual trousers."

"That will be fine. I need to get out of this dress, but I am a woman and women hate shopping." After she noticed Kristen's look of shock, the Queen winked at her. Kristen smiled.

"Is there a book store close to where we are going?" She asked Kristen, "I read a lot."

"You have a library My Queen, but yes, 'The Page Cage' is on the way."

When she was ready to jump in the shower, she asked Kristen how close the water tower was that fed the shower. She felt like an idiot when Kristen told her the water towers only fed hydrants and homes had wells.

When she was showered and done she was led by Kristen to her bedroom. Melanie stood and stared at her room. Just the bedroom was larger than her living room, dining room and kitchen back home. There were ornate stands on either side of the bed and the bed itself was huge and very comfortable looking with a yellow pastel canopy. There were two windows on either side of the bed with the same color drapes as the canopy. There was a couch near the door and two chairs and a table against another wall. There was a vanity next to the window that went the entire length of the wall. The closet, larger than her bedroom at home, had a mirror that ran from the floor to the top of the door. There were light globes in the closet, at the mirror, and three above the vanity and the bed. And one above the chairs and couch. You could hold a peewee football game in this room. She sat at the vanity and was watching her hair being brushed. She was not too pleased by what she was seeing. She really missed her makeup right now. "I suppose makeup is not possible, right?"

"I'm sorry, My Queen, I thought about it, but I didn't want to anger you and get the wrong colors. I did bring mine in if you want to look through them."

"Will they make me look as beautiful as you?"

Kristen smiled, "I have been told that, but I must be too accustomed to looking at myself because like you, I don't think I am."

Well you snot-nosed little brat! "So you're saying I can't recognize my own beauty because I'm too accustomed to looking at it?"

"That is the same issue that each of us have, Majesty."

She was enjoying this little confab with Kristen and was beginning to like the young lady. This ought to be a really nice shopping trip. "Kristen, how old are you?"

"Twenty-four, Highness."

"Oh, my. I took you for sixteen, or seventeen."

"As do most, Majesty. It makes the purchasing of wine and beer a good laugh."

Melanie compared her hair to that of Kristen's and decided Kristen's was a tad bit lighter red than her own, and it was considerably longer. So much so that Melanie felt sorry for the woman and wondered how she found time to wash it. She also appeared to be about an inch shorter than Melanie. She had a smooth complexion but there was an almost undetectable scar just above her left eye that she was attempting to hide with bangs that came to her brows. "Are you married?"

"Not for the lack of a certain man's trying."

"Not your type?"

"When he respects my mind, who I am, and what I do more than he does my figure, who he wants me to be, and what he wants me to do, then I will say yes."

The hair was finished, the makeup was on and it was time to go down and see if those pesky sup guests ever left, even though she knew all but Frances were staying the night.

As it turned out all shops closed at ten, so she made her excuses and she, Kristen, Phillip, Gary and Ursula left. She was introduced to her new limousine. A very strange contraption indeed. She had seen them before. Bicycle cabs. This one had a canopy that no man would be seen under, but there was enough room for four comfortably. She chose to ride a bicycle instead. She picked one from the lot Kristen had given her to choose from. Ursula, the Queen's pocketbook, rode in the contraption. The sun had set long ago, but she was pleasantly surprised at the lighting of the streets. She began to ogle the shops.

Silver Mountain Sisterhood

Brie reached the apartments and found Sister Heather with her head still buried in whatever she was doing.

"Brienne Thurss, you stop running through these halls this minute."

Brie stopped, took a deep breath and spit it out. "One of my friends just told me the Queen is dead, beheaded by the King." She never took her eyes off the sister, and could tell by the expression on her face that it was true. "Why did I have to find this out from a friend?"

"You just calm yourself down young lady, and take care of that tone. This doesn't affect your life in any way and there was no need for you to know yet. We were going to let Silver Mountain know on the new day. Did you pass this information on?"

"The entire assembly Sister, and it does affect my life and the lives of my friends. Who are you to decide to withhold this kind of information? All of Mother feared this woman, not knowing what she was going to do next."

"Are you finished?" The High Sister was now angered, "Do you have anything else you wish to insult me about? If you do, now would be the time. You want to be a sister, but you can't see the situation we are in. Not having a Queen on Mother. Everyone feared her? Life on Mother can't exist without a Queen. There has never been a Queen that died before her time. How long must we wait before the next Queen arrives? Must we wait the normal lifespan of Pamela? Will we be able to last that long? There is more to consider here than just whether we should tell Brie and her friends, such as worldwide panic."

"There was no panic Sister," Brie lied, "There were tears and sadness, there was eagerness to pass the word, but there was no panic. The only panic I felt was that the sisters betrayed me. You betrayed me."

Sister Heather slammed her fist on her desk, "This discussion is over. Get out."

"You have lost faith in humanity, Sister. We will survive because we will ourselves to."

"I said we are done." Sister Heather said angrily as she stood.

Brie left and headed to her room. She stopped at Sister Grandma's and poked her head in. She saw the sister sleeping soundly and the breathing was steady.

When she reached her room, she prepared herself for bed and climbed in. She lie there with her hands behind her head thinking on the day's events. She tried to take her mind off what just happened, but she was unsuccessful. She didn't think she would get much in the way of sleep tonight. She tried to think of pleasant things and more enlightening talks, but she kept coming back to the talk with Sister Heather.

She chuckled to herself about a comment her dad made to her one night as he was tucking her in. She was only eight at that time and had been having trouble getting sleep. Her dad told her to picture sheep jumping over a fence and in the morning she could tell him how many she counted. Little did he know the reason she couldn't sleep was because she had been stealing candy from his secret bag. At eight years old she thought counting sheep was hogwash, now she thought it might not be a bad idea to try it.

It failed, to no surprise. She thought of taking a walk in the garden. She loved the feeling of the soil slipping between her toes, but instead she swung her feet off the bed and into her flip flops that the sisters didn't like. They didn't mind the flip so much as the flop. She walked as quietly as she could to the kitchen to steal one of Sister Ellen's cupcakes, but found them gone. What a bunch of piggies. She laughed. She found some hard boiled eggs, grabbed one and took her egg, plate and salt to the table.

She thought back on her talk with Sister Heather, trying to decide if the sister was seeing her view in any way, but she didn't put much stock in it. Children should be seen and not heard. That wasn't going to happen to Brie. The sisters have always said she had the voice of a lion.

As Brie was peeling her egg, which was not peeling well at all, obviously made by one of her friends because they forgot to put salt in the water, she felt the brush against her leg.

"Hello, Muffin," she pulled the chair next to her out and the calico cat hopped up and tried hard not to show any interest at all in Brie's egg. Brie pulled a small piece off and sat it on the chair in front of Muffin. She watched as Muffin chewed and swallowed the egg and then began cleaning herself which would probably only take an hour for a piece that small.

This was a law that had Brie's full support. No one was allowed to have a dog or a cat that wasn't spayed or neutered. Only breeder farms were allowed to have them otherwise. They were expensive, too. Cats cost twenty-seven dollars and a gold half and dogs were thirty dollars. The sisters had two cats, Muffin and Cupcake. Brie wished they had a dog. She liked dogs and missed Einstein, her sheepdog on Earth. *I wonder if he's been here yet.*

Brie was beginning to feel a little heavy in the eye and thought it would be a good time to try again to get some sleep so she cleaned up, said goodnight to Muffin and headed down the hall. She stopped at Sister Grandma's room and peeked in and found her still sleeping soundly, so she headed to her room, lied down and was sleeping in minutes.

Dawn's Landing, Sisterhood

Sister Tillie began making her way up the steps to His Holiness and his suite. Having thought on the topic he had given her to think on, she realized there was nothing to think of. It was the worst decision she had made since becoming the High Sister. She deserved to be stripped. She knew that it should be her that talked with Kate's husband, but she also knew His Holiness would take that responsibility on himself.

When she reached the door, Sister Tillie went to her knees and said a silent prayer to Mother for His Holiness. To guide him in this decision and those to come. To give him the words to free Michael of his sorrow. She said no prayer for herself. She didn't deserve one.

She knocked on the door. She heard the footsteps and felt the rush of air as the door opened. There was no greeting, as there normally would have been. There was no melodic voice that welcomed her, or his magical use of the word 'sister'. There was only, "Rise."

"Have you thought on that which I asked you to?" He continued.

"No, Holiness. There was no reasoning for the decision that was worthy of thought."

He saw the tears and knew she was prepared for what was coming, so he saw no need to sugar coat it, "You will report to Sister Beth on the new day and tell her this. You have been stripped of your duties, and she is to see me."

"Have I been banished, Holiness?" She asked, struggling with her voice.

He had to give her credit, every ounce of her was crying, but she was holding it together on the outside. "That will be Sister Beth's decision, not mine."

"Thank you, Holiness. The sisterhood . . .

"Don't thank me. It is Sister Beth's call. I will not speak against, nor will I for you. Goodnight."

She went to her knees but the door closed before she could get there.

Market Square

Shopping with this woman was a riot, Kristen was keeping her in stitches (*oops! I made a pun*) as they went from shop to shop, trying on this outfit and that. This would at least set her up in the clothing and makeup area, and she got that handled on her first day. Kudos to Ursula, as she was dishing out funds without blinking an eye. Interesting woman. I am her third Queen and much to Melanie's surprise, Ursula had liked Pamela, saying she was good to her staff even toward the end.

The most expensive item Melanie bought was a pair of dress shoes for her meeting with His Holiness, that cost her two dollars, a gold half and a silver quarter. She could shop forever. She was a little skeptical at first as she had asked how much money she had.

"You have eleven hundred thirty-three dollars and a gold half, Highness."

That would not even pay her mortgage payment on Earth, so she asked what upcoming expenses she had.

"This is the Queens funds, Majesty. I realize it sounds like a lot, but Queen Pamela never spent her money, so much of it carried over from her."

Umm, it doesn't actually sound like a lot, but thank you.

Kristen later told her she will find herself having an excess of funds more often than not. Queens of the past, except Pamela, would use what they needed in the month, and just before the Queen's taxes would arrive she would send the Queen's purse off to give the remainder to the sisters to help the children.

When she had done as much damage as she was going to, they all packed up the cabbie and began the bike ride back to the Mansion.

As they entered the door, the King and Kevin were the only ones still in the room. The Own, according to Kevin were getting some sleep as Phillip and Gary were due to be relieved in less than three hours. Sister Frances was upstairs in the reading room.

"We are ready to retire as well, Mel," said the King, "But we wanted to bid you goodbye until we returned with your daughter. We will be leaving prior to your waking."

The desire to hug the two men was strong, but she wasn't sure that would be proper so instead, "I thank you both so very much for my safety, and I look forward to your return." With that, the two headed upstairs. Melanie headed up shortly after, stopped at the reading room to tell Sister Frances she wouldn't be saying anything important for the rest of the night. She perused the books and picked one out, and once Kristen was done loading her drawers and closet, it took no time at all for Melanie to fall asleep, reading.

Silver Mountain, Sisterhood

When Brie woke to the smell of bacon, she realized she overslept and bolted out of bed, slipped on her sandals and raced down the hall to the kitchen, pajamas and all. "I'm sorry I'm late, Sister."

"No harm done, Brie," said Sister Helen, kindly. Brie, Sister Helen and Sarah finished preparing breakfast for the school kids and started dishing up and passing out plates and slowly the rumbling from all the talking, each trying to be louder than the other, began to diminish as they began using their mouths for eating instead of joking and laughing.

Once the breakfast crowd had finished and was off to school, Brie and Sarah began cleaning up and Sister Helen headed off to begin waking the 'Young ones'. When she and Sarah were alone, Brie spoke, "Sarah, I need your help with something." As they were washing dishes and had the kitchen to themselves, Brie explained her need and plans to Sarah. Once they had finished the dishes, Brie saw she still had twenty minutes or so before they had to start breakfast for the sisters and other kids, so she darted off for the showers.

When she arrived back at the kitchen, she smelled the biscuits and saw Sarah working on pancakes and gravy and Sister Helen peeling and slicing potatoes, so Brie began working on the bacon and scrambled eggs. The buffet was set just in time, as the first person that showed up for breakfast was, to no surprise, Mark (Sandpit stomach) Harris. They filed in steadily and Brie and Sarah were kept busy with replenishing the bowls and helping the little ones dish up. No babies came in last night so no one needed to be fed. Babies never lasted long here anyway. They were usually accepted within hours. During breakfast, Brie also solicited the help of Mark and Henrietta for today's project.

Once everyone had finished and started off for their chores, Sister Helen, Sarah and Brie cleaned up and then headed off for their chores as well. Sarah was teaching reading to the little ones today so she might take a little longer, but there was no hurry. On her way out front to sweep the marble walkway, Brie was stopped by Sister Helen.

"Brie honey," Uh oh, "I just wanted to say that you are the sweetest, most kind and conscientious young lady we have had here since I have been here, but you are wrong this time. This is news that needed preparation."

"I don't believe that I am, Sister. Mother is not your world. We all belong to her. We all deserved to know when you knew. This is nine eleven type news." This drew a quizzical look from Sister Helen, but Brie continued, "I've studied my history, Sister. This is one of the reasons there is no government on Mother. We have the right to decide for ourselves."

Brie knew it was rude to do so, but she didn't want to antagonize the already volatile and strained relationship that was beginning between her and the sisters, so she turned and went out the door.

She finished all her chores and those of Sister Grandma and went to get her for their walk. Happily, while they were walking, Sister Grandma didn't mention the news or the conflict with Sister Heather. She just scolded Brie on her inability to get her chores done and they talked about Mother a lot.

Sister Grend said, "Brie, I want to go to Murphy's and get some chocolate today," so Brie went with her, helping her cross the street, irritating cabbies. Ridiculous looking contraptions anyway. You could almost walk faster.

Sister Grandma picked out the chocolate she wanted and told Mr. Murphy that she wanted a pound. Mr. Murphy bagged it up, handed it to Sister Grandma and said, "That will be. . . but the sister was already on her way to the exit. He just looked at Brie, smiled, shook his head and reached for his ledger.

Brie asked, "How much does she owe, Mr. Murphy?"

"She is up to two dollars and a silver quarter, Brie. Would you let Sister Heather know, please?"

Brie checked her pockets and found one dollar and a gold half and gave it to Mr. Murphy. "I will pay the rest and leave a deposit for her the next time I am in."

"You are a remarkable young lady, Brie," Mr. Murphy said, shaking his head.

"Have a nice day, Mr. Murphy."

Brie took Sister Grandma home and to her room, and to no surprise was refused when Brie asked for a piece of the chocolate. "I'm not made of money, young lady. Go buy your own."

"Yes, Sister."

Brie left Sister Grend to her chocolate, checked in on Sarah's home schooling and saw she was nearly done. She went to Sister Heather's office and started to knock, when the sister looked up and said, "What is it, Brie?"

"Sister, I would like to go to Dawn's Landing and meet Sister Tillie."

"I will not stop you, but you will be disappointed if you hope to alter our thinking."

"I understand Sister, and I apologize if I have come off as being too disrespectful, but I will not alter my thinking either."

"You are willful, Brie," the sister said angrily, "A train leaves Tuesday with an opening, pack what you will need."

"Thank you, Sister." *Three days and I will have a chance to meet His Holiness.*

Brie went to the kitchen and began to make sandwiches. Henrietta came and helped. Mark gathered a couple of baskets and when Sarah finished, they were off. On the road, Brie ran things through her head what she was going to say when they got there. She was right, she knew she was. She could feel it in her heart.

Dawn's Landing, Queen's Mansion

The King was true to his word. When she woke, he and his army were gone. He left a token guard of two hundred under the command of the Princess, but the balance were gone. Tents, supplies and all.

Breakfast was an omelet with ham and peppers, potatoes and orange juice. It was delicious but was not prepared by Theresa. The morning cook was a man named Arnold. It was just her and Sister Frances and the conversation was about the likelihood that Frances would be relieved today in favor of a more seasoned scribe. She and Melanie would, after breakfast, go to meet with Sister Tillie and set up a schedule for her training.

"Will I be meeting with His Holiness, as well?" Melanie asked.

"I confess, I'm not sure, Highness. If you want to, I'm sure you will not be refused, but His Holiness usually prefers a scheduled meeting."

"Then I won't dress up. Have you met His Holiness, Sister?"

"Yes Majesty, and it is not a meeting I will soon forget. His Holiness is a wonderful man, and you get an elevated feel in his presence."

The conversation continued through breakfast and Melanie was careful not to say anything that would cause Frances to have to put her fork down in favor of her pen. When the conversation ebbed, she thought on the nightmare she had last night. She couldn't remember the last time she had such nightmares, but thought it might have been when she was ten.

As Arnold and Pierre were cleaning up the table, Melanie alerted Willard and the captain, who had been chattering in the foyer, of her intentions to meet the sisters this morning. Marie informed her that another member of the Queen's Own had been raised last night and should be here by sup.

Melanie went upstairs and on her way to make her bed, passed by Kristen's room and poked her head in the opened door. Kristen was sitting at her vanity brushing her hair.

"Good morning," Melanie greeted, causing the poor woman pause. Kristen turned toward her.

"Good morning, My Queen. Did you sleep well?"

"I did, thank you, though I had a bad dream. Sister Frances and I are going to meet the sisters this morning. Would you do something for me while I'm gone?"

"Of course, Highness, what would you have me do?"

"I would like a tour of the house and grounds when I return and have a list of everyone that works here."

"It will be done."

"Thank you."

When Melanie got to her room, she found not only had her bed already been made, but the room was spotless. She proceeded down the hallway and came to another room. Spotless. She continued, checking each room, and found who she was looking for, about five rooms down from her, stripping a bed.

She walked in. "Hello!" Melanie nearly heard the thump before she witnessed the movement. "Oh for Pete's sake, girl. Get off your knees. No kneeling in this house."

"My apologies, Majesty. I am new yet."

"What is your name?"

"Angelina, Highness. Angelina Surcott."

"I am pleased to meet you, Angelina. Perhaps later we can talk a bit."

"Yes, Highness," Angelina replied with a fearful look of trepidation.

"You haven't done anything wrong. I would just like to get to know you."

"Yes, Highness."

On her way downstairs, Melanie popped her head back into Kristen's and told her of the talk with Angelina, and asked her to calm the girl down.

"I will speak with her, Majesty."

Melanie went back downstairs and found all was ready for visiting the sisters. The captain was waiting for her at the door to the front walk way. "Are you ready, My Queen?"

"Let's hit the road. How far is it?"

Marie pointed to one of the three story structures near the north gate of the city. "Okay, now I want a car."

Marie chuckled and responded, "You and the sister will be riding in the cabbie, Highness."

Melanie was certain if they ran into any steep hills, she and Frances would have to get out and push, but she got in anyway. She was amazed at how comfortable and cool it was. There were drapes on all sides with window slits to let the light in and there was more leg room than she had thought there would be. The cabbie started slow, but then got up to a pretty good speed. It would give her a good opportunity to see some of the city. Melanie asked Frances, "What's the date today?"

"Friday, June 32nd, 531, Majesty."

32nd? Yet another question I need ask.

The cabbie weaved down one street, then another, and Melanie would ask about this building or that building. Some streets were residential, some had parks. Mothers were walking strollers; children were playing ball. A soldier had two men and their bicycles pulled to the side. She wondered if he caught them dragging down main street. All considered, it was a very interesting ride.

Sisterhood

When they arrived, they started up a solid white marble walkway that looked like no one ever walked on it. It was immaculate and it led to steps that were bordered by six bronze statues with plaques at the bases. One of the statues was of a King Jonas of Dakota, one was of a Holiness whose name she couldn't even think of pronouncing and four were of former Queens Celise, Isabel, Colleen, and Cynthia. Frances waited patiently as Melanie stopped to read every plaque.

King Jonas was the first King to capture a wilder alive and transported her across the Great Sea and across the continent to Dawn's Landing and the Holiness in the year 192.

The Holiness whose name she couldn't pronounce was simply identified as the fifth Holiness saying he was Holiness from the year 177 to the year 212.

Queen Cynthia was Queen from the year 112 to the year 148, Queen Isabel from 148 to 172, Queen Celise from 172 to 212, and Queen Colleen from 212 to 224.

Melanie had finished admiring the statues and headed into the building. The first thing she saw were steps directly in front of her that ran up and were wide enough for twenty people to walk side by side with hand rails on both sides and right down the middle. On either side of the staircase was a walkway that led into the center of the building. She noticed that on the other side of the staircase they connected into one very wide hallway. Sister Frances led the way to the hallway at the right of the staircase.

At the first room they passed, two sisters were talking and noticed them and they converged on Francis rapidly and began crying in a group hug. Francis introduced them as Sisters Marilyn and Carol.

"Good morning, Majesty," said Sister Marilyn.

"Good morning, Majesty," repeated Sister Carol.

I wonder if the President ever got tired of being called Mr. President.

"Good morning, Sister Carol, Sister Marilyn."

"We are so sorry for the difficulty you had getting here, Highness," Sister Carol said, "We certainly hope that we can give you a better impression of life on Mother."

"I appreciate your kind words but I am saddened more by the losses than I am for myself."

With that, she and Sister Frances proceeded to the next room which was their destination, but Sister Frances looked a little surprised at who she found sitting behind the desk.

"Sister Beth, I have brought Queen Melanie to meet Sister Tillie."

"I have been raised to High Sister, Sister Frances. My apologies that you found out in this manner and please accept my condolences for your losses and my sincere apology that you had to witness such carnage, and to you, My Queen that you were received to Mother with such violence."

Frances looked speechless, so Melanie spoke up, "Thank you Sister, and please accept my apology and condolences that my arrival was so costly to the Sisterhood. Would it be possible for Sister Frances to be excused so that we might allow her time to freshen up and regain herself?" That should give her time to get the scoop from the other sisters.

"As you wish, Majesty. Sister would you be so kind as to ask Sister Eloise to handle your scripture for a little bit?"

"Yes, High Sister, thank you," Frances was off.

After a few minutes of cordial chat about the sisterhood and Dawn's Landing, Melanie felt Sister Beth to be a kind and gentle woman. Another sister entered and was introduced as Sister Eloise, who had been Queen Pamela's scribe.

"You will find her quite informative, My Queen. She is blessed with twenty-seven years of knowledge."

Say what? Melanie thought that had sounded like Sister Eloise was being appointed permanently.

"What we will do," Sister Beth continued, "Is have you here each day and gradually help you adjust with Mother's presence. We will be spending several hours a day sporadically having you merge with Mother and explain what it is you are feeling as was told to us by former Queens. We will naturally break for a lunch and sup."

Say what? Melanie was having second thoughts about the kind and gentle Sister Beth. That had almost sounded like a command.

"We will have you read past Chronicles so that you may adapt to the patterns of past Queens. We will have you meet with the Kings from other lands so that they may share with you each of their concerns about their respective kingdoms. I am sure you understand that we are down four sisters, so King Brent's request will have to be temporarily put on the back burner, so to speak."

Say what? This woman absolutely is trying to show Melanie who is in charge. Back burner?

"Is there anything you would like me to go over in more detail about the way we will progress or have I made the training clear?" Sister Beth ended with a smile.

Melanie stared at the woman in disbelief. She was infuriated at the condescending tone this woman just addressed her with, and judging by the vibration the wooden chair was making that Sister Eloise was sitting in, she guessed Sister Eloise had recognized the expression on Melanie's face as being less than friendly, and knew what was coming.

The High Sister's eyes and those of Melanie stayed locked as Melanie spoke.

"You will assign Sister Frances as my scribe. She has several more days of knowledge of this Queen than Sister Eloise. I will be here every moment that I feel I need to be educated on being connected to Mother. I will eat and sleep when I feel a need and if I happen to come here when the sisters I need help from are busy, you will escort me where I need to be. When I require information from the knowledge of former Queens, you or one of the understaffed by six Sisterhood, which include the two my King promised me, will read the past chronicles of Queens and get me that information. I will adapt none of their patterns, because I am not them. When my Kings from other kingdoms grace me, I will have knowledge of that long before you, and I will ask THEM if they would like to see the sister's apartments. You will get me every tidbit of information at your disposal about the wilder. I want to know their hair color, why their eyes are yellow, how they connect to mother, what they are feeling when they are connected, when the first wilder was discovered and what size bra they wear. Is there anything you would like me to go over in more detail about the way we will progress or have I made myself clear?"

The High Sister was showing signs of fury now, and she was still locked on Melanie's eyes, but before she could provide her own response, another voice spoke. It was a man's.

"When you ladies (both the High Sister and Sister Eloise hit the floor so fast, Melanie thought they might have melted through the chairs) are finished with your little power contest, I would like to introduce myself."

'The King and Queen don't kneel to each other, Majesty, they kneel only to His Holiness.' Melanie turned and looked at the man, so angry she was determined to be defiant. What she felt was respect. More respect than she had felt from any man. Ever. Defiance departed out the back door and she melted off the chair and was on her knees.

"My apologies, Holiness. I have had a bad few days."

"Please rise, My Queen."

Melanie tried to rise but her whole body was jelly and she went back down. She tried again and managed to stand up but was still very unsure on her feet. She gave an embarrassed chuckle. She looked into his eyes. The two sisters were still on their knees.

"Perhaps, you and I could take a short walk, Highness."

The pope of the pope just called me Highness.

"I would be honored, Your Eminence. Please call me Mel."

"I will call you Majesty, Highness, or My Queen. I will not call you by your given name unless you were to call me by mine. I have long ago forgotten what that name is however, but I am certain it is not Eminence."

The Holiness continued toward the High Sister, "It will be as the Queen commands. I will send word to the King."

"Yes, Holiness," came from behind the desk. He and Melanie left the room and headed further into the building down the wide hallway. Everyone they came across was on their knees but they just kept walking and chatting.

"This need you have to learn about the wilder mind might not be a healthy quest, Highness, but it is past time to make them a priority. I do not believe that all of the wilder are evil. Holiness Poppyo wrote that the wilder King Jonas brought him was very respectful and kind, but admitted animosity towards the Kings and Queen. She wouldn't speak of why.

"I believe there are wilders inside Dawn's Landing living normal lives like everyone else. Anyone that connects with Mother and is not our Queen is technically a wilder. That is the definition given when they were first discovered."

"Yes," Melanie responded, "But my understanding is that they connect and then stay connected and it drives them insane in less than five hours. That makes them dangerous."

"That's my fault. That refers to Queen Pamela. Queens of the past have been connected much longer than five hours. You can't reshape an entire mountain in that little time. I believe what drove the Queen over the edge was an attempt to merge with something Mother didn't want her to."

"Like what?"

"I know not, but there is a temptation that you will feel eventually to go there, I know I have."

Fear surged through Melanie. Did he just say he was a wilder? As they exited the back door, Melanie looked at the feet of the Holiness and saw he wore shoes. He had just admitted to being a wilder. Melanie surveyed the grounds and found everything cemented. No dirt anywhere. She tried to decide how far she would have to run to merge.

"They cemented everything in after Pamela," the Holiness offered, "So that they could better control her during visits, not knowing that the Queen had the ability to 'Store' Mother's power, and just out front."

"What?"

"When we came outside, you looked at my feet and then looked all over the grounds. The nearest soil is just out front. I'm not sure if I am one, Highness. I don't believe I am insane. I don't believe in violence and I do not hate as they do. This is why I don't think they are all evil. How did you think I knew you would be the next Queen even before you arrived? A magical ball in my apartment, maybe?"

"By definition, you are a wilder. You connect to Mother and you are not a Queen."

"I agree. I too feel I am a form of wilder. My appeal to you is that you accept that there are many wilders on Mother and they are, myself included, worthy of your attention. My question to you is, are you up to the challenge? I believe there are many that are simply hiding the fact out of fear. It is not a secret how the sisters feel about wilders.

"Wilders have the same connection feeling that you do," he continued, "You feel like your feet or hands are falling asleep. A tingling sensation and it works its way through you. It is only the power that you can hold inside you that separates you from them."

"Wilders are better prepared for battle than I," Melanie said.

"Today, they are. The time will come however, when you will swat them like flies. I encourage you to merge as often as you can for as long as you can. There were no sisters to help Queen Emily when she got here. She simply learned."

"Stop the violence! Set them free"

Melanie turned around to confront the person that had spoken to her but no one was there. She looked all around and then looked at the quizzical expression on the face of His Holiness.

"Majesty? Are you well?" He asked.

"I'm fine," she answered. She was going to have to see a psychiatrist soon. Now she knew she was hearing things.

The conversation went on throughout the afternoon, when the Holiness expressed regrets that he had to leave to talk to a man who had just lost his wife. As the talk went on she became less skeptical of his words. He was insistent that she merge in solitude. He asked her to continue allowing the sisters to believe that it is the time the Queen is merged that causes the problem. Also, he wasn't quite ready yet for the people to realize that there might be wilders among them.

"I will be available for your questions daily," he continued, "You and I agree that wilders need to be a priority. We just don't agree on why."

It was getting late so she made her way out front to the cabbie with his words streaming through her mind. She saw that Phillip and Gary had replaced Willard and the captain. When she climbed into the cabbie she saw Frances sitting there doing some needlework. "Your wrists don't get enough exercise? I need to ask a question. Previous Queens. Is it always death that causes another to come? Have any other than Pamela failed due to stress or other issues… or…you know, I mean have any just completely lost their mind?"

"There are no chronicle entries of mental disorder, My Queen. Not even Queen Pamela is listed so. The Chronicles are very forthcoming about cause of death. Queen Colleen was assassinated, but the others were either a disease or natural death. Shall I have the sisters make a list of causes?"

"No…no, that's okay. Just a question."

Frances just smiled and they made their way home to sup.

Silver Mountain, 7th Street and Emily Drive

When they got to the Wickert house, Brie saw the boy sitting by himself on the front porch, staring into nothingness. He saw them walking up the walk.

"What do you want, Breathers?" He asked.

"Dave, we are going to have a picnic on the beach and were hoping you would come."

"You are kidding me. Which one of these babes is the one with the crush on me?"

"Stop it, Dave," said Henrietta.

"No one was talking to you, Hank!" Dave spat back.

"Come on, man. I don't want to be the only guy," said Mark.

"Please, Dave. Please come," added Sarah.

"Fine. I'll play along, as long as the lady Brie doesn't start one of her stupid sessions."

Dave went inside and came out shortly after, and they were all off. The conversation went exactly as she warned them it would with the insults flying, and the 'You want me' attitude. The ride was long, as they all lived on the Southeast corner of Silver Mountain and the Lake was more northeast.

When they got to the entrance, Brie saw the beach was not as packed as she thought it was going to be, and if this went like she suspected, that was a good thing. They parked their bikes and the officer at the entrance gate was a cheerful man in his forties, Brie guessed.

"A picnic lunch. Aw, yes. I remember those days well. Whistles?"

Everyone produced their whistles except one. "Henrietta, what am I to do with you?" asked Brie.

The soldier produced a whistle for Henrietta and they were admitted through the gate, and Henrietta offered, "They chafe my skin, Brie."

"Wear a real shirt, everyone knows you have boobs." Brie offered.

"Yes, but they don't know how much bigger mine are than yours," Henrietta mused.

Dave was laughing so hard, Brie thought he might hyperventilate. She resisted the urge to check out her breasts for a comparison, but out of the corner of her eye she saw Mark was showing no such resistance. "Really, Mark?" she said.

Mark tried to look as if he was looking at the sand, but Sarah slapped the back of his head, laughed and said, "Busted".

"Busted? Now that's pretty punny, Sarah," Brie said.

They set up the baskets on the beach and Brie sat next to Dave and handed him a sandwich. The idle talk went on for a few minutes, but Brie and Dave didn't join in. Dave looked over at her and saw her looking at him and she made no attempt to look away. "What?" He said loudly.

"How old was she?"

"How old was who?"

Brie didn't respond, she just stayed on his eyes, not looking away. He matched her stare for stare, but after about ten seconds she saw the first tear. Then the eyes got wet. "It's none of your business, Breathers." She realized everyone had gone silent and was just looking at the two of them, but it was too late to stop now.

Dave stood up to walk away, but Brie was up and blocking his way. "It is my business, Dave. It is all of our business. If we didn't care about you, we wouldn't be here." He moved left, she moved right, he moved right, she moved left, he made a fist and made to hit her and she stuck out her chin. "If it will make you feel better, do it, but I'm not leaving your side, Dave. I'm not!" The tears exploded down his cheeks and he began to bawl loudly. "Thirteen," he was screaming. "She was my sister. Where were you, Breathers? Where were you when the sand pit was sucking her down? Where were your damn meetings then?"

She put her hand on his shoulder, but he jerked away. "Don't touch me, don't ever touch me."

Sarah and Henrietta were on him fast. Fastening hugs and sharing in his tears, even Mark joined in. The crying went on for minutes that seemed like hours but Brie never budged. She stayed in front of him and let his anger fly at her. With the other three attached to him, he continued to let it out. Insult after insult and name after name. She stood her ground, never flinching and never saying a word, her own tears flowing for him.

Finally, it subsided and sheer exhaustion took over and he collapsed to the ground and all three of his attachments collapsed with him. She sat down in front of him and they locked eyes. "I love you, Dave," she said.

"I love you, Dave," said Henrietta. "You can call me Hank whenever you want."

"I love you, Dave," said Mark.

"I love you, Dave," said Sarah as she kissed him on the cheek.

Dave opened up after a time. He and his little sister had been wrestling in their front yard, when they were swept. When they woke there were two soldiers on horses staring down at them. The soldiers took them to Silver Mountain and the sisters. The sisters were nice but gave them no hope that they could be re-united with their parents. The sisters worked hard to ease their fears and 'Chelle seemed to be handling it better than he was, but when he went to bed he heard the commotion in the halls and followed the crowd out to see his little sister sinking in the sand pit. She didn't even say goodbye, she just stared at him. He tried to run to her but two of the sisters held him down while another tried to get his sister to grab the rope she threw at her. By the time the sister tied the rope to herself and jumped in, his sister was too far gone.

On the walk back, each of them would talk to him about this or that and reassured him that they were available anytime he needed to talk and even when he didn't. They each called themselves a friend for life and all swore an oath of friendship. He swore one back. Brie said nothing. Just listened. I think they're finally getting it.

When they did bring her in on the conversation, she broke the news to them that she would be going to Dawn's Landing and that she wanted the four of them to take over for her. Dave looked surprised, but said that he would do all he could.

"I'm very sorry about all the things I said, Brie. Thank you for letting me talk this out to someone." Brie gave him her best smile and it was sincere.

By the time they dropped Dave off and said their goodbyes it was getting to be late afternoon and Brie and Sarah had to get back to help with sup. Henrietta and Mark stayed behind to spend some time at Dave's.

When they neared the apartments, Sarah grabbed Brie's arm and said, "Something's wrong."

Brie looked and there were many people on the front lawn and many soldiers were lining the marble walkway.

"No!" she screamed. "Sister Grandma."

Sisterhood

She pedaled as fast as she could, leaving Sarah to catch up. She turned up the walk, dropped the bike and charged up the steps.

"Slow down, child. Show some respect!" said Sister Grend. Brie gave her a big hug. A soldier was coming out the door and everyone except the sisters went to their knees. Brie was confused but soon realized it was the king. *He's here! The King is here. Oh how I wish I could speak with him.*

"Rise, Princess."

Brie sneaked a peek to her left, then to her right but no one was getting up. There was a tap on her shoulder and the King said, "That would be you, girl."

He called me Princess, the King called me Princess. She stood.

"Rise, all of you," he continued and everyone stood.

He looked her in the eyes and she looked into his. My word, is he a handsome man! The King was over six feet tall. His biceps bulged. He was square jawed with dark brown hair protruding from his head gear. He had a well-trimmed short stubble beard, and those deep brown eyes of his looked like they were seeing right into her brain.

"The Queen has sent me to fetch you," he said.

She found her voice, although she wasn't sure where, "Majesty, I thought the Queen was dead?"

"Not that evil bitch. The new Queen. Queen Melanie, your mother."

My mom's a Queen? Are you kidding me? Who cares? It's mom. I get to see mom.

After the initial shock was over, she had the sudden urge to go pack, but she knew Sister Helen was waiting to start sup.

"Will you be eating with us tonight, Majesty? May I prepare something for you?" She asked him.

"You may not. I will be joining you as well as my captain and whomever you care to join us, but your days of preparing food are done. While your meal is being prepared, you will need to go pack. You will be staying at my home tonight as we will leave from there at first light."

"Right away, Majesty."

Brie took off to pack and she was none to slow about it. She was not careful about what she stuffed where. She noticed a soldier standing outside her door, and looked at him questioningly.

"I am Devin, Highness. When you are ready, shout my name and I will have some men carry your things to the wagon."

"Thank you." *Did he just call me Highness?*

When she was finished, she double checked and triple checked every drawer and closet shelf and knew she had everything, so she said, "Devin!"

Two men immediately stepped into the room and picked up the bags like they were nothing and hauled them down the hall. She went back to the dining area and saw everyone staring at her, some in awe, some jealous, some in fear. Mom will not be Pamela. She sat down opposite the King and next to the captain and began her meal and the best talk she had experienced in some time.

HIGH COUNSELOR

Silver Mountain, King's Mansion

Brie was awakened by a kindly woman by the name of Samantha. Samantha was a member of the King's staff, and married to one of her mother's Own. She was pretty, but looked a little stressed or worried. She looked a little older than her mom, appearing to be in her forties.

"The King has asked that you awaken my Princess that you may shower and eat. He hopes to be gone by first light."

"Thank you so much," Brie glanced out the window and saw it was still dark out but she got up, gathered her clothes and headed off for the shower. *It's going to be so good to see mom again. I miss her.*

Many things went through Brie's mind in the shower. Would her mother try to prevent her from becoming a sister? What would happen at Silver Mountain after she left? Would she ever see her friends again? All of her questions went unanswered though as Brie made her way downstairs.

At breakfast it was only herself, the King, his captain, Sir Kevin, a woman, a boy, and one other man. It was the officer Brie and Henrietta had met on the street last eve. *Now this is one good looking puppy,* Brie thought. She could definitely see herself in his future if he weren't already spoken for. He was kind, had a great smile, magical eyes and a gentle nature. She shook herself from the thought. She was going to be a sister. A High Sister, eventually and maybe one day the Supreme. She would change the sisterhood when that happened. No more hiding things.

"This is Martin Trist, Princess," the King said, "He has answered the call to become one of the Queen's Own. This is my wife Jackie, and my son, Peter."

"Good morning, Highness. It is good to see you again," said Martin.

"Good morning, Princess," said the King's wife, providing a curtsy. Her son, at her side bowed, in a mannerly way, and said good morning as well.

"Good morning, everyone," Brie responded.

As breakfast started, Brie learned that Martin had been assigned to her personal safety during the trip, and would ride beside her. He was young, looking to be about twenty or twenty-one. Six foot with dark hair and smooth, slightly tanned complexion and very muscular.

"You can ride, Brie?" The King asked.

"I have ridden a horse before Majesty, but I don't remember him being as big as the ones the soldiers ride. I was only twelve."

"Those are warhorses, Brie. You won't be required to mount one of them. Sir Kevin can acquire a riding horse for you. All three wagons we are taking with us are horse drawn so we should be able to make good time. The Queen is very anxious to put her eyes on you."

"I miss her so much, Majesty."

Brie had bacon, eggs and a waffle in front of her and it was no small waffle. There was apple juice, as well. "My goodness, do I have to eat all this?" She asked.

"You will have nothing on Landing Road but fruit, crackers and water. Eat what you are comfortable with but there will be no meals until sup. As far as you missing your mom? It was a lot of work and arguments to keep her from coming here to retrieve you herself. She is not trained and the Own not staffed, otherwise she would be here now."

"Yes, Majesty."

She gave serious thought to whether she wanted to bring up her next topic or not, but decided she had no choice, she had given her word. "Majesty, I'm so ashamed to ask this, but there is a sister here at Silver Mountain that just turned eighty and has become a little forgetful and she owes money to Murphy's candy store. I gave him all my money and promised him I would bring the balance and a deposit on my next visit."

The King stared at her and said, "You are a good person, Brie. How much did you give Mr. Murphy?"

"One dollar and a gold half was all I had, Highness. She owed two dollars and a silver quarter."

The King reached into his pocket and pulled out five dollars and gave it to Brie. Brie had never seen five whole dollars since she had been on Mother. It was nothing on Earth, but it was a lot of money on Mother.

"Majesty, I can't accept this, please. It is important to me to earn my own way. I will be twenty in just three years, and I want to be a sister."

"You will accept it, that is your King's command and I will hear no more of it. What is this sister's name?"

"Sister Grandma... I mean Sister Grend, Majesty."

"Kev, when you gather a horse for the Princess stop by the City Watch and have Thomas check in weekly with Mr. Murphy and pay Sister Grend's debt. Make sure he understands Mr. Murphy is to be aware the Princess commanded it so."

Kevin was off and the King turned to the Princess, "I hope to dissuade you from your venture toward the sisterhood and work for me in the stead. I can use your services immediately. You will not have to wait the three years for the sisterhood. If you continue down the sisterhood path, I will understand, but I will still pay you while you are waiting to come of age."

"What would you have of me, Majesty?" Brie asked.

"We will talk of it on the trip. Martin, will you see to the needs of the Princess? I must go roust the men."

Martin responded, "It will be done, My King."

Dawn's Landing, Queen's Mansion

When Melanie woke, it was sunny outside. She stepped out of bed and walked to the door, heedless of what must have been a bed head that would have broken cameras on Earth. She tried to fix it as best she could and poked her head out and there sat Gary.

"Have you seen Kristen, Gary?" She asked, getting a look of disgust from him at her question.

"She has asked me the same question of you about every five minutes since sunup, Highness. The last time being about four minutes ago," He answered, seemingly flustered.

Melanie couldn't help but smile at the annoyed soldier, "Would you have her come in when she gets to you this time around?"

"Gladly Highness," he said, and then in a barely audible mumble,

"Would you be so kind as to keep her in there?" Melanie laughed as she was closing the door.

She pulled the clothes out that she was going to wear for the day, wanting to look presentable for the arrival of her daughter. As she pulled the shirt out of the closet and hung it with the rest that she had chosen, Kristen walked in.

"Good morning, My Queen," She greeted.

"Good morning, Kristen. Would you check and see if I can get an audience with His Holiness this morning, please?"

"Of course, My Queen. May I let Arnold know what to prepare for your breakfast?"

"I think I would like pancakes today, and if you would, will you have him let Theresa know that my daughter will be joining us for sup and she loves fish of any kind?"

"Of course, My Queen. I will be back with His Holiness' answer shortly."

"Very good, and Kristen please try not to annoy Gary too much on your way out," Melanie said with a wink and a smile.

"Don't let that old man fool you, Highness. He is obviously unaware of the mirror at the end of the hall or he wouldn't have spent so much time admiring my backside." Melanie laughed again and made for the shower.

When she got downstairs she found the table had been set for four. The Princess would be one, but she was unsure of the other two. She saw two soldiers she didn't recognize talking to a young woman whose face she couldn't see, near the fireplace. She thought the three might be her first visitors. *The woman was wearing a flowing short skirt, My God! I would give all my worldly possessions to have legs like that, and a loose fitting blouse that looked to be made of silk. Her hair looked just as silky, dishwater blond about an inch short of the shoulders.* Melanie headed in their direction to introduce herself and the woman turned to face her. Melanie did her best not to show her shock.

"Good morning, Majesty. This is William Marks, and Pedro Hernandez who have accepted my invitation to become members of the Queen's Own. Majesty, are you well?"

Despite her best efforts not to show shock, Melanie knew she failed. She was in the presence of a very beautiful woman. "I apologize, Captain. I did not recognize you out of uniform."

"My apologies as well, My Queen. I'm afraid I have anticipated your acceptance of a request I have of you. My parents will be arriving in town shortly and have asked to see me."

"Of course and I would love to meet them as well. Perhaps you and I can plan a trip since the village is so close."

"They would be honored for sure, and I will speak with them today. The Own is up to seven now and if Martin Trist has accepted my offer, eight this eve."

The Princess had told her that another member of the Own would join them. When she got back from the Sisterhood, they had dined with Michael Wainwright, a twenty-seven-year-old native of the King's force at Harper's Bay. Harper's Bay was the former residence of both the King and the Queen, until Queen Celise had moved to Dawn's Landing in the year 201. The Kings had stayed there until 313 when then King Willis moved to the new Mansion that he had built in Silver Mountain.

They sat down to breakfast and Melanie learned that William Marks was a member of the King's force stationed at Emily River. What a handsome brute this was. He was the same age as Melanie, thirty-five, was unmarried and had been with the King for fourteen years. Pedro Hernandez was twenty-nine and from Road Safety stationed right here in Dawn's Landing. He was married and grateful to the Queen for any opportunity to get out of the house she could provide. Everyone laughed at that, but Melanie wasn't buying it for one minute. Pedro had been credited with the slaying of one of the Beasts at the Garcia farm on her first night. He had mounted the Beast and was furiously slashing at the head, exposing its neck as the Beast was trying desperately to shake him off. With the neck exposed, three archers buried every shaft in their quivers in the underside, finally killing it.

Breakfast was excellent and Melanie was afraid she was going to have to cut back on her consumption in order to avoid dieting. She suddenly realized she hadn't seen an overweight person since she had been on Mother. The heaviest person she had seen was Darvon, but he could hardly be called overweight. He was just muscle with a Desiree bulge. Everywhere people went though, they either had to walk or bike. The best two exercises there were.

The breakfast dishes were cleared and they were all discussing Emily River, when Kristen returned. She took a seat on the couch to wait for the Queen to excuse herself, which Melanie did and went to sit beside Kristen. "His Holiness said that he has an early afternoon appointment and if you can find something to do during that, you can have him all day."

"Great, Kristen. Thank you. I will let the captain know and head over there. In the event I don't return by the time my daughter gets here, would you see that she gets settled?"

"Of course, My Queen."

Melanie told Marie of her plans for the day and went outside to find a bicycle. She, Frances, Gary and Pedro headed off for the Sisterhood.

Kristen ran upstairs to check the room her Queen had chosen for her daughter. Angelina had done a good job. Kristen found no dust, the floor was cleaned and new bedding was placed on the bed. There were an ample number of clothes hangers in the closet, all the drawers were empty and cleaned, the blinds were clean, and the vanity was emptied and cleaned. Everything seemed to be in order, so she went back downstairs and found a soldier at the door, talking to Pierre.

"Good morning, Commander," Kristen said, "What brings you?"

"I have come to introduce myself to our new Queen, Lady Kristen."

"I'm so sorry, Commander," Kristen said, "The Queen is not available, currently. I will be glad to tell her you called, though."
As politely as she could without embarrassing the commander, she continued, "I'm sure it may have slipped your thoughts since it has been so long between your visits, but no one may see the Queen without the leave of the Captain of the Own, and weapons are not allowed inside the mansion except those worn by the Own or the King."

"That would not include the Commander of the City Watch, Lady Kristen," the Commander said, "I command the city and can see who I want, and no one takes my weapons. Is she upstairs?"

Kristen was suddenly frightened and thought she had missed a recent directive, but her fear was soon quelled with the voice from the kitchen door.

"Perhaps you were not aware sir, that you are inside the Queen's Mansion, not a member of the Own, and yet wearing arms. Please step outside, remove your arms and then you may reenter."

It was one of the new Own, but Kristen couldn't remember his name. He was leaning on the door jamb eating one of Arnold's biscuits.

Another of the Own, the one that had arrived last eve walked past him, also carrying one of the biscuits. She knew his name to be Michael.

"Why the hesitation?" Michael said, "William explained the rules. Are you going out the door or through the window?"

"Do you know who I am?" The Commander asked the two. Kristen was not sure what to do, so she pulled Pierre slightly away from the scene.

"Can't say as I do," Michael said, taking a bite and walking toward the Commander, "How about you, Will? You know this man?"

"Nope," said William, still leaning.

"Your captain will hear about this," said the Commander as he turned and walked out.

"Now, this is a good biscuit," Said Michael, as he took another bite.

"My goodness," said Kristen, patting her chest as she walked to the back patio to check her Queen's chair.

Landing Road

Sir Kevin rode up with a beautiful horse for her. It wasn't as big as the other horses but it sure was pretty and sleek looking. An off white female with a few brown spots on the rump. Brie absolutely loved it. "Thank you, Sir Kevin." Brie was in the saddle and ready to go with a huge smile on her face to go along with her big eyes.

The group left for Landing Road just as the sun was about to rise, as the King had wanted. He is such a great man. Brie rode beside Martin and the King in about the middle of the column. The soldiers were toward the front, then the wagons, then Brie and Martin, then a few horse drawn buggies that Brie thought must be travelers. Behind the buggies on both sides of the column and intermixed in the center were about a thousand more of the King's soldiers.

"I am appointing you High Counselor to the Realm, Brie," The King said out of the blue. Despite the suddenness of it, the title sounded important. She felt a small amount of pride, but at the same time she had no idea what it was so she asked. "What is that?"

"You are already doing it," The King answered, "You just need to teach others to do what you do. I will have four counselors in each city and one in each village. You will need to work quickly as I have already suffered the Queen's wrath on this issue."

"Mom wraths a lot, Majesty. Her bark is worse than her bite though," Brie said as her mind began working on how to staff her new appointment.

The King shared a look with Martin and his captain. "Maybe on Earth, My Princess. I can assure you if she bites when she is with Mother it will leave a rather large scar. Work quickly, and start calling me Brent."

"Yes, Highness," Brie said, only half listening as she continued to stretch her mind. The King rolled his eyes and rode forward in the column leaving her bewildered at anyone being afraid of her mom.

Martin asked Brie, "How long have you been with us, Highness?"

"You can call me Brie, I'm no Highness. I have been here almost two years."

"I can call you Princess if you like, but I can't call you by your given name unless my Queen gives me leave. Where did you land? Inside Silver Mountain?"

"No. Just on the other side, but this side of the mountain itself. I awoke next to this dirt road that was going into the mountains. As it turned out it wasn't a road at all, it was just a path that horses had worn into the ground from all the travel. I walked the wrong way. Instead of walking this way which would have shown me Silver Mountain just over the hill, I went the other way. I walked for nearly two hours before I was found by soldiers coming back to Silver Mountain."

"My Princess, if I offend you with these questions I will stop. I'm just passing the time and have always been fascinated with settlers. Were you frightened?"

"I was so scared; my knees were knocking. The soldiers were very nice and tried to tell me what was going on, but when you are walking home from your high school football game with your friends, and then you're not, it takes more than a few kind words to calm you down. I thought about running from them, but then I figured if they were going to hurt me they would have already."

"So, they took you to the sisters?"

"No, not them. They took me to their camp on the outskirts of the city to their Commander, and he took me to the sisters. Everyone I ran into was so unbelievably nice. On Earth, if you were lost and stranded, most people would just drive right on by and only some would bother to call the police from their cell phones. I guess I knew right away that they weren't kidding by the way they were dressed and unsurprised to see me. I sure wasn't in Kansas anymore, Dorothy."

"Martin, my Princess," he corrected, "I've heard of these phones, they apparently made people lazy and less social. In some cases, a person was talking into these things while they were being talked to by a real person. That seems beyond a social issue. Just rude."

"Yes, I saw a lot of that when I was in line at a store and they were talking on their phone while the cashier was trying to get their attention. Nothing could be done about it though, it wasn't illegal and the talkers felt everyone was being rude to them by interrupting them while they were on the phone.

"People here are so nice," Brie continued, "I actually like it here more than I did on Earth. I miss my friends, but I made some new ones here. I miss my family too. I'm glad my mom found me."

"So when you were taken to the sisters?"

"That wasn't all that pleasant at first. They were certainly nice enough, but all the attempts to get me into a family failed. No one really wanted a fifteen-year-old girl, and I really didn't want a new family, I wanted my family. When I turned sixteen, I didn't have to go through that stuff anymore."

She was about to continue when she saw Sir Kevin riding toward them. When he reached them, he spoke.

"Highness, the King would like to know how the Queen feels about Venison."

"What's that?" Brie asked.

"Deer meat, Highness," Sir Kevin offered.

"There's a dead deer in the road?"

"No, Highness. They are alive. We mean to render them otherwise."

"Please, Sir Kevin. They don't hurt anybody." Brie pleaded, hoping she wasn't about to witness a massacre.

"They are too abundant Highness, and the Beasts cannot trap them. The other animals cannot catch them...and they feed the outlaws."

"No, my mother hates vezinon or whatever it is."

Sir Kevin looked perplexed, but said, "I will tell the King." He rode back to the front.

She and Martin rode in silence for a few minutes and then he spoke.

"You know they will kill some anyway, right?"

"I know."

"So you turned sixteen and what then?" He asked, continuing the conversation.

"I had to work at the apartments to earn my keep until I turned twenty, so I took a list of chores."

"That is where you met the young lady that thinks whistles are for losers, and you began to work on our teen suicide problem. How did that come about?"

"We had a boy from Georgia who was really struggling. He wouldn't talk to anybody or meet with families or even leave his room. He was with us about a week and one day we found his clothes on the beach. I felt so bad about not even having said hello to him that I made up my mind I would know every person that came into the apartments and spend some time with them. I would hold friend meetings in the back of the building. After a few weeks, people started coming to the meetings that didn't even live there. The sisters saw the space problem I was having and rented out the Town Hall once a week for my meetings, and people came, and then more people, and then more people."

"You are a remarkable girl, My Princess," Martin said.

"I really wish people would quit saying that, and just for the record? I happen to be a woman, not a girl," she countered.

Kevin reached the King, "The Princess has asked us not to kill the deer, Majesty."

Surprised at the statement, the King asked, "Did she give a reason?"

"She said they don't hurt anybody."

The King looked at Kevin and got a shrug. They rode in silence for a few minutes and the King said, "Very Well, have an archer put a shaft in the ground."

"Yes Highness," Kevin responded. As he rode away he made a whoosh snap sound. The King turned and threw his half eaten apple at him.

"I have been talking so much I am thirsty, is there water?" Brie asked.

Martin reached over to Brie's horse and pulled a flagon out of a bag draped over the back and handed it to Brie.

"How do I work this?" she asked.

Martin pulled his own out and showed her.

"I will know more about you My Princess, but I will give your voice a rest," Martin said. Brie's heart took a leap at Martin being interested in her.

They rode for a couple minutes in silence and Brie pointed and said, "Oh, look. Someone dropped an arrow. Should we pick it up?"

Martin smiled, "No, Princess. They will pick it up on the way back."

Dawn's Landing Sisterhood

Melanie had decided not to take His Holiness up on the all-day offer as she had a service to attend in the afternoon. The service for the sisters and the soldiers would be held as one service and all expenses, including pit or cremation would be borne by the King. The three travelers that had been killed would be separate services. She would also attend the clinics this afternoon to visit the wounded. One of which, as it unfortunately turned out was the fourteen-year-old driver of the wagon the sisters had been in by the name of Bethany Gregorian. She had been badly burned and suffered eleven broken bones. One of the sisters, between sobs, had referred to her as 'a mess'. Hope of survival was dim. Melanie had seen the girl fly through the air. Bethany's was the first wagon hit.

When Melanie, Frances and The Own reached the apartments she went to Sister Beth's office and found the sister working on a schedule of sorts.

"Majesty?" The sister spoke when she noticed the Queen.

"I am here to see His Holiness, Sister Beth. I wanted to stop by first and apologize for my behavior, yesterday. I am not usually that quick to anger. At least, I never was on Earth."

"We both suffer from the same dilemma, Highness. Until I accepted this position, I don't recall having ever been that bossy. Please accept my apology as well."

"Perhaps another day we could spend a few minutes getting to know one another a little better," Melanie said.

"I will look forward to it."

"As will I. Which direction is His Holiness, please?"

"Third floor, all the way to the back."

Melanie, Frances and the Own climbed the steps to the third floor, Where's an escalator when you need it? There was a waiting area of sorts outside the door of His Holiness, and Gary and Pedro parked themselves there and began perusing some reading material including something that had been outdated on Earth. Your average everyday newspaper.

Once greetings were over, His Holiness took her and Frances to the outside deck area where a table and chairs sat with what looked like a pitcher of tea. Melanie was impressed with the view. She could see the entire city. There were four three story buildings visible, but most of the buildings were single story housing and shops, with a few two story structures. The most impressive view was of the Horizon Sea. It stretched as far as she could see to the left and to the right, and when she looked straight out she could not see anything except a few ships. The ones closest to shore were emitting a steam, but the ones farther out had sails.

"This is the best part of my apartment. I love watching the sea," said The Holiness.

"I don't blame you, it's kind of therapeutic," responded the Queen, "I suppose learning about those ships is part of my training?"

"Yes, and about that. I think it would be wise to begin. The sisters know much more than I about the differences between Mother and Earth and they have the knowledge of seventeen Queens before you."

"I know, Holiness. I didn't mean to be so demanding of your time, but the carnage I witnessed on Landing Road has made knowledge of the wilder crucial to me."

"I understand and I didn't mean that I don't welcome our chats, but there is much to learn. Not just the wilder."

The conversation continued throughout the morning on the mind of the captured wilder. Melanie gained important knowledge and some not so important. The Holiness was steadfast in his belief that wilders lived within the cities. He believed they were reluctant to merge with

Mother for fear of being caught, but they were there. The Holiness, as a wilder, connects to Mother and thoughts appear in his mind, similar to the thoughts he receives when the Queen passes. On one of those visits the thoughts of the wilder living within the cities came to him.

A conversation began about the different cultures and yet single worship of Mother, and only one language, which His Holiness was at a loss to explain. He admitted having no clue why everyone on Mother heard the same language, but they spoke it on arrival. Immediately when swept. He said all insist they are speaking their home language, but another will say they are speaking theirs.

The conversation switched to faith and His Holiness explained what the swept had told him of the Earthly beliefs of the scientists and religious leaders and how the arguments back and forth were meaningless, as faith could not be swayed.

"Well, who was right, then?" Melanie asked.

"Both were right and both were wrong."

"Holiness, I don't mean to be daft, but they couldn't have both been right."

"Child, the religious leaders said God created man. They then said you should worship God, did they not?"

"Yes."

"The Bible was written. Was it written by God?"

"No Highness, it was written by man, but. . ."

"Yes, you were about to say God spoke to man and told him what to write. Put your mind back on Earth for a moment. If a man came to you and said God spoke to him, what would you think? Be honest!"

Melanie didn't want to admit to it, but lying to this man was out of the question. "I would think he was a little off, Holiness."

"Yes, and I don't mean to suggest that everything in the Bible was a falsehood, but it was written by man and subject to misinterpretation by those men, and subject to being misinterpreted again by the reader. Pardon my lack of knowledge of names, you had a man on Earth who parted a sea, did you not?"

"Yes, Holiness. Moses."

"Are you sure he was the one that parted the sea? I am sure the sea was parted, but are you sure it was he?"

"No Holiness, some things we have to take on faith."

"Do we now? Is he the same man that climbed the mountain and found the tablets?"

"Yes, Holiness."

"Wasn't one of those tablets directing you to worship no other Gods?"

"Yes, Holiness."

"Why would God write that, if you already had it right? And the burning bush that wouldn't stop burning? How was that possible? We worship Mother. Mother is a God. Mother can keep a bush burning. She can provide tablets, if she chooses. She is the one that tells me who the Queen is. She has never told me to worship no other. She provides you with the power to create. You are nothing when not merged with her. When you are merged, you could part a sea, you could raise a mountain, build a river or a lake. Mother's waters flow from your power, did you know that?"

"Yes, Holiness."

"Everything we do. Everything we have. Everything we are, is because of Mother. Have faith, my Queen. Choose your own path, but have faith in that path. If you can find one thing that we have that came from one other than Mother, I will prove you wrong, and it won't be subject to misinterpretation."

"The religious leaders said God created man," he continued, "They were right; God was and is a celestial being. The scientists said man was created from elements of the Earth. They were right. Earth was after all, and Mother is a celestial being."

Melanie's head was swimming and had no response that she could prove, the hesitation caused the conversation to ebb, so His Holiness excused them and said he needed to make this appointment.

Melanie and Sister Frances left and met Pedro and Gary outside the door. Pedro said a little boy came up, identified himself as a runner while they were inside and said the Queen was needed in twenty-four west. Frances had led the way and when they arrived Frances introduced her to two sisters that had a very large room to themselves, with fifteen, maybe twenty tables with huge books stacked five high on each. The sisters as it turned out, were the two assigned to find her family and they would need Earth information to begin the search. Melanie provided them with full names, their dates of birth, and city they would have last lived in. One sister said that was how they cataloged settlers. Melanie did not give them Brie's name.

"That is a lot of settlers," Melanie said looking at the books that covered every inch of every table.

"That is just year one, Majesty," one of the sisters replied.

Melanie had a sudden pang of guilt, but she would never give up looking for her family. When they left twenty-four west, they were treated to lunch in the dining hall. Melanie used the time to set up a tentative schedule with Sister Beth.

It was early afternoon when the four of them left the Sisterhood. The trek to the Town Hall took only about ten minutes, as it was located close by. The Town Hall was used due to the size of the service. On the way, she passed a gentleman being pushed along in a wheelchair. She decided to pass the ten minutes with a question for Frances.

"If a handicapped person lives on the third floor, how do they get up and down?" She asked.

"Why would a handicapped person even want to live on the third floor, Highness?" Frances asked.

"Some do, some even higher on Earth," Melanie answered.

"Sounds not very safe. How did they get up and down on Earth? Oh yes, I remember one of the settlers saying something about elevators. Did I pronounce that right?"

"Yes, very good. We had buildings called skyscrapers that had many floors. The elevators were the only way to go."

"What happened if a turbine failed or there was a fire?" Frances wanted to know.

"Um," Melanie was stuck and realized she had no idea why a handicapped person would live on the third floor, "Never mind."

She was surprised at the size of the Hall when she entered. There were chairs taking up two thirds of the Hall and they were all full. There were also several people standing to the rear. Lined up on both sides and in front of the chairs were caskets and urns. She also saw that His Holiness was standing at a podium speaking to the masses. She put it together that the man he needed see was Sister Kate's husband.

Melanie took advantage of the Holiness speaking and began at the first of the deceased, an urn, read the plaque, went to one knee, bowed her head and said her silent prayer. She continued this process all the way around the Hall, careful not to disturb the Holiness and spending a few extra minutes at some. The tears began at the first urn and never stopped.

Landing Road

"The High Counselor approaches, Highness," Sir Kevin told the King.

Brent turned and saw Brie and Martin coming and pulled out of the train to await their arrival. He also noticed the south flank had stopped inside the tree line. "Kev, have someone check that out." The King turned back to the arriving riders.

"Princess, what brings you up?" asked the King.

"Majesty, Martin tells me a train leaves daily from Silver Mountain in both directions. I would like to get a message to two people in Silver Mountain that would be key to my success."

"Come with me," said the King.

The King led Brie to one of the wagons in the middle of the column and instructed the boy to pull out, which he did. Brie recognized the boy as being one of the runners for the sisterhood.

The King opened the rear canvas and introduced Brie. "Brie Thurss has been appointed by your King to the position of High Counselor to the Realm. She has not had sufficient time to acquire a staff of her own and until she does, the sisterhood will assist her in her needs. She has need to send a message back to Silver Mountain."

Sister Maryann spoke, "I will log the command immediately, Highness."

"Compose the message in a way that states the urgency of the High Counselor, attach my stamp and send it back to Silver Mountain with my rider that I will assign." He then rode back to where they had left Sir Kevin and Martin.

Brie climbed into the wagon and explained the task the King had set forth for her. She explained at length what the message was to say and who was to read it. She also said there was a second message that was to be carried by every road sister to every city, village and farm throughout Queenland that a sister would come into contact with, and what that message was to say. A third message was to be sent to every newspaper in the Realm.

Brent arrived back where he and Brie had left their guards and asked Kevin, "What did you find of the flank?"

"Lieutenant Masters stopped the flank at the notice of three Riggers, Highness. They do not appear in an aggressive state, but he has left half the flank to keep them in sight until the entire train passes, with instructions to rejoin the main body when the train has passed the next corner."

The King answered, "Very well! We will lose sight of them before they lose sight of us. Have the rear command create a relay to keep them in sight."

Sir Kevin nodded and was off.

"Martin, run back to the sister's wagon and have them get back in the column as soon as possible. You stay with Her Highness." Martin nodded and he was off as well.

Another soldier rode up as Martin was leaving. "You sent for me, Highness?"

"Lieutenant, I want you to have three, no five of your men to ride back to Silver Mountain with a message. You can pick that up at the sister's wagon. Be swift. There are Riggers to our rear."

As the lieutenant rode off the King glanced back toward where the Riggers had been spotted, but the soldiers there were already out of sight. *I do not like this, why would Riggers who hate our smell be so close to the road?* To make matters worse another train was approaching from the opposite direction.

Brie was proofreading the messages when Martin rode up. "My Princess, urgency is upon us. The sisters must rejoin the column."

"What has happened?" she asked him.

"The King has asked me to get the wagon back in line, My Princess."

"...And The Princess will comply as soon as a certain member of the Queen's Own answers her question," Brie said with a raised tone.

Martin weighed whether to inform a seventeen year old that Riggers have been spotted and decided it would be her own fault for being so stubborn, so he did.

Brie responded differently than he thought she would. "Very well

Martin, but I will ride beside the wagon until I am finished proofing."

The last teenager he had mentioned Riggers too, screamed like a wounded animal and ran right into a biker. "As you say, My Princess."

With ten of the King's Own following him, Brent rode ahead to the approaching train. When he was about half way, he saw two men were riding out to meet him. He also noticed Road Safety consisted of a hundred at most.

When they met in the road, the King asked, "Why are you so few?"

One of the men, seasoned at least, said, "A coal shipment arrived at the docks yesterday, Majesty. Junction City's need is dire so Commander Burk sent out two trains to Exeter this day."

"Did he now? Then he shan't be surprised when only one hundred of his men show up in this train." He turned to the Own and asked one of them to notify Sergeant Andrews of Road Safety to have half of his men join the passing train, and to find Lieutenant Merritt and have his five men assigned to the High Counselor's missives join the train as well. "What is your name?" he asked the seasoned man from Road Safety.

"Sergeant John Hisle, Highness."

"You have Riggers to your right ahead, John. My men are watching them, but stay alert just the same."

John turned to the other soldier. "Alert the line," and said to the King, "Thank you Majesty. We will watch for them."

Brie finished proofing the missives and passed them off to the sisters. She and Martin began riding back to where they had started the trip.

"You seem to have a rather insatiable thirst for knowledge, Princess," Martin said.

"I don't like it when people keep things from me 'for my own good', if that's what you mean. I have the right to know, I have the right to be who I want to be, and I have the right to choose the path I want to take. . . and if you say even once that I am but seventeen, I will knock you out."

Martin threw his hands up in a mock defensive gesture and smiled.

The train was progressing without any sign of the Riggers and it was getting into the late afternoon. The tree line to the left was beginning to thin and the sisters had told her it was their favorite part of the trip, because the Horizon Sea would be visible and that meant they were close. Brie strained her eyes but couldn't see the sea yet. Soon they would be heading directly into the sun and Brie had packed her sunshades in with the rest of her things and she wasn't about to stop the train to look for them. "Are we there, yet?" she muttered to herself, knowing Martin couldn't hear her.

"About an hour out, Princess," Martin responded.

Dawn's Landing, Town Hall

Melanie had a sad visit with the friends and families of the deceased. There was no outward anger, but there were many tears. Melanie struggled most with Tessa Stanton and her twins. Tessa herself was holding up amazingly well with the exception of an occasional bout. Melanie however, felt like a waterfall. Tessa hadn't even known her husband was a member of the Own, and wouldn't have until he would have gotten here and told her. The woman broke down several times, but also displayed a large amount of pride in the man.

When the four of them left, Melanie asked if there was anything set up for wives and children. Frances assured her Queen that she needn't concern herself with that. The families of the Own that died in the line were very well cared for. Frances said that neither Tessa nor either child would have a financial concern for the rest of their life. Frances was also trying to dissuade Melanie from going to the clinic.

"It is getting time for the train to arrive from Silver Mountain, Highness. I'm sure you would rather see your daughter on her arrival."

"Brie will be there when I get back, Sister. I need to do this."

"Majesty," Frances continued, "The clinic will still be here tomorrow, there is no . . ."

"What is the matter with you?" Melanie interrupted with a little bit too much snap, "I am going to the clinic, if you don't want to go you may wait at the mansion." She felt immediate shame at her tone.

"Sister Frances means no harm, Majesty," Pedro interjected, "She is just trying to shield you from an uncomfortable sight."

"I am a big girl, Pedro," she answered him, "And this is important to me." She looked at Frances, "I'm sorry I snapped, Frances." The rest of the ride there was only silence, with the exception of an occasional 'turn here' or 'turn there'.

When they arrived at the clinic, Melanie was surprised at the design. Four roads ended at the clinic, connecting to a circular road that went all the way around it. The clinic was in the center of the circle, and it was no small building. It was very modern looking and there appeared to be an entrance on all four sides. The area around the clinic was plush grass, bushes and many trees. Benches, tables and drinking fountains throughout. There were also several statues that she would have to visit another time. Sitting at the benches and tables she could see, were mostly people in medical garb that must have been on break, considering the reading material and lunches. There were two very tall and exquisite looking decorative fountains. Along the top fascia read 'Clinic on the Round'.

When they entered, she didn't see what she expected. She thought she would see equipment out of the American old west, but what she saw was modern medical equipment, and what she witnessed was highly trained and well organized nurses that didn't seem to give a horse's ass who she was. Every attempt she made to ask about the victims, she was directed to ask at reception. She never heard so many nurses saying 'coming through' and 'excuse me', even when she lived on Earth.

Finally, she had found reception and asked about the survivors of the Landing Road battle, and was directed to the third floor. Of course!

On getting there she spent time with each victim, talking and apologizing and wishing them well, and they were for the most part genuinely appreciative, albeit surprised of her visit. There were burns, broken bones, lacerations, puncture wounds and head injuries, but none could compare to what she would see in the last room.

There lay Bethany Gregorian. A young girl that had been whisked from her Earthly home into a strange world full of strange places and strange people. Both of her eyes were swollen shut. A brace had been placed over her nose. There was some apparatus down her throat. Her head was wrapped in bandages. Her right arm and leg were in casts, her left arm was burned from shoulder to wrist. The rest of her body was covered but Melanie knew it must be bad as well. There were needles in her left arm and tubes leading to three bags on the pole. Melanie could only hope one of the bags had something in it to relieve the pain.

Two sisters were on their knees next to the bed, praying to Mother. A little girl had fallen asleep on the other side of the bed holding Bethany's hand. There were flowers and stuffed animals and uneaten candy bags in the room, none of which came from her parents and maybe never will. Melanie pulled Frances and the Own out of the room. She could tell by the expression on Frances' face the sister knew what was coming.

"Frances, go to the sisters and tell them we are going to have to reschedule. Then go to the mansion and have Kristen come immediately. Wait there for The King and Brie and bring them here. Gary, locate the captain and have her meet me here and let your relief know where to find you. Pedro, find me her doctor. We will be here awhile."

North gate

Brie had been staring into the Sea for near twenty minutes, but now turned her attention to the Beast wall surrounding Dawn's Landing and the structures within, the closer she had gotten the more her heart was racing in anticipation of seeing her mom.

"Be sure to keep the horse on the dirt shoulder until we get to the Queen's mansion, Princess. Horses are not allowed on the sidewalk or paved streets," said Martin.

"Do they break the pavement?" Asked Brie, realizing she had never seen horses on the pavement at Silver Mountain, either.

"No, they shit."

"Hey, watch your language, Martin." Brie said, sharply.

"Sorry, Princess. Just thought you had the right to know."

Brie initiated her angriest look and aimed it right at Martin. When they entered the city and began breaking off, Martin and Brie rode ahead to catch the King. "How far to my mom's house, Majesty?" Brie asked.

The King pointed to the mansion at the end of the road, and Brie jumped up and down on the horse trying to get it to run. It didn't.

"Come on horse, move it," she said. Realizing too late that she was trying to reason with a horse, using human language.

"We will be there shortly, Princess. Your horse has been walking all day," said Martin.

The King noticed Kevin laughing silently. "Are you laughing at the Princess of Mother, soldier?"

"I just got some dirt or something in my eye, Highness," Kevin answered.

"Best get that cleaned up before the Queen notices it."

Clinic on the Round

"There has not been much change, Majesty," the doctor said, "She is a little better in the blood pressure area than when she arrived, and she is alive. When she was brought to us by the King's medics she was barely hanging on and did pass away in the emergency room. The nurses worked on resuscitation for several minutes and did get her life signs back, but I urge you to be prepared for the possibility that we may lose her. "There are no guarantees I can give you, even if she does recover. The head injuries are severe, as are the spinal fractures. We may be looking at brain damage and the possibility of losing the use of her extremities."

"Is there anything I can do, doctor? Equipment I can get; specialists I can summon?" Melanie felt pretty useless right now and hoped to get good news from the doctor, but she had not provided any.

"We have everything we need, and as far as specialists, we are all specialists. Our knowledge and abilities are enhanced here the same as others. We still lose the battle at times. Bethany is a very strong willed young lady and her body fights hard. In all honesty, she shouldn't be alive right now."

"Thank you, doctor," Melanie responded, allowing the doctor to return to her other patients. After the doctor left, Melanie stood and stared at the crumpled heap that was Bethany Gregorian. The sisters were still praying, the little girl was still holding her hand and fast asleep. Melanie was not feeling much like a Queen. If she was so powerful, why couldn't she fix this?

Pedro spoke, "Majesty, if I may speak? Staying here will do the girl no good. We might even be in the way. She may be in this condition for some time, if the doctor tells it true."

"I appreciate your counsel, Pedro. I have already thought of all those things, but I'm not leaving."

Pedro looked at Bethany, the sisters, the little girl and back at the Queen. "I will make what sleeping arrangements I can for you, Highness." He headed for the nurse's station.

Melanie walked to the side of the bed that the little girl was on and looked down at her. Who are you, honey? Does Bethany know what a magnificent friend she has? Melanie could not figure out how she would go about lifting the girl onto a cot without waking her.

She was thinking on this when Kristen walked in. The first response of the Queen's Lady was one of shock at the sight of Bethany. Once she gathered herself, she asked, "What can I do, My Queen?"

"There is nothing we can do for Bethany except hope and pray, Kristen. Until further notice, I will be staying here. I need you here each morning, noon and eve to run some errands and report what has happened elsewhere."

"It will be done, My Queen," Kristen said as she stroked Bethany's cheek. Melanie nearly said something to the Queen's Lady, as she appeared to unknowingly be pinching a tube with a greenish hue. Her left hand was stroking Bethany's cheek and she was leaning on the tube coming from the wall with her right. Melanie didn't know what that weird looking hue was, but it was attached to the equipment that was attached to Bethany, so it must be important. It hadn't become necessary to say anything however, as Kristen departed the bed.

"Please have Theresa make some sandwiches and send some fruit, as well as a lot of coffee. If you can find one, I would like to see what is in that newspaper I saw at the Sisterhood. It probably wouldn't hurt to bring me a change of clothes, to keep on hand."

"The Daily is delivered each morning," Kristen answered, "I will bring today's copy with the sandwiches and change of clothes."

Two more sisters were approaching. "That will be all for now, Kristen."

Kristen curtsied and left and Melanie turned to the sisters. "Do you know who this little girl is?"

"Yes, Majesty. She is Chastity Gregorian, Bethany's sister," answered the taller of the two.

"Her real sister? Biological?"

"Yes, Majesty. Chastity was sitting in Bethany's lap when they were swept."

The nurse came in and went to the side of the praying sisters. The sisters rose and moved aside and the nurse began changing the bags on the hook. The four sisters exchanged words and the praying sisters left. *Shift change?*

Pedro returned with a cot on wheels and lined it against the wall outside the room. The nurse told Melanie that she had to 'dress' the burns, whatever that meant, and change the bandages and everyone would have to leave the room. Melanie looked at Pedro and nodded toward Chastity and the big man lifted her from her chair and carried her out. A second nurse entered the room with a cart and closed the door. Pedro laid Chastity gently on the cot.

The Great Sea, 'The Pristine Christine'

"Beaufort," the Captain of the Christine screamed.

"Twelve," came the response.

He was having regrets now that he had not gone to Queenland first. The storm was the worst he had ever been in and he traveled the seas endlessly. The Galleon was being tossed around as if it were a toy boat, instead of the hulk it was. Facing into the wind, it would rise and face the sky, as the wave arrived and then slam back down as it passed, and this had been endless. The sails had been lowered, the rowers, combined with the steam power, were simply not enough to propel the ship through this wind. At the best, the ship was holding position. The Sea was white and he felt like someone had opened a hydrant on him.

His orders were to travel to all lands and notify the Kings of the wilder woman that had boldly attacked the King of Caruso. The Supreme High Sister of Caruso didn't want the information delayed by the weekly packet deliveries. For a wilder to become this bold was not a good thing. They were a pain, for certain. Attacking settlements and trains was common, but all they generally took was food and clothing. They were tricky devils, for sure. They somehow could steal items while others stared away in the direction they had originally been seen. It had been decided they must work in packs, one distracting the soldiers with their fireballs, while the other snuck in behind. He wasn't so sure that was the case. He was pretty certain he saw one running like a deer, but none he told believed him, accusing him of abusing the sauce.

"Port," came the scream from the captain.

In any event, the Supreme High Sister had not specifically told him to follow a set course, she had simply said go to Queenland, Dakota, the Eagle Islands, New Texas and New Brazil. She didn't say in that order. Not specifically. No one would blame him for not wanting to be anywhere near that psycho Queen Pamela. She would probably fry him on sight.

"Straight on. Beaufort!"

"Twelve."

The storm had come up during the night. Swiftly, taking the crew by surprise. Once it was upon them it was too late to attempt to evade it. Judging by how long the captain had been screaming, it might not have been possible, anyway. It seemed to him, that he was looking up at every wave.

The captain was experienced, he could tell. She was screaming "Starboard" and "Port", "Bails to the Bilge, Batten that hatch, Beaufort," the latter of which was followed by someone screaming a twelve. Her eyes were everywhere at once. She was slight of build and what hair wasn't matted to her head was straight back from the wind, and what kept her on her feet the man couldn't see, but she appeared anchored by something to the upper deck. *I wonder if she really thinks she will make it through this.*

He should have made his journey land to land by HMS, but he had decided he could come out of this with a little more money if he only said he did. Traveling by the older sea vessels was considerably cheaper than the HMS. He would just tell the Supreme he had traveled by HMS and be reimbursed for those fares. Now though, he was criticizing himself for that decision.

"Starboard. Beaufort," she screamed.

"Twelve," came the response.

She ordered him below decks hours ago and he had obeyed, but he had come back up because he hadn't wanted to defile the below decks. At least up here, his stomach contents would be washed overboard. The wind and water hitting him in the face helped as well. The mast at the front of the ship had broken hours ago, but he thought the ship was okay without it. He continued to cling to the beams attached to the side, but it was taking every muscle he had left. He had tied himself off when he had seen her men had done the same, and like them he would occasionally lose his footing and be glad he was tied.

"Port," she screamed, "Secure that barrel." One of the sailors caught the rolling barrel and began to tie it to the railing.

"Straight on. Beaufort," she screamed.

"Eleven," came the response.

He dared not hope that the lower number was a good thing. Certainly the sea seemed no less dangerous, and he was no less wet. Times as these made him glad his death would cause no sorrow. He had no family and maybe two friends. He had been a loner since his sweeping. He started out his life on Mother as a runner for the Sisterhood. He became a wagon driver and after about five more years branched out as a currier. He was hired by Caruso Postal, but was fired within a year for losing mail. He then went back to his currier job and was still at that position now. Except his packages now consisted of Sisterhood pouches and he very seldom traveled inside Caruso any longer.

"Someone get me a flagon," the captain screamed.

"Aye," came the response.

She had been steering the ship into the waves for as long as he could remember. He wasn't sure how far off course that action was taking them, but if he ended up drowned, he didn't suppose he would care. He would have failed, of course. He would not have alerted the King of Queenland, nor the Queen. Everyone else knew. He knew he should have come here first, but the thought of being within sight of Queen Pamela, wasn't very appealing.

"Stay alert! Starboard! A little more. That's good, straight on! Beaufort!" The captain continued to bark.

"Ten," came the response.

Dawn's Landing, Clinic on the Round

"This is folly, Highness," Marie pleaded, "The girl will not be made better by your presence. Mother does not give you that power. Your training can't keep taking a backseat to items of the heart."

18

"Listen to me Captain, because I really grow weary of this conversation. I....am....not....leaving! There will be no need for the Own to be here. I can't imagine that anyone I have seen working here even has the time to do me harm. Continue to work on your staffing."

Marie had not let the non-uniform change her attempts to get the Queen to toe the line. Melanie knew she was just trying to get her to think on other things besides sadness and guilt. She had perhaps been a little gruff, but she really was tired of people trying to sway her.

Melanie put her hand on Marie's shoulder. "I'm sorry, Marie. I know you are just trying to help me, and I'm sorry I took you away from your family, but I can't leave. I just can't."

Marie hesitated a moment, but finally responded, "Very well, but the Own go where you go, regardless of your thoughts. They will stay outside the room and out of the way." Marie went to Pedro and Gary and gave them their instructions. She nodded at Melanie and left.

Melanie went back into the room and pulled a chair up next to Chastity, who had awakened and went immediately back to Bethany's side. The sisters had taken up the prayers as soon as the nurse had left. Melanie decided to break the ice.

"Hi, there. My name is Melanie and you are Chastity. It is good to meet you. I met your sister at a farm a little west of here. Do you live at the sister's apartments?"

Chastity nodded but said nothing.

"I would like to get to know you a little better. Do you go to school yet?"

Chastity shook her head but said nothing.

"How old are you, Chastity?"

"Seven," she finally answered.

"You know, back on Earth I had a son your age. Is Bethany your only sister? Do you have any brothers?"

"Andrew was our big brother. We were the ABC's," Chastity said.

"ABC's?"

"Andrew, Bethany, Chastity. ABC."

"I see. Where did you live on Earth, Chastity?"

"St. Petersburg."

"Oh, I lived in Phoenix. Do you know where that is?"

Chastity shook her head.

"It's in Arizona. It's hot there, but I'll bet it's hotter in Florida. Does it get hot in Florida?"

Chastity took her eyes off Bethany long enough to look at the Queen. "How would I know?"

Melanie felt like an idiot. Gregorian, meat head! St. Petersburg, Russia.

"I'm sorry, Chastity. We have a St. Petersburg in the United States, too. I thought you meant there."

"Oh!"

Melanie jumped with fright. Someone was trying to squeeze the breath out of her from behind. She looked towards the door to cry for help from the Own, but they were just standing in the door, watching with. . . with the King. Melanie bolted out of the chair and twisted in Brie's arms and hugged her back. Tears were flowing from mother and daughter, but happy tears for a change. Neither said a word. They just embraced.

Queen's Mansion

When Kristen got back to the mansion, she related the Queen's request for sandwiches and coffee to Pierre, and then went to the patio and grabbed the newspaper, made sure it was today's and headed up the steps to pack a change of clothes for the Queen. She packed a blouse and pair of pants, underwear, socks, and makeup. She put the book the Queen had been reading in the bag as well. She went to the closet to see if the clothes had been washed that the Queen had worn here. They had, so she packed those into a different bag along with the 'gift' the Queen had purchased on their night out.

She headed out the chamber door to go down and pick up the coffee and sandwiches and ran right into Angelina, almost knocking the poor girl over.

"I'm so sorry, Angie. I wasn't watching where I was going. Why are you still working, anyway? Where is Yanina?"

Angelina looked a little sheepish as if she was unsure if she wanted to answer the question, but then spoke. "I have not seen her, Kristen. I don't want to get her in trouble so I didn't say anything to Pierre."

Kristen tried to think back if she had ever known Yanina to miss work. The woman loved her wages, and would sometimes work sick.

"The Queen will not be returning tonight so just put your stuff away and get some rest. I will tell Pierre." This is peculiar, she thought to herself. Kristen went downstairs to pick up the sandwiches and found Pierre and Arnold were placing the sandwiches and coffee in a basket.

"Arnold, why are you still here?" She asked.

"Theresa has not come down yet," Pierre said. "We will be having words for sure."

"Have some with Yanina, while you're at it," Kristen said, "Angelina was still working upstairs. The Queen won't be returning tonight, so I told her to get some rest. If everyone has eaten, you should too, Arnold. I will go up and roust both of them."

"Would you give this to Fred," she asked Pierre, "And ask him to take it to the depot to be delivered on the next train to Desiree Garcia at the Garcia farm, please?"

Kristen went upstairs to check their rooms, thinking how unusual it was for even one of them to miss work, much less both. She got to Yanina's room first and knocked. There was no response from inside, so she opened the door. The bed was unmade but everything else looked like Yanina's room, right down to the vanity, but there was no Yanina. Kristen didn't think it proper for her to walk in to look for a note, so she closed the door.

She walked down to Theresa's room and knocked. No answer. She opened the door and found no Theresa. Everything in the room looked as it should, except the bed had not been slept in. She went back downstairs and waited for Pierre to finish giving Fred his instructions.

"They're not up there," she told Pierre, on Fred's departure, "Do you think I should notify the City Watch?"

"This seems a little strange," Pierre said, "I do think it would be prudent to notify the Watch, and I will tend to that, right away. I'm not sure what they can do at this early stage, but I will ask. You should take the Queen her bidding."

Kristen loaded the basket onto her bike and she and Pierre took off in opposite directions. On her ride to the clinic, Kristen thought of the possibilities that the ladies simply ran off, taking a dislike to the Queen, but why wouldn't they take their clothes, and how can they have decided so soon that they didn't like Queen Melanie? Maybe they were with each other. Kristen was certain Yanina liked women more than men, but Theresa always made eyes at any man that could walk, crawl or hop. She ran conversations through her head that she had with the two women and could come up with nothing that would lead to this. Kristen was getting a very uneasy feeling.

As she parked her bike and made her way up the stairs, she ran into Gary and Pedro who were on their way out.

"Excuse me sirs, might I ask a favor?"

"What is it?" Gary asked.

"Two female members of the house staff have gone missing. Would you be so kind as to check on Angelina when you get back? She is in the third room down from the captain's."

"Have you notified the watch?" Pedro asked.

"Pierre left at the same time I did to notify them, he should be back shortly."

"We will check on her," said Pedro, "Inform Her Grace. I will send word to the captain."

"Thank you so much," Kristen finished. She was unsure with all the problems her Queen was having, whether this was something she wanted to add or not, so she decided not.

Kristen headed back up the stairs. *Where were the Own? There were none of them there when I was at the mansion. If one of them were behind this, which one? The captain was with her family, Pedro and Gary were here.* She got to the room and saw the Queen was talking to a very pretty girl that was surely her daughter, since the King was here. That Kevin man was here, but he was with the King. Willard and Phillip were also here on duty for the Queen. *That left William and Michael.* She walked behind Willard and Phillip and sniffed as quietly as she could to see if she could smell either of the women on them. Nothing. Phillip noticed her sniff and looked at her curiously. "Where is William? I didn't see him at the mansion," she asked.

Phillip looked at her, sized her up and said, "Off buying you a dozen roses."

Guess I should have expected that, considering how little of my business it is where the Own are.

"Sorry, I'm a nosy sort and thought I could figure out who was working today. I thought he would be," she lied.

"Best you keep your nose where it belongs," said Willard.

She was about to apologize again when the Queen saw her and called her in.

"This is my daughter Brie, Kristen," the Queen said, "Brie, this is the Queen's Lady, Kristen Muller. She has been very helpful. Kristen would you take Brie to the mansion, so that she may shower and get a bite to eat?"

A bite to eat? Idiot! You told Arnold to get some rest.

"Right away, My Queen."

Kristen left the coffee and sandwiches, stroked Bethany's head a couple times, and led the King, Sir Kevin and Princess Brie downstairs to the bikes.

LOCK DOWN

The Great Sea, 'The Pristine Christine'

The man gained a new found respect for the captain. Not that he didn't think she was qualified as it was, but she did find a way to keep them afloat during the worst of the storm. The winds were still strong, but the Sea was visible now and very little in the way of white. Her men were in the process of replacing the forward mast that had broken and the rowers were working to get them back on course.

The captain was below decks trying to get some sleep and the sailor she had called Number One was directing the repairs and cleaning of the deck. Buckets upon buckets of water were being hauled up from below decks by rope. They had lost one dingy from above decks and some of the cargo had gotten wet below.

The man had made up his mind that his future voyages would be aboard HMS liners. The HMS fleet could cross the Great Sea in five days, sometimes four. They were powered by Queenstone and when seas were calm could travel at ridiculous speeds. He would have been back in Caruso by now, if he wouldn't have been so cheap with his funds. He would wait at Queenland for the next HMS voyage. They departed every two or three days, depending on travelers. An HMS could cross the Horizon in three days.

He would miss the camaraderie aboard the Cargo Vessels, for sure. It was never boring. HMS liners were all about speed. Getting people where they wanted to be, before they needed to be there. Always in a hurry, those ships. Number One had said they should reach Queenland in three days, so with luck he would be home in a little over a week. Depending on how long it took to find King Brent.

Each minute the sea became a little calmer, and Number One said the mast should be finished within an hour and they would be back at full power.

The man had made an error in judgment. The more time that passed, the more he felt so. His fear of Queen Pamela may turn out to

be the end of him.
Dawn's Landing, Clinic on the Round

Shortly after Brie and the others had left the clinic, Melanie bit into a sandwich and was reading the headlines of the paper.

"Queen Melanie Has Landed"

She hadn't gotten beyond that when a third sister came into the room. The sister was carrying a tome, bound in leather. The sister brought a chair in and set it close to Melanie. Sitting, she placed the book in her lap. "I'm Sister Tillie, Majesty. I'm your tutor."

"Tutor? I need a tutor?"

Sister Tillie continued, "Sister Beth has decreed that what time you had for the Sisterhood would be spent on developing and practicing your powers, Majesty. Training and development. The education process of your orientation to Mother would be conducted by me, at the Mansion or wherever you deem you need to be."

Now we're talking! You go, Sister Beth. "Very well, you may begin."

Sister Tillie began, "The Queen's calendar began on January 1st in the year one and the sweeping of Queen Emily De Shields. Queen Emily was in the shower at her house in Dagneux, France. She arrived on Mother fully nude and completely 'Awash' in Mother on her waking. There was no confusion with Queen Emily. In her own words, she knew who she was, why she was here, how much power she held. She knew where to find water, where to find food, and knew of the dangerous animals on Mother. Queen Emily set out for the water. . ."

Queen's Mansion

When they arrived at the Mansion, Kristen found a member of the City Watch talking to Pedro on the patio. Pierre was standing in the dining area watching them. "What goes here?" asked the King.

"Two of our staff are missing, Highness," Kristen answered him. When she did, Pierre held up a finger. *Are you shushing me, old man?*

"Did you warn the Queen?" The King asked.

"I did not want to alarm her, Majesty. I had no information with which to respond to her questions and she is so distraught of the girl."

The King looked at his captian and Kevin headed back to the clinic. "That is not your call, girl. The Queen sent her daughter here thinking things were well."

A sudden fear engulfed Kristen. *How could I be so stupid?*

Gary was coming down the stairs. The King summoned him and Gary joined the three of them. "In light of this news," the King said to Gary, "I would ask you to put Princess Brie under your protection until I can provide her with security."

"The captain has already instructed us so, Highness. She is on her way. Pedro anticipates an after-hours lock down."

Kristen noticed movement to her left and turned to see Theresa emerging from the kitchen. She was dumbfounded and speechless. Almost. "Theresa, where were you?"

"That is not your concern, young lady," Said the watchman from the patio. "Until we have finished our investigation, you will not have any communication with any other members of the staff without one of us being present." So, Yanina is still missing! That's why Pierre was holding up one finger.

"Well, I'm going to take a shower," said Brie, "Which way?"

Kristen led Brie up the steps followed closely by Gary and into the room next to the Queen's. "I'm afraid I may have gotten myself dismissed," Kristen said to herself.

"You definitely earned yourself a severe scolding, which mom does very well, but as far as the dismissal she's also notorious for second chances."

"Oh, thank you, Highness. Those words provide me with some hope, at least."

Brie dug through her bags and pulled out a change of clothes and headed to the shower at Kristen's lead. "I will tell you this, though," Brie stated, "Since you don't know me. I'm not fond of stuff being kept from me. I would think you could have warned me on the way here."

"My apologies, My Princess, I am not usually this unsure of myself."

"Apology accepted. What's for sup?"

"I will have Theresa prepare a fish, Highness."

Kristen left Brie to her shower and Gary to the door and went downstairs to have Theresa prepare sup. She saw the King now talking to another watchman and walked up, waiting for a break. Do what you're told. Start fresh. Ruffle no feathers. The watchman broke off his questioning of the King and looked at her.

"My apologies for interrupting, Sir. The Princess has asked me to have Theresa start sup. May I tell her?"

"Give her the Princess' instructions and ask her no question and refuse any statement not related to that preparation."

Kristen nodded and went into the kitchen and told Theresa what Brie would have for sup and walked out. She went back upstairs and began putting Brie's clothes away and setting up the vanity. Kristen's number one suspect in Yanina's disappearance right now stood to be Theresa.

The Patio

"When did you start your shift with the Queen today, Pedro," the watchman asked him.

"I arose just before sunup, my shift started then."

"Was Gary up when you got up?"

"I heard him shuffling around in his room. He's as quiet as a Beast."

"Was anyone else up when you got up?"

"The cook was in the kitchen making coffee."

"How did he look to you? Did he appear fresh, like he had been up for a bit?"

"No. He was still in his night clothes, and he did not look fresh in any way."

"How about that morning housekeeper? Was she awake?"

"I did not see her until shortly before the Queen awoke. She came down, ate her breakfast, and went right to work on the patio."

"And Pierre, when was the first time you saw him?"

"He came down just after Gary, if you ask me. . .," Pedro began.

"I didn't." the watchman finished, "How about the rest of the Own, anything different than their normal day?"

"Nothing that comes to mind."

"And the captain?"

"What about the captain?" asked Marie as she walked up onto the patio.

The watchman turned to her and asked her if she remembered who had been awake when she got up and she provided the list. "I need you to finish quickly with my men, they need sleep."

"Almost done here," said the watchman. He then turned back to Pedro and waited for Pedro to make eye contact with him. "Did you kill Yanina Svoboda?"

Pedro's hand slid towards his sword hilt, and Marie's rested on top of it. The fury in Pedro was fast and deep, but he gathered himself enough to answer. "No, but you might not be so fortunate."

"I think we are done here, Lieutenant," said Marie, "This line of questioning has gone beyond cordial."

"The amount of blood we found in that room leaves little hope we are going to find that woman alive, Captain. I will find out who did this, what they used, where Yanina's body is, and the motive for it. If I step on your toes while I investigate, oh well. If you are looking for a cordial relationship, buy a dog."

Sup table

Brie came down for sup with Kristen and Gary in tow and noticed a rather heated discussion going on out on the patio. The watchman appeared to be getting the worst of it from a little pipsqueak of a girl in a pretty skirt, with that soldier that was with her mom at the clinic.

The table was set and ready, with the King and Sir Kevin seated and watching the fireworks on the patio. There were two other place settings, so Brie took the one next to the King.

"If you will excuse me, My Princess, I must go apologize to my Queen," Kristen said after Brie had been seated.

"I would suggest you give her a little time to cool off and go see her, oh, I don't know. Next week?" answered Brie.

"I must see her now, Princess. I made a horrible error in judgment and I must atone."

Brie watched Kristen leave through the front and turned her attention back to the patio, where the pipsqueak had turned her back on the watchman and was walking in with the soldier. The soldier headed for the staircase and the pipsqueak was coming towards the table.

"Please accept my apology for the awful occurrence that you have been greeted with, Highness. I am Marie Mercer, Princess of Queenland, Niece to the King and Captain of the Queen's Own."

Oh, my goodness, my bad! "Hi, I'm Brie Thurss."

Theresa brought the plate in with the biggest piece of fish she had ever seen. "Wow, what kind of fish is this?" she asked Theresa.

"It is Spraig, Highness. I hope I have prepared it to your liking."

Clinic on the Round

With Sir Kevin having returned to the mansion, and Melanie fuming about the news being kept from her, she continued to listen to Sister Tillie's tutelage with Chastity in her lap sleeping again, and watching Bethany's breathing being done for her. She had sent Sister Frances to the Sisterhood to thank Sister Beth for her foresight in sending Sister Tillie, and to acquire the necessary paperwork that Melanie could adopt Bethany and Chastity, even though it wasn't legal to adopt until the parents had been proven deceased. Sister Frances had referred to the process the Queen would apply for as Acceptance. She would raise the girls as her own.

Did Bethany's lip just twitch?

Melanie stared at Bethany's lip and face and fingers and anything else visible and was determined not to be one of those 'jump for joy' people at any sign. She watched intently, but there was no discernible movement.

The education she was getting on Queen Emily was immense. These sisters really knew how to keep notes. Her thoughts strayed to the mysterious disappearance of her two staff members and wondered how that investigation was going, when she noticed Kristen on her knees at the doorway. She let her stay there while she told Sister Tillie she was going to take a break and walk around the building for some fresh air.

"Get up, Kristen, and come sit here and hold Chastity until I get back," Melanie said.

"My Queen I beg your forgiveness for my misjudgment."

"It is best we do not speak of that subject right now, I told you to rise."

Kristen stood and sat in the chair Melanie was in and reached to take Chastity, but the Queen wasn't looking at her. She was staring at Bethany. In a few moments, Melanie handed off Chastity and turned to Willard. "Let's go for a walk, guys."

Phillip, Willard and the Queen left the building and began to walk around the perimeter, which was no small stroll considering the size of the clinic. Melanie got to the grassy area and began taking off her shoes. "Highness, are you sure?" asked Phillip.

"I'll be fine," she replied. Mother was quicker this time. She got the same excited feeling and felt the same rush, but it was definitely quicker. Was it quicker last time as well and I just didn't notice because of adrenalin? So with Willard on her left and Phillip on her right, she picked up her shoes and they began their walk.

"It is eerie to see your eyes that color, Highness," said Willard.

"I can imagine," She replied.

"Danger comes. Set them free."

Melanie whipped around quickly, this time. Still, no one was there except Willard and Phillip. She looked at both of them and they were returning the look, questioningly. She decided against confronting them, but she knew she wasn't losing her mind. Someone was definitely talking to her, but she couldn't figure out who. What kind of danger? Free who?

Melanie felt a minor throbbing or vibration coming from the building. Several different ones actually. She searched and found the closest one and walked towards it. What she found was a small hatch. The hatch had three keyholes. One in the middle at the top and one on each side near the middle. They were not like any keyhole she had ever seen. There was also a combination type lock in the middle of the hatch. There was a steel grate over the hatch that looked like it was part of the building itself with two very large padlocks holding it in place. "What is this?" she thought, but said out loud instead.

"Queenstone cabin, Majesty. Queenstone is what powers the equipment in the Clinics," Willard answered.

Melanie thought on this as they continued the walk around the building, as well as Bethany having twitched again, who she was supposed to free and the possibility of wilders inside the city. She searched far and wide, and when she realized her thoughts had reached outside the city and past the Beast wall, she withdrew. They had walked all the way around, and she had thought about a second time around, but she saw the sun was setting, so she sat and put her socks and shoes back on without any dizziness or anyone having died and the three of them headed back up.

When they got back to the room, all were outside with the door closed, and they all were looking at her and smiling. "What has happened?" she asked.

"Two nurses and a doctor rushed into the room, Majesty," said Kristen. "We were ushered out and one of the nurses came back out and said the breathing device had shut down. She said it only does that when the patient has begun to breathe on their own."

Finally, some good news. Dare I hope?

Silver Mountain, Sisterhood

It had been two hours since the message arrived from Brie, but Sarah was nearly finished packing. It would be harder on Dave because he had been Accepted and he liked the Wickerts. She wondered if he had begun packing or would even answer Brie's request. She read the message again.

> *To Sarah Strong and Dave Hanson,*
> *The King has appointed me to the position of High Counselor to the Realm. He wants four counselors in every city and one in each village. Please have Henrietta and Auburn continue my work there and I will ask the two of you to come at once to the Queen's mansion at Dawn's Landing. I need your help.*
> *Love, Brie*

The message had the King's stamp on it. The King's! Sarah couldn't remember the last time she felt this important and needed, but she was sure it wasn't here on Mother. She had talked to Auburn and Henrietta as soon as she got the message, and Henrietta had gone to fetch Dave. Auburn had looked like a kid in a candy store, but Henrietta appeared more to be taking it in stride. Nothing excites that girl, anyway.

Sarah went downstairs to find out what time the train left in the morning and found Dave and Henrietta locked in an embrace, "I'm going to miss you, Hank."

"Oh, I know," she said and winked at Sarah.

"But the girls there are much prettier, so I pretty much have to go," said Dave, with just as much sarcastic wit.

The wink became a frown and Henrietta tried to twist and turn out of Dave's embrace and soon all three of them were laughing.

Sarah found out that the train wasn't leaving until mid-morning so she would be able to help with breakfast and say her goodbyes then. A certain person had their game room privileges taken away, so she, Dave, Henrietta and Auburn met in the community room and began reminiscing and talking of the future.

Dawn's Landing, Clinic on the Round

"I don't want to mislead you, Highness. She is by no means out of the woods," the doctor said, "If she becomes immune to the pain medication, she could conceivably drop back into a catatonic state. She seems at peace, right now. Her breathing is not perfect, but it is steady. We have removed the tube and will monitor her consistently. Nurses will be in and out of the room every minute to two minutes. We are not going to allow you to be in the room, but you certainly can sit out here if you want."

Melanie thought on this and told Sister Tillie and Sister Frances to return to the Sisterhood. She had signed the papers Sister Frances had brought her and she was now officially responsible for Bethany and Chastity.

She looked at Kristen who was standing with her arms on Chastity's shoulders, and then at Willard and Phillip, and they were all looking at her.

"You win," she said.

Kristen spoke first. "Doctor, may I get the Queen's belongings from the room?"

After having everything gathered and having made it downstairs, the five of them were making their way back to the mansion.

Queen's Mansion

Sup had been the most delicious fish ever. Brie was feeling pretty full and decided it was time to check out the mansion. She went up the stairs and took the left hall. There seemed to be a lot of bedrooms, because most all doors were shut. The ones that weren't were bedrooms so she assumed the rest were.

She came upon a room that wasn't. It appeared to be a library, so she went inside to check out the bookshelves. There must have been fifty books she had not yet read. One had a nice design on the cover so she cracked it open to see what it was about, hoping it wasn't romance.

"Princess?"

She let out a yelp and jumped with fright. "Don't do that!" she said to Martin.

"The captain has told us you are to go nowhere without one of the Own, Princess. Just thought you had the right to know," he smirked.

She swung with everything she had and slapped him, not caring for his sarcasm. He recovered but the smirk was still there so she stepped into it this time and slapped him harder. That one staggered him, but he recovered and the smirk was replaced by a smile. She decided she didn't like the smile, either, so she swung again. He grabbed her by the wrist and pulled her into him and kissed her hard. She pushed at him and twisted and punched and finally freed herself. She slapped him again with her right hand and then came back with a left and swung again with the right, but he grabbed it again and pulled her to him and kissed her again. This time she kissed him back, but she wasn't sure why. He released her and she swung as hard as she could and slapped him backward. She slapped him again, and then threw her arms around him and kissed him.

When Melanie and group were approaching the mansion she saw soldiers everywhere. There were four walking the yards, one at every window and two at every door. She helped Chastity down off the back of Kristen's bike, and put their bikes away. She made her way inside and saw the captain, back in uniform, talking to the King. She joined the conversation.

"What is being done to protect my family?" she asked.

Marie spoke first. "We are at eight, Highness. Martin Trist has arrived and Donovan Taggert has accepted my offer to become my second. He is on his way from Willow Wood as we speak."

"I have assigned twenty of my soldiers to the captain," said Brent, "They will be principally responsible for security at the Mansion but they will perform what duties the captain desires. The Queen's daughter. . ."

"Daughters," interrupted Melanie, "I have accepted Bethany and Chastity into my house."

"Very well. The Queen's daughters will be under guard. If the captain needs more men, she need only ask."

Melanie saw Brie coming down the stairs with her guard. *She at least is happy. . . she is very happy. . . she is. . . Oh damn!* She looked at the soldier, then at Brie, then back at the soldier. "Who is that man, Captain?"

"Martin Trist, My Queen."

"He looks a little young to be a soldier," Melanie said.

"He is but twenty Highness, but do not worry yourself he is quite adept with that sword."

That's what I'm afraid of. "Very Well. Thank you both." She looked back. "Brie?"

"Hi mom, wasn't expecting to see you. Did something happen?"

Don't say anything that might cause animosity. "Much and more. Bethany has begun breathing on her own and the doctors kicked us out of the room. I have also signed papers and have accepted Bethany and Chastity into my house."

"That's awesome. I have two new sisters?" Melanie felt the glee was sincere which made her happy.

"There is one thing more, Brie," She looked at Martin and said, "Sir, would you excuse us a moment?" Martin nodded and went to the captain.

I don't believe she has ever lied to me and she has never put on a stupid act. Melanie put her hands on Brie's shoulders.

"Mom, you're scaring me. What?"

Just do it! "Are you sure?"

Brie hesitated before she answered. She knew her mother could read her like a book. "Not in the least. I just met the guy, but I think what I'm feeling may be love and I want to find out."

"Okay, but if he hurts you I will have him hauled out to the grass and I will pull all of his organs out and feed them to the Riggers."

"No you won't, mom," Brie said, with a smile and tilt of her head.

"Don't bet his organs on it," Melanie said, without a smile. They gave each other a hug and Melanie went to be introduced to Martin.

Horizon Creamery

The watchman had stopped at the warehouse and found the produce was only delivered to the Queen's Mansion on Mondays and Thursdays. The Butcher said his products are delivered daily at the Queen's pleasure, but only for the evening meal as the breakfast items were provided by the dairy.

The foreman at the dairy had said the ice cart driver for the Queen's Mansion was a woman who started her route about two hours before sunrise. He was unsure when that would bring her to the Mansion, but she usually finished her shift about lunchtime. The watchman got her name and address.

When he got to the launderers, he was told that a young lady by the name of Angelina brings the laundry from the mansion with the help of Fred. He admitted he didn't know Angelina very well, but Fred he had known for years. They pick up the previous day's laundry and head back. None of his staff delivers to the mansion unless they get instructions to do so by the Queen's Lady.

The delivery cart driver was at the grocer when he got there. He said that the cook didn't want him disturbing the Queen's meals so he was to deliver mid-morning only. The driver said the cook, a man by the name of Arnold was a pleasant sort, but a little too meticulous with making sure the delivery was correct.

When he got to the gardener's house he was told they only work after lunch and are usually done by sup.

On his way to the Dairy driver's house he stopped at the 'Daily' and was told the cart leaves the printers early morning and stops at the various drop offs and the paper cabbies pick them up there. The watchman got the name and address of the cabbie driver for the area of the mansion.

He arrived at the dairy driver's house and found her reading at the window. He knocked, and in a few moments the door opened.

"Hello," he said, "I am Louis Maxwell of the City Watch. May I take a few moments of your time?"

The watchman explained why he was there, leaving out some of the details, specifically the fact that it was a murder, saying only that Yanina was missing and they were worried. The woman's answers were short and abrupt and the watchman knew there was something he was not being told. She claimed she didn't see anything out of the ordinary when she was at the Mansion. She saw a man walking two streets over was all.

"Is there any chance your husband could run your route tomorrow, so that you could come down and describe him to our sketch artist?"

"I have no husband and no use for men. I will be down after my run."

The watchman thanked her and headed off to the paper cabbie's house. That was curious.

When he got to the cabbie's house the door was answered by a woman wearing a sling.

"My goodness, what happened?" he asked her.

"I fell off the roof. We were trying to re-shingle."

He showed her his City Watch badge and before he could start his reason for being there a man came to the door, so he turned to him.

When he got to the man that had been seen two streets over the driver said he didn't see him and who would be out walking that time of the morning? The watchman had thought it strange, as well.

He finished his interview with the cabbie and headed home. This has been an interesting day.

Mansion patio

Brie stood at the table on the patio, looking at her mom's instructions for breakfast before she went to bed. Eggs and sausage and French toast. Yummy.

"Do I have dirt on my butt, Mr. Trist?"

Martin blushed and turned his head looking out over the yard area. "I can assure you, Princess. I wouldn't know."

"Very well, then. Good night."

"Goodnight Princess."

Brie was the last to go upstairs, and when she passed her mom's room she saw her dressing down Kristen, so she just waved and went to bed.

The watchmen arrived at the mansion two hours before dawn, and met with the King's guards. The Lieutenant positioned himself on the rear patio, with the two guards there, and his men stayed at the front with the guards there.

After about ten minutes of pleasantries the kitchen light went on and Arnold was seen putting things together in the kitchen. Five minutes more passed and the ice cart pulled up out front. The driver unloaded her goods onto a hand cart and she made her way up the walkway.

Arnold opened the door from the inside and the woman went in with her cart, followed by one of the guards and both watchmen. She wheeled it into the kitchen and began lining things up for Arnold's inspection. She kept looking at the watchmen and the guard. Arnold himself was curious, but he began his count of the goods, anyway. The Lieutenant noticed there were no others from the Queen's staff awake.

The Lieutenant watched the activity inside from the patio, but when they had entered the kitchen, he lost sight of them. Five more minutes had passed and the cabbie driver from the Daily rode up and stopped on the road toward the rear of the house. The driver brought up a newspaper nodded at the guards and placed it on the table of the patio.

"Good morning, sir," said the Lieutenant, "It is good to see you again."

"Good morning," said the driver.

"I was curious, what exactly happened to your wife's arm?" The inspector asked.

"She fell off the roof when we were trying to re-shingle."

"So she said. Almost exactly those words, actually."

"Then why did you ask? Never mind, I have a route to run." The driver started for his cab.

"Funny thing" said the Lieutenant causing the driver to pause, "According to our records, city maintenance is responsible for the roofing on your street. Why would you pay for something that is free?"

"Because I want it done right," said the driver, "I really have to go."

"Sure, just one more thing," said the Lieutenant, "According to your neighbors, a young woman matching Yanina Svoboda's description has been seen leaving your house several times just before you would get home. They also said they had witnessed you to be on several occasions, a little bit of a bully to your wife."

The man ran off the patio and in the opposite direction of his cabbie.

"I really hate it when they run," said the Lieutenant.

"Should we get him?" asked one of the guards.

"Not necessary," said the Lieutenant. The Lieutenant signaled one of the watchmen on the inside and he came and unlocked the patio door. The Lieutenant entered through the patio door and proceeded to the kitchen where Arnold was finishing up with the dairy driver. He noticed outside that his men already had the newspaper cabbie in irons and were walking him to the City Watch wagon.

He and his men took the woman outside so as not to wake the household, and he began.

"Yanina Svoboda kept a journal, Ms. Masters. My men were reading it when I was at your house, actually. It would seem that you and she were intimate. I guess you forgot to mention that. It also said that she had told you last week that your relationship was over. So, being upset, you decided to follow her one day to see who she left you for. Much to your surprise, it was the wife of your good friend Travis Green. The two of you would cross paths, what, daily? You became quite buddy-buddy."

The dairy driver sat in silence with her head down.

"You were very angry about losing Yanina," he continued, "But not nearly as angry as he would be, right? So, you told him one morning and found out how angry he really was. So angry in fact, that he went home and beat up a defenseless woman, who was so ashamed of her behavior, she took every punch.

"So, the two of you devised this master plan. He would deliver the newspaper to the patio just like he does every day, and then watch through the back window for you to arrive to distract Arnold and then he would sneak in and kill Yanina Svoboda."

"He wasn't supposed to kill her," said the dairy driver, "He was only supposed to hurt her."

"Yes, well. There were still two problems. Neither one of you knew which room was Yanina's nor how to make sure the patio door was left unlocked. You had that covered though, didn't you, Ms. Masters? You knew someone on staff that was going to be dismissed if the Queen found out about his past, so you confronted him and got the help you needed. Did you think we would conduct a murder investigation and not find out about a peeping Tom? Oh, that's right, she wasn't supposed to die."

The Lieutenant looked inside and saw the man coming down the stairs. He nodded to his men and they went inside. "Ms. Masters, you are under arrest for conspiracy and murder. I sincerely hope Mother has no mercy on you when you get to the Sisterhood." He placed the irons on the dairy driver. He sat her on the walkway, and saw his men coming out of the mansion, one on each side of the shackled Pierre Bernard.

"Well?"

"Sand pit, Lou. Him and the paper guy," said one of his men. Her family would not even be able to say goodbye to her.

"Stop by the dairy and the Daily. Have them come and get their things," he said with disgust.

"My Queen?" Melanie heard someone calling her Queen again, but rolled over and pulled her coverings up over her shoulders.

"My Queen?"

She realized that she wasn't dreaming and looked up to see Kristen standing over her.

"You wanted to be awakened at sunrise, My Queen."

"Thank you, Kristen. I'm awake." She lay there a few minutes after Kristen had left contemplating her day. One thing at a time. Shower.

By the time she got downstairs, the room was buzzing with activity. *Idiots! Don't they know its morning?* She saw Chastity sitting at the table and Chastity saw her. "I wanna go see Bethany."

"We will honey, right after breakfast. Did you wash your hands?"

Chastity jumped from the chair and ran upstairs and Melanie did a headcount. Kristen, Arnold, The captain, Martin, William around the table; Angelina on the patio, Brie coming down the stairs, a watchman sitting by the Brazier. When he saw that she had seen him, he bowed and asked her for a couple minutes of her time.

When the Lieutenant related his findings to her, she stayed steady and calm. Even when he confirmed Yanina's death, she felt a tug at the heart, but didn't cry or show emotion, "Thank you for your swift action on this, Lieutenant. It was kind of you to wait and inform me personally."

During breakfast, the captain would glance at her occasionally, but left her to her thoughts. Brie was teaching Chastity that the proper way to eat French toast was from the center out. Melanie's thoughts went to Yanina's family, Bethany, Sisters Tillie and Frances, Martin and Brie, and the King. The latter having already left to see his own wife and family, Pierre, and who would be the new head of house, and on and on. She felt sorry for Arnold, but she had lost her appetite and left half of her breakfast on the plate and walked to the patio, and picked up the paper.

High Counselor to the Realm

The newly appointed High Counselor to the Realm has announced a meeting to be held at Town Hall this Tuesday Eve at 7pm. All are invited as The High Counselor will be explaining the suicide issue that the cities are having and what we can do to help. The High Counselor has said that two Suicide Prevention Agents have been summoned from Silver Mountain to help answer any questions we might have. Within just the last month the city of Dawn's Landing has suffered six 'Death by suicidal means' reports from the city coroner. Silver Mountain over the same period has suffered just one with a larger population. Dave Hanson and Sarah Strong are the SPA's that will be. . .

"I wanna go see Bethany," Chastity said again.

Melanie sat the paper down and said, "Well, let's go then."

The Great Sea 'The Pristine Christine'

The ship was moving so fast that the man felt like he was leaning forward just to stay erect. The captain had said they should be arriving at Port Courage by the new day. In an attempt to make up time the captain and crew had forsaken safety for speed. They had left the ship at full speed all through the night which one of the crew members had said was like charging a Rigger blindfolded.

The captain and crew stood to lose a lot of coin if the cargo was late. The trip was not a total loss, however. He was able to find out why the captain kept screaming Beaufort. The term came from Earth and the crew member that was explaining it to him took him to mid ship and pointed up at a cone shaped thing about halfway up the main mast, and then two more on the port and starboard railings. He then took the man to a device shaped similar to a sundial located behind where the captain had been anchored. It had numbers that ran from zero to fifteen. The man knew he would never be a sailor because when the crew member explained how the cone shaped things reported the wind speed to the sundial gizmo, he hadn't understood one word of it.

The man knew, since he was standing here instead of floating bloated, that the captain had to be one of the best.

One more day!

Huntington Ridge

Donovan Taggert had accepted his captain's request to become a member of the Queen's Own. He had sent his belongings with the train from Willow Wood, but he had chosen to ride separate from the wagons as the train would stop two nights on the trip and if he went via the village of Pepper he could be there with stopping only one night.

When he had departed Pepper a few hours back, he had been pleased with his progress, but his pleasure had been met with dismay at the sight he beheld. Huntington Ridge had been the sight of a battle. There were ten, maybe eleven soldiers lying dead before him. As well as others not in uniform. It could not be Beasts as Huntington Ridge was on too high of a ground for them to climb, and they would have eaten the bodies.

He dismounted and began checking the faces of the uniforms. He didn't recognize any of them, which wasn't all that surprising since he had spent the last twelve years assigned to the Willow Wood detail. One, when he turned it over had been lying on top of a woman. He became proud of the soldier for protecting the woman with his life, until he saw the soldier had his hand on his sword hilt and the blade thrust through the woman's heart. Wilder!

He also saw many men, maybe as many as thirty scattered all along the ridge. These were not soldiers. They had the appearance of outlaws. Had these men joined with the soldiers to defeat the wilder? That scenario seemed unlikely. Had the outlaws and the wilder joined forces against the soldiers? That seemed unlikely as well. The King's men were well trained, but ten against 30 and a wilder? He doubted it. He would have to go back to Pepper and give them the news so they could retrieve their dead. They would have to sort it out. His duty was now to keep the Queen from harm.

He turned to mount and saw three men approaching.

"Hold where you are, swine," one said.

Well, this doesn't sound promising. "Do you have knowledge of what happened here, sir?" Don asked the men.

The three men looked at each other, and the talker said, "That's the trouble with you swine, you're not very bright. We killed us some swine is what happened."

"That wasn't very friendly of you," Don responded.

"We ain't your friends. Never will be. We come for the girl, but looks like we got us a little fun in the process. We'll be killin' ya, now," It was said so matter of fact like, that Donovan was momentarily speechless.

He regained himself, "Since it is your intent to kill me, perhaps you could be gentlemen and grant me a request."

The man smiled and said, "What would you have? Be quick. The Queen awaits us."

"The Queen? In Dawn's Landing?"

"Not that whore, the real Queen. We'll be riddin your fellows of that pretender real soon now."

Whore? "Since I am about to die, surely it matters little if you tell me where your Queen resides."

"You're right. It doesn't, but I'm done talkin," the man said as he drew his sword and charged.

Donovan drew his knife and threw it past the charging man and buried it deep in the chest of one of the others. He drew his long sword and parried the man's thrust and swirled and severed the man's head. The man with the knife in his chest said, "That didn't even hurt," and he reached to pull the knife free. Donovan said, "No, don't," but the warning came too late and the blood gushed from the man's chest as he wrenched it free and he fell to the ground, dead before he hit.

"Well, I guess you get to be the one that comes with me, then," he said to the last man.

With fire in his eyes the man charged Donovan brandishing a cudgel. Donovan swung to the side and brought his long sword down. The cudgel fell to the ground with the man's hand still attached. Donovan pulled him to the ground and pulled off the man's boots. He unlaced the boots and tied the lace around the man's arm tightly until it stopped gushing. The screaming man was put back on his horse and Donovan led him and the two spare horses back toward Pepper.

Dawn's Landing, Clinic on the Round

Melanie, Brie, Chastity and Sister Frances departed for the clinic, with Michael and Willard on duty for the Own. Chastity had chosen to ride with 'her sister' instead of her own bike, because she wanted to stay all day. Brie looked pleased as could be each time that Melanie glanced her way. As it had turned out, when Brie had awakened this morning she found herself with a bed mate. Chastity had been too frightened of the Mansion to sleep in her own room.

When they reached the clinic and went upstairs, Brie and Chastity went right into Bethany's room, while Melanie was met by a waiting Sister Tillie, "I took the liberty of checking with the doctor when I arrived, Highness and although she cautioned me not to 'Read too much into it', I was pleased with her words.

"They had removed the breathing tube last night, as you know. During the night her breathing became stronger, so they removed her from the induced coma. This morning one of the nurses tried to get her to drink through a straw. Her mouth closed on the straw, but she hadn't the strength to drink. The feeding tubes remain in place, but when it slows down tonight and more staff can be at the ready, they plan on trying again."

Melanie forced herself not to be too pleased and happy, thanked Sister Tillie and proceeded into the room. She found Brie talking softly to Bethany, introducing herself and promising to take care of Chastity until she was better.

Two new sisters were praying beside the bed, there were still three bags on the pole. Bethany's eyes looked ever so slightly less swollen, but still as black as pitch. Chastity had already claimed the unburned hand that had been encased in a cast with just the fingers exposed, so Melanie went to the sister's side and examined the heavily burned left arm and hand. As gently as she could she slid her hand in Bethany's palm and quietly whispered to her. "I hope you remember me, Bethany. We met at the Garcia Ranch. I am sorry for what you're going through. At the same time, I am proud of you for taking care of your sister in the absence of your parents. I have signed papers to accept both of you into my house, and hope you will accept me as a temporary mom."

She reached to wipe a smudge off Bethany's forehead, and jumped in fright when her left hand was squeezed. The jump frightened the praying sisters and they both fell backwards. She looked at Sister Tillie and mouthed silently, "Get the doctor!"

Sisterhood: Prison level

Sisters Alice, Tracie, and Kaye had been assigned to the trials of the Queen's mansion murders and the trial of Pierre Bernard was underway.

"Is your birth name Pierre Bernard?"

"Yes."

True! True! True!

One of the sisters scribbled on a notepad as she did after each question.

"Were you born here on Mother?"

"Yes."

True! True! True!

"Were you convicted by the Sisterhood of Pioneer Lake of voyeurism?"

"No,"

Lie! Lie! Lie!

"Have you at any time made a successful effort to see a female employee of The Queen's Mansion in her nudity?"

"No."

Lie! Lie! Lie!

"Have you at any time made a successful effort to see either Ursula Nielson or Angelina Surcott in their nudity?"

"No, I said."

True! True! True!

"Just answer each question yes or no. Have you at any time made a successful effort to see The Queen of Mother in her nudity?"

"No."

True! True! True!

"Have you at any time made a successful effort to see Yanina Svoboda or Theresa Tamm in their nudity?"

"No."

True! True! True!

"Have you at any time made a successful effort to see the Queen's Lady in her nudity?"

"No."

Lie! Lie! Lie!

The three sisters compared answers, saw that they matched, and the Trial Lead Sister Alice, entered into the Chronicles of Time: On July 2nd in the year 531 Pierre Bernard, Native, is hereby convicted of the crime of voyeurism against the person of Kristen Muller, Queen's Lady of 320 Celise Avenue, Dawn's Landing, Queenland.

Sister Alice turned to the watchman, "That will be all for Pierre this morning, sir. The conspiracy trials will start this afternoon, and the murder trials on the new day."

"Let's go, pervert," The watchman jerked Pierre to his feet, "Is he guilty this time, or no?"

"That is not your concern, Sir. Have a good morning."

Sister Alice led the other two out of the room and down to the next trial. Greed by a clothing merchant. This is ridiculous, there has to be more than fourteen trial sisters for a city this size. The Sisterhood hadn't been tested in over a year for those with the proven ability to detect falsehood. She will speak with Sister Beth this afternoon.

Pepper

When Donovan arrived at the village gates he was met by the two soldiers guarding it. "What have you here, Taggert?" one had asked.

"I have found some of yours lying dead at Huntington Ridge. Have your commander meet me at the clinic. The news is graver even." Donovan departed for the clinic. When he arrived he walked the outlaw in and explained the wound to the nurses.

Despite his wound, the outlaw was boisterous in his defiance while he was being cared for, shouting slurs and obscenities at the nurses and inviting them to check his privates. Donovan was growing impatient waiting for the commander, but couldn't leave the outlaw to create havoc at the clinic. After a time the commander came and Donovan related his story.

The commander left two men at the clinic and he and Donovan left for the gate. The commander sent two of his soldiers to Silver Mountain to ask the King for reinforcements. He told his Lieutenant to gather the men and follow after him and Donovan.

"I will show you the location, Commander," Donovan told him, "But I will not be able to join your search for these foul creatures. I must ride with haste and tell the Captain of the Queen's danger."

"I understand, Taggert. I am indebted that you returned to tell us of our losses."

As he and the commander were closing on the battlefield, Donovan heard the thunder of the hooves coming from behind them. He was surprised at the size of the host. Three hundred strong, at the least. He showed the commander the woman he thought to be a wilder, the two he had slain, and said to the commander, "I must be off, Commander! I will advise caution in your search. We have no knowledge of their size."

"Thank you for your concern, Taggert, but we have this."

As Donovan was riding away he heard the commander giving orders to clear the dead and remove the clothing of the outlaws and the wilder. Donovan realized what the commander was doing. He would have live soldiers take the place of the dead and await the arrival of a larger amount of outlaws that their leader would send out to check on what was keeping their comrades.

Donovan was now riding to Dawn's Landing with increased urgency.

Dawn's Landing, Clinic on the Round

"It was certainly encouraging to see her swallow," the doctor was telling Melanie, "We were more than a little concerned that her throat might begin to swell and we didn't want to add more to an already heavily medicated young lady."

"Are you thinking she might be ready to come home tomorrow?" Melanie asked without a smile.

The doctor looked at her incredulously, but then got the joke and smiled. "I will stick my neck out here, Highness, and say that I believe Bethany made the leap into a recovery stage today. I am going to leave her on the critical list for now, so that we maintain the staffing around her and I will check on her progress before I leave for the day."

Melanie took a chair away from the bed that was already overcrowded and Sister Tillie began again reading from the Chronicles of Emily. *I cannot imagine accomplishing the things this woman did without any history or knowledge or aid.*

Brie had Chastity hop off her lap, and she came and told her mother that she had to go to work. Those words came so strange to Melanie. Her fifteen year old daughter having to go to work. It was still hard for Melanie to accept her as suddenly seventeen. Melanie looked out at Michael. He nodded and went with Brie.

Kristen came in a few minutes later with a box and quietly pulled out three thermoses and placed them on the table between Sister Tillie and Melanie. One was marked coffee, one green tea, and one was fruit punch. *Gee, I wonder who that's for.* Kristen placed cups on the table, and waited for the Queen's pleasure.

"I'm good for now, thank you Kristen. What's with the sugar water?"

"Orders from Princess Brie, Majesty, for Princess Chastity."

"Very Well, thank you," Kristen once again went to the bedside and brushed Bethany's cheek, then left and Melanie went back to full attention on Sister Tillie.

North Gate

The captain had been busy since breakfast, having gone immediately to the King's command outside the gates. The commander, on the downside of middle age, had been none too pleased with the King's orders and even less so with the captain's choices. Despite his age, he was a rough man and Marie would not have wanted to face him in single combat. The King had also left instructions with him that a rider was to be sent to the training facilities at Harper's Bay to raise one hundred men with which to replenish his host. That would increase the size of his force by fifty, but the grumpy old man referred to them as 'Unseasoned fools who would load their pants at the first sight of Riggers.'

Marie had finished the Own and staffed the newly appointed positions of six guards for Princesses Brie, Bethany and Chastity. Not to be confused with the Own, the King had commanded that the guards would be referred to as Guards of the Realm.

She told all nine men that the Queen would be expecting them for sup, and departed for the second stage of the King's orders. The King had commanded that 4 patches were to be made and sewn onto the left shoulder of all uniforms. The first patch would be a hexagon of red background and a C W in white. One thousand were to be made for the city watch. The second patch would be square of green background with a single beige bar going from the lower left corner to the upper right. Four hundred of these were to be made for Road Safety. The third patch would be a triangle of blue background with crossing swords of silver. Twelve would be needed for the Own. The last patch would be a diamond of brown background with two silver fists, knuckles to knuckles. Six were to be made for the Guards of the Realm.

The Guards of the Realm would be under the captain's command for now, but in likelihood would branch off in the future. If Taggert accepted her request, the Own would be fully staffed this eve. The captain was gaining peace of mind, with each day.

City Watch Headquarters

Brie had wanted to go from the clinic to Town Hall, but Michael made her go to the mansion first. Brie picked up Pedro there, and Michael went back to the clinic. Brie and Pedro went first to the Town Hall so Brie could speak to the manager about Tuesday night's meeting. The manager was a very nice man and assured Brie there would be no problem as the Hall was not used on Mondays and Tuesdays. Brie made sure the seating was adequate and then she and Pedro headed off to the City Watch offices.

"I know these are not your favorite people Pedro, so you can wait outside while I negotiate."

"Where you go, I go, Highness."

When they arrived they got directions to the commander's office from a lady with a pencil in her hair at the front desk. They walked the hall and found the commander busy with an officer, so Brie sat on the bench outside the office and waited. When the commander finished with the officer, Brie and Pedro went inside.

"How do you do, sir? I'm afraid we haven't met. My name is Brie Thurss and I am the newly appointed High Counselor to the Realm, may I have your name?"

"I am Commander Bruce Burk, High Counselor. It is good to meet you. Kevin speaks highly of you, even though you stifled his deer hunt," The commander laughed. "How may I be of service?"

"I am going to need you to assign some of your men to a task, Commander, until I can hire my own."

The commander looked leery and said, "We have a thousand officers to cover a population just shy of two million, High Counselor. I'm not sure I can help you with that. What did you have in mind?"

"I am going to have the sand pits encased and bolted with security locks."

"All of them? Every pit in the city? How do people dispose of their waste?"

"Every pit in Queenland actually, but I only need you to attend to the ones in Dawn's Landing. For now, until I am staffed, you will have the officers open the pits twice a day for the citizens to dispose of their waste. It will be done at 9:30 in the morning and 7:30 at night, so the citizens can be prepared. You will counsel your officers to be cordial to the citizens as they are doing this, so that the citizens are not afraid to use the pits. I will bring you the keys to these locks as soon as the locks are built to my specs. You will caution the officers not to lose these. If they do, you will be responsible for the replacement and they will not be cheap."

Brie waited for the commander to acknowledge, but he just stood there with that dumb look she always got from Mark when she wouldn't let him eat what was left on other people's plates. So she spoke first.

"Have you need for me to write that down, Commander?"

"Why in the world of Mother would you think I would agree to that?" He asked finally.

"I hope you accept my apology, Commander, if that came out as a request. The days of suicide by sand pit are over. You will assist me until I am staffed, or I will have His Majesty read those exact words to you two days from now. I have other business to attend to, and I can't stand here and watch you mull this over. I will be back when the locks are complete. If it is necessary for me to send for the King, send word to me at the Queen's Mansion. I will be working from there until my offices are finished. Good day, Commander."

She and Pedro left the office, she waved at Pencil Lady, and when they got outside she asked Pedro if he knew a good place for a lunch on the way to the city planners.

He led the way and they walked in silence for a few minutes and he said, "Remind me to run, if I see you coming, Highness."

Clinic on the Round

It had seemed to Melanie that Kristen had just left as she walked in with lunch, but she realized she was so engrossed with Queen Emily that much time had passed. Chastity was sleeping, the sisters had gotten off their knees to make way for the nurse that was checking Bethany's vitals. The coffee and fruit punch were empty, and the tea half empty. Kristen sat the basket and new thermoses on the table and put the empties in the box she had sat down outside the room.

She stood there and Melanie took it to mean she had need of her so she tapped Sister Tillie's arm and stood to leave the room.

"Highness," said the nurse, "I would like to change the bedding and dress the burns, could you give me a moment?"

Melanie ordered everyone out and Michael had returned at some point, so she pointed at Chastity and he lifted her out to the cot.

She looked at Willard and said, "I am going to stretch my legs. I will need one of you to stay here with my girls," She looked at Kristen and said, "Let's take a walk."

Melanie, Kristen and Willard went outside, and at the edge of the walkway, Melanie took off her shoes and socks. For reason's Melanie would have to ask the sisters of, all the tingling stopped when she was fully merged, except the tips of her fingers, this time.

Kristen asked, "May I, Majesty?"

"Absolutely!" replied Melanie.

Willard and the barefooted Melanie and Kristen began their walk around the building. Melanie, when Mother was in her, began her daily wilder search, asking Kristen, "You have news?"

"Yes, Highness. The captain has given me this note to pass on to you," Kristen pulled the note from her pocket and handed it to Melanie.

My Queen,

I have accepted three more of the Queen's Own. If Donovan Taggert accepts, we will be at twelve. I have also, at the King's request, hired six Guards of the Realm that will be responsible for the safety of the Princesses Brie, Bethany and Chastity.

Further, I have taken the liberty to assume you want to meet each and have asked Arnold to assist Theresa tonight.

On that note, I must also inform you, because I'm sure they haven't, that Ursula, Kristen, and Angelina have been putting in extra time to cover for Yanina and Pierre.

My apologies as I'm sure this news is not welcome at this time and place, but I am trying to keep you as up to speed as possible.

With utmost respect,
Marie

Melanie had to admit, staffing the mansion had gone to the back of her mind, which was unfair to the ladies, so she finished her usual unsuccessful sweep for wilders and sat to put her shoes and socks back on and asked Kristen. "Who usually handles the hiring at the mansion, Kristen?"

"The Sisterhood provides the Queen with the help in this area Highness, but there's no hurry, Ursula and Angelina are doing fine. I will help where I can and it can wait until Princess Bethany is better."

"We are about to have a dozen new house guests. Go to the Sisterhood, explain our situation and our need and I will accept their assistance."

"Yes, Highness."

Kristen was off, and she and Willard began the climb to the third floor. Just before they reached the top she saw Michael leaning out the doorway.

"The Princess is asking for you, Highness," he said.

Melanie quickened her pace, guessing that Chastity wanted more fruit punch. When she turned the corner she found Chastity still asleep on the cot, with all three sisters conferring at the end of the hall. She looked at Michael and he began to smile. She darted past him into the room and found two nurses and the doctor surrounding Bethany. "I'm here," she said.

"I'm thirsty, mom."

Landing Gyro and Subs

Brie and Pedro had a Gyro. Brie had never had one before, but she considered herself hooked now, and it only cost her a silver quarter for two. She was still at four dollars, a gold half and a silver quarter and wondered what she would be paid for being a High Counselor.

The city planners told her there were one hundred and one sand pits in Dawn's Landing, and four empty buildings she could choose from for an office. They gave her a list of masons, carpenters, brick layers and locksmiths. She decided to start at the locksmiths because there were only two of them. At each one she explained that the locks would be encased in cement and how long the tubes would need to be that held the mechanisms, how many locks per pit, how many keys per lock, etc., and they should have their bids to the Queen's Mansion no later than midday on the new day.

When she left the locksmiths, she stopped at the first health store and made her way to the medication section. She perused the labels and made several notes on her pad. It took a good deal of time and she could tell Pedro was getting impatient. She explained some of the medication would have to be pulled behind the counter, depending on ingredients.

The two left and continued with the sand pit process with the masons and the bricklayers. The carpenters would have to wait until she decided on an office. She also asked the bricklayers to show how many men they would have to hire to complete the job in one week.

By the time she had finished with the bricklayers, she saw that it was getting into late afternoon and decided the offices and Sisterhood would have to wait until the new day. She and Pedro began making their way back across town.

Clinic on the Round

The afternoon had not gone as well as it could have for Melanie, but it was all worth it to hear Bethany talking. Bethany had asked for Chase and it took Melanie a bit to realize that had been a nickname Bethany had given Chastity. She had asked Willard to wake Chastity and Melanie had spent the next several hours keeping sugared up Chastity from jumping on the bed.

Melanie had given Frances the day off since she would be listening to the reading of Emily and there wouldn't be much scripture. Sister Tillie had borrowed paper and pen from the nursing staff and had become the scribe. Sister Tillie sent the praying sisters to inform Sister Beth and summon Sister Frances.

Bethany didn't want to talk about the battle of Landing Road, saying she knew the sisters were dead and was crying for them before she hit the ground.

Two doctors had pulled Melanie from the room to discuss what was next, so she sent Michael in to make sure Chastity didn't jump on the bed. She had noticed that Michael had picked her up and was dangling her by her britches over Bethany. Chastity was waving her arms at Bethany and explaining life at the Mansion.

She called me mom. Melanie felt the sniffles coming.

The doctors said they were going to be inducing sleep on Bethany and testing for grafting, re-casting, bandaging the head anew and it would be better if they had the room.

Melanie went in to explain things to Bethany and say goodnight. After Chastity said goodnight, Melanie cleared the room.

Sister Frances, Martin and Phillip all arrived at the same time. Melanie asked Martin and Phillip which one would stay with Bethany and Martin got his hand up first so Melanie, Chastity, the two sisters and the three Own headed back to the Mansion. Chastity decided it would be fun to ride with Willard, but the long sword kept hitting her in the head so halfway there she switched and rode the rest the way with Melanie.

The mansion was buzzing again when the group arrived. I hope we have enough rooms for all these people. She was obviously not going to be able to hear more about Emily tonight, so she sent Sister Tillie back to the Sisterhood. A headcount revealed she was missing a daughter and Pedro. She also didn't see Angelina or Ursula and assumed they were sleeping. Good, get some rest.

The captain noticed her and approached. "My Queen, we are near fully staffed and I would like you to meet three new members of the Own when you are settled."

"Lead the way, Captain."

North Gate

"Where are the stables, Sir?" Donovan asked the soldier at the gate.

The soldier sent him in the right direction and Donovan rode to have his warhorse cared for. She had been ridden hard and needed food and a brush down. The stable boy was a kindly one and offered to check the leg braces and saddle straps as well. Donovan was given a bicycle which needed to be returned when he picked up his horse, and directions to the Queen's Mansion. It would be a bit of a ride.

As he was leaving the stables he observed a soldier riding beside a young girl in the same direction he was going. He pedaled to catch up and noticed the soldier had seen him and was placing himself between the girl and Donovan. A guard, I wonder who this girl would be. Could the Queen be this young? The soldier said something to the girl and got off his bike and handed it to her, facing Donovan.

Beach Front Avenue

"Someone approaches us, Highness. I'm sure it is fine but I will check just the same," Pedro said to Brie.

Brie noticed the man coming. With the exception of the head gear he was dressed in uniform. Pedro was walking toward the man. She watched as they talked and saw Pedro stick out his arm and the other man grasped it in that ridiculous macho man shake that Brie thought was stupid. Why not just shake hands? Brie got off her bike and waited for the two of them to reach her.

"Highness, this is Donovan Taggert. He will be the second of the Queen's Own. He just arrived from Willow Wood."

The three of them began the ride to the mansion, and Brie decided she and Donovan Taggert would not get along. Pedro had asked him of his trip and after glancing at Brie, Taggert declined to comment. "How was your trip, Sir?" she asked him, daring him to blow her off.

"Slower than I had imagined, Highness. I had to double back on one occasion to consult with the commander of Pepper."

"Really, what about?"

"Battle strategy, Highness."

He wasn't lying to her, she could feel, but he wasn't telling her everything. She could feel that too. She continued with the questions for the remainder of the ride, but the man was calm and steadfast in his ability to dodge and parry the questions. This is going to be a tough nut to crack.

Queen's Mansion

The captain had done her social duty and introduced each of the Own as well as the King's newly formed Guards of the Realm and Melanie noticed the table had been set. It was too crowded inside, so she begged leave, eyed Chastity trying to get the Own to play tag, so she and Sister Frances went to the patio. The patio was quickly becoming Melanie's favorite part of the house. She had just sat and kicked her feet up when she saw Pedro enter with another man and Brie. She waved at Brie and stayed lounged.

Brie was looking all around the room. Too bad, so sad, he's with your sister, Melanie thought, knowing it was Martin she was looking for. The man that had come in with Brie and Pedro was being introduced to the others. Must be the man from Willow Wood. When the introductions were finished, the table was ready and Melanie got up and made her way through the crowd to her place at the table. The man was placed next to Melanie by the captain, and she herself took the seat to the other side of Melanie. The girls were sitting at the far end, giggling.

"Brie, Chastity has had enough sugar today, see that she eats well," Melanie said.

"Okay," was Brie's answer. Chastity's answer was arms folded across the chest in defiance and the pout look.

Sup was what looked like an entire pig. Dishes of pork roast were every two feet or so and the table had been extended out quite a way. There were also bowls of vegetables that looked to be carrots, celery, cauliflower and broccoli. The bread was Theresa's usual biscuit loaf. There were mashed potatoes, baked potatoes, fried potatoes and potato boats filled with cheese. There were three salads on the table as well, a leaf salad, a fish salad and a fruit salad. Gee, I wonder who requested that. Melanie saw Chastity asking Brie for it, and Brie pointed to the carrots on her plate, and Chastity returned to her pout face.

Melanie hadn't had much at breakfast, so she ate pretty well, talking with Donovan at length about Willow Wood, the King, the Own, Dawn's Landing and the girls. He was a good eater, for sure. He probably had three helpings of roast and practically swallowed the boats whole.

She was conversing with the Guard of the Realm, as well as her new Own. Besides Donovan, she met Albert Mason, a thirty nine year old veteran of the King's force who she would just call smart ass, since he was one. Albert, she had learned first-hand, was not one you wanted to ask silly questions of. Carl Niemann was known as a silent, but deadly man. He looked somewhat shy about talking about himself, flushing when the Queen of Mother actually talked to him, but those at the table that knew him, spoke of his heroism facing down a Rigger alone.

Finally, Doran Oberman had her laughing so hard, she thought she might leak boogers. Carl and Doran were also from the King's force.

When sup was finished and all were chatting over coffee and tea, Theresa, Arnold and Kristen began clearing the table. Brie had held Chastity's plate back as well as the fruit salad. It looked like Brie had set a goal for Chastity with her roast and mashed potatoes, because Chastity was shoving it down pretty good. As she was heading back to the patio, Donovan begged a private audience with her and the captain.

Melanie led the way onto the patio, and the three of them took a seat away from the door near the lawn, so as not to be heard from inside and Donovan began telling them the details of his trip. The battlefield, the wilder, the outlaws, the capture and return to Pepper, the trap being set by the King's forces, the disposition of the prisoner, and the things said by the outlaws, including the threats.

"If I might be so bold, Highness, as to speculate and share my fears?" He continued.

"Please," she said.

"I believe there is a wilder out there that fancies herself a queen. I believe since she sent these men to retrieve only the woman, that she has convinced other wilders to join her. I believe she has a substantial force of outlaws at her disposal. I also believe she has eyes and ears inside Dawn's Landing, judging by how sure the outlaw was of ridding us of our Queen."

Melanie sat in silence absorbing everything Donovan had said, running scenarios through her mind.

"Captain, would you be kind and send a couple of extra men to the clinic? They may decide I would be easier tamed if they had my children."

The captain nodded and went inside.

Melanie stared toward the street contemplating this bit of news brought to her by this man. Is he a doomsayer, or extremely wise? Did he misinterpret something or is he even possibly understating the danger. She saw Gary and two of the Guards of the Realm, hastily peddling toward the clinic. She heard the door open and close, but she felt in a trance.

"I'm ill prepared to do battle with even one wilder, Captain. I'm open to suggestion."

"Shut down the city, Highness. No one in or out without proper papers. Put the mansion itself in lock down. Notify the Sisterhood of this dire news and have them come in force to begin battle training. Put the City Watch and Road Safety under my command and let me worry on your safety and that of your daughters. Send a written message with every detail to the King with your seal, including the possibility that Huntington Ridge may have been an elaborate trap to ensnare the King's forces there. They would have been the closest force of size to the Landing. Encircle the Landing with the King's force outside the gates. Cancel all trains."

She's really only twenty-two years old? "Make it happen."

Melanie heard a commotion inside and saw Brie embracing a boy and a girl.

MOTHER'S CHILDREN

Queenland
Huntington Ridge

All the bodies had been cleared, the outlaws stripped, and his men dressed in their clothing. The toughest challenge for Commander Wyman was finding a female member of his host that would fit the wilder outfit.

The signal had still not come from the outposts he had stationed in the woods, and the men were growing anxious for battle. If the impostor had sent three men to pick up a dead wilder, the commander was certain she would send more the second time, and with luck also send a wilder along. He was in need to capture a wilder to gain information on the pretender. This had never been done on Queenland, and he didn't particularly enjoy the prospect of placing his men in that degree of danger. Everything would have to go perfectly to capture her. He had been over it time and again and hoped all of his men play their parts.

Wilder first, outlaws after, is what he had told his men. One attempt to capture and if it went awry she was to be killed. Then and only then do they take the outlaws. He ran scenarios through his head and wondered if he had gone over it enough. How many could there be? Is the pretender battle savvy? Would she anticipate an ambush, or did she think the men she had sent were on a bender? Would she come herself? Why does she need her dead wilder? It was too late for second guessing; the plan was set.

Silver Mountain, King's Mansion

"So, what's she like?" Jackie Jensen asked her husband as they were having breakfast.

"She seems kind and caring, though she is yet another that will not be rid of these Beasts," the King answered.

There was a knock at the door and he watched as Samantha made her way to answer. The man at the door was a soldier and Kevin immediately rose from his plate and went to the door ushering the man out. Kev is determined to give me a couple days with my wife, the King thought to himself.

"Does Marie like her?" Jackie asked.

"Marie has a job to do. I seriously doubt she has given her personal feelings for the Queen a thought." The King pulled the sweet roll back off Billy's plate. "Eat your potatoes first," the King told him, and then to his wife said, "I'm afraid I may have placed undo stress on her by giving her more to command. I forget at times her age."

"I have learned," Jackie responded, "that niece of ours shouldn't be underestimated." She didn't think Brent heard her as he was looking out the window at the conversation between Kevin and the soldier, trying to read lips.

"There are rats in the cellar," she said. No response.

"I'm pregnant," she said. Nothing

The King began to rise.

"Sit. . . down, husband!" Jackie said firmly.

The King sat and looked at her.

"Have you heard anything I've said?" She asked him.

"Of course I did. You said the rats in the cellar are pregnant." He continued to stare out the window.

"Samantha, draw the blinds, please," she said and Samantha closed the blinds. "Brent, how about if you trust Kevin to inform you of that which you need know, and just relax?"

"You're right, honey. I'm sorry." The King did not relax. Kevin would not have taken this long with the man, were it good news.

Port of Courage, Sisterhood

Finally, ashore and with that awful storm behind him, the man had thanked the captain and was at the Sisterhood, booking passage on the morning train to Harper's Bay, but there was none. He went to the stables and rented a horse and was now on the road, after taking the time to grab some water and snacks.

He estimated his arrival at Harper's Bay to be shortly after the sun was at its peak, another three hours on the skiffs from there and he should be in Dawn's Landing. If the brainless planners had done a better job on the design of the Port, they could have fit skiffs in there and he could have been in Dawn's Landing by mid-afternoon, instead of having to go all the way around the bay.

He had abandoned his hopes of telling King Brent first, because the trip had made him eager to get home, so he would tell the Queen and then be off to Silver Mountain. He was elated and further convinced to notify the Queen first, by the news from the Sisterhood that Queen Pamela was no more.

Dawn's Landing, Queen's Mansion

Melanie was thrashing and trying to scream but her mouth was full of sand. The pit was pulling her down and there was nothing for her to grab. She tried to touch Mother but couldn't. Her hand touched something. She grabbed for it and got it. It was someone's hand. Someone was trying to pull her out of the sandpit, but the hand was too small. It was a girl's hand, not one of the Own. The hand was tugging and pulling with all its strength, but Melanie kept slipping down.

"I wanna go see Bethany," came the voice. Melanie's eyes fluttered and she began to wake from her slumber. Chastity was trying to pull her out of bed.

"I wanna go see Bethany," Chastity repeated.

"Okay, honey. Go find Kristen for me."

Chastity ran from the room, and Melanie swung her legs over the edge of the bed. *Last night's news must have been more troubling than she thought, to have given me that horrible of a nightmare.* She stood and made her way to the washroom and splashed water on her face.

Kristen walked in, or rather was being ushered in by Chastity. "What's going on downstairs, Kristen?" Melanie asked.

"My Queen, everyone is in the mansion except Princesses Bethany and Brie and four of the Guards of the Realm. Two of those are with Princess Bethany and two are with Princess Brie at the Sisterhood."

"Why is she at the Sisterhood, do you know?"

"I did not think it my place to ask, my Queen."

"Very well. I'm not very hungry, would you take Chastity downstairs and ask Arnold to fix her something non sugary?"

"Can I have a sweet roll?" Chastity asked.

"You will eat what Arnold prepares for you. I don't want you trying to jump on your sister's bed today."

"I'll be good, I promise."

"I will hold you to that. If you are you can have a sweet roll tomorrow."

Kristen took the pouting Chastity downstairs and Melanie began preparing for her day.

When she got downstairs, Chastity was finishing what was left of a sausage scramble, the Own appeared to be in a meeting in the study and the two Guards were watching a man and a woman that were on the couch. Melanie went into the kitchen and asked Arnold for a piece of dry toast and a cup of coffee.

She found Kristen sitting with Sisters Frances and Tillie and asked, "Who are the two on the couch?"

"They are waiting for your blessing, my Queen. They were sent from the Sisterhood to fill the opened positions at the mansion," Kristen said.

"Excellent," said Melanie, "What is going on with the trials, does anyone know?"

Sister Tillie started to answer but glanced at Kristen and stayed silent. "Okay, I will find out later. Kristen would you get the two and take them to the patio. I will talk to them there."

Kristen left and Melanie looked at Sister Tillie.

"Pierre was found guilty of voyeurism yesterday morning and the Queen's Lady is the victim. The Sisterhood would like your counsel on whether to tell her. This morning, the newspaper man and milk woman were found guilty of conspiracy. Pierre was found not guilty. The murder trial was also this morning. The newspaper man was guilty and the other two not. His Holiness has not pronounced sentences yet."

"Sister Tillie, would you run to the Sisterhood? The High Counselor is there as we speak. Tell her what you have told me and follow her instructions. How can Pierre and the woman not be guilty? Can you find that out for me as well?"

"I will try, Highness. Trial sisters are not usually willing to discuss their decisions, but I will tell them you wish to know," Sister Tillie said and departed.

"I have put your toast and coffee on the patio, Majesty," said Arnold.

"Thank you," Melanie and Frances went to the patio and met Kristen there with Franklin Adams and Kristi Davidson.

"I wanna go see Bethany," came the usual demand.

Melanie said, "You stay off the bed, and obey your guards." She nodded at the Guards and they were off, and the interviews began.

Silver Mountain

"Eleven soldiers defeating thirty outlaws is not unheard of," said the King, "but they had a wilder with them. Something is amiss, here."

Kevin responded, "The usual excursions of Commander Wyman are a compliment of twenty, which leaves nine unaccounted for. They could have given chase or been taken, and we are only assuming she was a wilder."

"She was either a wilder or one of my men shoved his blade through the heart of a harmless woman. Which do you think more likely?"

The King was deep in thought with the puzzling news. "Leave three hundred to shore the City Watch, shut down today's train and have Road Safety watch the gates. Send five hundred to Huntington Ridge. I want everyone else ready to march in two hours." The King had been wrong before, and he hoped he was this time, but he had an uneasy feeling this pretender had just out maneuvered one of his best commanders. Why would they have concerned themselves with Pepper?

Dawn's Landing, Queen's Mansion

The interviews were done. Melanie had Kristen take Kristi to Angelina and Franklin to Ursula. Then, each of them toured the house with the new hires. While finishing her third cup of coffee and talking with Frances about the new employees of the Mansion, Melanie's thoughts went to Bethany and her recovery. The recovery was almost going too fast.

Kristen rejoined them and contributed her thoughts of the new hires. It was obvious from her comments that she liked them both.

"May I talk with you a moment, Kristen?" came the female voice from the doorway. All heads turned, and saw Brie looking at Kristen.

"Yes, Highness," said Kristen, but realized her mistake and looked at Melanie. Melanie nodded and Kristen and Brie walked out into the yard.

"Give way," Melanie commanded Brie's Guards and they both retreated to the edge of the patio. Melanie noticed the beginning of tears on Frances and instructed her to go inside. Sister Tillie took a seat next to Melanie and began her readings. No one was witnessing except her and the two guards. Melanie had a feeling she would be able to tell when Brie hit the topic. Yup, there it is. Kristen had her head buried in her hands, but to her credit it wasn't a total freak out.

The girls' conversation went on for a bit and Melanie found her thoughts straying to the readings of Emily. Every word she heard and every sentence uttered gave her more respect for this remarkable woman. *I will never be that great of a Queen.*

She noticed two men at the sandpit, measuring something. *That's queer!* The guards, thinking they were a little too close to the girls, headed toward the pit, but the girls had begun working their way back to the patio, so the guards stopped and waited.

Brie had noticed her mother's interest in the bricklayers and said, "They are here at my summons, Mom. I will be locking down the sand pits. I left Sarah and Dave still haggling with the Sisterhood, so I have to get back. I can explain later. May I borrow Kristen? She may be able to provide help."

Atta girl! "Sure, I'm heading to see Bethany anyway, so I will see you two at sup."

Melanie had thought about interrupting the meeting of the Own, but decided against it, so she sat on the patio listening to the reading of Emily. On occasion, Emily would talk about her children and Melanie found her thoughts going to the Sisterhood and their search for her family. She had heard nothing yet, but she had convinced herself to be patient.

Eventually, the meeting ended and Melanie, the two sisters, William and Albert were on their way to the clinic, along with Sister Meredith that had identified herself as one of the sisters who would be teaching her to defend herself. Melanie had Fred taxi her and Sister Tillie, so that the sister could continue to read.

Harper's Bay Shipyard

It took a bit of work, but the man finally convinced the commander of Harper's Bay of his need to get to the Queen. The commander had told him there was no way in or out of Dawn's Landing any time soon, by land or sea. After several minutes of explaining what had happened in Caruso, the commander agreed to lead the skiffs himself.

After a disagreement about passage, and the commander's comments about commandeering the boats, a fleet of three left Harper's Bay and began their trek to Dawn's Landing. The commander had said that if the man had gone alone he likely would have been arrested on sight and never gotten to the Queen, whereas he and the four men he had brought along were all known to the port watch.

The breeze was strong and the small boats were cutting well. The man was hoping he would be facing the new Queen before her lunch plate was clean.

Huntington Ridge

The reinforcements from the King had arrived and relayed the King's concern to the commander. There still had been no signal of approaching riders. Commander Wyman felt the blood rising in his cheeks. It wasn't embarrassment, it was anger that he had allowed himself to be duped by the pretender.

"Leave twenty men to watch the ridge, they are to use caution if the ridge is approached. No guessing. They need to know they can overpower them or stay hidden. If no one comes by nightfall, they are to return to Pepper. I want every scout, archer, horseman and foot ready to march in ten minutes. We are going through the woods. If the Pretender is marching on Dawn's Landing, I mean to get to her first."

Dawn's Landing, Clinic on the Round

It was mid-morning when they reached the clinic, and when Melanie got out of the cabbie, she looked up and saw an absolutely perfect blue sky. Not even a wisp of a cloud. She wished she was at the apartment of His Holiness to look upon the Horizon Sea today. There was a slight breeze, the temperature must have been around seventy-five. A perfect day for a picnic, but that would have to wait for another day.

When she reached the upstairs, she went to the nurse's station prior to seeing Bethany, to get a report on what the testing had revealed. The nurse was very positive and genuinely impressed with Bethany's recuperative ability. They were planning to begin grafting this afternoon.

"How much grafting will there be?" She asked.

"The back, from the buttocks to the head is burned the worst, but Bethany herself only seems to be concerned about her arm. I suggested to her that it would be easier to do it all at once. If she were to change her mind later and want the back done, it would be harder on her. She said she would think about it."

"The head and the casting?"

"The breaks seem to be healing well, but we placed her in new casting to be safe. We don't want her rolling in her sleep and aggravating it. The bandage has been removed in place of a half skull. She didn't care for it when she woke, but it gives her more maneuverability to see her surroundings. She seems more concerned about her appearance being a disappointment to you, Highness, than she does her health."

"Have you checked her pain tolerance? I am only asking because I don't want her to become addicted."

"Medical medication is non-addictive, Majesty. All medical medication contains soursop."

"What's that?"

"It grows on the Eagle Islands and Southern Dakota. It is a fruit, I believe. It has properties that somehow counteract addiction. You could talk to the labs about that, I'm not sure how it works, but it does."

"Thank you," said Melanie and she made her way to Bethany's room. She found both the girls fast asleep, so she sat and listened to Sister Tillie continue with the Chronicles of Emily.

North gate

"Have you covered all possible approaches?" Marie asked the commander.

"We have scouts in every direction, Princess. Some as far out as five miles. Unless they have developed wings they will not surprise us."

Marie scanned the defenses. There were soldiers everywhere patrolling the tree lines on the outside of the Beast wall and in the front. Archers had taken up position behind the wall and on the battlements. The snares were nearly complete and if everything worked according to plan they will face only the outlaws. The wilder queen would be netted and lifted and unable to merge. Things never seem to go according to plan though, so she rode off to check the shelter.

If the defenses failed, the Queen and the three princesses would be whisked to the shelter, hopefully to stay there until the King's forces arrived. All the Own had been told the plan and given their instructions on lifting and wrapping the queen, to prevent her from attempting to take on multiple wilders. The Guards of the Realm were to grab Princess Brie and Chastity and the rest of the Guard and the Own would meet at the clinic to carry the bed of Princess Bethany and its attachments to the shelter.

Two things were left to do. She had to have the clinic supply her with Queenstone, and she had to have a doctor and nurse volunteer for the shelter.

When she got to the shelter, the masons were finishing the interior wall. The exterior wall was just thick enough to stop the fireballs, the debris would explode in on the interior wall, but that wall would hold. Another hour and it would be ready. She made her way to the clinic.

Business District

Brie had finished with the Sisterhood, the final result being the King's taxes would be raised on the businesses only and those increases figured in prior to profit, so the owners wouldn't even feel it. The bricklayers would get their extra men and she would be able to keep those men employed after the pits were finished, as Pit Guards.

She and the SPA's would draw a salary, the expense of which would come from the King's taxes and the Sisterhood itself would fund Brie's office space and Town Hall lease. Kristen, Sarah, Dave, herself and the two tagalongs made their way to the business district to examine the three offices. She didn't want to stop, once she started, so she asked the Guards to find a food court for an early lunch.

The guards led the way to an area where the road divided with a center median full of food choices. They all sat and surveyed the assorted shops. The Guards wanted to go to Burger Heaven, figures, so she gave them her gold half, Dave just wanted a pretzel, so she gave him the silver quarter and he was off to Mr. Twister, and she and the girls went to Sally's Salads.

The food was fantastic and the conversation light for the most part. Everyone loved the perfect weather they had been having but knew rain was needed. Sarah decided she needed to travel to New Texas to see the Mountains of Pecos. She had seen a painting and wanted to see if the artist exaggerated.

Dave asked Brie, when they were staffed here, if he could be assigned to a village because he liked small towns better. She assured him he could pick one, since he was the first to ask.

"What about you, Kristen? Any childhood dreams?" Brie asked.

"More than anything when I was growing up, I wanted to be a breeder. I love animals, all animals. They always accept you for who you are and never expect anything from you. They love me too. Most will walk right up to me and just sit there like they own me," she giggled, "now, though, after having met my Queen, all I think about is how to make her day easier. I really love her, Brie."

"Yeah, she grows on you. Just like bacteria."

Sarah and Dave saw the humor and laughed but Kristen wasn't laughing.

"I didn't care for that," Kristen mumbled.

"Sorry," Brie said, "I love her too, and that was callous."

Lunch was finished, so the group cleaned up the table and headed off to the business district. Brie, Sarah, and Dave were making comments on every building they passed, making mental notes of where this shop was or that business was, or what a nice, scenic area those houses are in, and oh my gosh, we have to bike that hill sometime.

Brie would glance casually at Kristen on occasion, but found her mostly staring straight ahead and pedaling.

Clinic on the Round

Chastity was the first to awaken. She looked at her sister, and then at Melanie, climbed up into Melanie's lap and went right back to sleep. About ten minutes later, Bethany woke and Melanie stopped Sister Tillie. "How are you feeling?" she asked.

"Ugly!" Bethany responded.

"I don't think a day has passed that I thought you ugly, maybe your vision needs work."

"I can't see me," Bethany said.

"That might be a good thing, right now. You're kind of ugly."

"Hahaha. Ow! Ow! Ow!"

Oh, shit! "Sorry, honey. I keep forgetting about that."

"It's okay. It's this darn pad I'm lying on. If I lay still, my back feels kinda wet, but if I move it really hurts."

"You are making some amazing progress. Even the doctors think so."

"I'm really thirsty," Bethany announced.

Melanie motioned Frances to the water and Frances gave her a drink. Bethany looked at Frances and the tears started. That's okay, get it out.

"I couldn't save them," Bethany said.

"That's not your fault. I couldn't either and I'm the Queen," Melanie said, soothingly. The tears were really flowing now and Frances started to head back to her but Tillie grabbed her arm and Melanie motioned her back to her seat. *She has a strong heart, this girl. No wonder I love her.* Melanie watched carefully to make sure the crying didn't turn into painful sobbing, but it remained silent tears with lots of sniffing. Melanie placed Chastity with Tillie and grabbed some tissue and began dabbing Bethany's tears. Melanie kissed her forehead and placed tissue over her now brace less nose and allowed her to blow her sniffles. With the swelling gone down Melanie could see the brown of her eyes.

"This isn't very classy of me," Bethany said.

"Wrong! I love seeing so much heart in you," Melanie responded.

"Are you mad at me for calling you mom?"

"I'm not. That filled my heart with love and I'm extremely honored."

Clinic Shelter

The captain had her doctor, her nurse, and her Queenstone. She now left the clinic and headed to the west docks, where the runner said a man from Caruso was demanding to see the Queen. It was a jaunt and would take her far from the Queen, but his need was reported urgent.

Offices of the Counsel

Brie had decided she liked the office on Moon Street the best, so she made the notes she needed to, and what the carpenters would need to do. She went outside and looked up and down the street at the businesses, shops and parks. Then she walked to the edge of the property and looked up and down Heron Avenue and made notes of those businesses and shops. No parks on Heron.

Brie gathered her group and they were off to the carpenters. She paid close attention to everything that was around the office, that she might partnership with to help offset the labor. Sarah pointed out the postmaster and Brie noted that. Dave saw a griever building and she made a note of that. There, there it is, not more than three blocks from the office. A care center for the elderly. Brie made a note of the address and the group continued on.

They arrived at the carpenters and Brie, Sarah, Dave and Kristen went inside. The Guards walked the grounds.

Clinic on the Round

Melanie went out for her midday walk and took Sister Meredith with her. She left Chastity in the care of Frances and Tillie who were bringing Bethany up to date on events at the Sisterhood. Bethany had been taken off the serious list and had been reclassified as recovering.

Melanie tapped into Mother and listened as Sister Meredith gave her the information from former Queens that had been used for their defense. She searched for these items and places, found them, and played a bit with moving them around. She found herself easily multitasking, working with Sister Meredith's words, crushing limestone, searching for wilders, moving shale, positioning stone, and using magma, which was tricky but fun.

She noticed two of the Own walking with a doctor carrying something to a brick building she hadn't noticed before. She disconnected from Mother, and walked to the building.

"What goes, Gary?" she asked.

"Just a precaution, Highness. If we are attacked, and if the impossible happens and they do make it past our defenses, you and all three of the princesses will be here, and they will have to get through all eighteen of us to get to you."

"I see. So then, this is Bethany's well-being that you are working on now? I'm assuming that's Queenstone?"

"Yes, Highness, and this is the doctor that will be in there with you."

I love my Own.

"Thank you for caring, I'll try to behave this time."

As they were walking back to the clinic, a thought came to her. "Sister, is there any way that I can touch Mother, besides being barefoot?"

"Of course, Majesty. If any bare part of your person touches any part of Mother, whether it be the ground, grass, tree, water or rock, you can connect. You are connected to Mother at all times, just by being here. You just don't realize it because the air is made up of too many parts, and the touch is extremely weak. When you arrived on Mother, you were frightened and confused, but you had the sense you belonged here, am I right?"

"I remember that, yes."

"Eventually you will learn that you can hold Mother's power even when lifted or standing in a structure. It will seep, naturally, but the air itself touches Mother which provides you the ability to 'store' it, shall we say. Each second that passes, will make that power a little weaker.

I believe it was Queen Gayle that said it equivocated to holding your breath under water. The Chronicles dictate past Queens have not been as modest as you in their dress and the Sisterhood believes although no queen has confirmed it, that they stayed as exposed as was appropriate, in the event they needed to connect, but never wore shirts with sleeves or high necklines and only wore long gowns or pants at formal functions, or if their travels took them to frigid climates. I only knew Queen Pamela and Queen Shirley, and personally, I never saw either in anything but shorts. Queen Pamela was always bare from the bosom to the belt and Queen Shirley a barebacked halter top. I personally think that the more skin exposed to the air, the longer the storage, but the other sisters tell me I think too much."

"Had Pamela or Shirley ever given birth?"

"Majesty?"

"Never mind, I will keep your words in mind and test it for you one day."

Melanie was frustrated with herself for not taking the advice given her and meeting with the Sisters earlier, but nothing could be done for it now. She would simply have to get smarter in her decisions. She and Meredith went back inside the clinic.

Dock Three West

"How long ago was this?" Marie asked the man.

"Three weeks, Captain. I'm afraid I have no news on the King's present condition."

"It took you three weeks to get here from Caruso?" Marie asked sarcastically.

"No Captain, I traveled to all lands to inform all Kings."

"In doing so you made the decision that the one person that needed to know the most, needed to know last?"

"It was an error in judgment on my part, granted. . ."

"You are a fool, sir. I question that you have judgment of any kind. Commander, take this imbecile back to Port of Courage and have him gone from here."

Marie turned, mounted her bike and made haste back to the Queen.

This bodes ill. That pretender entered Queenland right under our noses. Probably right through Dawn's Landing.

Marie was dead certain the attack was coming. This news pretty much assured it. It also gave her pause of Donovan's fear of vermin inside the Landing. The pretender probably spent days here gathering what she needed.

Deepwater Wood

"Re-form the line," Commander Wyman screamed.

The archers released another barrage into the massive army, and then another. "To the next ridge. Quickly, now."

As soon as he and his men came upon the enemy, he'd sent riders to alert the Landing. He simply did not have enough men to even put a dent in the masses, but he meant to slow them. This was the largest march he had ever seen. The men must have been ten thousand, and he could see rocks and fireballs coming from five different directions, and his men had already killed two of those Earth cats. How in the world did she tame animals?

"Form the line. Loose!" The archers released, and more of the enemy fell.

"Re-form the line. To the next ridge." It was a simple process. His mounted kept them from being attacked on retreat and watched for the animals. His archers would retreat from hill to hill firing, retreat, firing, retreat and so on.

"Form the line. Loose!" His goal was to slow them down as much as possible through the woods and then feign a permanent retreat. He and his men would then wait for the army at Rainbow Pass. One could not traverse that pass more than ten wide. He had sent the supply wagon ahead with everything they would need to dam the pass with the dead bodies of these assassins. The arrows traveled much farther than the fire, so it was easy to stay out of range of the wilder. With Mother surging through them they could throw farther than any ten men, but still not as far as an arrow could travel.

Dawn's Landing, Business District

That is enough for one day, Brie thought. Everything was coming along nicely and she wanted to check in on Bethany. The group began heading back toward the clinic. Kristen had become her normal self again and hadn't called Pierre an asshole for over an hour.

Dave and Sarah had made good notes. She was kind of proud of them. The only thing Brie had left, was to work up a plan for how she was going to get counselors in other cities. Dave had his mind set on a small village, and Sarah would be heading back to Silver Mountain. Brie herself wasn't going to be able to leave the Landing anytime soon. It was going to require some thought.

She was surprised at how much she missed Martin right now, as well. Just thinking about him made her insides feel like they were fluttering. She wondered if he was thinking about her. Ever. At all. He needed to get off his duff and ask her to a play pretty soon or she might have to shame herself and ask him.

Clinic on the Round

The captain and Brie's group arrived at the same time at the clinic. Brie went right into the room, Sarah and Dave took seats outside the room and began comparing notes. All the Own and the Guard began chatting in the hall, and the captain and Kristen headed for the Queen. The captain trumped Kristen and spoke first, telling her of the man at the pier and his news.

"So, I need to go to Caruso?"

"No, Highness," said the captain, "The King has not been reported dead, so he is still King."

"What about that wilder?" Melanie asked

"I do not believe she is still there," said the captain and she related that she thought the attack on the Caruso King was a test. She then informed the Queen of the rest of her beliefs.

You're only twenty-two, really? Melanie thought as Marie was providing her insight.

"If your theory is right we have traitors in Dawn's Landing. Do I read you right?" Melanie asked.

"I can't say, Highness. I will say it is more likely than not. If she came through the Landing, and has the ability she is reported to have, she may have turned some."

"Captain, please don't take this as a personal affront. If you think the threat is real, I think it would be prudent to inform the King."

"I do not take it so, Majesty. I agree and have already sent a rider."

"Good," Melanie said. She looked at the Queen's Lady, "Kristen please ask the doctors how long they will be working on grafting today."

Then, looking back at the captain, "Captain, what is your best guess on how much notice we will have?"

"The commander has men in the highest trees about five miles out, Highness. Two hours, tops."

"Be honest, Captain. Please. Will my girls be safe?"

"If anything happens to any of them you may kick what's left of my dead body."

"And mine," the rest of the Own and guards said in unison.

Kristen returned with the doctor. "Highness, we can start when you are ready," the doctor said, "And end it the same. We haven't gotten the okay from the Princess yet, however."

"Wait here," Melanie said and made her way into the room. She chased the sisters, but let Brie and Chastity stay. She told Bethany everything that was going on, including the threats, and the need to get all the grafting done and why. She tried hard not to leave anything out, and ended it with, "I love you very much, and what you wish, is what will happen."

The room was silent while Bethany was thinking it through. She looked at Brie and got a nod. She looked at Chastity and Chastity said, "I don't want you to be burned anymore, Bethany."

"Let's do it, Mom," Bethany said, and Melanie told her she would have to tell the doctor. Melanie called the doctor in and Bethany told him. The doctor left to get the nurses.

Deepwater Wood, Rainbow Pass

All the miner sticks were placed. Every man was exactly where he was supposed to be. The commander and his men were at the mouth of the pass opposite the approaching army, waiting. His lookout had given the signal that the enemy had entered the pass. Stay calm, don't panic. Wait for it. Minutes seemed like hours, but eventually the lead riders appeared around the bend. He stayed hidden but waved to his man at the top of the cliffs. That man waved to another.

The explosion was deafening as the miner sticks went off almost at the same instant. Boulders the size of houses, trees, dirt, rocks, everything imaginable was raining down on the enemy. The ones in the front panicked and were trying to clear the pass, coming right at him, and then he saw her. "Mount," he screamed. "With me."

He and his men charged into the pass right at the approaching force. He could see the fear in their eyes. The wilder stepped on the back of her horse to jump. He saw the net drop and snare her out of midair. She hung suspended there, while he and his men tore through the enemy line. They were not as adept with the blade as his men were and were falling fast. Some fell to the blade, some to the shaft. One man freed himself from the carnage and charged at the net in an attempt to free the wilder, but the commander cut him off and knocked him from his horse. The man stood up and took a shaft through the cheek for it.

The battle was done quickly. The enemy lay dead, all except one. "Wrap her! Bind her well and put her in the back of the wagon. Mason! You're with her."

"Casualties?" He asked.

"Miller burned his thumb on the fuse, commander," replied his man above.

"Tell him to stick it up his ass, maybe he'll be more careful next time," The commander was extremely happy that he had no injuries, but he didn't have time to show it. "To the Landing. All speed!" The commander rode to the wagon that contained the wilder.

"Free her face, so that she may breathe. A dead wilder will do Her Grace little good."

Mason pulled at the covering over the woman's head, freeing it. She looked up at Mason and spat. Mason cold cocked her, and looked at the commander. "What? She's breathing."

The commander told Mason the road would be rough and to make sure she doesn't bounce out. He then picked three men to run relay and report any change of direction or speed of the enemy.

Pepper's forces put the horses to the whip and headed for the Landing.

Dawn's Landing, North gate

"As you wish Highness, but I beg you that we not stay long," the captain said.

Melanie, Brie, Chastity and the twelve Own made their way to the battlement. The six Guards had stayed with Bethany, to handle the bed if it came to it. She was tossing around in her head what she would say to all these men that would be doing battle for the Landing. When she brought it up, Brie was all for it as was 'I wanna go' Chastity, but the captain had said the men were good men and she didn't need to worry whether they thought she was grateful.

To Melanie it wasn't a matter of whether or not they thought her grateful. It was in trying to convince herself she was worthy. Maybe what to say would just come to her, but she felt ill at ease about sitting at table with all these men out here waiting for the inevitable.

Off in the far north there was a semblance of a cloud that looked more like smoke, on this otherwise cloudless day. She could hear the everyday hustle bustle of the city behind her, the clanks and clinks of the forges, the hammering of the carpenters, and the squeaky wheels on some of the bikes. Wasn't she just doing the dinner dishes? How long ago was that? Is this just one very long dream?

They reached the battlements and she began to climb the cement steps. She was surprised to find her thoughts concerned about there being no hand rails. Who cares at times like these? She took the final step and looked out at the Beast wall and beyond. The Beast wall had been lined with men with bows and some with crossbows. There were swordsmen there as well. Beyond that, men were lined along the other side of the road. Everyone facing the trees in anticipation. The commander riding the ranks.

To the east, more of the same. Men lined with their backs to the wall, facing the wood. Some archers, but mostly swordsmen. Some men walking their horses, some eating, some sipping from their flagons.

To the west, two men were playing rock-paper-scissors. There she saw the back of a man in a tree staring west towards her very first friend on Mother, Desiree Garcia. *I wonder how she is.* There was no activity on the road, having been closed, but she remembered with sorrow when there was.

Out in front, a man by the road had seen her. He drew his sword and went to his knee. Another saw him, looked at her and did the same. One by one the men were kneeling to her. Her! Within minutes the entire force was on a knee.

"Dang!" said Brie, in wonderment.

There were no words Melanie could say to these men that would make her feel worthy of them.

"Please rise," she shouted. "Thank you for who you are. Thank you for all you do. Thank you for this protection you provide myself and my daughters and the citizens of the Landing. You are strong men and women. You are good men and women," She walked toward the opening in the battlement so they could see all of her, "Good husbands and wives, good fathers and mothers. I can only hope that someday I might be able to prove myself worthy of you. I beg Mother give you strength!"

Melanie went to her knee and bowed her head to them. Chastity and Brie saw her kneel, and copied her.

The roar of the cheering masses was deafening and a chant began to the west first and then encompassed the entire camp.

"Queen Courageous!"
"Queen Courageous!"
"Queen Courageous!"

The captain was exhilarated herself, but she knew the men were facing the wrong direction and she needed to turn them around. Chant or no, she needed to get the Queen off the battlement. She walked over to the Queen and laid her hand gently on her shoulder. The Queen looked up at her and understood. She rose and began toward the steps followed by the girls.

Descending the steps, the chant continued. Brie climbed back up and ran back to the opening.

"I love you all," she screamed. The roar began anew as she made her way back to the steps, passing Chastity who was running to the opening to copy Brie.

As the roar was dying from Chastity's words, the Queen herself climbed the steps and blew a silent two-handed kiss to the men and the roar became thundering.

Queen's Mansion

Melanie, Brie, Chastity and the Own began their way back to the clinic to get their bikes. They then rode back to the mansion. Melanie met with Franklin and gained assurance that the panic room was set and ready for the staff and the two guests. She learned that the password for the day was 'Ursula' and related that information to the Own.

Melanie looked at each of the Own, each member of the staff, and the two guests and hoped that once this started she would be able to see each of them again. She instructed Sister Tillie and Sister Meredith to return to the Sisterhood and not come back until she sent for them. She and Sister Frances walked to the patio and Melanie sat and picked up the newspaper, looking over at the two layers of bricks that had already been laid at the pit. Four men were working at a ridiculous pace and Melanie knew right away that Brie must have set a deadline.

Brie and Sarah were sitting in the foyer, Dave was entertaining the captain with a story, Kristen was playing tag with Chastity, and the Own just stood at the windows and doors. It looked like it would on any given day. Melanie prayed to Mother that this day would be just that.

She saw Donovan walk out the front to meet with a soldier that was making his way to the mansion. As much as Melanie was hoping and wishing, she knew that this wasn't good. Donovan was asking questions and the soldier was answering. Were it good news, it would have been the other way around. Donovan left the soldier and went right to the captain, excusing Dave. The captain did not look all that disappointed in the news. She made her way to the patio and Donovan sent two of the Own out the door.

Marie came onto the patio and said, "A rider has arrived from Pepper's forces, Highness. They have engaged the enemy at Deepwater Wood."

Melanie's heart lurched. "How far is that?"

"By horse, without stopping, about four and a half hours. The rider also said the King left Silver Mountain this morning with a thousand horse and two thousand foot. If the Man's timing is accurate, the King should be here just after sup, well ahead of the enemy."

"Have you forgotten something in your report, Captain?" Melanie asked.

"Nothing that can't wait for another time, Highness. The King will be here soon and he will handle it."

Melanie was afraid she wasn't going to like the answer, but her girls were involved in this and she wasn't about to let up. "I gave Gary my word that I would try my best, Captain. I do not appreciate partial information."

She could see that Marie was struggling with herself, unsure if she should tell her Queen the rest of it. It became obvious to Melanie that the pretender was not alone, and Marie thought by giving the Queen the information, it would make her task of keeping that queen alive substantially more difficult.

"How many?" Melanie asked, trying to let her captain know that she had figured it out. Judging by the look on Marie's face, telling her how many wilders were with the enemy wasn't even all of it.

"Five Majesty, but as I said it won't present a problem for the King."

"That might be, Captain, but you're about to tell me what will."

Waiting for Marie to decide to tell her, Melanie tried to look unconcerned. Kristen was standing in the doorway listening, so Melanie gave her a big smile. She tried to read some of the chicken scratch that was scribbled onto the notepad of the trembling Frances. She looked out at the bricklayers, looked up at the sky, but the answer was not forthcoming. "I will not ask again, Captain."

"Earth Cats, Highness. Hundreds of them. Some striped, some brown, some black, but mostly spotted."

What? How? How does she control animals?

"Kristen, please get Sister Meredith for me," Melanie said, but Kristen wasn't there.

"I will fetch her, Highness," said Phillip and he disappeared into the house.

"Frances, do you have any idea how a wilder can control an animal?"

"No, Highness. I do not believe that ever came up with King Jonas' wilder. Nor do I remember reading anything in the Chronicles."

Melanie kicked off her shoes and went to the lawn.

It was getting near sup and Marie wasn't sure how much longer to let the Queen stay connected with Mother. It had been near two hours, if not more. She kept walking through the house, speaking occasionally with one of the Own, or watching Princess Brie practice swordplay with Martin and the oaken swords, Chastity cheering her on. She is pretty good, this was not her first practice. Phillip had no luck finding Kristen, so Marie had sent him after Sister Meredith. The news must have frightened the girl so much she fled. It was a shame because the Queen liked that girl, but Marie could hold her no ill will, Marie herself was a little shaky.

Phillip finally returned with Sister Meredith and the sister went right to the Queen, and touched her shoulder. The two of them talked for a bit and the sup bell chimed. The Queen didn't disconnect and surprisingly, Meredith didn't seem to be bothered by it. The Princesses sat at the table with the guests, leaving just her and the Queen. Her Grace continued the talk with Meredith but began moving toward the patio.

The conversation ended before Marie could get the gist, but the Queen had put her shoes back on, Meredith headed back to the Sisterhood, and sup began. The Queen was her cordial self, thanking Marie for sharing the news, chatting with Dave and Sarah, laughing at Chastity and Brie fighting over the same piece of lobster. The Queen ate well and excused herself.

Melanie asked every member of the house staff and the Own, and both daughters if they had any idea where Kristen had gone or where her boyfriend lived, but none knew. She cursed herself for not asking more about the man when they were discussing him. She cursed herself for being so hard on the girl when she had tried to shield her Queen from Yanina's murder. The captain had been right. She did indeed have her whole life ahead of her and probably just broke. Melanie was going to miss her horribly, though.

Feeling sorry for herself was going to have to wait. There was a soldier in front of her on his knee. "Rise sir, no kneeling in my house. You are?"

"The King's Commander Bud Wyman, Majesty. Of Pepper. I have come to you bearing a gift."

"I am pleased to see you safe, Commander. The news that had

preceded you left me with fear for you and your men. Your safety is gift enough."

"You are too kind Highness, but if you will come with me to your front, I may be able to change your mind. My men have captured a wilder. She lies without."

By the Grace of Mother. This is good fortune. "Lead the way, Commander."

The Queen, Frances and all twelve of the Own with swords in hand went outside to a wagon at the Mansion front. In the bed of the wagon lay a woman wrapped and bound.

Melanie locked eyes with her and saw the woman's hatred. "Captain."

Two of the own physically pulled the woman from the wagon, where she stood in front of the Queen.

"On your knees, wilder," said Donovan.

"Never to that bitch," said the wilder.

The woman's head snapped so hard from Marie's backhand that Melanie wasn't sure it would straighten. As she was falling, Marie said, "Then on your back, it matters not to us."

Melanie asked, "Who are you?" No answer. "Why are you so filled with hatred?" No answer. "Where is your Queen?" The woman spat at Melanie.

"Hold!" she screamed at the Own, three of which were drawn to behead the woman.

Melanie kicked off her shoes. When Mother had filled her she said to the captain, "Remove the wraps."

"Highness. . . ?"

"Remove the wraps please, My Captain."

Marie readied her sword and nodded to Gary. He and Carl yanked the wraps from the woman's feet, none too gently.

"Fill yourself," Melanie told the woman.

"You don't scare me, bitch," said the woman, "And neither do your pet swine."

Her eyes glazed and then went yellow, but the sneer on her face began to change to fear. She shook her head vigorously and the look turned to determination and then back to fear. A tiny whimper came from her mouth and she shook her head again. A trickle of blood dripped at the tip of her left nostril.

"Get out of my head, you whore," she screamed at Melanie. Her eyes were bloody now. The woman began to shake violently, and her head flew back in agony and she screamed more.

"Hold her up, please," Melanie said as if she were idly chatting.

Michael grabbed one arm and Willard the other, and the woman screamed more. Blood was flowing freely from her right ear, and she screamed more and then collapsed. The Own did not let her down gently, they dropped her.

"She shit herself, Highness," said Albert, holding his nose.

"Wrap her up, take her to the Sisterhood. Frances go with them. Interrupt His Holiness on my command. They are coming for him first, then me. The object is to eliminate him first, so that he won't be able to tell anyone who the new Queen is when they kill me. Her rule will go uncontested."

Melanie headed back into the mansion, not bothering to put her shoes back on, the captain at her side. Melanie said to Marie, "I don't believe your uncle will be able to help us, Marie. He rides into a trap."

Landing Road, East of the Landing

"The wilder is pinning down the foot, Maurice. Take ten of the archers over there and see if you can take her out," the King said to the commander.

The commander gathered ten of the bowmen and they weaved their way into the woods. There was a good five hundred yards separating the foot from the horse now, as the King and his cavalry were pushing forward into the ambush. Earth cats and outlaws lay dead in the clearing and on the road, but mostly it was a ragged bunch of outlaws, united as they were, swinging their clubs, rusty swords, cudgels and maces, that they needed to weave around.

The King swung his long sword, striking one of the black cats that leaped at him, hitting the cat square between the shoulder blades. The cat growled and staggered but came at him again. The warhorse kicked the cat, sending it sprawling. Guessing there must be easier prey, the cat charged off seeking a different rider.

The King saw his captain pulling his sword out of the chest of a dead outlaw and rode over to him. "Kevin, if we hear the horns, we may have to leave the foot to work their way clear. If the pretender sent this size as an ambush for us, I can imagine how big the main force must be."

"I agree. If not for these bloody cats, we would be gone from here. These men die easy," Kevin said. "I must ask my Queen for the names of these cats, they might be good hunting," Kevin looked around in all directions, "Though maybe not in this quantity."

"I don't understand how they are so easily trained. Their attacks are calculated. They do not go after the outlaws," said the King, "We need to down them quickly and be gone from here."

The King was about to ride back into the fray when he saw Kevin's eyes. He followed those eyes and saw her. A second wilder, sitting atop a Rigger at the crest of the hill to the west. He was not excited that the wilder could tame Riggers.

Is this the fake queen? Surely not one so young.

"Which would you have, Kevin, the Rigger or the wilder?"

"I live for the hunt, My King. I will take the four legged creature; you can have the two legged one."

The King looked out upon his men. Some had noticed her but were too busy trying to stave off the cats and outlaws to care. He looked back at the foot, to see how they were faring, but the rocks and fireballs kept raining down on them. Then he heard it.

Yakyakyakyakyak, that heart wrenching, blood freezing, laughing bark of the Riggers coming from the woods in front of him. He looked at the mounted wilder. She just sat on the hill watching. The cats had stopped their attack and were pacing back and forth with their eyes on the woods. The fighting had diminished to nothing as the outlaws and soldiers alike stared into the woods. Then, from the woods behind him, yakyakyakyakyak.

This may be our end.

"If you die before I do, I will speak to you no more," he said to Kevin. The clanging of the battle had stopped. There was an eerie silence with the exception of the snickering and hoof stomping of the warhorses with the smell of the Riggers in their nostrils. He looked at the foot. They were standing with their backs to each other, swords up and facing both woods, mindless of the rocks and fireballs that also had ceased.

A woman's scream came from the wood by the foot. Loud and long. Then out of the wood burst a Rigger with a woman's head in his mouth, her body dragging behind. The Rigger was shaking and twisting the head of the woman and blood was gushing from its mouth. The screaming stopped, as with one final shake the head ripped off and the body fell limp.

"WheeeeeeeEEEEEEE!" Came the deafening whistle from the mounted wilder. Riggers, thirty strong charged out of both woods. He and his men silently prepared for death, swords at the ready to make it a costly one for the Riggers, but the Riggers weren't interested in his men. They were ripping into the cats. The cats outnumbered them three to one, but it didn't seem to faze the Riggers. They would shake off the cat that pounced on their backs and continue to rip the ones in their jaws. The Riggers were as big as riding horses, and this would be carnage for the cats.

The outlaws were panicking and bolting for the woods, but his men were slowly coming to their senses and charging after them. He heard the war screams of the foot as they charged toward the battle. The King himself was still concerned about these Riggers. Once they finished with the cats, would they turn on his men?

"They will not harm your men," came the voice behind him, "See that you return the favor."

The King turned his warhorse toward the Rigger who was staring at the wilder. She wore brown and green camouflaged shorts, a camouflaged top and head covering. The top was sleeveless and the midriff bare. She had a knife tucked into her calf high boot, a whip and a short sword at her belt. She had fingerless riding gloves holding the reins of a makeshift harness. The Rigger didn't look threatening in any way, and the warhorse was not afraid.

Two major things differentiated this wilder from a normal wilder. Her eyes were not yellow, they were silver, and the red locks coming from under the head covering assured the King her name to be Kristen Muller.

"I must admit, my lady," the King said, "I am a tad baffled at the moment."

"Yes. Well, we have stayed hidden for over five hundred years, My King. I can understand your confusion. We must make it a topic for a later time, however. Mother is in need of you. A large host marches on her as we speak. I will clean up the road and clearing. Mine will eat well for months."

She patted the neck of the Rigger. "I trust they will not gorge themselves and become useless to Mother's cause," she said, more to the Rigger than the King. "Please have your dead and wounded cleared and be off. Mine will take the rest, and please apologize to Mother for me. Haste of your need forced me to run off on her without proper notice."

"Are you speaking of the Queen?" Kevin asked.

"I am speaking of your Queen, our Mother. We are Mother's Children."

Dawn's Landing, Queen's Mansion

When the Queen had told her that she had learned from the wilder of the ambush laid for her uncle, Marie laughed inside. Then after thinking on the size of the host marching on Dawn's Landing, she realized it would be no small army lying in wait for the King, either. She began to fear for him. It had been two hours since they had gotten the news out of the wilder, and there had been no sign of her uncle.

Everything was set for the shelter. Chairs had been moved in and cots, if the battle lasted long. She had relinquished command of the King's forces to Commanders Wyman and Birch, so that she may focus solely on the protection of the Queen and her girls. The attack was only minutes away, Commander Wyman was sure. The size of the enemy would have made short work of the avalanche. None of the outriders had sounded an alarm yet however, and some of them were as far out as five miles, and the commander's relay had not yet emerged.

The Queen herself had split her time between sitting alone on the couch and standing alone on the lawn, her face a constant picture of concern and deep thought. Was she training herself? Was the time she spent on the lawn used to load her mind with knowledge? Princess Chastity was still cheering on Princess Brie, who had taken up the lessons anew with Martin after the Queen had finished raping the Wilder's mind. Ursula had done her best to become Kristen for the

Queen, but the Queen was so deep in thought that she hardly noticed.

The sky was becoming a light slate with the setting of the sun. It was still mostly clear and there were no stars visible as yet. The temperature was still warm and unfortunately, the breeze was coming off the Sea so they would not have the additional benefit of smell as a warning.

Marie walked out front and took a deep breath. The air smelled sweet. It was an absolutely wonderful afternoon. She heard a commotion from the gate and looked that direction. It wasn't the enemy or the horn would have blown. She told Willard she was going to check it out and to watch the Queen and she made her way toward the battlement.

Before she even got half way there she saw the train of horses coming through the gate, too many of which were taking the road to the grievers instead of the one to the clinic. Then she saw her uncle riding toward the mansion. She ran to catch up. "Hello, uncle. It is good to see you well. Where is Sir Kevin?"

"He is helping my men spread the word to the Landing defenses of a new unexpected ally. I must share the news with the Queen and your Own as well. What news of the enemy?" The King asked.

"Nothing as yet. Commander Wyman does not think them far, though."

The King dismounted and he led the way as they entered the mansion.

Melanie had been on the lawn filled with Mother, when she saw the King walking in. She ran in the house, throwing caution to the wind about being appropriate and threw her arms around the King. "It is so very good to see you, My King."

The King, after getting over the initial shock said, "It is very good to be seen, My Queen. Not too long past, I was doubting that possibility."

Melanie broke off and instructed Theresa to fix the King a plate. She and the King sat at table, with the Own gathered around and Melanie gave him the details of Commander Wyman's gift. The King listened intently as he was eating, and showed periods of pride, anger, frustration and glee as the story was unfolding. When the Queen got to the part about having lost her lady and the feeling it gave her of having lost a member of her family all over again, the King interrupted.

"She is not lost to you, Mel," the King said, "Although I believe you may need to replace her as the Queen's Lady. Kristen is a wilder . . . ."

Before the King could finish, the Own erupted in anger, Brie gasped, Chastity looked like she was about to cry, and the staff were in shock.

"Quiet down, please!" the Queen ordered. She looked at the King and waited.

He continued, "As I was saying, Kristen is a wilder that fancies herself a Mother's Child. She said 'We are Mother's Children'. I take that to mean there are more than just her. Her eyes were silver, Mel. Silver! And she saved our bacon. She rode a Rigger. The calmest I have ever seen. It was like they belonged to her. They obeyed her. There were sixty maybe, and they killed the wilder that had my foot pinned down and the cats that were creating havoc amongst the mounted.

Further, she said to Kevin when he asked if she was talking about you, 'Your Queen, our Mother'. You are Mother to her. She knew of our need somehow, which is why she left without telling anyone. She asked I apologize for her. She was not dressed as the Queen's Lady, she was dressed as a warrior."

"Where is she now?" Melanie asked.

"She asked that we come to you with all speed. When last we saw her, she and her Riggers were dragging the bodies of the cats and outlaws into the woods."

Melanie's emotions were conflicting. Anger, frustration, happiness and relief were fighting a battle for her heart. She was relieved and happy that Kristen was alright, but at the same time, angry and frustrated that she found out in this manner.

"Did your wilder perchance happen to enlighten you on which of the approaching wilders was the play queen, that I might introduce her to my blade?" The King asked.

"She is not amongst them," the Queen said nonchalantly, her thoughts still on Kristen.

Everyone was talking at once now, hurtling names and obscenities at the woman, but Melanie's thoughts continued with Kristen. She hoped to see her again before she left.

"I must go confront her," she said softly into the loudness.

The King and Marie appeared to be the only ones that heard her, as they both just sat and stared at her.

"I am not sure you need come, Mel," the King responded. "This is something me and mine can handle. Once the battle is ended. I will gladly bring you her head."

"You cannot come with me, My King," she told him.

"Is that so? May I remind you all I need do is wrap you in a blanket, if need be? This woman is a threat to my Kingdom, and she will be mine."

"This woman is a threat to Mother, Brent. The captain has news to share of Caruso that trumps the threat to Queenland. This is my fight, my responsibility and my duty. She will feel you coming, the quantities will alert her and she will be waiting for you. I must do this alone."

"Alone?" said Marie, "We go where you go, Highness."

"Marie, thank you so much for all you have done. I will have Ursula pay you all handsomely for taking care of my girls while I am gone, but as far as the Own?...... You're all fired."

Leaving the Own with their jaws hanging and the King angrily finishing his sup, Melanie went to the patio and stared at the bricklayers working late. There was enough moonlight that a lot of the work could be finished. Seeing this aroused Melanie's pride in her daughter. She turned out pretty well. Dan would be proud. Dan. Melanie felt the tears begin to surface in thinking of the loss of her husband, still thankful to Brie for telling her, as hard as it was.

People were going home from work, oblivious to the approaching danger, confident in her and the King. A man and a woman were walking hand in hand along the street beside the mansion slowly, looking at the stars and the moon. A dog was barking down the street and two neighbors were chatting on the sidewalk across the way. These are good people. They deserve peace.

Chastity came out and climbed in her lap and Melanie gave her a big hug. The two of them sat in silence, both thinking of Bethany and the grafting.

BarooooooooooBaroooBaroooBarooooooooooo, sounded the horn from the gate.

MIND RAPE

Queenland
Dawn's Landing, Clinic on the Round

With Chastity in hand and Brie on the other side they made their way to the clinic. Melanie wanted all three together, to make it easier on the Guard. The Own had not taken her up on her offer to protect her girls and she couldn't say she blamed them. She had been gruff and passionless. The King had left at the sound of the horn. She had no idea when the Own left, but found all their patches on the table. They were soldiers not babysitters, and probably had joined the King out front.

There was still no sound of battle, and she was sure they were probably an hour or so out yet, depending on how much slower the host was than the scout who had warned of their arrival. Brie looked worried for Martin or for her mom, Melanie couldn't tell. Chastity was now skipping between them, seemingly unconcerned about the threat or just assuming Melanie would fix everything. Melanie herself was worried for the High Holiness, the King, her girls, the staff, everybody really. She was glad Kristen wasn't here or she would be worried about her, too.

They reached the clinic and found that Bethany's room had been changed to the first floor. The grafting had stopped when the King's wounded arrived. She greeted the six Guards, explained the conversation to them that had occurred at the table and asked them how they felt about it. All six agreed that they were separate from the Own and worked for the King in a capacity to protect the girls. She thanked them very much, kissed all three of the girls and said she would be back as soon as she could. Chastity cried which started the other two crying. She reminded each of them of the panic room password and made her way back to the mansion.

She looked out over the city and saw the lights going out one by one and the Sea shining from the reflection of the moon. *This is my home now.* The City Watch was gathering people and ushering them into their homes, making slow calculated rounds so they didn't miss anyone. When she was passing Colleen drive she could see all the way to the Sea. The docks were quiet and empty with the exception of a few of the City Watch. There was no one on the entire street all the way down.

She walked up the walkway and could see her pack on the table and Franklin and Theresa waiting at the door. Theresa told her what foods she had packed along with the lightest clothing she could find in the Queen's closets and drawers. She also urged the Queen to take something warmer because Black Mountain was bitter cold in the fall. Melanie wanted to travel as light as possible, but thanked Theresa anyway. Franklin went over the map with her, pointing out the villages and cities she would pass on the way. He also handed her a packet of money from Ursula for lodging and food. She thanked him and told him to have somebody on the third floor at the windows facing the gate. If the gate was breached, he was to get everyone in the panic room.

She left the mansion and walked to the gate, taking in her favorite street that had endeared her to Kristen with all the clothiers. She eyed the bench she and Frances sat at for over an hour talking about Earth. To the right was the clinic and the lawn where she had given her word to the Own that she would try to behave. Behind her and to the left, the Sisterhood with all the lights out except one on the gate side on the third floor. She looked at the clinic and where she imagined the girls to be. I love you! She kicked off her shoes and put them in the pack. Then she exited the gate.

North gate

The King looked over the troops one more time. The archers were to the front, facing the trees, with some of the foot intermixed to keep them from being overrun. More archers, armed with longbows were at the battlements. Inside the Beast wall were some of his best foot as the last line of defense, the mounted were lined along the sides of the column. This was going to be eye opening for the enemy who were expecting no more than fifteen hundred. The King and his forces were not supposed to be here.

He saw out of the corner of his eye some of the men going down and then back up and then he saw her. Walking as if there were no one around as casually as could be, right through his men. She must be going to hide in the guard tower until they pass. Not a bad plan. The hiding part, not the journey. He watched her until she disappeared in the woods. His man at the guard tower hadn't come in yet, so the King had no doubt she would make it.

"So, are any of these cats good eating?" Kevin asked him.

"Can't say as I know, but you really need to get a different hobby. There are other things besides hunting," the King answered.

"Such as?"

Before he could answer, a rider came from the wood shouting "They are upon us. Stand ready."

She didn't make it. "With me," he shouted and charged his warhorse toward the woods. The warhorse had not taken two steps when yellow streaks could be seen through the trees. He and the Own and all of his men charged at the wood. He heard the explosions from the fireballs. He felt a pressure in his ears, then the hair on his arms bristled, a horrible hissing sound emitted from the woods as the sky lit up and became as bright as daylight. Blue flame seared everywhere. In less than a second a loud thunder and the very ground shook so hard the warhorses were falling, including his. The brace did it's job, as the horse tumbled on his leg. His men were losing their balance and falling as well. Mother herself shook and shook. More yellow streaks and again followed by the blue flame and again followed by the thundering quakes. Yellow streaks and blue flames continued, with resounding explosions after the flames. The explosions that followed the blue flame were deafening.

Screams of agony could be heard coming from the woods. He abandoned his horse, drew his long sword and charged at the woods. More yellow streaks, followed by the thundering, quaking blue flame. More screaming and the sounds of cats growling in pain. Shrieks of pain and agony filled the woods he was charging.

Then silence. The only noise being his breathing and the sounds of his boots hitting the ground and those of a thousand men behind him. His legs would not move fast enough. He developed a thirst for blood as he knew his Queen to be dead. His thoughts went to his wife, as he feared failure. I love you Jackie, we may have to meet again another day.

A couple of younger men had caught and passed him and Kevin and the Own were pacing him. He couldn't help but think what he would do for younger legs. More than anything he wanted to strike the first blow. They burst out of the trees and came upon a horrendous sight. There were dead everywhere, most cut in half at the waist. Cats as well. There must have been a thousand dead. He charged anew, hopping the dead bodies, toward the ridge ahead and when he reached the top he stopped. More dead over the rise.

With the help of a full moon he and Kevin searched the valley below and saw the cloud of dust from the retreating enemy, moving away in the trees to his left. Kevin pointed a little to the right. There walked the Queen like she was out for a Sunday stroll coming from the trees and walking across a glen. He followed her with his eyes and she entered the opposite tree line. He was about to turn away when he noticed them. Eleven men and one woman had entered the glen and taken the same path into the tree line, about three hundred yards behind the Queen.

He turned and walked back to the field and met one of the company medics.

"Can you tell what happened to these men?" he asked.

"With the exception of an area the Queen had been standing there is no blood, Highness. These were cut in half and every vein, artery, and organ was seared shut before they even had time to bleed. This one," he picked up the top of a woman and turned it over exposing the cut. Pointing at a dark spot a little off the center of her opened torso, he said, "That's her heart. Whatever did this was a flame hotter than anything known to us," The medic took in the whole field, "Whatever did this," he repeated pointing at three massive craters, "Could cut Mother in half."

"How were you able to determine where the Queen was standing?"

The medic walked the King to the area. "These small blackened craters? Fireballs. I have seen them around our own dead after a wilder attack. If you look out toward the larger craters, they are directly behind a dead wilder."

The medic walked him into the trees behind where the Queen had been standing. He saw there five dead cats and about twenty dead men, all having bled out. The Own had her back. "One other thing, Highness," said the medic. "Some of these men," pointing out toward the field, "just died."

"I'm thinking they all died," said Kevin.

The medic gave Kevin a quizzacle look, "I mean they weren't put to the sword, or hit with whatever this power is the Queen has. They just died. Judging by the eyes and the smell in their trousers, I'm guessing fright. In any event, whatever happened here could not have been pretty to the enemy."

Commander Wyman joined them and the King asked him if he wouldn't mind handling Silver Mountain for a time. The commander said he would, so the King gave him his instructions and the foot to be spread out amongst the Landing, Silver Mountain, and Pepper. The King also told him to open all cities back up to the trade only, but no travel.

"And you, Highness?"

The King pointed at the dissipating cloud of dust, "I need to meet whoever commands that cowardly force. Kevin, have the men fetch the horses."

"What of these?" The Commander asked, pointing at the dead.

"Burn them."

"The ally you spoke of; will she want any?"

"She is on her way to join the Queen, or will be shortly. I believe she felt they had enough to eat for one day anyway."

Corcoran Hills

Marie edged her way over to the oldest of the former Own and asked, "Have you seen such, ever?" She thought back on the sights she had seen on the plateau, her fearless Queen standing firm with the fireballs being hurtled at her and the last second diversion, causing them to fall harmlessly to the ground. She thought on the pressure in her ears and sound and sight of that blue streak that exploded out of the Queen's fingers and lit the very sky and almost sent the troup flying from the force of the air. She remembered the sight of the wilders, cats and enemy soldiers being cut in half by that streak.

"Neither seen nor heard of, Captain," Gary answered. "I admit, had I not been otherwise occupied, it might have caused me to piss my pants. You are aware that our Queen knows we follow, right?"

"It would have been simple to just duck the fireballs, yes. They would have ended some of us. I am just not sure how she knows. We are none of us bare to Mother." Marie had gone over with each, the need for stealth and wearing their gloves in the event they were knocked to the ground. She had checked anew after the battle, to make sure none had exposed bare skin to Mother. None had.

She saw Willard, who she had given the point to, stop and slip his long sword from its sheath. She worked her way forward to where he stood. "What have you?" she whispered.

She stared forward with him. His eyes unwavering ahead to the path. Then she smelled it, too.

"Mother worries of your harm and wishes you to return to the safety of the Landing," came the voice hidden in the trees.

"We are no longer the Own and go where we please," answered Marie, staring forward to catch sight of the speaker, "Show yourself. We do not talk with trees."

Kristen and her Rigger emerged from the trees. Marie was taken aback at the sight of this woman and her attire. She was dressed as a warrior and not the Queen's Lady and in so appeared a totally different woman.

"Put away your blades, you make mine uneasy. You would not like them uneasy," Kristen said.

"My group are all well trained, yours will find us formidable enough."

Kristen looked angered at that comment, but then the semblance of a smile appeared on her lips, "Perhaps we should test your theory, Captain."

"When you two are done with your pissing match, I would like to be back on my way," came the third voice from behind Kristen. Kristen bolted from her mount went to both knees facing the Queen, folded her hands in her lap and stuck her forehead to the ground. The Rigger turned to the Queen and went down on all fours, lying beside Kristen with his head on the ground. Realizing she was no longer the Own, Marie dropped to one knee and bowed her head. The rest of the group followed her lead.

"My apologies, Mother," Kristen said into the ground, "I did not feel your approach."

"The rocks and twigs were hurting my feet, which hurt enough right now, so I put my shoes back on. It is good to see you safe Kristen, but we have much to discuss. Captain, I am somewhat disappointed in the lack of respect for my commands."

"We followed your commands Majesty, but we have a new life now and choose to travel," said Marie.

"That's the best you could come up with?" asked the Queen. "Please rise, all of you." All did. Surprisingly, even the Rigger.

"I was hoping to come up with better, Highness. I thought I would have more time," answered Marie.

"Kristen, Marie, walk with me," said Melanie as she turned and headed back the way she had come. Marie walked in beside her, Kristen went first to the Rigger, said something, removed the harness and joined the other two.

"Look ladies," started Melanie, "I have never before had so many people quite this dedicated to me. My husband, bless his heart, and my kids when I didn't interfere with their friends. I hope you can understand how much I appreciate the devotion, but you can't come with me, you just can't. This woman possesses something that gives her control over the minds of others, including animals. I haven't figured out yet what that is, but there is no way ten thousand people would suddenly turn into a fighting force full of traitors to the King. More than one King, actually. She can't know I'm coming. She can't see a woman riding a Rigger. She can't see twelve soldiers who just happen to be accompanying me."

"I see what you're saying Highness," said Marie, "And if she did come through Dawn's Landing, she would have taken this very route and therefore probably has spies in every village and city along the way."

"You must not lodge under your real name, Mother," interjected Kristen.

"Thank you for seeing my dilemma. According to Franklin's map, Cotter's Cove is right over the next rise. I will be staying there tonight. If you choose you may leave now, or I will put you up for the night and you can leave in the morning."

"Yes, Mother," said Kristen.

"Thank you, Highness," said Marie, "I will take a vote," Marie headed to each of the Own, leaving her and Kristen alone.

"How many of you are there?" Melanie asked.

"I don't know, Mother. We keep ourselves secret even from each other," Kristen answered, "If the threat is strong enough, they will show."

"Threat to Queenland?" Melanie asked.

"Queenland is not our concern. Mother is."

"Then why did you help the King?"

"He had three thousand, I had but sixty. I had hoped by freeing up his army, we could both provide for your safety. By the time I arrived at the ridge where you met the enemy, the King's men were stacking bodies, so me and mine followed your trail."

"How is it you walked barefoot with me at the clinic and I wasn't able to determine your connection?" Melanie asked her.

"I will teach you that on the way, Mother," Kristen responded. "How are your fingers?"

"My fingers are fine, and I thought you understood me, Kristen. You are not coming!"

"Oh, I am coming Mother. With you or yards behind. It doesn't matter to me," said Kristen, "How, as a single traveling woman do you plan on getting past the gate guards? Had you planned on playing the part they will think you to be? Because one may hire you."

Melanie hadn't thought of the gate guards. Of course they will think her a prostitute and send her away without entry. Just as she started to think this through, William walked up in everyday garb and said, "Are you ready to go, wife? I grow weary of sitting around."

Melanie, now frustrated beyond reason, asked William, "Were you aware we had a daughter?" pointing at Kristen.

"I did, but not that we had two."

Oh, for the love of God! Melanie, knowing he meant Marie, just sat down where she stood, holding her head in her hands.

Cotter's Cove

The soldier saw the others approaching and walked up to meet them.

"Greetings, welcome to Cotter's Cove. Why is your business so late?"

"We have orders of transfer to Junction City," said Donovan, "We will stay here tonight and be on our way in the morning."

"... and who are these?" asked the guard.

"A family of travelers that asked for our protection on their journey."

"Where are you headed, sir?" the guard asked the travelers.

"We are going to visit my sister in Chesapeake," answered William. "We were hoping to catch the next train that direction."

The guard studied the foursome, looking in their eyes and then said, "Very well, the Cove Cave is the only lodge open this late. Maggie will have the train info. Best hurry. I heard thunder in the distance. Might get a little wet" He pointed the direction they should take and the group was off.

Melanie had to admit defeat. They were both right. She was going to need help, she would not have made it past the guard.

They got to the Cove Cave and the proprietor was glad to have them. Business had been bad and only a third of the lodge was occupied. They took seven of the rooms. One for the daughters, one for the husband and his wife and five for the soldiers. While William and Donovan were booking the rooms, Melanie pulled Marie and Kristen aside. "I owe you two an apology. You were right and I was wrong. I don't want the woman to know we are coming, but I will not interfere with your advice on getting me there."

"Mine are pacing us in normal packs of three," said Kristen, "unless we are threatened or attacked, I am willing to admit that Marie's tactical knowledge is superior to mine."

"Very well," said Melanie, "I guess that puts you back in charge, Marie."

"Okay then, you Kristen will call me sis, as I will call you. This is mom or mother. William is dad or father. The train doesn't leave until mid-morning, that will give dad time to rent a wagon and the rest of us time to get some clothes that will better pass scrutiny. For now, we need to get some sleep. It will be a long journey."

Luckily the rooms had duel beds, which she hadn't thought of until William actually opened the door. Most of the guests at the lodges were merchants, soldiers or hunting buddies that were not interested in sharing a bed. Melanie wasn't sure how much sleep she would get with the things occupying her mind, but she would try to do as Marie asked.

Rainbow Pass

The King had anticipated catching the enemy at Rainbow Pass, but they knew they were being followed and were pressing, fast and hard, to outrun the Queen. If they knew it was only the King and his measly three thousand they probably would have turned and fought.

Rather than fall prey to the same result the enemy had suffered at the hands of Commander Wyman, the King decided to end the chase and make camp just short of the pass. On the new day he would have men check the cliffs for foul play and would then turn the march into a tracking, instead of chasing.

The Queen had killed more than she knew. The King's scouts were continually finding dead that had been dragged into the woods. The medics said some of the men had, and some had not, died of the wounds they had suffered at the hands of the Queen. Some had been put to the sword, some died of various organ failures, one of these was an exploded bladder. One of the Queen's strikes had taken his leg and half his penis, searing both shut.

They had also found the last wilder, who had been stabbed in the chest and throat and everywhere else except her right arm, which wasn't there. These men were doing away with their wounded in favor of speed. No cats had been found, which bothered the King but only because he couldn't think of why.

The King lay in his tent, thinking on the day's events, decided he was going to boost his forces from each village and city they passed in tracking the enemy.

Dawn's Landing on the New Day, Clinic on the Round

Brie and Chastity were playing at finger puppets waiting for Bethany to get out of surgery. Brie had not slept well. All she had thought of was her mom and Martin. She had gone two years without seeing her mom and now after not even half a day, she was missing her.

The soldiers and that commander had come back from whatever had happened that had caused all the lightning and thunder in the woods. Brie and Chastity had watched from the windows of the clinic and Brie thought it meant rain, but when she looked up she saw nothing but stars. Her mom wasn't with them, nor was the King or Martin. She knew inside she wouldn't see Martin again unless it was with her mother. She kind of missed that Pedro guy, too, and Kristen. Who would ever have thought her a wilder?

Chastity was sad too, so Brie let her have a sweet roll this morning. If things go well in surgery, she will be back to normal. She was a kid. Kids are resilient. The doctor had promised Brie that if the surgery went well she didn't see any reason why Bethany couldn't be moved to the mansion at some point today. Brie, all through her life, had wanted a sister and now she had two, and they both were so lovable.

The bricklayers had asked if she wanted the shelter torn down now that the threat was over, but the doctors wanted to keep it in case something arose in the future. She was eager to get outside and see what was happening with the sandpits, but she wasn't in the state of mind right now to leave Bethany and Chastity.

"What's taking so long?" Chastity wanted to know, so Brie looked around for another game that would distract her. She picked up the newspaper and began reading some of the less gruesome news to her.

Cotter's Cove, Cove Cave

Melanie woke to the sound of running water. She saw William shaving. It was strange to see a member of the Own without a uniform, much less without a shirt. This particular member was solid muscle in looking at his back. He also had thick, brown hair without any touch of grey. "Good morning," she said.

"I apologize for waking you, Highness. I should have left the door closed after the shower."

"No worries, William. I was having some pretty horrible nightmares. It is good to be shed of them." She kicked her feet over the edge and tried to make her hair resemble something that wouldn't cause the poor man to lose his appetite for breakfast.

She walked to the window and looked out. It was raining, but not as horrible as the day at Darvon's that she was wearing Desiree's dress. She looked out over the village and was pretty impressed. This was a quaint and cozy little burb. There were no two or three story buildings but she couldn't imagine that they needed any. The population here couldn't have been more than five or six hundred. There was a park across the way with two women sitting and talking on a bench under a canopy while their kids were playing in the rain. An ice cart was parked in front of the lodge. A man on a bicycle had stopped to talk to a soldier and they were laughing heartily. Further down the street a man was opening his shop. Enough admiration. Time to get ready for the road. William left, so Melanie headed to the shower.

"We are going to have to come up with a different name for the Queen," Marie said to Kristen, "Melanie is not that uncommon, but it would be better to be safe. Pick one," Marie handed Kristen a note with three names. Marge, Diane and Alicia.

"Marge and Alicia do not fit Mother, so Diane," Kristen decided.

"My thoughts as well," said Marie and she left the room and headed for the lobby. She poured herself a cup of coffee and waited for William to finish with Donovan. William handed Donovan some of the money the Queen had given him last night, and Donovan headed toward the Village.

"Are you confident in this man's ability to be discreet? Remember, the pretender probably came through here," she said to William.

"I have known him since my youth, if he even blinks wrong, I will know."

"Good, good. The woman's name is Diane. Be as quick as you can. The Queen will want to make that train. Make sure the wagon has a tarp to cover our weapons," William left and Kristen was walking towards her.

Kristen looked around to see if anyone was close enough to hear, and said to Marie, "I must find a way to slip out of here and tell mine to stay clear of Road Safety on the trip."

"You don't 'slip out' against the King's men. You should have thought of this last night. Damn it!" Marie made no attempt to hide her anger. Kristen was fuming and ready for a fight but the Queen had joined them.

"Keep your voice down, what's the problem?" Melanie asked.

"My sister forgot to tell her friends about Road Safety, Mom. This can be a problem. She can't simply walk out the gate to tell them.

Village watch are more stringent than those even in the cities."

"Let me think on this. In the meantime, a little less noise when you are resembling real sisters, please," Melanie walked over and poured herself a cup of coffee and thought on the dilemma. She looked outside and saw the rain had stopped and wondered how William was doing procuring a wagon.

"Go get Martin," she said to Marie.

Williston Cards and Documentation

"Will, how you doing, buddy?" Asked the man behind the desk. "Where's your uniform?"

"Shutup, bonehead!" William whispered, "I am working for the King as a traveler. A friend of Jackie's has witnessed a murder, and the King needs her hidden away until the trial sisters are finished with him. I need temporary papers for her. I told him I had a friend in Cotter's Cove that would help."

"Why doesn't the King have his own people for this sort of thing?" The man asked suspiciously.

"He does, but he wants no one in Dawn's Landing or Silver Mountain to know her whereabouts, or who she is. He doesn't even want Jackie to know."

"Do you have any idea how suspicious this sounds?" The man asked, looking around.

"Yes, but I told him you could be trusted to keep it discreet, and he is insistent on that." William watched the man's eyes, there was no deception. He was Walter.

The man looked at William trying to decide if he was being set up. After a few moments, he said "I am going to do this for you this once, but you will take my name off your list of recommendations, and if you are doing anything that will end up hurting my wife or kids, I will find you, soldier or no. Trust that I can."

"If any harm comes to you, Shelly or either of those two little munchkins, I will slay the bastard myself, trust that I will."

West gate

Kristen stood facing the tree next to the gate. Marie had been right, the guard presence was skeleton at breakfast time. Kristen looked around making sure no one was watching and kicked off her shoes, stuffing them in her trousers. She filled herself and nodded to the tree.

Marie watched for Kristen's nod and when it came she darted out the gate. "Help! Help!" With Martin chasing her, she swung to the right and ran as fast as she could. She looked over her shoulder and saw all four gate guards chasing them and behind them a blur of a woman making for the woods. She slowed slightly, allowing Martin to catch her. When he did, she turned in his arms giggling as best she could. Martin pushed her down and the two of them began frollicking and rolling around on the ground.

The guards did not appear all that amused and began chastising the two. Melanie ran past them and turned on them. "Are you just going to stand there while this animal mauls my daughter? What kind of guards are you?"

"We're the kind of guards that watch for real threats, lady. Not some teenager with hormone issues. Take them back inside, before I call the Watch."

Melanie turned and started pummeling Martin with both hands, and then looked into his eyes and when his met hers in between ducking, she faced away from the guards. When she knew her eyes had turned, she looked at him and spoke to him.

"If you ever hurt her, I will kill you, don't think I won't," She released Mother and continued punching at him, but she knew he got the message about Brie. The guards were enjoying the show and when Marie jumped up, that was the signal that Kristen was gone, so Melanie grabbed her and began forcing her toward the gate.

"I'd be careful of that one if I was you, boy. She comes with a shoe up your ass," one of the guards said to Martin and they all laughed as he walked back in.

Marie had run ahead, and when Martin caught Melanie he said, "I love her. If that was an attempt to scare me away, you failed. You will always fail," he took off after Marie continuing with the act.

Melanie watched him run after Marie. *That was the perfect response, Martin. I wish you two well, but heed me.*

Rainbow Pass

The pass had been cleared and they had started out early tracking the enemy. They had not come across any more dead through the pass so they must have finished weeding out those that slowed them. Kevin was holding the reins of one of the scout's horses. The man was attempting to read his maps to determine if there was a route that could be taken to cut off the retreating enemy. "Majesty," said the scout, "an army that size will need to divert here," he pointed out the area to the King. "But this path over the mountain is narrow and in some places only a single horse may pass at a time. I believe they will not attempt it in their haste. They will take their force over Cherokee Ridge where they can pass easier. It will be dangerous, but both come out in the same valley. If we take the mountain pass, we should be in the valley a half day sooner."

"Then that is our destination. Tell the point."

The man rode forward. The King watched him ride off and saw they were entering a large meadow with tall grass blowing in the wind. The sky was ominous to say the least. A rain should begin within the hour. Hopefully, it will rain on the enemy as well, or they will be putting even more distance between them and their pursuers.

His horse whickered and snorted. "Hold," he shouted and the men stopped and looked at him. When they saw him draw his long sword, they all drew theirs as well and looked in all directions.

"Archers to the fore," he shouted towards the back.

Kevin's head looked like a windsock in a storm, and the rest of the Own began positioning around the King. The archers came riding from the back. The wind was favorable and the rain near. "Burn it," he said, pointing to his left and an archer lit his fire shaft and fired it into the grass. The blades caught fast with the steady breeze, and the flames began moving away toward even higher grass.

"Shoot anything that moves," he told the archers and they didn't have long to wait. Cats were bolting from their crouches in panic and dying where they stood as shaft after shaft and bolt after bolt took them out. It was the most lopsided battle the King could remember as the cats had nowhere to go that would free them from the flames. They just stood there and got shot. A wilder stood with a fireball and took two bolts through the heart and one through the eye for her trouble, not even having time to release her arsenal.

The rain started and the field turned to a smoke out and the archers, no longer being able to see, ceased fire. The rain became heavier and the fire was soon out. The King and his men began a slow progression through the field, finishing kills here, retrieving shafts there. Soon he was convinced they were either dead or gone, and the march continued after the enemy. It would appear Commander Wyman had his wilder count wrong.

"Majesty," Kevin said, "Do we want to cut them off?"

Brent looked at him and asked, "What are you thinking?"

"I am thinking there is only one place they will be going."

Kevin was right. The enemy would lead them right to the head wilder. He would be able to get to her before his Queen. He instructed a man to ride forward to the scouts and have them follow the enemy.

Dawn's Landing, Clinic on the Round

Surgery had been a huge success. Bethany had her cast removed from her right leg in favor of a pretty blue brace. Her right arm had been recast. There was a very small bandage on the back of her head and she had less hair on the right side than the left, but the burns on her left arm and back were gone. The skin looked kind of stretched in places but it was the same color as the rest of her skin. Her eyes had been drained and didn't look swollen at all, and the girl was in good spirits, laughing without pain and holding Chastity's hand.

Brie brought her as up to date as she could remember on mom, the King, the lightning and thunder, Kristen, who Bethany hadn't officially met yet, but Bethany's attention was all on the fact that the doctor said she could leave this afternoon. She told Brie that, it must have been a hundred times, always followed by 'you're not going to forget, are you?'

Brie told her sisters she had to check on how things were going with the bricklayers and Sarah and Dave and she would be back this afternoon to get them. "You're not going to forget are you," asked Bethany, for about the twentieth time.

"I'll leave my sister here as a hostage," Brie answered and they all laughed.

As she was walking out with two of the Guard she heard Chastity say, "Thank you for the sweet roll," which made Brie smile as she made her way to the bricklayer's offices.

Cotter's Cove, Depot

Melanie was now Diane Marks. Her husband was carrying her luggage and placed it in the wagon. No one had seen or heard from Kristen and the train was about to leave. The ten former Own had become merchants seeking trade and were now horsed and looked the part, except Michael that looked absolutely ridiculous dressed as a children's toy merchant. He looked more like a Christmas tree.

The wagon was enclosed so they would be able to get past the gate without anyone noticing one of her daughters was missing. Exiting cities and villages was not nearly as difficult as entering. Diane was inside the wagon, studying her papers. She was a thirty-eight-year-old mother of two and wife of a clothier from Dawn's Landing. She was born February 2nd, 493. She read that over several times and had it committed to memory. She studied every aspect of the papers, thoroughly. Neither of her daughters had yet reached the age of twenty and therefore didn't need papers. She thought it very unfair how both the daughters got to be younger, whereas she needed to portray someone older.

She had to admit, the Own were all as cool as popsicles in August. Every member of Road Safety that came up to any of them, rode off with a smile. William had checked in with the wagon master and the man was not even interested in seeing Diane's papers, much less count kids. Everything was at the ready and Diane watched as the first wagon began toward the gate. She looked in every direction, but could see no Kristen. She gave up hope as Marie urged the horse team forward. She climbed up on to the front and sat beside her. Next stop, Exeter.

Dawn's Landing, City Center

Gregory Dane had been with City Watch for six years now, and he still marveled at what a great job it was. He worked for City Watch in the most important city on Mother. Yet, he had never set eyes upon a Queen. He sat his bike biting off a piece of beef pull, and watching four children playing soccer with a makeshift goalie. He smiled as it reminded him of fun he had been having lately with his neighbors and their children in the same park.

Tweeeeeet....tweeeet....tweetttttttt.

He turned and made hastily toward the sound of the whistle. He was pumping furiously, hoping to reach the victim or comrade in time. He turned a corner and saw a soldier lying on the ground alongside four others. He hopped off his bike and checked the soldier. Dead. His throat had been cut. He rolled him over and saw the patch of a Guard of the Realm. He began the process of checking the other men and found them reaking of salt water. Sailors.

A second watchmen arrived and they began checking the surrounding area. They found a whistle with a broken chain lying about twenty feet in the direction of McGowan Park. A lady in a house across the street came out and waved at the officers. She was very nervous. Greg hurried to her home.

"That poor girl," she said. "They took her, dragging her kicking that direction," she said, pointing toward McGowan Park. "That other watchman was chasing them. Him against twenty or so."

"Did you blow the whistle?" The watchman asked her.

"No, 'twas her. Blowing for everything. They jerked it from her and threw it over there somewhere. She bit one of the men hard, and he was screaming and dropped her, and she kicked one so hard in the you know whats that his feet came off the ground. She poked one in the eye too, and he was bleeding bad, but there were too many and they just run off with her. I woulda helped, but my baby's inside. The watchman that was chasing after them was limping bad. I doubt he caught up."

The two watchmen left their bikes and ran hard toward the park. They passed two dead sailors before they got to the park and saw as well what had caused the man that had been poked in the eye to bleed so badly. His eye was lying beside him.

They ran into the park, following the trail of blood. They passed two more dead sailors, and then came upon a group of four, one of which was the other soldier. He was still alive, but barely. He had lacked the strength to pull his blade from the dead sailor's body.

Two more watchmen caught up, but the trail of blood ended here. They began a search of the area, but found no signs of anyone being dragged. One of the watchmen stayed with the dying guard, one went for the medic, and the other two followed the path toward the docks.

Cherokee Ridge

When the King and his men reached the ridge, one of his scouts was waiting, "They turned, Highness. They make for Junction City."

Brent looked out onto the plains and mesas before him. He could not imagine why they would take a chance, passing that close to a big city. Junction City was the largest city in Queenland. The forces there would be large as well. "This may be a ploy to shake us. Trying to decide how we think. They will turn again," he hoped.

"Take this message to Commander Fryman at Emily River. She will give you half of her command. Follow us. Catch us, if you are able," The scout was off.

"Darvon and I hunted the Earth Elk there," he said to Kevin, pointing at the next mountain range. "There is a stream and falls for bathing. We will camp there for the night. They should be past the area and won't see the fires. Kill what you can on the way. We will eat meat tonight."

"Do I have to?" Kevin asked, with a smile.

"No, you don't have to. Maybe I'll just eat your horse, and you can walk from there," the King responded, with as much sarcasm as he could manage. He rode to the front followed by his Own and met with the point. He told them their destination and they headed down the slope. The King waited to the side and nodded or greeted each man as they passed and there were a lot of them. It took nearly an hour for all the men to pass and when the rear guard was in front of him he told them all, "Make no attempt to hide our tracks. I have sent for reinforcements and I want them to find us."

The King and the Own rode forward and took their place towards the front and they made their way in the wake of the enemy. The King absolutely loved this part of the land. The majority of his hunting was done here. Animal life is sparse because it is surrounded by mountains, so it makes for a fun hunt. When he, Jackie and Peter would have any time to themselves, this is where they would camp. The weather is nearly always nice, the water in the streams is pure and the fish are to die for, because of it. The water at the falls is far from being cold, nearly tepid, which makes for a great shower. Villages are sparse and cities nonexistent, and the mountains make for great hiking. When it does rain, it is nearly always at night, which makes sleeping that much better.

South Exeter Road

Melanie couldn't see the road in front of them because of all the wagons, but it looked as if it was headed into a line of trees. She leaned right and then nearly collided heads with Marie leaning left, also trying to see.

"Husband, does the road narrow?" She asked William, who was riding beside a member of Road Safety, talking of the golf course being built outside Junction City.

"It does. The tree line comes right up to the road ahead. The wagons are stopping," William answered.

That is where she'll join us, Melanie thought.

"We will be resting and attending your team here my lady, while we clear the woods," the Soldier said. "We don't want any surprises as we pass. It would be a good time to stretch your legs, if you have the need."

She won't be joining us there. Melanie climbed down and watched as many of Road Safety rode forward, in a branching pattern disappearing in the woods ahead. It was very pretty here, but especially where the woods came right up to the road. That was camera worthy, if there were cameras on Mother. She had never seen so many different shades of green. She looked around and saw no one was near so she said to Marie, "I thought maybe she would join us there."

"I'll be honest! I don't care what my uncle said, I don't like her. I don't appreciate her hiding herself from you. It is deceitful."

"It is something she and I need to discuss, but it will be between her and I. You will show her the respect she deserves as an ally, and I will here no more about it. Am I clear?"

"Yes, M..mom."

Melanie watched as William and Marie loaded the water buckets and were tending to the team. She walked around between the wagon and the members of Road Safety, trying to act like her legs needed 'stretching', went forward and made idle conversation with William and Marie about how long the train would take to get to Exeter, and what lodge they would be staying at. She wanted to take her shoes off and see if she could feel Kristen but the eyes of Road Safety were everywhere.

Yakyakyakyakyak came the bark to their right. All of Road Safety went immediately to the Rigger side of the train.

"Merchants," one of the soldiers shouted, "get to the other side of the wagons. Everyone else get into the wagons. Hurry now." All the travelers and merchants on horseback rode to the side opposite the bark, and the walkers were climbing in their respective wagons. Everyone's eyes were on the woods where the bark had come from. Everyone's except Marie. Hers were scanning the opposite side, and Melanie understood. She and Marie saw the tree branch shake at the same time. "Father," Marie shouted, loud enough for all to hear, "scaredy-cat, ran into the trees."

"Where?" Asked the soldier nearest.

Marie pointed the direction and two of the soldiers rode quickly to the area. At the edge of the wood they stopped and were looking in all directions and one looked up. "Get down from there girl, and be quick about it."

Melanie watched as Kristen climbed down amidst the scathing words of the soldier. The soldier picked her up by the front of her shirt with one hand and swung her over his saddle to ride behind him. They rode back to the wagons. The soldier was a sergeant and was not very kind in his words to William ending with a threat of a King's fine if she strayed more than ten feet from the wagon. William took the tongue lashing without back talk, all the time holding Kristen by her locks with her sobbing and crying 'Ow, papa' every five seconds. William looked at her angrily and said, "Get in the wagon and stay there," which she did.

Road Safety returned from the barking side and one of them told the sergeant, "They were just fighting over a cat they killed, Sarge. They wanted nothing to do with us and dragged it off."

Dawn's Landing, McGowan Park

They had been running so long they were both beginning to suck hard for every breath. They were but two against they didn't know how many but they must be gaining on them. They had to be. The sailors were dragging a girl that would not exactly be helping them. They rounded a corner of the park path and saw them. Greg pulled out his whistle and blew for all he was worth, while they continued the charge.

The sailors heard the whistle and split up. Six turned to face them with their short curved blades, while the other five continued on with their package. The other watchman gave one final blow of his whistle and spit it out, drawing his long sword. He charged into the band, screaming at Greg, "Get them."

Greg charged through, swinging his long sword while passing and taking one sailors arm off. He continued going, chasing after the retreating five. He caught them around the second bend. They dropped their bundle and turned on him. He took a slash at his left side and felt the blood running down his side. He hit that man with the hilt of his sword, knocking him down. Another jumped on his back, and two charged at his front. The other was helping the downed man up and grabbing a blade from his belt.

Greg swung his hip and drove his long sword into the groin of the man on his back. That man fell off, freeing the watchman for the others coming at him. A female watchman charged out of the brush and drove her sword into the ribs of one of them. Greg swung and took out another with a stroke across the thigh, causing the man to drop like lead. The female slashed the neck of another and he dropped his blade to hold his neck and she finished him. Greg took the last out with a thrust through the chest.

Two more watchmen came from the other direction and stood over what was left of the sailors, waiting for them to flinch. "Did you pass Walters? He had six," the watchman asked the two.

"We finished that batch off, he's hurt bad, but the medic is with him."

"She may be not far off dead," said the female watchman, as she knelt next to the unwrapped package. "Not breathing well, and it looks like she might have put up more of a fight than they cared for. Her face is a mess and there's blood everywhere. Can't be much left in her."

"She is one of the Queen's daughters," Greg said, "These killed a Guard of the Realm to take her, maybe a second. He wasn't looking well when we left him."

"He died," said the medic that arrived with three other watchmen, "there was nothing I could do for him," He went first to the girl laying in the burlap, opened his pack and got help from two of the watchmen and began putting pressure on her slashed abdomen, legs and ribs in an attempt to stop the bleeding.

"This looks dim," he said to the others.

Clinic on the Round

Bethany was elated when the Guards helped her stand. The brace on her leg was actually two braces, broken in the middle so that she could bend her knee. She still wouldn't be able to walk by herself, but she would be able to walk. She was cleared to go home to the mansion. Brie had broken her promise and didn't come back, but Sister Frances came to sign for the Queen.

"I'm so ugly. Does the cabbie have a covering?" she asked Sister Frances.

"Yes, Highness," said Frances, "But you are far from ugly."

"My right eye has puffed up again and I am hairless on one side. What would you call it?" she asked Frances with a smile, "Get out of the way, Chase. Gosh!" The Guards were helping her out the door and Chastity was trying to help but was just getting underfoot. As she was making her way to the cabbie she saw that boy and girl that were always with Brie pedaling quickly toward the sea.

"Those are Brie's friends, where are they going so fast?" she asked anyone who would answer.

"I don't know, Highness. I am sure they left word with Franklin. You can ask him," Sister Frances offered.

McGowan Park

The lieutenant came up the path and asked the female watchman, "Have you left any alive?"

"The man with the broken ribs is alive Sir, and the one with the thigh wound."

The lieutenant walked over to the two and saw the one holding his ribs with blood seeping through his fingers. The wounded man looked at him defiantly, and said, "I need a doctor, I know my rights." The lieutenant looked at the second man who was desperately trying to stop the bleeding in his leg. He was not looking at the lieutenant, but instead looking away while pressing on his wound. The lieutenant walked over and stood next to him waiting for the man to look at him. He did.

The lieutenant kicked the man hard in the wounded leg, and the man screamed in pain while trying to stop the gushing blood. The lieutenant reached down and grabbed the man by the hair, jerking his face up.

"What were your intentions with the Princess?" the lieutenant asked.

"We was just following orders," the man screamed, "No one said she was a Princess."

"She was accompanied by two Guards of the Realm, did you think her a hooker?" The lieutenant stared at the man's face and saw indecision. His eyes shot from the lieutenant to the man with the broken ribs. *Oops. Thanks for telling me whose order.*

He looked at the medic pumping furiously on the Princess' chest, and walked to the man with the broken ribs and knelt beside him. He grabbed his hair turning his face towards the Princess.

"Looks pretty dead, doesn't she?" He asked the man.

"Kiss my ass," said the man.

"I don't think that I will. I don't think you get a doctor, either. You did kill a Princess of Mother, after all. I will get you a doctor, if she lives and you tell me what your intentions were."

The man laughed at him. "Now that I think about it, I guess it don't hurt all that much, after all."

The lieutenant punched him hard in the ribs. The man wrenched in pain and bit his tongue. The lieutenant punched him again. The man doubled over and went to his side. The lieutenant sat him back up and looked into his no longer so defiant eyes. "Say when," said the lieutenant and he punched him again.

"Stop, please," the man said. "It was you, asshole. She was an enemy to the watch. Your boss told us to take her and hide her."

South Exeter Road

Melanie was learning a lot from Kristen during the ride, including how to hide herself from wilders. She also found that Kristen had no control over Earth's animals. The only animals native to Mother that would not heed her were the Beasts, which Kristen called 'too stupid to live'. Kristen felt there was a child that controlled the birds, because they would not heed, or else it was just that they spent too much time not connected to Mother.

She said she felt the children dated back over five hundred years, but she had no way to prove it. Mother 'Imprinted on my mind' the need for secrecy, but that she also was 'given' knowledge that there were others, just not who they were. Melanie tried to dig info out of her about the correlation of the color of the eyes, but Kristen was clueless. She said she had heard Road Safety saying not all wilders they came across were yellow eyed, but the violent ones were. The others would just turn and run like the wind. She also explained Melanie's tingling fingers when around Kristen. Melanie learned her finger tips would tingle around one of the Children, just as theirs would around her.

"Mom, geez. Dad's calling you," came Marie's call from the bench. Melanie realized William had been calling 'Diane' and she had forgotten her name. She made her way to the front and peered out. "Sorry, honey. I guess I dozed off."

"The Sergeant would like to apologize to Kristen for his harshness," William said.

"That's not necessary, she had it coming. She has always been afraid of monsters, despite our best efforts," she said to the Sergeant.

"Just the same, my lady, it would make me feel better, I am not usually that gruff," said the Sergeant.

"She's a scaredy cat," said Marie, "Half the time she wets herself."

"That is a shameful thing to say about your sister, young lady. You apologize, right now." chastised Melanie.

"Yes, Mother. I'm very sorry, Sergeant."

"Not to him. Ugh, you are a spiteful thing," said Melanie.

"Enough!" said William, commandingly, "Kristen, get out here."

Kristen poked her head out between Marie and Melanie, pinching

Marie hard on the side. "Dad, since she was so mean can she wash her own undies. Those poop-stains are really getting bad."

"I am very sorry, if I hurt your feelings, young lady. I said some things that were uncalled for," said the Sergeant.

"That's okay, I will stay in the wagon from now on. I'm sorry I ran," Kristen disappeared back inside.

Melanie looked at William and saw that he had found the ability to look embarrassed to the Sergeant. The Sergeant said to William, "I have a couple boys their age. I feel your pain." The Sergeant rode back to the front.

Dawn's Landing, McGowan Park

Dave arrived first and saw the soldier with the medical insignia on his uniform, leading a procession of litters out of the park. All were completely covered and each being carried by four of the watch. He said to the medic, "I want to see her."

"That's not going to happen, son. She was beaten badly anyway and her face took most of it. Until the princesses are officially adopted, only the Queen will be allowed viewing. King's law."

Tears welled up in Dave's eyes and Sarah ran up behind crying heavily. They both watched as the procession passed. The litter with the breast humps and a bloody covering passed and Sarah's sobbing became heavier. She moved toward the litter and touched the shoulder, but the watchman told her gently to back away. She walked over to Dave and the two of them embraced and tried to console each other, but it was failing.

Queen's Mansion

"Why are there so many soldiers outside?" Bethany asked no one in particular. They must really be afraid for our safety to station that many men here. I wonder why.

Frances, after finishing her conversation with Franklin walked over to the girls, fighting hard not to cry, "Sit down, girls. I have something to tell you."

Bethany stood her ground, looking into the eyes of Frances and then at the hand wrenching Angelina, the lousy attempt Theresa was making at looking busy, the look of sadness on Ursula and then back to Frances. She sat next to Chastity and stared at Frances, defiantly.

"Sometimes people leave us and there never seems to be sense in it, or a reason for it," began Frances, "I'm sorry to have to tell you this. Brie is gone."

"Gone?" questioned Chastity, "Gone where? Whatdayamean? When is she coming back?"

"She's dead, Chase." said Bethany, staring at nothing now. She put her arm around her sister and held the bawling child as hard as she could.

South Exeter Road

Melanie was giving Kristen a break, so that she could eat a little something and she had joined Marie on the bench. She sat admiring the woods, the sky, the streams they passed, and all their vibrant colors. Colors, she surmised, that were no different than their counterparts on Earth, with the exception of the pollution. Colors only seemed more vibrant here. Smells only seemed sweeter, because a person was smelling with heightened senses. There did not appear to be desert here either, at least not on Queenland, so there was not a good deal of dust.

"Marie," she asked after looking around to see who might be listening, "Have you ever heard of a problem here with haboobs?" Melanie took it as a no since Marie's eyes went down to her chest. "Haboobs, not high boobs, h-a-b-o-o-b-s, it is a storm of sorts with sand instead of rain."

"I have not heard the word before, mom. I have not heard anything of a sand storm either. I would think the Span may have some though."

"The Span?" Melanie asked.

"Pearson Span. It joins Queenland to Dakota. It takes up as much as two times the area of the Great Sea, but is mostly sand. There are probably bodies of water, but they are the size of lakes and are sparse, one cannot carry enough water to cross it. Many have tried, but there has been no report of their success."

Something else to store and learn about from the Sisterhood. They sat in silence for a while and Melanie did more gawking at the scenery and the magnificence of Mother. What a thrill it would have been for the whole family to take this in together. She will never see her husband again, but thank you, Mother for reuniting me with Brie. She wasn't totally certain she wanted to know what, if anything happened to Matt and Todd. So many people were swept here without ever seeing any of their family again. She had Brie, so the odds of finding Matt or Todd would be astronomical.

She watched the soldiers pacing the wagons, with their eyes constantly searching the woods. She saw the wagons, lined perfectly, continuing to roll along with the merchants and acting merchants riding alongside. She searched for the Own and each was jabbering with someone on a wagon, another merchant or a soldier, just playing the part to perfection. William himself, had become quite chummy with the Sergeant as they rode together, even now. She wasn't totally convinced that it was all an act, though.

"Mother, you must eat," came the voice from the wagon bed. Melanie agreed, feeling a little on the hungry side, so she joined Kristen in the back of the wagon, and pulled a sandwich from their pouch, taking it up to Marie and then grabbed one for herself. Kristen pulled one out and stuck her head out the back of the wagon, looking for William. When she found him she turned to Melanie and said with big eyes and a ridiculous grin, "I think father has taken a new wife."

She turned back and said out to William, "Papa," and held the sandwich out. William and the Sergeant rode up behind and William reached and took the sandwich and just glared at Kristen. She got it right away and fetched a sandwich for the Sergeant as well.

The Sergeant took the sandwich and said, "Thank you, sweetheart," nodded at Melanie and said "My Lady". The two rode behind for a bit, and Kristen turned toward Melanie and made a face and mouthed, "Sweetheart?"

William and the Sergeant rode back to the side and Melanie said to Kristen, "Don't do that, you crack me up enough as it is. I would hate to try to explain why I suddenly burst out in laughter."

"Yes, Mother."

The wagon stopped. Melanie looked forward and saw they all had. She also saw the Sergeant riding forward. After a few minutes he rode back, stopping at each wagon and telling each what was going on.

Melanie tried to read his lips but couldn't make it out. When he got to William he whispered something and continued back along the line. When he was far enough gone, William rode to the back of the wagon.

"There are animals in the road ahead," he said.

"What kind?" asked Kristen.

"He didn't know. He said he has seen them before, but only at a distance," answered William.

Kristen slid out of the back of the wagon, slipped off her shoes, faced the wagon and looked around to see if anyone could see her eyes. Melanie looked forward and signaled to Marie to close the flap, which she did and then reached and grabbed Kristen in an embrace, placing Kristen's head between the canvas and her own.

The power surging through Melanie was intense. She felt everything. She saw everything. She was a Rigger racing through the woods to get a look at the animals in the road. She could see through the Rigger's eyes. All the color was gone. Everything was gray and oddly shaped, but she was quick and surefooted. It felt funny to run on four feet. She was careful not to be seen by the soldiers. She saw one and worked herself a little further ahead to avoid him. She snuck slowly toward an opening and looked between the trees and saw them. Her mouth began to water and she felt empty in her stomach.

Melanie tried to distinguish what they were, but looking at them through the eyes of a Rigger portrayed them distorted. Whatever they were, made her hungry. She watched, trying to get the Rigger to hold still and stop shaking his eyes. She waited for calm, waited . . . there she could see. Buffalo, Bison. Good enough. She was in Kristen's mind.

"Leave them."

"You do not belong here, leave my head."

"They are protected, you must leave them be."

"Protected by whom, we have a right to eat."

"They are few, they are peaceful."

"Leave my head."

"Please, Kristen."

"Leave my head. Now!"

Melanie retreated back into herself and released the hug of Kristen, and looked at her. Fear surged through Melanie as she realized she had hurt Kristen. The girl's nose was bleeding and her right eye was too. No blood was coming from her ears but her whole body was shuddering.

"Lift her now!" she told William and he lifted Kristen into the back of the wagon. "Keep the soldiers away," she told him.

She put Kristen's head in her lap. "I'm sorry, I'm so sorry." She began daubing the blood with her shirt and saw that there was no more flowing and the shuddering was slowing. Kristen's eyes had returned to their natural color. "You violated me, Mother. I feel filthy."

"I'm so sorry, Kristen. I thought I was just talking to you. I'm so sorry."

Kristen got up, crawled over to a corner, tucked her legs between her arms and started crying.

Melanie crawled over to her and said, "I'm sorry, I didn't mean to do that evil thing. I guess I should have had you teach me kindness first and how not to hurt those I love." She went up front to the bench and signaled to William to meet her up front.

"They are buffalo," she told him, "they are harmless as long as you leave them alone. The wagons should be able to pass by without a problem. Ask the Sergeant if you can ride up front with him and then tell him that." William rode back to the Sergeant.

Melanie looked at Marie, but Marie wouldn't meet her eyes. "It was wrong of me," she said.

"I am here to serve, Highness," Marie whispered. "I will do as Mother commands. I do not like her, but yes, that was very wrong."

Melanie went back to Kristen.

Dawn's Landing, Queen's Mansion

The work was almost finished on the majority of the sandpits. Sarah sat with Dave watching the pit wall behind the Mansion being seal-coated. "I'm sorry you lost your sister and I'm sorry you lost a friend. Both in such a short time, but if you continue to mope around and make her death without meaning, I swear to Mother, we will be done."

"What chance do we have now, Sarah? She was the rock. We were only pebbles."

"I for one, will not let them win, those that did this. This little pebble has become a boulder, and I am going to roll over anyone in my way. Project Breathers will go on and you can either hop on or get out of my way."

"In that event," said Dave, "until the King gets back, I hereby elect you High Counselor to the Realm."

Franklin walked out on the patio and announced that sup was ready, so Dave and Sarah rose and went to the table. No one was sitting in Brie's spot, or the Queen's, and they took their usual spots leaving those two chairs empty. Bethany was doing her best to keep Chastity from crying and was for the most part doing a good job at it.

Sarah knew the best thing for both right now, was to let it out, but she also knew they needed to eat. Brie, in this spot would test the waters, so to speak. Sarah, if she hoped to take over for Brie as High Counselor would need to do the same. She had to be careful though that she didn't come off as trying to replace Brie.

"I was wondering if I might get an audience after sup, Highness," she said to Bethany.

"Of course, Sarah. I can't promise full attention, but I will try."

City Watch, Main Precinct

"Somehow these sailors, or the person that hired them knew of your spat with the High Counselor, Commander. I realize you are a busy man, but for the safety of the Accepted, I must ask you to search your memory for who might have seemed more interested than they should have been."

"Look Lieutenant, you are right. I am very busy. Regardless of that, I would be hard pressed to believe anyone in this office would be involved in the murder of a Princess of the Realm."

"Princess of Mother, Sir," the lieutenant corrected. The lieutenant found it difficult to believe that the commander would be that confident. Half the time he would not even be aware of who was working in the building, much less who might have overheard the disagreement. He also was not pleased with the commander's offer to have another investigator help with the case. The other investigators had much larger areas to cover than he did. His area was crimes at the Mansion, the Sisterhood and it's plaza, and the clinics and grievers. The others had entire sections of the city.

"If there is nothing else, Lieutenant. I have much work to do."

"Of course, Commander. My apologies for taking up your time."

18

The lieutenant left the office and made his way to the front door. He stopped at the front desk to plant another seed in his garden. "Marjorie, you didn't happen to notice anyone lingering outside the commander's office the last time the High Counselor was here did you?"

"A lot of people walked by Lieutenant, but no one stopped," said pencil girl.

"Okay, thank you anyway."

The lieutenant left the headquarters and headed for the grievers. He stopped at a sandwich shop and got a sandwich to eat on the way. He took the rear exit and made his way down the alley to the next street over and continued his journey to the griever. He took a side street and entered a coffee house. He ordered his coffee and paid the kindly clerk.

The man watched the lieutenant enter the sandwich shop and knew he would take the rear exit if he had any suspicions at all of being followed. He did, so the man continued shadowing him. He must change his ways and get over himself. He's not as smart as he thinks.

The man followed the inspector down the alley and watched him switch streets. He watched as he turned down a side street and entered a coffee shop. The man moved to where he could see both doors and waited. An old man with a limp and a twitch came out the front and headed away from the main street. A woman came out the back and headed down the alley way. The man waited and saw the lieutenant come out the back door again and head down the alley way. He followed. When they got to the next street, the woman went left and the lieutenant went right. The man continued to follow his mark.

The lieutenant, having changed into a disguise, left the coffee shop and made his way back the way he had come, limping as best he could. He turned and grabbed the bike his compatriots had left for him and began his way to the grievers. So far, so good.

South Exeter Road

"I must leave you Mother," Kristen said. "I don't like leaving you having to explain the loss of a daughter, but I can no longer attend you."

"I understand. I worry for your safety and that of the Own, anyway. I know you need time and I know words are stupid at a time like this, but I honestly did not know what I was doing."

"You are right, Mother. Those words are meaningless. I am sorry, but I must leave."

"Do you want us to create a distraction?" Melanie asked.

"No, we are almost at Exeter. I will leave from there."

Melanie nodded and went back up front to Marie and the bench. "She will leave us when we reach Exeter," She put all her strength into trying to hold back the tears, but she saw Marie's eyes catching them.

They rode in silence the rest of the way and before long they saw the buildings of Exeter on the horizon. Melanie's thoughts went to her own failures. She wasn't much of a Queen. People would get hurt around her, or worse yet, she would be the one that hurt them. She had to find a way to get the Own to safety. They were pretty head strong, though and she didn't put a lot of faith in her chances.

"I am tired of hurting people or being the cause of it, Marie. I would like you to ask the Own to go back to the Landing or their families. I think it will mean more to them if you ask. I will of course be there to provide you with support. What I have to do, I can't be worrying about loved ones."

"I totally understand, Highness. We will let each make their own decision and ask them individually. The Own no longer exist, so I can't command them, but I think your request deserves their response."

They crested the last rise and all of Exeter was visible. Larger than the Landing, it took up the entire side of a mountain. It had two lakes, one to the East and one to the West. A river flowed just this side of the city, and a long bridge spanned it. There was a walkway on both sides of the bridge, and it was occupied by walkers and bikers. The gate to the city was the bridge, and houses were built right up to the river on the other side. The King's forces occupied this side, and it was no small outfit.

The tree line ended at the crest, so the entire rest of the way was open plains that had been well maintained and kept low. The Beast wall was halfway between the crest land the city. Warhorses and cattle grazed inside the wall and it looked like wildlife was doing a good job outside, although she couldn't see any now.

The buildings were pretty much the same as the Landing except there were a few that looked to be six or seven floors. *Hope those aren't the lodges.* She had a lot of thinking to do and didn't want to spend all her time climbing stairs.

The first of the wagons was passing the Beast wall which prompted her to stick her head in the back bed and ask Kristen, "Will you say goodbye, Kristen?"

"Yes Mother," Kristen answered, "I don't hate, I just need to be with mine."

As the wagon passed the Beast wall, it was the first time she had actually taken the time to look at it. It was only about four feet high, but it was at least four feet thick as well. There was no way a Beast would be able to step over it, and leaning on it wouldn't make it go much better.

The river was wider than she had thought it was going to be, but considerably less swift as well. A lot of the people standing on the bridge were fishing and having fun doing it. Fathers and sons, grandfathers and grandchildren, women and men, it was a place for family outings. There were even boats with fishermen and women. Melanie tried to get a look at the lakes to see if they had the same activity, but they were too far away.

The lodge they had decided on was almost right on the other side of the bridge. She could see the sign already and they were only half way across. Luckily, it was only a two story building.

Right next to it was a restaurant called the Gobble Hovel, so she already had her mind made up about sup as well.

Pearl Mountain

The King had been right, the enemy had turned again and headed up the west slope of the next mountain. The Kings forces had set up camp, and Kevin's boar was being roasted on one spit and deer on the other two. There were campfires everywhere along the south side. He had walked quite a ways and congratulated his men on a great march. He saw rabbits, turkeys, ducks, deer, and even an elk being cooked over the campfires. His men would eat well tonight.

He had checked with the trackers about their ability to continue to follow the enemy and he had been assured even a torrential downpour could not cover that many tracks. He had sent out perimeter guards with instructions that they be relieved to join in the festivities in a few hours.

It was the King's plan to be underway at the first sign of light. For tonight, he continued to walk the camp and rejoice with his men, continually telling them not to let the fires die so that Emily River would be able to find them.

As he walked the lines his thoughts strayed to the Queen as well. How was she faring? He wondered what the Own had come up with for a reason when she learned they were following. He had no doubt that a woman, that bright, knew right away. It was just a matter of time before she would put an end to the game, because the Own would have suspected she knew. It was just a child's game of wills.

Then there was the new found ally. How would that have gone over with his Queen. Would the strong willed Queen's Lady and the stronger willed Queen's captain create so much conflict that the Queen would have to choose? Or more likely, would the Queen sneak away while they were arguing with each other? He chuckled at that concept a little too loudly as some of the men looked over at him.

How fared the High Counselor? The girl even shocked him when he learned of her first commands, and he knew what she was capable of. He was more than ashamed that a seventeen-year-old girl thought of something he should have pondered ages ago. Already having hired two SPA's as well. She was definitely a nose to the grindstone type of girl.

When was the last time he had been graced with visiting the Holiness? Never before had he entered the Landing without begging an audience. Never before this Queen that is.

He hadn't decided how he felt yet about the Queen taking on the responsibility of two new Accepted yet, either. She was far from trained and developed, but he had to admit fear was not something that occupied space in the woman's head.

"You're going to give yourself nightmares thinking that hard."

The voice surprised the King and he realized his captain was right. He had been thinking too hard. "The only nightmare I ever have is dying on an empty stomach," he retorted to Kevin.

"Well then, for sure you will not die this night. The boar is ready, and our mouths water waiting for you to stop dreaming of Jackie."

Exeter, Gobble Hovel

Marie, who didn't look like a turkey leg type of girl, devoured the last of the meat that was attached to the bone and Melanie was sure she would try to consume the bone as well. She had to admit, considering the size of her former captain, the girl could put it away. Melanie and William each had a hot turkey sandwich, smothered in gravy. Kristen, her mind being absent, picked at her salad sparingly.

Melanie, filled with so much shame for what she had done, was having a tough time finding words to engage Kristen in conversation. William and Marie, thankfully were not having the same issue. William, having been informed of Kristen's impending departure, thanked her for teaching him that not every wilder on Mother is a threat to his Queen.

Marie, being the outspoken, blunt, truth speaking person she was, told Kristen that she didn't care for her and would feel better if she were gone. Kristen had responded that she understood totally and that she had been an only child and had become unpopular and introverted and was used to people feeling that way about her. She held no hard feelings for Marie, thanked her for her honesty and said if she did have a sister she would want her to be Marie. Marie had excused herself from the table at least three times to attend to her allergies.

Exeter Lodge and Pool

When sup had finished and they had returned to the Lodge, Kristen had changed back into her warrior outfit and each of the former Own had, with as much stealth as possible, gradually worked their way into the Marks' room for the meeting. Once everyone was in, Kristen said her goodbyes and gave them each a hug and said with sincerity, that she hoped to see them again someday. When she had come to Marie, Kristen held out her hand but Marie gave her a hug instead. Melanie knew she would never get another hug from Kristen but she was able to apologize again and wish her well. When Kristen left, an uncomfortable silence encompassed the room.

Marie began, one by one, talking to each of the Own and telling them each Melanie's wishes. She saw a lot of nods and began to hope that they were understanding her feelings, but when Marie had finished with the last of them she approached the Queen and said, "No deal, Highness!"

"What? Which one? I will speak to him."

"All of them, Majesty, 'I am no longer their captain' 'I can't tell them what to do.' 'They are grown men and can go where they want.' 'I think I'll hang with the cute redhead'. 'Go if you wish, I'm staying', the answers were endless and all said the same thing."

There was a silence that followed as Melanie absorbed all the dissension to her wishes and she struggled with her worries of harm coming to them. She couldn't find the words that she need for rebuttal, so instead she asked, "Which one thought I was a cute redhead?"

Dawn's Landing Sisterhood

"I realize I'm asking a lot Sister, and I have no issue with you asking His Holiness if you so wish, but I need the truth from these men and I can't wait for trial. I don't believe the intent was to kill the High Counselor and I think her Majesty's Accepted may be in danger."

"I appreciate your concern for the Accepted, Lieutenant," responded Sister Beth, "but we are horribly short staffed in Trial Sisters, and I don't see this as a possibility. I will take you to the courts, but we will abide by their decision. The holding cells are packed, right now and some are being doubled up. You and your fellows are a little too good at your job."

Sister Beth led the lieutenant down the hall and to a staircase leading down to the prison cells. They found two of the three courtrooms in session even this time at night, which didn't give the lieutenant much hope. Sister Beth led him to what looked like a conference room and they entered, finding three sisters coming to a decision. Sister Beth took a seat on the bench inside the door and motioned for him to as well. He watched and waited. He had been waiting all day for this opportunity. All he had to do now was find a way to get Sister Beth out of here and he would be set. He was about to talk with three people that were impossible to corrupt. Their minds couldn't be controlled by some wench from Caruso. They couldn't be bought. They couldn't be influenced. Whatever was in their head that made them beyond reproach, he would like to bottle.

One of the three began to write in a ledger, one made notes in a book marked *'His Holiness', Capital Crime? I didn't know we had any pending,* and the other rose and began checking the calendar. Without raising her head, that one said, "What can we do for you, High Sister?"

Sister Beth stood and said, "I'm very sorry to disturb you Sister Sally. This is Lieutenant Louis Maxwell, inspector of the City Watch. He has a request."

"No," Sister Sally answered before he could ask.

"I wonder if it would be possible to have one minute with you, Sister," the lieutenant asked.

She looked at him and he averted his eyes toward Sister Beth twice. All had finished and were now looking at him. Sister Sally walked over to him and looked at his eyes. She stared in his eyes, it felt like she was staring right into his brain.

"If Sister Beth would be so kind as to fetch someone to take our parchment and the wilder to His Holiness, you will have one minute."

Wilder? They've captured a wilder? "Thank you so much, Sister."

The lieutenant waited for Sister Beth to leave, making small talk about how he admired their work, but as soon as Sister Beth left, he turned to Sister Sally and said, "We have a problem."

"Yes, we do," Sister Sally said. The other two sisters made a sandwich out of her and all three were now staring into his eyes. "Is your name Louis Maxwell?"

"Yes, Sister Beth already said that."

"Just answer the question yes or no. Are you an inspector for the City Watch?" asked Sister Sally.

Oh, Mother! I'm on trial. "Yes" I'm worried about making them believe me, and they're already ten steps ahead of me.

TREASON

Exeter Lodge and Pool

Melanie stood at the window looking out and William walked up beside her and looked to see what drew her attention. "The sandpit looks funny without bricks around it," she said to him. Being on the second floor had given her a reasonably decent view of the city. It was a normal city with normal activity, untouched by the turmoil that had surrounded Dawn's Landing two days past. There did not appear to be any fear on any of the faces and there did appear to be more smiles than she had witnessed at the Landing. Many families walking or riding together, sisters actually being able to get out of the Sisterhood to mingle, City Watch without headgear, lovebirds sitting by the fountain, and a little girl sitting on the grass of a park, giggling at the Abedi surrounding her.

Her thoughts went to Kristen and whether she had made it out of the city without being seen. What a mess I have made of that relationship. Shame filled her once again as it did all last night when she was trying to get to sleep. Melanie didn't know what she must have been thinking when she raped the poor girl's head, or if she was even thinking at all. There was so much she still didn't know about being a Queen, so much still yet to learn.

"The High Counselor vowed to have them all enclosed by year's end," William responded, "I was hoping, Highness, since the train doesn't leave for Walker until late morning, that I might interest you in a walk to relieve some of the pain in your heart."

"Please stop calling me that. I don't feel very high and we need to play our parts. I rather enjoy the disappearance of those titles," she looked at him and saw his request was sincere, "I would love to go for a walk with you."

She heard the shower shut off and said, "I would like to take a shower and grab a sweet roll first, if that's okay?"

"I will await you in the lobby," he said in response.

Melanie went to her bags to gather her clothes for the day and turned to him as he was walking out, "Have you a desire for the clothes I should wear for our walk?"

"None," he said but realized right away, when he saw the smile on her face that he should have said something else and he flushed.

"I meant, I have no desire," he said, but when her smile turned to a deep frown, he realized that was an error as well.

"What I mean is........" He rolled his eyes, shook his head, turned and walked out.

Melanie's frown turned back to a smile, and she heard Marie.

"That was mean!" Marie said as she stood outside the washroom shaking her wet hair, with a grin that looked like that of the Cheshire Cat.

"You shouldn't be eavesdropping on your parents," Melanie said, smiling back.

"Yes, mommy!" Marie sat at the vanity and began brushing her hair and Melanie entered the washroom.

When William got downstairs, he poured himself a cup of coffee and grabbed a city map from the lodge racks and headed to the tables. He saw the merchants all sitting at a large table, nodded to those that noticed him and sat and opened the map. He found a botanical walk, a craft park, and the Exeter Museum that would suit just fine to take his Queen's mind off her ill doing.

William had come to like little Kristen and felt a genuinely parental attachment to her, though he never would have said so to her, not wanting to assume himself in such a lofty way. He didn't care for the way she touched Mother, not being the Queen, but she was a good girl and had no ill intentions, so he could have lived with it. He had been upset with his Queen for what she had done, but couldn't help but feel sadness for her, and he believed her when she said she didn't realize what she was doing. He wondered how Kristen fared today.

The merchants, Martin and Doran, arose from their table and walked to the coffee and when they reached his table, Doran asked, "Did you sleep well last night, sir?"

William felt a little suspicious about the question, frowned but answered anyway, "Fine, thank you"

"Nothing... came up... then, that caused a lack of sleep? Good." He and Martin continued toward the coffee to get out of William's reach, so William fixed them with an angry glare instead. The merchants at the table were all laughing as silently as they could, but Michael was having a little difficulty hiding the tears running down his face.

On the way back to the table, Martin said, "I wish you safe traveling today, Sir, and hope nothing... arises... that might cause you or your ladies discomfort," causing the merchants table to erupt anew.

Disguises or no, William was about to challenge them all, but stayed seated as Marie was approaching.

Packard Forest

Kristen sat with her back to the tree, pulling the reed apart thread by thread, as her Riggers were finishing their feast. She hoped she hadn't done anything to end the deer population. In the normal Rigger pack of three or four the deer were pretty safe, as the Rigger couldn't match their speed. When her pack of sixty surrounded them, though, they were easy prey.

She watched as a group of those black Earth birds with the red chests fluttered through the trees and wondered if they nested near. She felt the graws crawling around underground waiting for the leftovers. Occasionally, one would pop his head out of the hole to see if the Riggers had finished yet.

Between the trees she could see a storm approaching from the west and knew it to be heavy rain with lightning and thunder. Her's would have to move soon, as she could tell from the trunks of the trees that this little opening was accustomed to being under water. She would take them up the face of the mountain they were coming to and have them find her a place to stay dry.

The degradation was starting to wear off from her mind being invaded, and she knew in her heart that Mother's intent was to save those furry things, and not to cause her harm, but she was still not ready to be with people yet. She had thought about returning to the Landing and helping to keep the girls safe, but then she would have all the demands for answers from the Sisterhood and the distrustful looks from the Watch. The best thing for her to do was to be with her friends and let them take her places she hadn't yet seen. Besides, she had been called. She couldn't leave Mother.

She stood and began making her way toward the mountain, knowing that her friends that hadn't finished yet, would join her when they were of a mind. Some that had already finished were walking with her now. They walked unhurried toward the face of the mountain already beginning to incline. She kept her eyes up, hoping to spot a cave or an opening or something with an overhang that would provide protection from the storm that was closing in. Just atop the first ridge she saw what looked like a dark shadow that may have been a cave, so she headed off in that direction.

Halfway to the shadow, she stopped. More graws. Thousands upon thousands she felt, all around her. One of the Riggers walked up and nudged her face with its maw. She made a face and waved her hands between her and the Rigger and grabbed its snout. *Drink. Your breath is awful.* She felt for the graws. *Join.* Nothing, but they meant her no harm, they felt . . . friendly. *Join. Nothing.* She moved amongst them, burrowing with them. In and out of their ranks, searching. *Join. Nothing.* She gave up and continued toward the mountain focusing on that, but trying to figure out this new development as well. *They are native. Why can I not merge with them?*

She reached the opening and saw that it was a cave, but she hesitated. She was feeling something she had not felt with her friends. *Fear.* Something was in there, she could feel it. Something powerful. She merged with the Riggers warning them to get back and they began inching cautiously, slowly back down the slope. She stood her ground and slowly felt her way in with her mind, trying to determine what this threat is. Slowly she went, inches at a time. The deeper she went the more fearful she became. The power was immense, not equal to Mother, but close. Was it coming from one source or had she stumbled upon a nest of wilders?

"Are you coming in, or are you just going to stand out there and get wet? Gonna rain, ya know."

"Who are you?" She asked the man.

"Name's John David Mathews, but my friends call me J D."

"I find it hard to believe you have friends. You are after all, hiding in a cave."

"Oh, I wouldn't exactly say I'm hiding."

"If you're not, then why not come out? I will introduce you to my friends."

"Ha-ha! Are you as pretty as you are witty? Do you think yourself a match for me, or your pets a match for mine? This is my man cave. Come in and accept my hospitality, or be gone from here and take those Riggers with you."

Kristen had felt the man's power. He could easily have done her in, had he wanted. Cautiously, she edged toward the opening and peered in. A man sat at a fire, cooking what appeared to be a duck. He was older than she by as much as twenty years with a touch of gray on his otherwise dark brown hair. He wore a camouflaged outfit that looked a little too tight. A pair of boots sat beside him along with a long bow and he held in his hand the biggest dagger she had ever seen, with the duck on a spit above the fire. He carved a piece off and stuck it in his mouth and was pleased at the taste.

Show no fear. She stepped out into the open and the man looked up at her. "Well, you certainly are as pretty as you are witty, and you are no wilder. Who are you?"

"I am Kristen Muller. Since you have given me your name, but take care of your questions, Sir."

"Very well, you may put your bedroll over there, and keep a blanket close. It will get cold and damp in here when the fire goes out, and don't even think of using me to warm yourself."

Kristen was aghast and began stretching her neck and looking in every corner and passageway of the cave.

"Looking for something?" He asked.

"Yes. I am looking for the wine casks that you have obviously intoxicated yourself with, if you think I would come near the likes of you."

"Good, then we are in agreement," he sliced off a piece of the duck and held it out to her.

She took the meat and began eating. It was delicious. She studied him, careless if he saw her or not. His eyes were silver, the same as her, so he was probably not a wilder. He knew she wasn't. "What makes you so sure I am not a wilder?"

He looked at her before answering, "As you grow older, you will learn that the one color that a wilder cannot turn her eyes is ours. An experienced wilder can even match the Queen's eyes. As fortune would have it there are very few wilders that live long enough to become experienced."

"I thought the only male that could touch Mother was His Holiness."

"No you didn't." He was right, she knew there were males. She had felt them.

She thought of her friends. *He means me no harm. Find a place to keep yourselves warm and dry.* She felt the Riggers moving off. "Do you live here then?"

"Nope. As I said this is my man cave. It is where I go to escape the nagging of my wife and bickering of my children. I have a farm on the other side of the mountain."

"What do you farm?"

He sliced off two more pieces of meat and handed her one. "You're eating it. At least partly. I breed and sell fowl."

"You take a lot of chances exposing your abilities, some would wish you harm," she said to him.

"True, but I have a bargain with two hundred thousand graws and I don't think those that mean me harm would get anywhere near me. They love fowl, did you know that? The feather is to them what Spraig is to us."

"I think I would like to be a friend of J D," she said and when he looked at her, she threw her hands up and continued, "Just friends, I will be able to control myself."

He smiled and handed her another piece.

Exeter, Mancini Nursery

Melanie thought the colors of the flowers and plants native to Mother were vibrant and not all that much different than those of Earth in respect to types. She doubted roses were 'swept' but there were plants in this garden that resembled them greatly. This was a fabulous idea of William's. She loved flowers and had a garden of her own at home. Well, on Earth. Home was the Mansion now. Some of these bushes had little yellow buds on them, but by far her favorite was a tall plant that twisted around a pole and had huge Lily like flowers hanging down from it. She wanted to lift one and look inside, but she was not familiar with the plant and didn't want to break it.

"Thank you for bringing me here, William. That was kind of you." When she didn't get a response, she turned and saw him outside talking to his new best friend, the Sergeant. They were looking west toward the sky. Curious, she walked out and followed their eyes. The skies to the west were full of thunderheads, and they didn't look all that peaceful. She walked over and slipped her arm in William's, looking at the sky.

"I was just telling your husband, my lady. You may be in for a rough trip. Hopefully, they won't call off the train. Storms like that sometimes frighten animals who end up stampeding the wagons, but for that short of a trip, they may not."

"How far is it to our next stop, honey?" She asked William.

"It is five hours to Walker. A short jaunt for a train, but we will get wet for sure."

"Good, I don't wish to be delayed seeing my friend, and thank you for bringing me here, you know how much I love flowers," she turned to the Sergeant, "Will you be leading us again, Sir?"

"No, my lady. I'm sorry. We only ride every other day, otherwise we would never see our families. Speaking of which, I must finish my errands. Good day to you both."

Stroke of luck there, no questions about Kristen.

Melanie's next stop on her walk with William was a craft shop where she found herself a nice pair of sunshades, a handmade belt pouch, and a map of Mother. She stopped short on her way to the cashier. There was a stand there of souvenirs and novelties totally dedicated to Queen Melanie. There was a necklace with an eighteen on it signifying her as the eighteenth Queen of Mother, headbands, leather wrist bands, and wallets with 'Queen Melanie' written on them. There were hats, scarfs and shirts as well. She wasn't sure how she felt about this, but didn't think she liked it. She saw William eying the hats and scarfs and fixed him with a stare.

He put the items back, paid for her goods and they made their way toward the museum. "It might not hurt to reconsider, Highness," he whispered. "We are supposed to be tourists after all."

"We are not tourists, we are a family of travelers going to visit friends, and I will not have you parading about with my name on your head." When she saw him puff up like a dirigible and crack his wry smile, she continued, "I didn't mean you personally, I meant the Own."

What is wrong with you? That was horrendously mean. "I'm sorry, William. Sometimes my mouth goes to work before my brain catches up. I didn't mean that the way it came out."

"No need to apologize, Diane. I wasn't offended."

The museum was absolutely fascinating. She saw items from the past that had been the forerunners of today's technology and how they worked and what powered them. Some of the first toilets, that were identical to Desiree's, stoves, kilns, ice chests, even the progression of the common bicycle. The changes made to bows and arrows and knives and swords were also on display. She was definitely going to hit the museum when she got back to the Landing, but William called the tour as it was getting on toward time to depart for Walker.

On their way back to the lodge, Melanie watched the approaching storm and knew this wagon ride was going to be anything but pleasant.

Horseshoe Mountain Range South

It had been some time since the King had marched with his men through this strong of a storm. They would normally just stay in camp and wait it out, but he didn't want the enemy to get too far ahead. He had his cloak pulled as tightly as he could around him and he was still drenched. The rain was bad enough, but the lightning and thunder added to an already miserable ride.

They had left at sunrise and were only about an hour out when it started. They had to travel slowly, to give the warhorses a fair chance at not stepping in a rut. It was near noon now, and they were just getting to where the enemy had set up camp last night. He peeked from under his hood and saw the skies were starting to lighten to the west and north. Another hour, maybe two and they would be free of this mess.

Commander Fryman, had herself led the two thousand additional horse from Emily River, and rode beside him now, with Kevin and the Own. She had always been a fierce fighter, challenging all comers at training sessions. She had laughed in the faces of the men that showed any frustration at not being able to best a woman. "Halt the march,

Commander. We need to give the horses an hour's rest. Have the packs brought under the thickest trees. Have the men take shelter as best they can as well."

The commander rode to the front and halted the march. She sent two men ahead to halt the scouts as well. There had been no lightning for many minutes now so she sent two of her surest footed up the tallest trees. The rain was beginning to subside, so she expected the King wanted to wait it out now.

The King walked over to a clearing under some heavy trees to inspect the enemy campsite. He sat on a stone that their commander may have sat on and looked around for anything that might have shed light on their thoughts. He saw nothing, and again asked himself the same question he had asked himself twenty times, if once. Why the feint to Junction City?

He picked up a stick and began doodling in the damp soil, then he changed his doodling to a drawing of Queenland, He poked a hole here and one there, depicting the cities. Once he had his rendition complete, the King stared at it. Kevin stared at it. Commanders Fryman and Crawford stared at it. None of them provided any insight. He drew a line from the Landing to their current location, and a lighter one, straight north in the same direction, assuming the retreating army knew where they were going. He then drew a small fork off to the east, signifying the feint, and they stared at it more. The smartest way would have been to give Junction City a very wide berth, as he had indicated in his drawing. They had not done that.

They had feinted toward Junction City and then turned back to their original course, not giving it a wide berth, but moving over eight thousand ragtag soldiers within twenty miles of the largest army in Queenland.

Commander Fryman noticed the man she had sent to stop the scouts had returned. "Rogers? What have you?"

"The scouts are less than a mile ahead of us, Commander. I gave them your orders and they stopped right away. The lead scout instructed me to inform the King that the enemy has slowed, considerably."

The King looked at them and they were all looking at him, each bearing the same thought, they were not chasing a retreating foe. That foe was leading them somewhere. They were ahead of the storm, so there would have been no reason for them to slow, unless they didn't want to get too far ahead of the King. It came to him then that the enemy still thought the Queen to be with him. The enemy commander was trying to get the Queen to the Pretender. It was his or her belief that the Pretender would be able to do her in.

Dawn's Landing, Landing Brick and Mortar

True to their word the bricklayers had finished the enclosing of the sand pits on time. Dave and Sarah were at the warehouse of the bricklayers, addressing the workers and thanking them for their diligence. Those that would now be laid off were the focus of the meeting, but billing was the main topic that the foreman wanted to discuss.

"Where would I send the bill, my lady?" He asked.

"High Counselor," corrected Dave.

Sarah placed her hand on Dave's arm and whispered, "Don't get pissy."

She addressed the foreman, "You may send that to the Sisterhood, to be paid from the King's funds. Make a notation on the billing that it is payment for 'Project Breathers' so that they can categorize it properly."

Once the foreman left, she offered continued employment to the laid off workers as Pit Monitors. All but a few accepted the position graciously, so she began explaining what their duties would be. In less than two days the gates would be installed by the carpenters, as they had done their measuring and cutting while the bricklayers were laying the stone. She would need the monitors to start immediately.

Once that was completed, she and Dave left for the locksmith to make sure everything was still on schedule, and from there they would go to the carpenters. Dave would be in Dawn's Landing for a while as she would leave for Silver Mountain on the trade train leaving on the new day. Her plan was to solicit help from some of the thousands that Brie had been working with over the past year, train them and send them off to complete the projects in other cities.

Two people had applied for the suicide prevention agent position that Brie had put in the newspaper, and she and Dave were pleased with their desire. They were a little older than Dave and Sarah at twenty-five and twenty-four but Sarah felt they would be fine for the position. No one had applied yet for the counselor position. Dave would begin working with one of them as early as the new day. With the exception of hiring, everything was on the exact schedule Brie had set.

Queen's Mansion

Bethany didn't like all these soldiers around. She didn't like the group of sisters that were here this morning bothering the staff. She didn't like everybody that was trying to make her feel better. She didn't like anything. She wanted Brie back. She had a big sister for a lousy week. She felt silly and selfish, because she knew Chase missed her more. For Chase, things were about to get worse. When the braces came off the leg and the cast was removed from her arm, Bethany was going to have to go back to school, which would leave Chase with no one during the day.

Chase wouldn't talk to anybody, and not more than a few words to Bethany. She picked at her food, cried herself to sleep, and said mean things to people that tried to help her.

Mother was gone, that Queen's Lady was gone, Brie was forever gone, leaving Bethany to make decisions, and she didn't want to make decisions. She was only a kid. She needed help and short of going back to the Sisterhood to live, she couldn't imagine where that help was coming from. She liked the mansion, she liked her new mom and didn't want to give it up, but she had Chase to think of. She made her way to the patio, or as she had taken to calling it the ponder-o, sat and began to try to think of what to do.

Sisterhood

Whatever specific thing the Sisterhood was looking for, the lieutenant had been cleared of. That was an interesting experience to be sure and he understood why there were so few repeat offenders.

Whatever it was, the sisters had learned from that wilder, had sent them on a mission. The prisoners awaiting trial on minor offenses had been released for a later trial, with instructions not to try to leave the city. There were now only three trial sisters handling all the high, felony and capital cases, with the other eleven along with ten of the jailers moving around in the city, asking questions.

He sat now outside the apartments of His Holiness, waiting for his turn. He could only hope His Holiness would slip and tell him something of what is going on with the Sisterhood. He would need to make a decision, and soon, on what to do with the Accepted of the Queen if His Holiness refused any advice.

The door opened and four sisters came out and began making their way down the stairs. The lieutenant stood, in anticipation of being called, but instead His Holiness came out the door, followed by two sisters. The lieutenant went to his knee and waited. His curiosity was about to bust his brain.

"Please rise, Inspector. My apologies for keeping you waiting. I am desperate for a walk, my legs are stiff. Would you care to walk with me?"

"It would be my honor, Holiness," the lieutenant responded, but hesitated when the two sisters stepped in front of the Holiness and confronted him.

One of them spoke. "Were you at any time, given a word to use before addressing the Sisterhood?"

The trial sisters that had confronted him downstairs had given him three words when they cleared him. One to give if he was asked, one to listen for and one to give if that word was correct.

"Subsequent," he said.

"Silo," came the correct response.

"Sizing," he finished. He wondered if it was significant that they all started with an "S".

The four of them began descending the stairs, and he looked at the Holiness and said, "Holiness, I don't mean to offend, but this is all a little dramatic, don't you think? What would these two girls have done if I didn't have the proper words? I am armed, after all."

"The Sisterhood is a mystery, even to me Inspector. These two 'girls', as you say, are not. They are prison guards and at my side at all times.

Had you not the proper words, armament or no, you would be lying on the floor with serious injury. Please do not test my words on this. I have been placed on threat watch, and my safety is their sole responsibility. What brings you to me?"

"I was hoping to solicit your aid in the protection of the Accepted of the Queen, Holiness."

"The Accepted are no longer your responsibility, Inspector. Neither is the investigation into the death of the Princess Brienne Thurss. The City Watch has been disbanded, pending the return of the King. All current members of the Watch that have been cleared now report to Sister Beth. The sisters are at the office of the commander, as we speak."

Holy mercy of Mother! What is going on?

"Holiness, this is my case. I have already put much work into it. I can solve it."

"I am certain it has already been solved, Inspector. Please report to Sister Beth."

City Watch Offices

Sister Sally and her trial sister partners had been asking the commander the questions that needed answers, while the two prison sisters waited to the side. Most of the questions had simply been dodged, but everyone he did answer, he answered with a lie.

"I am afraid that your answers have lacked the conviction that we were hoping for, Commander. I will have to ask you to attend the Sisterhood," Sister Sally said.

The commander smiled at the ridiculous women standing before him.

"Get out of my office," he said, "I'm not certain who you think you are, but I have work to do, and I am tired of your attitudes of being in charge around here. You're not. Get out! Now!"

"I will ask you again to attend the Sisterhood, Commander. Rise and come with us," Sister Sally said more sternly.

The commander rose and said, "Don't say I didn't warn you."

He grabbed Sister Sally's arm and began to force her toward the door, but didn't get a full step taken before he felt the excruciating pain in his lower back from a punch. He fell to one knee and saw the palm of the little hand come up under his nose. He felt the pain and the blood trickle down into his mouth. He was dizzy and his vision went blurry and then everything went black.

Queen's Mansion

"I don't want that young lady going down on her knees and re-injuring that leg," His Holiness said to the sisters, "You are to go in there and tell her I wish her to stay on her feet."

"That we will not do, Holiness," said Sister Sheryl, "We will not leave your side, even for that long. I will make arrangements to have her notified."

They made the last turn and began their way down Mansion Drive. The Holiness noticed there to be, at the least, a hundred men surrounding the Mansion and he wondered if they had all been cleared. As they approached, the soldiers took a knee to His Holiness and he told them to rise. Sister Sheryl signaled one of the soldiers to them.

"Do you have a word?" She asked the man.

"Marker," he said.

"Mill," she replied.

"Mixing," he finished.

"Have all these men been cleared?" She asked him.

"To the man, sister."

"Please go inside, Sir. Tell Princess Bethany Gregorian that His Holiness wishes an audience, but only if she promises not to take a knee."

The Holiness stared out from his position, and saw that things had not gone well at the offices of the Watch. Four soldiers were carrying a man on a stretcher surrounded by five sisters, heading for the Sisterhood.

Soon we will know if all this secrecy is really necessary, His Holiness thought.

The soldier came back out. "Her Highness said she would be honored of your audience Holiness, but ordered me to help her to a knee."

"Let us hurry, sisters," said the Holiness, "So we may get her back on her feet." His Holiness did not have the legs to run, but he walked hurriedly into the mansion.

"Rise," He said as he crossed the threshold not caring if everyone had made it down or not. "Help her," he instructed anyone who would listen.

With Bethany back on her feet, His Holiness asked whether they could lounge on the patio and Bethany agreed.

"Please accept my condolences on the loss of Princess Brie, Highness."

"Thank you."

"I'm afraid I have to rush right into this, Highness. The sisters want me back in the Sisterhood before sunset."

"Please, rush away," said Bethany pointing at the floor behind him.

"Rise, Princess Chastity. I'm very sorry for your loss," He said.

"Thank you, Your Grace," Chastity said.

"Back to it, My Princess, I'm afraid I must send the Guard of the Realm away. They were hired to protect the High Counselor, not the Princesses. We have a new High Counselor and the Guard must attend her."

"I understand and agree," said Bethany.

"I will add two of the men surrounding the Mansion to their number to make up for the two we lost. I am also going to spend the King's money in his absence and employ twelve as your personal guard and twelve to attend Princess Chastity. The rest, I must use elsewhere. I'm sorry. If you like, we have room for all of you at the Sisterhood."

"We are not leaving until mom gets back," Bethany responded. Chastity nodded.

"I thought that might be your response, therefore I am also sending educators here daily. The less you leave the Mansion, the better, for now."

"Thank you."

"My apologies, Highness," said Sister Sheryl. "We must get His Holiness back to the Sisterhood. I will have Sister Frances stop by and give you updates."

"That is kind, thank you." Bethany went to stand and His Holiness asked her to stay seated.

Sisterhood

When the Holiness got back to the Sisterhood he found Sister Beth in a meeting with two soldiers. He waited until she noticed him and then took a seat in the waiting area. The sister ended the meeting rapidly and dismissed the soldiers. She stepped around the desk and went to her knees.

"Rise," His Holiness said quickly, "What's the latest?"

"The commander is downstairs in the interview rooms with Sisters Sally, Brittany and Tricia. Sister Sally seems convinced that the commander is the only one in the Watch involved in any treason. She knows there is much more to do but she feels strongly about it, and I trust her judgment. All the soldiers talked to so far were all found tremendously loyal to the King."

"Good, but we can't let up. The investigation needs to continue until complete. From the docks to the clinics. We need to have every question answered the Queen might even think of. She loved that girl and when she finds out, Pamela will look like a two-year-old. Where is the lieutenant?"

"He is finishing his statement, Holiness."

"I have a job for him and for Sister Tillie," he told her.

"Sister Tillie?"

"Yes, she is to be your assistant. You can't run the Sisterhood and the city. You need to choose, and have her handle the other under your guidance. Everything has to be back to normal as soon as possible. I don't want so much as a mouse slipping through this investigation, but speed is critical so as not to alarm the populace.

"Further, I need two sisters for home schooling of Princess Bethany. Neither she nor her sister, are to leave the mansion unless necessary. Those sisters need to be from the prison guards, but not to say so in the event we have a repeat. Sister Frances may know, but no one else. She will be the liaison to the Mansion."

The lieutenant had finished his statement and was on his way out. "Inspector!" The Holiness called.

"Yes, Holiness?"

"I am putting you in command of three factions of the King's force.

The Guard of the Realm, and twelve each guards of the princesses. You will select these men tonight before you go home and instruct each on their duties. The names of the guards for the princesses need to be different so they are not confused about who will be held responsible if a princess so much as breaks a fingernail. The twelve for each princess and six of the Guard may stay at the Mansion. All others are needed here. They are to report everywhere they take their charges each day to you, Inspector."

"Isn't this micro managing just a tad, Holiness?" The lieutenant asked.

"Indeed, I am the one that will be responsible for answering the Queen's questions when she returns. I will do everything possible to make sure I only need to face that wrath once."

Walker, Vista Villa

That was, in Melanie's memory, the worst ride she had ever had. The lightning was bright, even inside the wagon. She couldn't imagine what it must have been like for those drivers and riders. The thunder was enough to make her ears still ring, and the rain so heavy that the road became rutty and rough. Poor Marie was absolutely drenched, despite her cloak. Melanie felt bad about not letting her ride inside for periods, but she had no idea how to handle a team of horses.

The rain had stopped as abruptly as it started, just as they were approaching the gate. Their lodge this time, was well up the grade of the mountain and if they were walking could probably have reached it in a half hour, but having to take the twisting roads, would take considerably longer.

William had stopped at the dispatcher to get info on tomorrow's train and had not caught up yet. Her brain told her the earlier the better, but with what they had just been through on that ride, her heart told her to let them rest a day. She knew every day this woman went unchecked would be a bad day for Queenland.

She had been riding with Marie since about the halfway point of the trip, feeling she had no right to sit in a dry wagon, while they were getting soaked. She could still feel her hair matted to her neck, but also saw a patch of blue sky, giving her hope. She removed her cloak and helped Marie out of hers, and threw them in the back.

They reached the lodge and the merchants went inside to get rooms while mom and daughter waited outside for dad. Melanie stepped down and around the wagon and was awe struck by the beauty. The lodge was elevated enough to provide not only a view of the city but the entire landscape. She would have hung this painting in any room of her house.

When she looked toward the east all she could see was mountain, but to the south from whence they came, she could see almost all the way to Exeter. Woods, glens, the river twisting and turning, the mountain passes and all. To the west she took in the whole city and the forest beyond. To the north, there was a huge lake inside the Beast wall, butted up against the mountain, but instead of a normal waterfall, this lake was being fed by a leaking mountain. Water trickled down in to the lake from what must have been a hundred different streams. It was absolutely beautiful. The most beautiful sight of all though, and she prayed for calm weather so that she could ride through it, was where the road and river forked. The river was swallowed up by the woods, but the road forked northwest through a blue forest. Deep blue, similar to the Jacaranda trees of Earth but even more intense. She wanted so badly to see one close up.

William walked up beside her. She looked at him and said, "Every time I see something of Mother's creation, it becomes the most beautiful thing I have ever seen."

"Enjoy it while you can, once you get on the other side of Junction City, forests become scarce. They are replaced by plains and mountains, and not those formed by former Queens. Mountains natural to Mother. Many of them hide things."

"What kind of things?" She asked.

"Dangerous things. You will need to stay close to us north of the Junction."

"What did you find out from the dispatcher?" Melanie asked him.

"Two trains depart on the new day. One leaves a half hour before sunrise and arrives in Junction City about an hour after sunset. The other leaves after breakfast and arrives at the village of Apache Falls about sup time."

"What is your advice, husband?"

"I suggest we take the later train, so as not to appear in a hurry. It will be less strain on all as well."

"Nah. We'll take the early train."

William threw his arms up and stormed off to the lodge. Melanie and Marie watched as he entered in a huff.

"I forgot how much fun it was to be a wife," Melanie said to Marie with a huge smile.

Marie chuckled, "So wives on Earth were no different than here, then."

The two of them grabbed the bags and headed into the lodge and found William arranging for a room, so they sat in the lobby and waited. When he finished he joined them, grabbed all the bags and headed down the hall. The two ladies followed dutifully, giggling at each other.

When they got in the room, Melanie apologized for her misguided humor, and explained that she would of course, go with his recommendation.

She had not noticed any eateries around the lodge so they were restricted to the lodge cafe, but they were all hungry enough that it mattered very little. When they had the room set up for the night and had freshened up from the downpour, they headed back toward the lobby and the coffee shop. The merchants were already filing in when they arrived. The Marks family was fortunate enough to get a window table, so she was able to gawk again.

Vista Villa Café and Grill

Marcus saw the Queen and her fake family enter the eatery, took a drink of his water and placed his order with the server. He didn't spend too much time watching, not wanting to be seen staring, but he was unsure who this man and girl was that was with her, and until he was sure, he would bide his time.

He had caught up with her at Cotter's Cove, but by that time these two and one other were already with her. When they left, the other was not with them, which made Marcus curious. Who was the girl that was with them and what happened to her, and why was the Queen traveling without her guard? No matter. It just made his impending contact so much easier.

Marcus had disguised himself as a merchant, to stay close to her, and await his chance. His food came so he thanked the server and began his meal. He would finish the meal and go to the lobby, and watch for when the 'family' came out. He almost thought he had his chance at Exeter when she was walking with just the man. She had been in a garden alone, but that Sergeant had been there. Another opportunity would come up, he just needed to be patient.

Marcus finished his meal, paid his tab and proceeded to the lobby. He chose the couch and picked the Walker Press and opened it and pretended to read it. Two of the other merchants he had been riding with approached. He gave them a smile and a nod.

"Marcus, how goes it? Quite a rain wasn't it?" asked the one that had introduced himself as Carl. Carl sat next to Marcus and picked up a magazine.

"Even my eyeballs are wet," responded Marcus, "How are you two doing?"

"My saddle is so soaked, it is bigger than my horse," answered Michael as he sat on the other side of Marcus.

That's curious. Three chairs available and they chose the occupied couch. The conversation went on for about a half hour. The family had headed back to their room several minutes ago, but Marcus wasn't able to break away from the conversation to see which room they had entered.

"Are you continuing on, Marcus?" asked Carl, "We never talked about where we were going, I am headed to York."

"That's remarkable," answered Marcus, "I am going there myself."

"You're not going to the docks, I trust. I was hoping to have them to myself," said Carl.

"No! No! I never go near them. My business there has always been inner city."

Marcus felt a prick on his side near Carl. "Funny thing about that," said Carl, "York has no dock."

You're a moron, Marcus thought to himself, the Queen goes nowhere without her guard. Marcus tried to stay calm even with the dagger at his side.

"We are not looking to draw attention to ourselves," said Michael, "We simply want to have a chat. It is time for you to stand up and walk down the hall. If you make a scene, you are a dead man. Are we clear?"

"It is not what you think. I mean her no harm," pleaded Marcus.

"Good to know and if found to be true, you may live to see another sunrise," Carl said.

The three made their way down the hall and stopped at one of the doors, where Michael knocked.

The girl from the family answered the door, looked at the three of them and the dagger and stepped aside for them to enter. When Marcus walked in, it became obvious that the girl and the man were surprised at the visit, both looking at him curiously. The Queen was nowhere to be seen.

"What have we?" asked the girl.

"He's been with us since Cotter's Cove, Captain," said Michael.

Captain? Thought Marcus, I am indeed an idiot.

"His glances toward the Queen at every stop, left us little doubt that he knew who she was," said Carl.

"How unfortunate for you," the captain said to Marcus.

The Queen came out of the washroom and Marcus went immediately to his knees, placed his hands in his lap and his forehead on the floor. "I come to serve, Mother," he said.

"You are?" Melanie asked.

"Marcus Landon, Mother."

"Stand up. Where are you from, Marcus?"

He stood. "Oregon City, Mother."

Melanie studied the man, who had the appearance of being a harmless farmer. "What caused you to break your vow of secrecy?" She asked.

"I don't know the cause, Mother, I just knew it was time."

"How do you serve me?"

"Mother, I mean no disrespect or harm, but if you would fill yourself, please."

Melanie tried to decide if the man was trying to lead her into a trap awaiting her outside. Is he so sure he can overcome her and the Own? "Carl, would you be kind enough to check outside for a secluded spot?"

Carl was skeptical but he began to leave and was stopped by Marcus, "That won't be necessary, Mother. You may fill yourself here," Marcus said.

Melanie looked at Marcus suspiciously, but decided to give him the benefit of the doubt. *Merge.* Mother was in her instantaneously. There was no period of filling, no tingling, no blurred vision, she was just full of power. Marcus' eyes were blue as she was told hers' were when she would just merge with Mother.

"Captain, what color are my eyes?" She asked Marie.

"Blue, Highness," Marie answered.

Melanie released Mother and asked Marcus, "How was that possible?"

"I am never without Mother, I retain her and I project her. I can also block you if there is a need. I have no power of my own, Mother. I would not be as valuable as yourself in hurtling fire, but as a sniper I am unparalleled."

"How so?" The captain interjected.

"I can fire an arrow through a squirrel's eye at a thousand yards."

"Beast shit!" said Marie, "No bow shoots that far, much less accurately."

"Mine can. Given the opportunity, I can prove it," Marcus said.

"You carry no bow, nor did we see as much as a long knife," Michael said.

"Mother, with your permission?" Marcus said to Melanie.

Melanie nodded and Marcus opened his thigh pocket and pulled out a six inch round piece of what looked like a form of metal tube, black with the strangest runes carved into it. The runes began to glow and a shaft protruded out of each end and grew to a length of five feet or so, clicking with each section. Marcus pulled what she thought was a length of string out of the end, but she had never seen this kind of string before. He tied the end of the string like substance to the opposite end of the shaft. Melanie watched in awe as the string tightened itself and began bowing the shaft. When the bowing finished, Melanie saw that Marie was still unconvinced and listened to Marie's next question.

"You admitted to Her Majesty that you are useless in battle. How have you the pull strength to fire a thousand yards?" Marie asked him.

Marcus looked at Melanie, obviously looking for approval to answer.

"Let's be clear, Marcus," Melanie said, "I have developed the ability to harm those close to me and generally mess things up, so Marie is in charge of this expedition. You will answer her every question and follow her every command, or you will go home."

"Yes Mother," Marcus said to Melanie and then turned to Marie. "The bow does not require that much pull, and I never said I was useless, I said I would not be as valuable as Mother. I do not have the ability to hurl rocks or fire, but you will find me adept at hand to hand."

Marcus unstrung the bow and grabbed the center. The runes stayed bright, but the bowstring had retracted. Both ends of the bow retracted as well, and immediately expanded again into what looked like a well-crafted walking stick that Marcus demonstrated as a battle staff. He then made one end retract, and he held a sword of sorts, though Melanie couldn't imagine it cutting through anything.

"Can you make more of these?" Marie asked him.

"I did not make this one, Captain. It found its way to my fish hook when I was ten. I assumed the last bearer had placed it there for me to find. I believe it might fall to treason to design and further would serve no purpose." Marcus handed his sword, staff or whatever it was to Marie and when she took it, the end retracted, the runes went dark and disappeared and Marie was left holding a hollow cylinder.

"I see your point. How close to The Queen do you need be for her to benefit?" Marie asked him.

"That I don't know, Captain. I knew only of my gift to her, not more."

"Very well. We leave on the second train, tomorrow. Ride with the same merchants you have been. As far from our wagon as you can manage without drawing the eye of Road Safety. You will not contact the Queen or acknowledge her in any way or at any point from here out. If she has need of you, she will summon."

"I understand."

Marie went to the door and listened, opened it a crack, and then peered out. She opened it all the way and said, "Out, all of you."

Horseshoe Mountain Range North

They had camped on a rise out of the tree line. Things had not gone the way Brent had hoped. The plan had been to gain as much ground on the enemy as they could yesterday, and hope the enemy would take it as an invitation, but instead their commander rallied his troops into a quicker pace and maintained the same distance.

This was going to be a hard day for riding. The majority of the clouds had dissipated but the air was no less like walking through hot water. A stifling humidity made worse by not the slightest breeze caused Brent to sweat profusely even when standing still and he couldn't imagine it being any different for the rest of his force. A stream was going to be a critical find on today's march as water would be at a premium.

Brent thought back on last night's meeting in the command tent and Commander Crawford's repeat of the King's thoughts that the enemy commander might be under the impression the Queen was with them. He was trying to lead the King's command north, not knowing the Queen had gotten the information about Black Mountain from the wilder. Every question that came up about Crawford's comment, he was able to provide a totally logical and probable response to. All but one. The one that had been bothering Brent for two days now. Why the feint?

The answer he didn't want to think about involved the pretender and that ability she had to persuade or control the thoughts of others. She had found a way to convince ten thousand men and women along with an unknown number of wilders to march on the Queen of Mother which would have been a death sentence for a hundred thousand if they were to march on her while she was filled. He wasn't stupid enough to believe that she wouldn't have at least attempted to control some of his force at Junction City, maybe all.

Before they even had reached the campsite last night, he had sent five men he knew to associate with friends on the Junction City force to the city to try to 'feel out' their friends. He had asked them to ride with haste, there and back. If they rode with minimum sleep, they should get back shortly after midday on the new day. They also had a parchment they were to deliver to one of the commanders, if they felt nothing was amiss.

He wasn't sure what the Queen's progress was. Had she come to her senses and let him handle this traitor? If not, had she joined with the ally? Did she allow the Own to provide her with protection, or were they still just following? If she was still on her quest, where was she?

He was unlikely to get an answer to any of his questions, and had his own issues anyway. The pack had arrived to pick up the command tent, and it was time to continue the chase. Kevin and the Own were already mounted, Commander Crawford had the Van this day, and Commander Fryman would be bringing up the rear. He mounted the warhorse, gave the signal forward and the King's force began anew.

"Suppose we do a feint of our own?" Kevin said as they began the descent.

"I grow weary of these games", the King responded. "I am tempted to leave the packs to catch up at their own speed, run these yokels down and be done with them. I will be thinking on this during the ride."

Dawn's Landing Sisterhood

Dave was alone. Really alone. Sarah and her Guard had left at sunrise for Silver Mountain and he was carrying on in her absence. He would have to make the decisions when he got to his post anyway, so he may as well get accustomed to it.

The carpenters and locksmiths should be done by the end of the day, and he would have to station the workers. He and Sarah had decided on two shifts per pit. The pits would be opened from mid-morning to early afternoon and from sup to sundown. The signs had already been placed. It would be an inconvenience at first for some, but they would adjust. Settlers would have no issue at all as they were accustomed to once a week pickup.

Today's agenda involved two interviews and the questions had been started by Brie and finished by him and Sarah. Sarah had felt the reason both applied for the SPA position is because it paid better, but she also felt that once people learned it required travel, they would re-think.

Dave would conduct the interviews at the office borrowed from the Sisterhood since Breathers Manor was not yet complete. While he was there he had been talking to some of the settler children listed by the Sisterhood as high threat as well as those listed as high risk. High risk settlers were those the Sisterhood had deemed needed immediate counsel and high threat were those that had been confined as inevitable. These were essentially on psychiatric lock down.

Once the interviews were complete he would head to the sculptor and give him the depiction that he and Sarah had put together of Brie, which would be erected at Breathers Manor. He and Sarah would confront the King when he returned about having one erected in every city. Sister Beth thought that was a little extreme and Dave had witnessed that day, the fury of Sarah Strong and heard words coming out of her mouth that Dave had never heard before.

His Holiness had finished the meeting with the soldiers. The death of Brie Thurss had put Dawn's Landing in peril. After the initial shock was over and the Queen's pain had subsided, her rage would kick in, and the structures within the city would be at risk. He had decided the conspirators would need to be moved so that their trial could commence. The Sisterhood at Dawn's Landing was stretched too thin and he couldn't wait for things to get back to normal.

The soldiers he had picked would transport the prisoners to Pepper, with his parchment directing the Sisterhood there to commence with the trial right away. He had been up front and honest with them, explaining the potential threat from the Queen.

The sisters had uncovered another conspirator at the docks, but he had decided instead of prison he would hack up the sisters with his blade and very nearly paid for that misjudgment with his life. He was in no condition for travel, so the sisters were treating his injuries at the Sisterhood and his identity and crime were being kept secret. Once the docks were finished the sisters would move to Road Safety and the King's command outside the gate. Dawn's Landing would be considered cleansed and this mess would be ended. Sister Tillie's first command to the City Watch was that they were not to associate with Road Safety or the King's force until the investigation was complete.

The City Watch was as close to being back to normal as it would get. The streets were being patrolled, crimes were being investigated, fines were being imposed, order was being kept, and citizens were being served and protected. The only hole right now was the inspector position. He was waiting for Louis Maxwell to accept it.

The High Counselor had left for Silver Mountain this morning. The Guard of the Realm with her, so the lieutenant shouldn't be much longer. Hopefully he got along with Sister Tillie well enough that he would retain the inspector position as well as his current position as Commander of the Guard. The Holiness found himself pacing the halls, knowing it wouldn't make things happen any faster, but it did help him think.

As His Holiness approached Sister Beth's office in his pacing, he caught her sitting, slumped over her desk with her head buried in her hands. Had he misjudged? Was the stress getting to her? He approached the office and entered.

"Sister?" he said questioningly.

After she had gone to her knees and been encouraged to stand up, she said, "Holiness, I just received a missive from the Sisterhood at Kingston, Caruso. King Thomas has succumbed to his injuries. He is dead."

"That is sad news, indeed," His Holiness confirmed.

It would be awhile before the Queen would be able to get to Caruso to appoint a new King, so the standard election would have to occur in the meantime. It was a pretty common practice as Queens were very seldom able to just drop what they are doing and run. The former King's Commanders nominated their choices for King, and the Sisterhood accepted them and whoever had the most nominations became Supreme Commander until the Queen arrived and made it official. There had not been a Queen in the history of Mother that went against the recommendations of the commanders.

"Send a parchment back with my seal. So they don't think the Queen is ignoring them, explain her situation, and that the Queen is marching against the usurper that killed their King. Also explain that Her Majesty's own daughter has been murdered while she was on that march, which may create more of a delay, as she does not yet know. Wish them luck and ask for their prayers for the Queen's success. Send that immediately with my condolences."

He left Sister Beth's office land saw the lieutenant in a meeting with Sister Tillie, so he went there and waited for them to finish.

"I know it is going to put a strain on you, Lieutenant," Sister Tillie said, "And I very much appreciate your cooperation in this."

"I will be fine, Sister," the lieutenant said, "It will actually be less territory than I had before, without the Sisterhood being part. Anything occurring at the docks will put me further away from the

Mansion than I would like to be, but it has been quiet there lately anyway, and shouldn't be an issue."

"I would like to thank you as well, Lieutenant," His Holiness interjected. "We are close to returning to normal routine in less time than I had dared hope. Your staff is complete?"

"The Guard of the Realm is on Landing Road with the High Counselor, the Arm of Mother has surrounded Princess Bethany and her educators on the patio, and Princess Chastity, Sister Frances and the Queen's Heart are at the park across the street," The lieutenant informed him, "For the record, I had nothing to do with the names of the respective guards, they were picked by the Princesses."

His Holiness chuckled and then said, "I would rather the Princess stay inside the Mansion, Lieutenant."

"I expressed your wishes to Princess Chastity, Holiness. She called you an old fuddy-duddy and said you must have been boring as a kid."

For the first time in what seemed like months His Holiness was hysterical with laughter. It so elevated his heart he didn't want to stop.

Walker, West gate

Melanie sat in the wagon with Marie, the two of them discussing the news they had just been given and watching William trying to dig information out of Road Safety. This morning's train to Junction City had been canceled and according to Marie, the only reason for that would be turmoil within the city, and the city itself being on lock down.

For a city being as dependent on trade as Junction City was, this was nothing to shake off. Marie had said it needed to be something horrible to have shut down a city that size and since the Queen was accounted for, she couldn't imagine.

William was not the only one trying to squeeze info from the soldiers. All the merchants were, as well. It did not appear any were having luck, however.

"Do you have a plan, Marie?" She asked.

"Not yet, Majesty. I am thinking on it though. This would be a horribly bad time to expose ourselves, so the challenge is going to be getting out of Walker, not getting to Black Mountain."

Melanie followed Marie's eyes to two men walking into a grocer. It was Donovan and Albert. Marie handed the reins to Melanie and said, "Wait here, mom. I'm going to get us a snack."

Melanie's eyes went to William, Marcus, Martin, Pedro and then back to Marie heading to the grocer. She, herself was unsure how to proceed from here. She didn't want the head wilder to know she was coming, but the situation might be decided for her. She couldn't wait here for whatever the problem was to be cleared up. The woman had sent a lot of people on potential suicide missions and every delay might be another life.

Melanie's thoughts of the suicide missions made her mind wander to Brie, wondering how things were coming along for her. She made Melanie so proud. She knew Dan would have been proud too. Dan would have absolutely loved Bethany and Chastity. It was hard not to. What a couple of sweethearts. She looked over at the sandpit by the grocer. Your time's coming. Brie will be here soon.

William was walking back to the wagon, either having given up or beginning to think he was making the soldiers suspicious. He kept looking towards the assorted merchants, who were each working on their respective soldiers. Melanie glanced toward the grocer, but Marie still had not emerged from the shop.

William climbed onto the wagon and Melanie, after looking to see if anyone was close, told him about the grocer.

"That's good, because I have nothing," William said.

"Then we must hope that Donovan and Albert talked to a less dutiful soldier, because I can't delay. I need to end her."

Donovan and Albert emerged from the shop and went back to where they had left their horses, and shortly after Marie came out carrying a bag of Beef Pull, which didn't surprise Melanie. The girl seemed to live on it. Marie climbed into the back of the wagon and inched her way to the drape.

"Is anyone listening?" she whispered.

William looked on one side and Melanie the other and William said, "No. We are alone."

"Junction City is engrossed in a rather large battle, right now. The train wasn't gone even for an hour this morning before the rider reached them, closing the road."

Melanie's thoughts went right away to them having been discovered and the woman marching on her, instead of the reverse. Apparently, as she followed the conversation with William and Marie, that turned out not to be the case. Junction City was at war with Junction City. A couple of lieutenants had staged a coup against a commander of Junction City's forces. The rider who turned back the train had received his orders from one of those lieutenants. Both William and Marie were visibly shaken by that seemingly useless bit of information.

"It would be nice to talk to that rider, instead of getting hearsay," Marie said.

"Asking after him would put our position at risk," replied William.

"Why does it matter who sent the rider?" Melanie asked.

"The rider would have been sent by the person concerned about the safety of the innocent people in the train, Highness," William answered, "It is disturbing that the Commander was not the one concerned. I believe your friend has corrupted certain elements of the King's force there. You should know, by the way, Junction is the largest force in Queenland and it has two Commanders."

"Then we must go there and aid the King's forces," she said.

"How will you know who to aid, Majesty?" Marie asked, "They are all in the same uniform. No, we must be gone from here and go around while they are engaged."

A soldier was going wagon to wagon talking to each. "Is he telling everyone what is going on?" Melanie asked.

"No. He is probably determining whose destination is Apache Falls, and turning the rest back to the lodges," William answered. "Some are pulling out and heading back into the city."

"Should we go on to Apache Falls, then?"

"No. There will be few wagons and the same amount of Safety. It will be harder to sneak away," Marie answered. "We will head back to the lodge and go for a walk along the mountain paths. The City Watch will be thinner near the mountain."

"Where are you folks headed?" The soldier asked.

"We are visiting a friend in Chesapeake," William answered.

"Well, the road to Junction is closed, so there will be a small delay. Maybe tomorrow. Head on back to the lodge for today."

Marie poked her head out of the back and became a typical teenager, "Why, what's going on?"

"That's not your concern, young lady. You folks enjoy your stay." The soldier moved on to the next wagon and William turned out of the column and headed back to the mountain.

"Holy Cow, is it muggy!" Melanie said as they made their way. Walking through the mountains in this stifling heat didn't sound too appealing. The trip itself, back to the lodge, seemed longer than it even did on the original trip. Melanie saw Marie was deep in thought, so the ride went without conversation. She distracted herself with the everyday routine of the city.

The Queen was right, thought Marie, it is very muggy and they wouldn't be able to take any horses through the mountains. She was unable to think of a way to even acquire any without exposing themselves. Once out of the mountain passes, it was still going to be a long walk to Black Mountain carrying everything on their backs, through this heat. Despite the thoughts going through her head, she was looking toward the mountain, at every twist and turn of the road, trying to decide the best passage.

First things first, and the first thing was how to get their weapons out of the wagon without being seen. Everyone's eyes focused the other direction would be good, but there was no way to make that happen. She was just going to have to figure out the best way to do it, using what she had available. "Dad!" She voiced a little too loudly, causing the Queen to jump in fright. William made his way toward the wagon and Marie continued, "Get everyone together to huddle around the wagon on the pretense of talking about the road closure. We must be the last to break down the wagon."

William rode up next to Gary and Pedro, and then back to the wagon. She watched as Gary and Pedro began working their way in amongst the other merchants. Marie pulled the wagon over on the road and got down and began checking the right rear wheel. William dismounted and fell in beside her. Once the last wagon had passed, Marie got back to the bench and fell back in line. She continued her scanning, but was scanning the city, instead. When she found what she had been looking for, she allowed herself a moment's rest.

Within minutes they were in line for breaking down and Marie leaned close to the Queen and whispered, "You and I need to go for a walk, Highness. We are going to expose ourselves to the Sisterhood and have them aid in getting us out the gate, fully armed, in uniform and with horses."

"I don't want her to know I'm coming," Melanie replied. "Can we trust them?"

"I don't know what secret the sisters hold, Majesty, but they can't be swayed. Any attempt the pretender would have made to do so would have been rebuffed and she would either be in prison or dead."

"Dead?" Melanie giggled, "Those little bitty women?"

"Underestimating those 'little bitty women' has been costly to many, Highness. They can be quite deadly."

Melanie couldn't stop giggling, but she trusted her captain. "I am ready when you are."

Walker Sisterhood

Sister Ekaterina Dokhov had been High Sister of Walker for fourteen years now and this was the first time in her memory that the returning road sisters had not known the reason for the road closure. Sister Janine, the lead sister on the road, had told her she had asked but was being given lies and speculation.

That had been two hours ago, and she had feverishly been reworking her schedule for the week, and would have to do so again tomorrow, if things didn't get cleared up. She had sent a runner to the Road Safety commander with her parchment, but he had returned without a reply. Sister Ekaterina was in need of a walk, anyway, so after she finished her schedule, and saw to the family that had been waiting, she would have a talk with the commander herself. Nothing quite brought out the truth as well as surprise.

She finished the schedule and summoned the family, hoping to be quickly through whatever the issue was and be on her way. "Welcome, I hope you are making it through this thick heat well. My name is Sister Ekaterina, or Sister Trina, if you prefer. How may I be of service?"

"Thank you, Sister. It is plenty hot for sure. My name is Marie Mercer, Princess of the Realm, niece to King Brent and Captain of the Queen's Own."

That last title shook the sister into a sober stare at Melanie. Melanie returned the stare and said, "I will be blunt, Sister Trina. We have a perilous situation and discretion is foremost. No one must know I am here."

"Indeed, and I will be blunt as well. Why would the Queen of Mother allow herself to be out with only two members of the Queen's Own?" She looked at William, "Assuming, Sir, that you are also claiming to be one of the Own? Why would she allow them to be dressed so, and why in Mother's name would one so powerful need to hide? Who are you, and be cautious, I am in no mood to be lenient to anyone that would dare to impersonate the Queen," She signaled a sister in the hall and when she entered Sister Trina instructed her to fetch five other sisters, spouting their names so quickly that Melanie couldn't even catch one of the them.

"I appreciate your caution, Sister," said Melanie. "But I assure you I am Melanie Thurss from Phoenix and I am in need of your help."

Sister Trina wasn't swayed. Her look at the three was still intense. She continued to study the trio.

This woman does not even know fear, Melanie thought. She will not be easily convinced. Marie's idea to bring Marcus was looking pretty smart, right now.

Five sisters entered the room and Melanie noted that Marie became extremely nervous. "Stay calm," Melanie said to her.

Two of the sisters faced off with Marie and William and just stood staring at their eyes, the other three looked at Sister Trina. "Sister Kelly, this is Melanie Thurss, Queen of Mother." She had said it in a doubting fashion and the three sisters now stood in front of Melanie. Sister Kelly stood in the middle and all three stared at her eyes.

"Is your name Melanie Thurss?" Sister Kelly asked.

"You were just told it was," Melanie answered.

"How about you answer the question yes or no? How would that be? Is your name Melanie Thurss?"

"Yes"

True…True…True

"Were you swept from Phoenix?"

"Yes"

True…True…True

"Were you swept to Dawn's Landing?"

"No."

True…True…True

Sister Kelly turned to Sister Trina and said in an astonished fashion, "She tells the truth, High Sister."

Well, that was a ten on my weirdometer, Melanie thought, and watched as Sister Trina told the sisters to return to their duties, and then turned to her and asked, "Who is the man in the lobby?"

"Sorry, you ran out of your question allowance for the day. It's my turn now. You seemed pretty certain I wasn't who I said I was. Have a lot of impersonators, do you?"

"There is one, My Queen. We found her out about a month ago, but she slipped away before we could get her. She's here and we will find her."

"She's not here, and things are worse than you think. Marie?"

For the better part of an hour, Melanie listened as Marie filled Sister Trina in on everything that had happened at Caruso, Dawn's Landing and Landing Road, the battle of the Ridge, the wilders and all of it, but when she got to the part about Kristen and Marcus, the news stunned the sister so fully she let out a yelp.

"Children of Mother are just a myth, a campfire story," she said to nobody in specific.

"We have not the time to keep proving things to you, Sister. I'm sorry," Melanie interjected. "As I said, we need your help, and speed is critical."

"Of course, My Queen. What may we do to help?"

Marie continued on about her Queen marching on the pretender and not wanting to be seen coming, causing the pretender to flee, the need for secrecy, the speculation about Junction City and where the pretender was, and ended it with their need to ride out the gate.

"Our prisons are full of traitors right now, so your speculation about Junction City is probably true," Sister Trina said. "Very well. We will have the twelve of you escort a prisoner to Exeter along with a sister. The King's force doesn't even know all of Road Safety, much less City Watch, so they will have no reason to question you. When you are out of sight, you may turn and continue your journey."

"Who is the prisoner?" Marie asked. Sister Trina looked at Marcus.

Melanie looked at Marcus and thought, that's not a bad idea, he does look kind of shady. Which still left the problem of the sister. She looked at Marie, William and Sister Trina and saw they were all looking at her.

"Oh, no you don't. I am not wearing a potato sack."

PACKARD RISE

Queenland
Packard Rise

The enemy had gotten cocky and slowed their pace considerably, which was the play the King had employed. He had slowed his forces to a crawl, at least the forces that followed the enemy. He had sent Commander Fryman to the east and Commander Crawford to the west, both as fast as their host could ride, to circle the enemy and halt this game of wills. The King knew where the last place the pretender was known to be and he grew weary of whatever the commander of this supposedly retreating foe was playing. The captured wilder exposed the usurper's base of operations to his Queen.

The scout said the enemy had changed direction and were heading at high speed right at Junction City. They had detected Commander Crawford and were now sincerely fleeing. The King had ordered full charge, leaving the packs behind. He was close enough now that he could hear the screams and the clash of steel, coming from Packard Rise. Commander Crawford had either caught them or chased them into the waiting forces of Commander Fryman.

When he reached the top of the last rise, he saw that the latter was the truth of it. Commander Fryman was in the midst of the fighting, slashing this cat, parrying that outlaw, screaming encouragement at her men and archers who were trying unsuccessfully to take out way too many wilders. As he watched, one of those wilders went down from a shaft in the back of her head. Many of the outlaws had turned to repel this new assault from the rear and Commander Crawford.

"Let's end this," the King shouted and he charged down toward the battle, knowing the balance of his force was on his heels. He drew his long sword and urged his warhorse through the throngs of cats and outlaws, charging after the first wilder he could reach. Her lousy aim cost her to lose her head, and he turned after the next.

Commander Fryman was sick of these cats, and ready to make them her main concern, but she knew the key to victory was killing every wilder in the batch. The problem was they had dismounted and were now hiding amongst the outlaws, so the archers were firing blind, and these damned cats were attacking the archers. Out of the corner of her eye she saw two outlaws break free of the battle and ride east, toward Junction. She found two of her men still mounted and pointed the cowards out and the two men chased after.

She needed to find a way to rid herself of these cats, so that she could move on the outlaws and wilders. She had seen Crawford had joined the fray and the King shortly after, but even so they were greatly outnumbered, and that didn't appear to be improving with the number of her men that were falling to these animals.

Commander Crawford had taken his men in a reverse wedge formation into the battle, not wanting to spread the enemy out. Only one wilder had fallen so far, and he had kept his archers on the elevated ridge, with instructions to do their best at picking out the hidden wilders, while he and the rest of his men charged into the battle.

He brought his long sword down across the neck of the spotted cat and in the same motion, across the chest of the nearest outlaw, or whatever they took to calling themselves these days. A striped cat jumped at him, knocking him from his horse. His leg brace worked perfectly keeping him from being pinned by the falling warhorse. The warhorse, as it was falling, kicked the cat senseless and the cat was staggering and trying to keep its balance, but was not given enough time as Commander Crawford's long sword came down on its neck.

The Commander saw a mop of brown hair attached to a woman's head fly, and knew there was one less wilder to worry over. He turned just in time to parry a cudgel and sever an arm, but was too slow to stop the brown cat and he was down and had lost his grip on his sword. He forced the man's severed arm into the mouth of the cat, causing it to delay enough for him to shove his dagger into the neck. The cat growled and stumbled away, and he regained his sword.

The cat had Commander Fryman pinned and she slashed wildly with her short sword trying to free herself, but the spotted cat had her thigh in its mouth and wasn't letting go. She stuck the sword in the eyes of the cat. First the left then the right, but it continued to rip at her leg. The bite got through the armored padding and she screamed in agony. One of her men, who she would have to kiss later, heard the scream and slipped his long sword in the jowls of the cat and began sawing away. Another soldier was hacking furiously at the body. The cat died finally but the teeth were still buried in the Commander's thigh.

"Medic!" one of the men screamed and the three of them tried desperately to pry the head of the cat from her leg, when she saw them. Three more cats running right for them.

So this is where I die. Please, Mother, let me reach my sword. She prayed, and screamed at her men at the same time to save themselves, but they turned to face the cats, swords in hand. They are good men, she thought.

Yakyakyakyakyak. She watched as the charging cats stopped in their tracks and turned too late to prevent the onslaught of Riggers that were starting to chew them to pieces. A wilder was riding one, carrying a short sword in her left hand and a whip in her right. She knew this to be the ally the King had spoken of. "Help her!" She screamed at the two men that were trying so hard to pick up the jaws that they had dropped.

She watched the girl ride into the battle wearing nothing but shorts and half a top. No body armor of any kind, and the commander was suddenly ashamed of herself. She tried to stand to fight anew, but arms grabbed her and pulled her down. The medic told her to be still and began cutting the cats head and pulling her trousers down.

The King was dodging and slashing at outlaws and cats, but was getting no closer to the next wilder. He dodged a cudgel and shoved his dagger into the heart of the outlaw that had wielded it, but couldn't wrench it free so he just released it and swung his long sword at the next man. He thought he had heard Riggers, but it probably was just memories of his last battle.

A cat knocked him down, but Kevin's short sword was already buried in it to the hilt. The Own were ferociously fighting and the King realized that the outlaws, at least closest to him, had each wanted to be the one that did him in. They were falling in their attempt, but the cats and fireballs were presenting a problem.

He heard what sounded like a whip and then a woman screaming. Then he saw her. Kristen was riding her mount and dragging a wilder behind her headed out of the battlefield. She was a bloody mess. She had taken slashes on her thigh and her arm. The Rigger had a knife sticking out of its hind flank. A fireball flew over her head, but she kept dragging the wilder.

The King lost sight of her as he was in a battle for his life and would have to thank her later, if he was able. He was back to back with Kevin and they were swinging at anything or anyone that had managed to get past the Own. He parried one thrust but another took him across his left arm. He took that man in the throat. A man charged from his left, but he was downed by the long sword of one of his Own.

He heard Kevin grunt, but had no time to look as a cat burst through the line and was coming right at him. With all his strength he swung at its head and struck it flush, causing it to collapse on one of the dead. He drove his blade through its heart. The Own were losing ground, the sheer number of outlaws were forcing them back.

Commander Crawford saw from his elevated position, the ally dragging the wilder to a bunch of Rigger pups, and releasing it there and then charging back into the battle. She did not look in a good way. He could pay her no more mind though as he was locked in battle himself. Two wilders were causing most of the problem, driving his men away from the main battle and the King, but the cats were too many to focus on the wilder problem. There was a moment's rest and he looked quick to determine how his forces were doing.

A man wearing camouflage was walking toward him from the rise, as casual as could be. When he got to the commander he raised his left hand in greeting and said "Hey! How ya doin'?" and continued to walk past. A cat charged the man, but collapsed as the ground gave way beneath it and the cat was engulfed in what must have been a hundred graws. The commander had never heard a cat scream, but this cat was screaming. The commander was trying to follow the man, but became a little busy with a cudgel-bearing outlaw. He did the man in and noticed the camouflaged man was heading toward the two wilders. He lost track of him as well though, as he once again became otherwise occupied.

Just as he was thinking things were looking up, they got worse. Fireballs were flying out of the trees in front of him, and a lot of them. Over the two wilders, over the outlaws and into his men. The fireballs were exploding in the ranks sending his men flying. They were being thrown towards the King's forces as well. He caught a sword with his own blade, pushing it aside and shoved his blade through the outlaw.

Cats were collapsing everywhere, so he made the decision to have his men push into the outlaws to reduce the wilder's target. He was about to signal his archers to fire on the trees when he saw a long black blur fly over their heads and into the trees. A woman fell with the black shaft protruding from her skull. She no sooner hit the ground than another black blur hit the trees and another wilder fell.

His ears went deaf as all sound stopped, then he experienced the strangest pressure in them followed by an awful hissing sound. Blue flame erupted from behind him and the trees exploded with a deafening boom. He was knocked off his feet and he saw that no man or horse was left standing. Only what was left of the cats, the Riggers and the ally.

More blue flame, more deafness, more pressure and another explosion in the trees. The Queen was here. A sheer wall began to rise behind the trees. It was rising in all directions. More flame. His Queen was multitasking. No one would be climbing it. No one was escaping. May the best force win? He looked toward his archers but couldn't see her. What he did see was twelve men and a woman, slicing away, killing everything coming at them. Nothing was getting past them.

One of the men was using a black sword that was nothing more than a blur, and this was no ordinary sword. Whatever it was, seemed to be sawing men in half, bones and all and doing the same for cats.

The trees were on fire and women were screaming and falling out of them aflame. They tried to run, but they were consumed by thousands of graws. Riggers were ripping the cats to shreds, but the outlaws were not giving up. They got back to their feet and the battle began anew.

The attack from the trees hadn't lasted long, the King thanked his stars, because his men were being hit hard. The Queen, or at least he thought it was the Queen, but what he saw was a sister in a grock, had attacked them with that wicked flame of hers. He was too busy to notice the first bolt or whatever it was, but when he was on his rump, he watched the second one. The blue flame wasn't thrown; it simply went where she pointed. The deafness and ear pressure went unexplained. He had no idea where she drew it from. He became too busy to watch any of the other blasts.

The Own were still pressing the outlaws, but not with the ferocity they had been. They were pushing forward due mainly to an absence of many of the cats. They were still present, but not so many of them. Kristen's Riggers were winning that battle and they were getting help from the strangest source. The King himself had seen two cats totally engulfed by graws, of all things.

Some of the outlaws were trying to flee, but there wasn't anywhere for them to go. Some turned back to fight, but with their heart not in it, were being slain. Others were surrendering. The battle was beginning to wane, but was still fierce in some places. As his forces and the Own were handling the stragglers near him, he surveyed the battle ground.

He turned towards Kevin and found he had taken a dagger to the shoulder. He led Kevin toward the medics. Kristen was lying atop a wilder pulling her knife free, but she looked a mess. There wasn't much of her not covered in blood. The King hoped it was mostly wilder blood. He saw Commander Crawford and his forces pushing hard toward the fiercest fighting still left. He saw Commander Fryman's forces taking and disarming prisoners, but he saw no sign of the commander. He wasn't liking the looks of that. Some man the King didn't know was closing on Kristen, but she didn't seem concerned. The Queen still stood atop the rise, looking down upon the carnage. He wasn't sure what she was doing dressed like a sister. The Queen's Own stood about thirty yards in front of her amid what must have been forty bodies of men and six or seven cats, some of which appeared to be cut in half. There seemed to be one too many of the Own.

The King and Kevin found a medic working on Commander Fryman. She was pulling her trousers on. "Are you okay, Amanda?" the King asked.

"The medic tells me I get to keep both legs, but one will be uglier than the other for a while."

"How do you plan to lead and direct your men, when you place yourself so deep in the battle?" the King asked her.

"You're one to talk," she responded.

The King had no response for that and was being poked at by a medic anyway, so he turned his attention to the medic. "It is fine. I must speak with the Queen."

"It bleeds. The Queen can wait," said the medic. The medic began working on his arm, and the King looked toward Commander Crawford's men and saw that the fighting there was nearly at an end. He looked toward where he had last seen Kristen and found her lying on her back amidst the dead, with that man kneeling over her, trying to stop the bleeding in her leg. He also saw another of the medics closing in on them.

The Queen still stood where she had been in that ridiculous outfit. He surmised that she wanted to check on things in the battlefield, knowing her as he did, but Marie was standing with her and probably told the Queen no, knowing her as he did. Two of the Own were making their way towards him, probably dispatched to do so by Marie.

The Packs had made it through before the Queen raised the land and were making their way down the slope toward the battlefield. The King's warhorse had been clawed by a cat, but one of the soldiers was placing a salve on the wound, and it would soon be able to carry the King once more. Four wilders had been taken and wrapped and were huddled together, circled by several of his men, all of which looked like they were hoping the four would try to run. Riggers and graws were not even bothering to drag off the cats, they were all just feasting where the cats had fallen. There were pups among them as well.

He heard Commander Fryman talking to two men. The men were telling her about having chased two that were fleeing the battle, but they had needed to slay them as they were unwilling to return peacefully. No one had gotten out. Everyone that had been involved in the battle was still here. The Junction City forces, if they were traitors, would have heard the Queen's explosions. They would be unable to join the battle however, with no way past the Queen's walls. Was that the purpose of the walls? Did she know of treason?

If not for the Queen and Kristen this battle may have been a two or three day skirmish, without a guarantee of victory. It would have been an easy matter for treasonous forces to intervene. The King had a feeling he had others to thank as well. The man with Kristen was a mystery and the King had been too busy to pay attention to his contribution, but he was certain, judging by Kristen's reaction to his presence that he had helped her.

The King didn't have the advantage of being on a rise, so he couldn't see how many of his men had given their lives in the defense of Queenland, but he was certain the amount would wound him to the core. Just thinking about it made his desire to shove his blade up the pretender's ass unquenchable. He was definitely going to need more forces, because she would have to be a blubbering idiot to send all her strength against Dawn's Landing. This force would have been no more than a test. If they had succeeded, great, but she hadn't expected them to. What the King would face at Black Mountain would make this host look measly. He was going to have to get through three obstacles to even get near the bitch. At least three. Her wilders, the cats, and the host. There might even be more she hasn't shown yet.

Oh, my goodness! Melanie looked down on the devastation below and her stomach began to churn. So many dead. She kept running into the same three words, so many dead. The Own were unscathed, but she could see the King had taken wounds, and Kristen? What is wrong with that girl? Charging into the fray without any armor or protection, and who is that man who stands over her?

She watched as some of Kristen's new friends consumed the bodies of cats, leaving nothing but blood splotches. They were even eating the bones. Melanie shivered. She wanted to go down and talk with her and tell her she misses her but Marie forbid it, saying it was still unsafe. Marie had sent Gary and Donovan to meet with the King and tell him about Junction City, but they were still weaving amongst the dead, not even half way there yet.

Melanie had managed to do it again and not follow Marie's request, but this time she thought she may have actually saved lives for a change, instead of costing them. It would have taken Marcus forever to pick off those wilders in the trees, and they continued to rain fire down on Brent's forces. Marie had been infuriated at her, screaming for her to stop. That she was broadcasting her presence, but Melanie thought lives were more important than stealth. Melanie had to hand it to Marie though. For being so young, she was sure savvy. The sheared walls were a brilliant idea.

Once she had blown up the trees, a bunch of outlaws and cats came charging at her. Marie had been right and if the Own had not been so good at what they did, she would be feeling horrible right now. With the help of Marcus, the Own dispatched the charging force without as much as a scratch.

A soldier was approaching from the western section of the King's forces, and Marie headed down to meet her. Melanie watched the two for a few minutes and then they both came up to Melanie and the soldier, a female, took a knee.

"Rise, what brings you?" Melanie asked.

"My apologies, Grace. I am Victoria Lopez, a medic with Commander Crawford and I have come to beg for a stream that we may clean wounds."

"No begging allowed. Where do you want it?"

Melanie went to work on the stream bed, the rocks, the inlet, the low area that would become the new lake, and opened the underground stream and the water began to flow freely. This was the part of being a Queen that she loved. She was helping others and no one was dying. She watched as soldiers that must have been medics were running to the stream to fill flagons, bowls, buckets, and assorted other water holding items. She had never felt more helpful than she did right now, and for a change held a small portion of self-pride. She realized, with the stream and the lake this would soon be a new village and maybe one day a city, well maybe too close to Junction City to become a city, but a village at least.

Marie was still refusing to allow her to go see Kristen or Brent, so as gracefully as she could in her potato sack, she sat and began to go to work on the lake bottom.

The King cupped his hands in the stream and splashed water in his face and stood and faced the two members of the Queen's Own. "How certain are you?" he asked.

"Not the least, Majesty," said Donovan, "We're just at a loss at what else could cause a rebellion of this nature. There are two lieutenants involved. Our best guess is that's about five thousand of your force against five thousand of your force."

Gary added, "The order to close the highway came from one of those lieutenants, not the commander."

The King grimaced, as he could have gone all year without hearing that tidbit of news. Commander's Tate and Yakamura had held the posts at Junction City for eight years now, and there hadn't been one incident worth mentioning. They had been doing a great job, and Tate was one of the few having been mentioned as his successor. Tate, having fallen to the pretender's will, hurt the King's heart. He would find out soon whether the fail-safes he had installed at every Sisterhood would fall into place. During issues such as this, the Sisterhood was supposed to take control of the city. He would have to wait to see if it had actually happened as designed. There were so many sisters at Junction City, that it took three buildings to house them all.

"Thank you for the information. Please tell my Queen I will attend her as soon as the medic gives me leave. So that she doesn't become concerned as I know she will, it is an arm that took a minor injury. Nothing more."

He saw Donovan and Gary look at the wrist to elbow minor injury, nod to the King and begin the trek back to the Queen. The medic began placing pressure bandages over the stitches of the wound and had started wrapping the arm. He saw that the prisoners had been confined in a single area and were being watched by some of Commander Fryman's men. The four wilders had been kept in a different spot, wrapped and bound and he guessed they were hurtling obscenities as they were now being gagged.

The dead outlaws, nearly six thousand, were being dragged by tens and fives by every warhorse available to the burnt tree line where they would be burned later. The dead soldiers, nearly a thousand of them were being wrapped in their respective bedrolls, labeled and for now left in a line. Even for him, this was a gruesome sight.

The ground suddenly shuddered and he and every one of his men, steadying themselves, looked toward the Queen who was sitting on the grassy rise. He saw her raise an arm and heard, "Sorry!" Nothing appeared affected so he went back to the work of his men. His men were ignoring the cats, so he assumed Kristen had asked them to leave them, but when he looked back over to where a medic had been working on her, she hadn't been moved and was still being stitched up. She was out cold, so the pain had either caused her to faint or the medic had given her the opium powder.

This was going to take the balance of the afternoon and into the evening to clean up and he would need to find his scribe, because the sisters would want numbers and names for the Chronicles. He turned to one of the Own and asked him to find the man and have him begin his report and log it as the Conflict at Packard Rise.

"Conflict, Highness?" The man asked.

"That is correct. I am declaring war on the pretender. Have him note the date and time of the declaration, as well as exemption from the King's tax and a dowry started for every fallen soldier and their direct family beginning with the first thrust of Commander Fryman's force." The man went in search of the scribe.

The medic had finally finished so Brent made his way to his warhorse, mounted and headed toward the Queen.

Melanie saw the man approaching, but she didn't recognize him. He was no soldier. A tall man of about fifty. He seemed to be an aloof sort, walking without haste. Marie had stopped him a good distance from the Queen and had been talking to him for some time. She couldn't hear the conversation, but it appeared Marie was reluctant to give him audience and he was just as reluctant not to be given it. The conversation had gotten heated and Marie's hand went to her dagger, but the man had just laughed at her and folded his arms across his chest. Melanie had a very uneasy feeling that if Marie pulled that dagger, she would die where she stood. She didn't want to usurp Marie's authority but Melanie was very frightened for her.

Melanie stood. "Let him pass," she said.

Marie didn't even look at her, she continued to stare at the man and he continued to stare back. Neither was backing down, but Marcus had gotten the same feeling Melanie did and his hand slid slowly into his pocket. The man broke his stare with Marie and looked directly at Marcus, and his eyes went silver.

This man holds power. A lot of power. Holy marbles! A shit load of power, she thought. She spoke again, but this time to the man. "Stand down, Sir. I don't want to hurt you."

Melanie knew her eyes to be red without needing to ask, as she was fully prepared to cut the man in half. The man looked at her and she was suddenly unsure of herself. This man held power she had never felt in another, and she knew he was knowledgeable in its use. She felt the anger rising in Marcus and she laid her hand on his arm.

"I gave my word to a friend, that I would speak with you for her," the man said to her without looking at her, his eyes back on Marie, "And I never break my word."

Marie, to her credit, was not the least bit intimidated and continued the stare down and the Own had not taken their eyes off the man, but they made no threatening move towards him. The one she worried about was Marcus. The fury in him was immense. She kept her hand on his arm and squeezed lightly.

"Then you understand the power of one's word. Good," she said to the man, "Then you will understand as well that you are not in charge of this situation, I am. If I see so much as a whisker pop out of the ground from your little buddies, I will saw you in half like butter and drown every one of them. You have my word."

Nothing. The stare down continued, but then the man's eyes returned to the brown they had been. He continued to stare at Marie though, not an ounce of fright in those eyes. "Captain, stand down!" She said giving Marie an opportunity to save face, but she didn't take it. She stared into the man's eyes her hand still on her dagger.

Melanie did not feel this would end well, unless she did something. She got up and walked toward the man, but Pedro stepped in front of her. She moved to the left and William blocked that path. All the Own now stood between her and the man, Marcus still at her side. Still filled with rage. Melanie stuck her hands between Pedro and William and it took all her strength, but she pried them apart enough to get her head in. "Who is this friend you have given your word to?" She asked the man.

"My friend, Kristen," the man said.

"You could have said that right away and this would have all been unnecessary," she responded. "Kristen is a friend to us as well and the name would have given you an audience."

"She is in a bad way and did not share that information with me before she lost consciousness."

"I understand, and now you know you cannot intimidate the Own. Good job. What is your message?"

"She said she loves her family."

This shook Marie, she looked like she was about to cry.

"Take me to her," Melanie said to the man, and she began flailing at Pedro and William. "Get out of the way, damn it!" Marie's head was hanging, but she nodded at them and they moved. Melanie released Mother and followed the man down the rise.

"What is your name?" She asked.

"John David Matthews," he answered.

"You are not a Child of Mother, but you are no wilder, either," Melanie informed him.

"Kristen has told me I am not one of the Children."

"She is correct. If you were, I would know," Melanie said to him, "The silver of your eyes, tells me you bare no evil, though. How have you gone undetected?"

"I never usually go anywhere except my farm," he said. "You will swear to me you will tell her family she loves them?"

"She speaks of us. I am Mother, specifically. William is dad, and that girl you were in a stare down with is her sister. The Own in general."

Now it was John David's turn to be shocked. He obviously had no answer to that, which was good because they had arrived. The Riggers had Kristen surrounded and she re-connected to Mother and felt their fear for her. They were not going to be letting anyone near her. *I love her. I am her friend like you.* She told them. She turned to the Own and told them to stay back from the Riggers and she began weaving her way through, patting one on the maw as she passed.

When she got to Kristen a female medic was sitting next to her, doing nothing. "How is she?" Melanie asked the medic.

"She will be fine, Majesty. She has lost more blood than would be preferred, but not so much to cost her life. These Riggers will not let me leave, however. I do have others to attend to. I sent for a stretcher, but they wouldn't let them in."

"Go get one and some to bear it," she told the medic, and explained to the Riggers. The medic slowly stood and watched as the Riggers spread out to make room. She left and went immediately to fetch a stretcher. Melanie couldn't figure a way to sit with all the men looking at her, so she went to her knees and kissed Kristen on the forehead, and then felt it for a temperature. Not that she knew what she would do if she found one.

"Would someone get me some water from the stream, please?" she asked. She watched as William headed toward the stream. She picked up Kristen's hand in her own and surveyed the damage. Kristen had a long bandage on her left leg that looked long enough to have been caused by a sword, her right arm in the bicep area had a huge bruise but no bandage, probably from a club, and her forearm had another large bandage all the way around. *Bite? Wouldn't have wanted to be that cat, if it was.*

William returned but was not allowed through, so Melanie told the Riggers to go and eat and drink, that they were in the way. She also assured them that no one would harm Kristen, and she would always let them know of any changes. Melanie thanked Mother for giving her the smarts to ask Kristen how she communicated with her friends.

Reluctantly and slowly the Riggers began moving away, and William brought her the water. John David came with him. Melanie poured a little in her hand and ran it along Kristen's lips and her forehead and eyes. Kristen began to stir. Melanie dangled the flagon over Kristen's mouth and let a few drops trickle, and her eyes began to flicker.

"Move it!" came the command from the returning medic, and the Own began to spread and let them through. Carefully, they lifted Kristen onto the litter, but Kristen inhaled loudly and said, "Ow! Ow! Ow!"

The medic shook her head and asked herself, loudly for all to hear, "How did she wake up so quickly?"

Oops! Melanie realized the water was inadvisable, but no one ratted her out so all was good. They lifted Kristen and began walking toward what looked like a makeshift trauma area near the stream. Melanie and the Own, John David, and Marcus followed as well as the King who had at some point joined them. The King was shaking the hands of John David and Marcus, introducing himself, she guessed.

Melanie had so many questions running through her head for just about every person that walked Mother, but she realized it was futile to think about. She would just have to pick things up as she went, but this John David guy was going to continue to be a mystery. He was just not the type to open up. The King had walked at her side leading his warhorse.

"You look extravagant, Sister Melanie," he said with a smile.

"Shut it!" she said, "What are your losses?"

"The scribe is still at work. I would appreciate the walls staying until the new day. We will camp here tonight, so my men may rest. There is much to clean up and much to burn."

"No burning," she said, "You will find a sandpit inside the tree line the bodies have been dragged near."

"When did this occur?" he asked.

"I apologized for the shudder."

"Oh, that's what that was. I'm not sure the High Counselor would approve of a sandpit in the middle of nowhere."

"She'll get over it. What are your thoughts of Junction City?"

"My thoughts are that this is a delay I did not need. The pretender is doing a good job at creating distractions. She is a coward and should just bring it." The King thought some more and then continued, "I am broken. Commander Tate is a fine man, as is Yakamura. I am saddened that I must kill them, but if the speculation is true, they will die on the new day. The city should be under the control of the Sisterhood in times like these. We will need to see. Lieutenant Taggert spoke of many acting under orders of the Sisterhood."

"Marie prefers we continue to travel in disguise with the trains. She feels the wilder Queen....."

"She is no Queen!" the King interrupted angrily.

"Sorry, the wilder woman may have scouts and spies everywhere and Marie thought we were better hidden in the trains. I will have her speak with you. If you are going to Junction City, she may make me wait on what you find."

They had reached the trauma center and Melanie was disgusted with what she saw and became even more infuriated at the wilder woman and her minions. Every delay was just going to create more of this, but she knew it would be unwise not to accept the help offered. The King stopped the procession following Kristen long enough to introduce Melanie to his commanders. Both tried to rise to take a knee but Melanie physically held them both back down. *Where is Frances when I need her?*

"The injured do not kneel," she commanded.

"I'll sign off on that," the King said in support.

"Death comes. Set them free."

Here we go again, Melanie thought as she checked her surroundings with as much stealth as possible, so that none thought her daft. There was once again no one around that had spoken. Something occurred to her, and she hoped it wasn't true because then she would need psychiatric help.

"Mother?" She worded in her mind, "Set who free, Mother? I don't understand. Are you saying more death is coming this day?"… "Mother?"

Melanie thanked the commanders for their service to her King and they were back underway following Kristen. When they got to where the medic wanted her, Kristen's eyes were open and Melanie smiled at her and fulfilled her promise to the Riggers. She heard the yakking in the distance.

It got crowded around Kristen in a hurry, as both Owns were commending her on what a great warrior she was and wishing her well and touching her head, it became so crowded that Melanie could no longer even see the girl.

"Excuse me!" she said loud enough to make it known they should spread out, which they did. Melanie worked her way up and caught the eye of Kristen who immediately began to chuckle.

"Sure glad I taught you fashion, Mother," she said to Melanie.

"I am making it mandatory that all women dress as sisters, henceforth. I thought I should lead by example," Melanie retorted.

"Where do I go to become a man?" Kristen asked, causing everyone including the King to laugh. Good. Melanie thought, as quick witted as ever.

"How's the pain? Do you want me to ask them to give you something?"

"The pain is fine, it's the healing that hurts."

Melanie saw the look on Kristen's face. The look of realization that she had just said something she probably shouldn't have. Melanie had no intention of bringing Bethany's recovery up in front of so many, but it was a topic she would cover when she had Kristen alone. Kristen took a chance on being discovered before she was intended to. Kristen diverted the attention from herself immediately.

"JD, thank you so much for bringing them," she said.

"You were a little groggy, but I heard Queen and your loving family. The Queen figured the rest out," John David answered.

"Poop stain, you fared well in the battle I see," Kristen said to Marie.

"I wasn't as bold as you, bed wetter. I stayed under the protection of the Queen."

The King was looking totally baffled and said, "This is above my knowledge, so I will speak with my commanders. Kristen, thank you for those you saved, we will speak again."

"I will look forward to it, My King," said Kristen, "Brother, how long have you been with Mother?"

"Just recently, sister," said Marcus, "It is an honor."

"For me as well," said Kristen and after a moment's hesitation, uttered, "I must rest."

Kristen was out like a light, Melanie let the Riggers know she was resting easy and they should continue to feed and drink and she asked William, who was the closest to her, what was being erected near the shear wall.

"That would be the command tent, Highness," he told her.

"Would you take me there that I might change?"

"I will go back to the horses and bring your pack," he answered. He grabbed Willard and Phillip and they were off after the horses.

"Are you injured, Grace?" one of the medics asked her and she realized it was the polite way of saying get lost, so she answered that they were all fine and began ushering everyone out of the trauma area.

Melanie asked Marie to take her to the wilder prisoners while she was waiting on William to return, so Marie led the way to where the women were. The Own surrounded them and Marie faced them with Marcus. John David had stayed with Kristen. Melanie studied the women and they looked like ordinary women. They weren't dressed like hicks, they didn't have disheveled hair, and they weren't covered with dirt. They just looked like the housewife next door that she had coffee with once in a while. They wore the same types of clothes that she wore. Well maybe not today's grock, but normally. One looked to be in her thirties, two were twenty-five or so and the other looked about twelve. She wasn't, but she looked it.

"Would any of you care to answer questions for me? I really don't want to enter your head by force," she asked. "Nod your head for yes, or shake it for no." All she saw was hatred and four quick shakes. Melanie felt tears starting. "For the love of Mother, what has she done to you?" She turned and walked away, not wanting them to see her cry, and made her way toward the outlaw prisoners. "Martin, please run ahead and tell the guards to keep their eyes on the prisoners, that I will think less of them if they kneel."

As she was walking toward the outlaws, she saw the King still talking with his commanders and William just now descending the slope with Phillip, Willard and the horses. Martin returned and said, "The guards requested you not attend. They said the language was not fit for a lady, but if you must to please stay behind them." Melanie nodded and continued on.

When she arrived, she worked her way up between two of the guards and stopped in between them. She looked over the bunch methodically, No, not that one, nope, no not him, not her either, there, he's the one I want. She pointed the man out to Marie, and Marie walked into the gaggle, not caring whose hand she stepped on and asked the man once to stand, which he naturally didn't. He hadn't looked up once and had no idea Melanie was even there. Marie pulled her dagger, grabbed the man's ear and he bolted to his feet and walked toward Melanie, still not looking at her. Marie pushed him down in the front, and returned to stand next to Melanie.

"My name is Melanie Thurss, I am the Queen of Mother. Are you the commander of these men?"

The man finally looked up and smiled, once again just a regular looking young man with a very nice smile. "Well, will you look at that? The queen bitch herself, and dressed in a way that I don't need to mess with zippers. Came ready for a real man, I see. How about you let me have a look under that sack, sweetie?" His men began to laugh, but the Own were not laughing. She could not see any of them, but she could feel the tension.

"Sure," she said to the man.

The man smiled more and looked around at his men, with his best macho look, and the men began with their cat whistles. The man stood and began to walk towards her.

"Leave your trousers, though. I so need you ready for a real woman," she said to him.

The man took his trousers down and started at her again.

"Underwear, too," she said. The man hesitated, but pulled his shorts down and began walking toward her.

"That's good, pumpkin. Right there," she said to the man. "Now lie on your back and I will straddle your head and you can have a look, okay?"

The man looked back at his men, showing his best cat that ate the canary look, and lay down on his back.

Melanie looked back at the Own and said, "Hold him down."

The man tried to bolt, but the Own had him back in place in seconds. He looked afraid, very afraid.

"Now I am coming honey bunch, and it will only take me four steps. If you are smart about it, you will have a nice look under my sack, but for each step I take you have to say two words. I am so ready for a real man, so I hope you can remember the words. You will have to shout these words out so all your men can hear them because I might give them a look too, and my captain is hard of hearing and might make a mistake.

"Those words are right eye, left eye, right testicle, left testicle, and my penis." Marie became eager to abide, drew her dagger and went and stood over the man.

"I'm waiting, sugar bear. So are all your men. Please let me come to you. I am so ready for a real man. Please say the words. I am only four steps away, so close. It's been so long, I just can't stand waiting any longer."

Melanie looked at the prisoners and they were all looking horrified, except a few of the women and they were just not looking. "Line up, boys. Everyone gets a look under my sack."

Slowly, one by one the prisoners began to descend to a knee. The commander was crying, and not silently. "Are you going to keep me waiting? I need you now," she said to the man.

"No, Majesty. Please, I beg you. I was only showing off."

"So, you're not a real man then?"

"No Majesty, I'm nothing. Not even worthy of your notice."

"Then perhaps you can explain to the Queen's Own why you are not on your knees."

The man was begging each member of the Own to let him kneel

to his Queen. Gradually, they released him and he rolled over on his knees, but his eyes never came off that dagger.

"Look at me!" she said to him.

"No Majesty, please. I don't want to look."

"Stand up." She saw the prisoners begin to stand and turned on them. "No one was talking to you." They all went back down to their knees. She looked back at the man and he was standing in front of her with his eyes closed. "I said look at me!" she demanded.

He opened his eyes, slowly and looked at hers and began to shake so bad the Own were having difficulty holding him up. "Tell me what scares you more, that coward that sent you to die...or these eyes?" She merged with Mother and felt the eyes blurring and changing. The man watched her eyes and whimpered and grabbed his chest.

"Please, Majesty. I'll do anything. I can help you. I know things. Please let me help."

"Are you sure you don't want to look under my sack, first?" Melanie asked with a head twist and puckered lips.

"No, Majesty, I'll never want that again, I promise."

"Fetch my King," she said brusquely, intentionally. She heard someone trot off, but kept her eyes on the man. "When my King gets here, you will swear your fealty to him and answer his questions."

"Yes, Majesty."

"Get down on your knees and stay there, until he gives you leave to rise," The man crumpled to the ground. She looked over at the prisoners and the few that had raised their heads to watch were now trying to bury them in the dirt. She looked at Marie who still held the dagger in her hand and the testicles in her eyes. Melanie touched her arm and shook her head. Reluctantly, Marie put away her blade.

A puddle materialized under the man, and Martin and Gary stepped away in case he shit.

She saw the King coming and started toward him, stopping him just short of the prisoners. "It's fear. That's how she controls them. They fear her more than anything. Well, at least they did. If they don't do what she says, they die," she turned to Michael, who had been the one that went for the King, asking him to announce the King.

"His Highness, King Brent," Michael said.

"My King," Melanie said, with volume so all could hear, "These men are eager to provide information about the usurper. Please ask the questions you seek. If they lie or don't answer, bring me some piece of them. Beginning with this man. He is the commander."

"As you command, My Queen," the King said, looking at the puddle. Melanie cocked her head, smiled at him and began her trek to the command tent where she saw the horses and William and Gary waiting. The Own with her were silent on the way to the tent. Albert was next to her, so she asked him. "Why is everyone so quiet?"

"I don't know about the others," he replied, "I'm trying to avoid shitting myself."

"That's gross!" She said giving him a look of disgust.

"We could use your help," Kristen said to JD."

"This is not for me, little one. Too much violence and I don't interact with others very well. Kind of a loner. Besides, I need to get back to the old ball and chain. I'm sure she wonders what happened to me, by now. I will stay with you until the Queen brings the wall down, but then I must leave you."

"I am going to miss you, JD. I don't think I know anyone that has cared about me like you do."

"You do actually, you just haven't realized it yet. That King cares for you, as well as that young lady that is so over bold. The guards are fond of you as well, but the Queen, Kristen. That woman's aura around you is bright. Her heart aches, though. She has said something or done something to you that causes her grief."

"What makes you so sure? Marie hates me. She has told me as much."

"Do not be deceived by words, as I have been many times. She cares about you," he said. "I just know stuff," he continued. "Don't know how, but things just come to me when I am with others. It is why I am a loner. People cannot hide the truth from me about their feelings."

Kristen thought back to a conversation she had with Mother about His Holiness, "Mother speaks with you."

"Ha! If only she would. I have many questions," John David laughed harder as he thought about something other than the current talk.

He received a nudge in his back and turned to see the muzzle in his face. He turned back to Kristen, "It appears someone thinks I am taking up too much of your time. I will see if I can find us something for sup." He got up and walked off toward the soldiers.

Melanie pulled the jeans and shirt out of her pack that she wanted to wear and entered the tent with Marie. The Own closed the flaps and stood guard at the entrance. As she pulled the sack over her head, she said to Marie, "I need to know what's going on with you."

"Highness?"

"Don't even start with the stupid act, please. You know what I'm talking about."

Marie hesitated, but then said, "I don't feel you are getting the respect you should, and I am just having a little trouble accepting it."

"A little trouble? It appeared to me you were going to castrate that man whether he cooperated or not, and that friend of Kristen, John David? Holds more power than any I have run into and could have killed you with a simple thought. You are the captain of the Queen's Own. If you are going to continue along this path, you need to resign. I assure you, I am more worried about the harm that might befall you than I am the lack of respect. If you were to die because someone didn't respect me, how do you suppose I would feel?"

"I apologize," Marie said. "One doesn't think about the effect her actions might have on another. It is true that I am easily angered of late. I don't particularly like myself. I said mean things to Kristen, and I have thought mean thoughts of others. Perhaps being your captain is above my skills, or maybe I am just too young for the post. I will speak to Donovan, and ask him to take the position."

"Wait a minute. That's not acceptable. You will resign because you can't contain your anger and can't distinguish between threats to my honor and threats to my life. That resignation I will accept, but resigning because of your age or your skill? That I will not sign off on."

Melanie had finished dressing and was brushing her hair, and stuck her head out the flap, and laid eyes first on Doran. "Doran, would you be kind enough to locate Sir Kevin?"

She closed the flap and looked at Marie. "When Mitchell died for me, I cried harder and longer than I ever have. Not even watching my grandpa slowly slip away caused me to cry that hard. I will cry again. Because I know that before this is over I will suffer more loss, and you are all too hard-headed to accept my request to stay out of it, but by all life on Mother, I will not lose one of you to such a petty thing." She had a horrible knot in the back of her hair that she couldn't brush out. One of those things her mother had called a rat. She handed the brush to Marie and asked, "Would you see if you can pull that out?"

They sat in silence as Marie was pulling hairs apart and brushing. Pulling, brushing and after a few minutes she heard Sir Kevin calling from outside and she told him to enter. She filled him in on their conversation and asked his advice.

"So, you want me to understand the view of my Queen and at the same time understand the view of my King's niece. Nuh uh! You're both adults. Act like it." He turned and walked out.

Melanie sat there in total shock. How dare he? Of all the nerve! She suddenly felt Marie shaking behind her, and turned to look and Marie was trying very hard to suppress laughter. Melanie stood and put her hands on her hips and Marie said, "Does this dress make my butt look bigger than Marie's?" She finally broke and was laughing hysterically, and then Melanie realized she had put Kevin in an awkward position to which no answer would have been the right one, and she started laughing, too. It felt so good to see Marie laugh.

Marie became somber and looked at her, "I will try to control my anger, but I'm not sure about the respect thing. I don't think you would have any better luck with any of the Own in that area."

"I will take the anger promise and we will continue to work on the rest," Melanie responded, "But you and your charges need to start working some things into your heads. First and foremost being that I abhor violence. I'm not stupid. I know that some things like this battle will bring it out, but the days of thinking everything can be solved by removing heads will go away. I will not stop until it does."

They stepped out of the tent and Melanie saw several soldiers frolicking in the lake and a few were dangling their feet in the stream, this side of the lake. There were still many surrounding the prisoners, and the King was still there and had been joined by his two commanders. The trauma area seemed to be the busiest, with soldiers teasing the wounded and the Riggers surrounding Kristen, who was sitting talking to the female medic but looking like she was free of pain. Some bodies of the outlaws were still being dragged to the pits, but the cats were nearly all gone. The graws were still working on a few, but the Riggers that weren't with Kristen were just basking in the sun oblivious to them.

The wilder prisoners still looked defiant, trying to wiggle free and receiving the hilt of a sword for their effort. The Queen knew they were not being controlled through fear like the outlaws were, but she was not comfortable doing again what she had done to the previous wilder and Kristen, so she may never know.

She wanted to tour the wounded and thank them for their service to the King, but she knew that would displease the medics that were trying to keep them motionless. She started walking toward the King's dead and there were a lot of them.

She started on one end and went to her knees at the first man and touched his head and said a silent prayer for Mother to accept him. Men, women, head injury or no, she would speak to Mother about each. She crawled the line and it didn't matter to her how long it took. She was only about twenty or so in when she realized it had become quiet, she thought she may have lost her hearing. She looked at the Own and all twelve were on a knee, with their long sword stuck in the dirt. She thought they were joining her in prayer but when she looked around, every soldier had done the same. The King's Own, the outlaw prisoners, those at the lake, the medics, the wounded, Marcus, John David, Kristen, and the King. The wilder captives had stopped their struggling and were watching her. The graws had stopped munching and were now all above ground and there were thousands upon thousands staring at her. The Riggers were all laying muzzle to ground looking at her. Only the warhorses remained standing, and there was not so much as a snort even from them. She felt if a leaf dropped, she would hear it. She ignored them and continued her tribute to the dead.

John David had to admit the Queen was a remarkable woman, honoring the dead as she was. Taking the time from her thoughts and quest to say a prayer over each. He had no problem taking a knee to this woman. She was everything the little one said she was. He watched her touch the head of each, hesitate and then move to the next. She had stopped only long enough to look at everyone looking at her. Then he heard a chant starting to his left and in no time engulf the entire camp, all the way to the lake.

"Queen Courageous!"
"Queen Courageous!"
"Queen Courageous!"

Melanie was stunned at this repeat by the King's men of what they had done on the battlement that day at Dawn's Landing. Everyone was chanting, even the King. It was embarrassing, but she didn't want to insult them. She had to put an end to it, though. It had become deafening. She walked over and took Marie's long sword and marked the woman she had last prayed for and walked to an opening and created a flat rock just under the ground and elevated it just enough that everyone could see her, and threw her hands up and began a silence motion.

Slowly the chant died off and she said, "You honor me . . ."

The chant exploded again and it took longer this time to quell, but eventually lessened.

"But I am not the one that should be honored. You should be honored for your service to my King," she pointed at the dead. "They should be honored for the lives they gave," she pointed at the wounded. "They should be honored for continuing to press through the pain," she pointed at Kristen. "She should be honored for the Riggers and the courage she showed each of you." she pointed at John David, "He should be honored for bringing his friends to our aid, so do not chant to me.

"I am but one of the team. Honor yourselves, give honor to your fellow soldier, to your commanders and your King. Honor your allies, for there are many. Pay homage to the fallen and the wounded. Know that you are the most fearsome fighting force on Mother who will accept no defeat. Know that courage comes from each of you and projects to the man or woman next to you, but do not chant to me.

"My road is clear. I must stop this evil woman who has put the fear of her in human beings like yourselves, who think they are fighting the good fight." She pointed at the outlaw prisoners. "Farmers, merchants, peddlers, carpenters who are so afraid of her they have been convinced they need to fight or die. For that, we must put an end to her. For what she has done to the innocent, for that I will need your help, but do not chant to me.

I must end the poison that she has infected these poor women with," she pointed at the wilders. "She has filled them with hatred and rage and has sent them forth to die, knowing they cannot succeed. Ordinary women, such as your wives and mothers and sisters that, unfortunately for them, she has found to be able to touch Mother. Look at them. Do you really believe they were born full of hatred? I must stop her. We must stop her, but do not chant to me.

You are the mighty. You are the brave. You are the soldier. The commander. You will show this woman that her fear will not reign. Her injustice will not triumph. You will show her that she has chosen unwisely where to spread her evil, and I will be with you when you do, but do not chant to me."

Melanie allowed her perch to be absorbed back into Mother and as she was descending the entire encampment erupted, and she needed to suppress the desire to cover her ears. She headed back to where she had left off but the noise continued and may even have gotten louder, if that was possible. She lifted Marie's sword and handed it back to her and she once again went to her knees and the encampment went berserk. The walls were the problem, she suddenly realized. The sound was bouncing back off of them. She saw a few of the Own were wincing and the wilder women were covering their ears as were the outlaws. They will go hoarse if they continue.

"Set them free."

Melanie looked at the outlaw prisoners. Was she supposed to set them free, after what they had done? She wouldn't! She couldn't! "Set who free, Mother? Please help me understand."

One of the wilder guards was walking toward her holding his ears as well, and he went to his knee and waited for her to finish her current prayer. When she did, she smiled at him and he spoke, almost screaming.

"My apologies for interrupting, Highness. It's the wilder women." He looked like he wasn't sure he was believing what he was about to say to her, "They have asked that we lay a tarp, that they may kneel to ask forgiveness" It was so loud Melanie didn't know if she misheard the words or the man misspoke them.

"You mean pray to Mother? Yes you may," She screamed back and started to the next man, but the soldier was still there. So she looked at him again.

"No, Majesty. They want to kneel to you... and... their eyes, Majesty. They're silver."

Melanie almost swallowed her heart. Stay calm, stay calm. "I am busy, right now. Tell them when I am finished they may," she continued her homage at the same pace she had been. *Wait a minute! How can their eyes be silver if they are wrapped? Am I supposed to set these wilders free? How can I possibly do that?*

"Marcus," she screamed to him. He looked at Marie and she nodded and he approached the Queen.

"Yes, Mother?" he asked.

"Can the wilder women draw on your power?" she screamed at his ear.

"No, Mother. Just you. Well Kristen can and that John David man, but I blocked him. He made me angry."

"Who can draw on you, specifically?"

"You, the Children, or realistically anyone whose eyes are silver, but no wilder."

"What about a wilder with silver eyes?"

"A wilder cannot be silver, Mother. They can be any other including yours, but they can't do silver."

"How sure are you?"

"Dead sure. It is not possible. A wilder with silver eyes is not a wilder, but a servant of Mother. Not you, Mother, Mother that we worship. John David is not one of Mother's Children, but he is a servant of Mother. He can defend himself or his little friends, but he can't do evil or his eyes would turn."

"You are dead sure?"

"Dead sure."

"Go look into the eyes of the wilder prisoners and return to me."

Marcus went to Marie and she nodded and went with him. Melanie continued on. The noise was finally starting to subside, but she already had a pounding headache. There was a line waiting to speak with her, so she was going to have to finish this after sup. She had Albert mark her spot, and went to the limping Commander Fryman.

"I am so sorry for bothering you with something so trivial, Highness. I was wondering if we might have some water with which to bathe."

Each person she met with had a legitimate request and she would fill the requests as they came up. The medics refused bathing in the stream, the cooks needed stones to keep the food hot, soldiers wanted different areas leveled for bedrolls. The horses needed their own troughs, and so on and so on. Each time though, she continued to glance toward the wilder prisoners. The conversation Marie and Marcus was having with them was lasting awhile. She could only hope Marcus had blocked them. The King himself was back with the outlaws.

She hadn't realized that the line had ended, but she checked with Donovan and he went to ask Marie if the Queen could approach. She saw Marie shake her head, but then motion to the guards who began laying down the tarp. The women were one at a time walked to the tarp. They went immediately to their knees and buried their faces in the tarp. Marie nodded at Donovan and he signaled Gary and they were off.

The women were surrounded. If this was a hoax they would die together instantly, but Melanie tried to see the good in them. She spoke as she got there.

"You wished to speak with me?" she asked.

In unison, all four women jerked in fright not knowing that she was upon them. Between the crying and the talking into the tarp all at once, she couldn't understand a thing. Gently, she said "Silence." The crying continued, but silently and their muttering stopped.

"Look at me," she said and one by one and fearfully, they each lifted their head and looked at her. She decided to start at the left.

If not for the already unbelievable things she had witnessed, the magic, the abilities, the knowledge, His Holiness and his talks with Mother, Kristen's scary healing talents, she would have sworn she was thinking the impossible. These women had been hypnotized. Mind controlled in some way, and she must have said the keyword when she was speaking to the soldiers. She tried to think of any uncommon word she might have used, but could come up with none.

She had been right, though. Every one of these women had a family or a husband or children that they hadn't seen, but they didn't know in how long a time. They all had a vivid memory of their families, but not much memory of their service to the usurper. Melanie's heart nearly broke as each asked if they would be allowed to see their families before they were beheaded. Melanie finally understood Mother. It was the wilder she was supposed to free. She just couldn't figure out what she was supposed to free them from. It wasn't like they were imprisoned. They just lived in the wild. Or was she supposed to free the wilder with the usurper? How? She had no idea what she had done.

Melanie asked Marie to speak with the Own and Marcus about this new development, and she would be back for their counsel. She herself, went to Kristen who was already up and walking along the creek with John David. When she reached them, she waited to be noticed and saw Kristen smile at her approach.

She explained the happening with the wilder prisoners, and asked Kristen if she had ever heard the like. Kristen said that she had not, but John David said that he was able to control thoughts and that she, the Queen, was as well. He used words such as reading and willing, but basically a form of mind rape had been used, and you first "read" the kind of person they are, then you "will" them to your thoughts and then "mold" it to their conscience. It took a while to complete the process, as John David had done it once to his candy eating son, but it made him so sick and ashamed of himself that he undid it right away.

Melanie continued to drill him with question after question, and thought she was beginning to understand the head wilder. She brought Kristen in on the questions, and when she had finished she had developed a full package with which to share with Brent and Marie. Kristen had unknowingly provided her with how the woman controlled the animals, she had figured out herself how she controlled the outlaws, and John David had explained the wilder issue. She thanked them both and headed for the King.

As much as she thought the King would love her to death about this new revelation, he was anything but excited, saying how she did it provided him with nothing of strategic value. The fact was she could do it, and he needed to combat three elements of an enemy. He also said the Queen was kidding herself if she thought they had seen the strength of the woman. He finished by saying it didn't matter to him what she threw against him, he meant to be the one to pierce her black heart.

The cooks had gone around announcing sup and the King said he would be eating alone with his commanders and his Own, and that he would appreciate it if the Queen would host Kristen, John David, soldiers by the names of Darin Michaels and Antonio Martinez, a medic named Sharon Willa and anyone else she thought deserved it in the Command tent. She said she would.

Melanie went to Marie and passed the buck, included her request of her Own, entirely, and Marcus, and headed to the Command tent to greet each as they entered, grabbing Kristen and John David on the way.

During the walk, Kristen informed the Queen that John David would be leaving them as soon as the walls were down and why.

"I wish I could go with you, John David," Melanie said, "I dislike violence myself, but I cannot ask these men to do my work. This woman uses people in the worst way and I must put an end to it."

"It has been an honor to meet you, My Queen. I must admit, I knew the time would come when I would be discovered and I fully expected to have to fight for my life, but my friend insisted that if I would just meet you, then that suspicion would be quelled. I trusted my friend, so I came with her. When she saw that female commander in the battle for her life though, she just charged without a word and left me standing there all by my lonesome. I had just come down to say goodbye, but as it turned out my friends were a little hungry, so we stayed for a snack."

"Kristen is a wonderful young lady and you could do much worse for a friend," Melanie said, "And I hope one day, I will be so honored to be considered a friend of you both, but until then please accept my invitation to visit at your leisure."

Melanie stopped, stunned. Kristen had no bandages, no bruise, and not so much as a scar. "That is amazing."

"Mother, please. Do not ask this of me. It is painful and drains me."

"Ask what?"

"To cure the injured," Kristen answered.

"No chance. Each one of those men and women represent one person that won't die. They are too injured to go on, so they can't come with, and therefore won't die. I don't suppose I can convince you to go with John David?"

"My place is with you, Mother."

"That's what I thought."

When they got to the command tent, no one had yet arrived, for which she was thankful so that she could greet them individually. She hadn't said anything to the King, but she felt he could have waited for his strategy meeting until after sup and been here himself to thank those that needed to be commended, and why was he so cold to her?

The King sat alone at the stream, tossing stones, and absorbing the news he had learned from the outlaws. The commander of the City Watch of the Landing had been turned. The attempt on His Holiness was known, as well as the attempt on the Queen. However, the relationship of that commander and the Queen's daughter was not. The King had been told, but he had no time to deal with it as the Queen was walking toward the enemy when he was told. This was ill news. He suddenly feared for the High Counselor. He knew he had to tell the Queen of his fear.

His commanders sat beside him having brought him some sup and he knew he needed to eat, but his appetite wasn't there so he mainly just picked. The commanders just sat silently and ate, knowing when he was ready to talk he would, and they were right. "I worry for the High Counselor," he finally said.

"What's a High Counselor?" asked Commander Fryman.

"It is a new position aimed at ending teen suicide and eventually all. She is quite good." answered Commander Crawford. "Why so, Highness?"

"She and the commander of the City Watch are at odds and with him turned, it does not bode well for her."

"She has six guards, Highness," said Crawford.

"And he has a thousand," the King responded.

"No," said Crawford, "They are good men, My King. Trust in them."

"I am just not sure how to tell the Queen of my concern, or even if I should," the King said.

Commander Fryman looked at the King and said, "Honesty will keep the relationship you have with her in better standing, and as for how? Words usually work."

The King shot a glance at Fryman, "Don't make me smack you, Amanda."

Sup was a rice mixture of some sort that looked like a rice pilaf, but had a different taste. After seeing it, Melanie realized she was probably restricted to army rations of a sort. The forces, being on a march wouldn't exactly be able to store foodstuffs, and she had closed the area in and any game inside the walls would have been left to the four and six legged allies. This was good, though. It filled her with a certain amount of pride to be eating what the King's men were eating.

The conversation had been light and jovial. There had been no battle bragging or talk of it at all. The female medic, who as it turned out was a settler five years past, had been a stand-up comic on Earth and was displaying her abilities, keeping everyone laughing hysterically. She had to stop at one point as she had Doran laughing so hard he actually choked on his food. For a short time, the medic had stripped all of their worries.

When she had finished eating, Melanie changed seats with William, so she could talk with Marie and asked her what the Own thought of the situation with the wilder women.

"I know how you hope this to end My Queen, but it cannot be. The women are enemies of the realm and the King's responsibility. Beheading is not out of the question, but it is more likely that he will just turn them over to the Sisterhood at Junction City."

"But if I speak with him, surely he will be open, don't you think?"

"I don't believe anything you say will sway him. They are just as responsible as the outlaw prisoners in the deaths of men loyal to him. I am sorry and truly saddened that the play Queen did this to them, but they did commit acts of treason. The Sisterhood is there for a reason, and if they are not guilty they will be found so. It is not for you to decide."

Melanie tried hard to understand what Marie was telling her but it did nothing to ease the knot tightening in the pit of her stomach. These poor girls, having not had freedom of choice, would be punished for something they had been forced to do. Not wanting to ruin the mood, she got up and walked from the tent.

She tried not to look toward the girls or the outlaws, but realized she was not a twelve-year-old and needed to face the issue. The outlaws were eating, but took a knee to her as she walked past. The women saw her coming, sat their plates down and buried their heads in the tarp, surrounded still by the guards.

She walked up to them and told them that they were enemies of the realm and that she wouldn't be able to help them, their fate being in the hands of the King. She will speak with him only about allowing them to see their families. They all began to sob but thanked her for speaking for them.

Melanie saw the King sitting with his commanders at the stream and he appeared very distraught, but it was something she needed to address. She walked toward them and stood waiting a discreet distance to be noticed. Commander Fryman noticed her and the three stood and looked at her.

"I would like to apologize for interrupting your sup," she said, "But I would like to speak with you about the wilder prisoners."

Fryman and Crawford looked silently at the King and buried their heads back in their plates. The King himself looked at her and said, "This is not a topic you want to breach. It will not end as you hope. They killed my men. They are traitors. Killers on Earth were allowed to walk because they were suddenly cured?"

"No, of course not. I am not asking for their freedom, only that they be allowed to see their families before they are sentenced."

"Bunning, Spenser, Adams. They took fireballs through their hearts. Williams lost the left side of his whole body. Four men we weren't even able to identify. No one allowed them to see their families before they died. Do not bring your soft heart into play here, My Queen. They will not walk away from this."

Fury flowed through her. 'Soft heart?' She started screaming, "Retaliation? Revenge? Avenging the fallen? Is that who you are? You call yourself a King? You are no better than they. Kill. Kill. Kill. We are not killers. You have said many times you want to be the one to kill the pretender. Is that how you think? Kill?"

"It is now," he screamed back, "War has been declared. The enemy has been identified, and the enemy will fall. All together or one at a time. It matters little to me."

"You are letting her control the field. You are letting her control you. We are supposed to be the good guys here. You have let her teach you hatred, and she needed no effort. You have allowed yourself to be manipulated like a three-year-old."

"By the Lands of Mother, you will not talk to me this way. You are a housewife from a city on Earth. You have no knowledge of the ways on

Mother and no knowledge of War. Do not profess to me about hatred. We were perfectly content and this was brought upon us."

Sarcasm flowed through Melanie's next words and she couldn't stop it. "She started it. Would you listen to yourself? Do you want me to get you a lollypop?"

The King's eyes were filled with rage as she knew hers were. The screaming had been louder than she thought as the entire encampment had been watching the verbal skirmish. She felt a little embarrassed about the things she had said to the King in front of his men. This was not the place for this. She walked up to him, stood on her tiptoes and kissed him on the cheek, turned and walked away.

"Well," said Commander Fryman, as the Queen was walking away, "That was certainly unexpected."

"Do shut up!" said the King as he turned and walked the other direction, leaving Crawford and Fryman finishing their meal. Both looking as if it was a cool, clear day in wonderland.

The King walked away from everyone, wanting to be alone. Was his Queen right? Had his distaste for the pretender changed who he was? Had he turned into a madman? He didn't want to admit it, but he had found his new Queen to be wise in her views of people. He knew he was only King at her leisure and she could replace him on a whim, but she hadn't. She had, in fact, kissed him which left him perplexed.

She was right, and he knew she was. The outlaws had become enemies simply because they thought they were fighting for someone fearful, someone powerful. It wasn't until they came into contact with the real Queen, that they realized they had feared the wrong woman. They knew what they were doing though, who they were fighting for, but the wilder women had not been in control of their thoughts. They were being driven by her, controlled.

The King had reached the south wall and sat at a tree with his back to it and looked out upon his men. He was proud of these men, as well as his commanders. He was proud of his allies, and very proud of his Queen. The proper and legal thing to do was to turn the wilder women over to the Sisterhood. It was their job to determine guilt and innocence, not his. His Queen had the truth of it. His feelings toward the wilder had turned to hatred and hatred was not an emotion that was healthy to one's soul.

He had over a thousand prisoners and on the new day when the walls came down, if he was not in a battle with other forces waiting without, he would leave a hundred men here with the bodies of the dead soldiers and march everyone else on Junction City. He would get that city under control first, then talk to the Sisterhood about the traitors, and then resume his march on the Pretender that he had dubbed Blackheart. First, he would need to find his Queen and beg her forgiveness.

Melanie was at the edge of the lake with her feet dangling in the stream. Surely the medics wouldn't object to that. The water felt cool on her feet and ran between her toes. What an amazing feeling that was. The Own were with her, but had given her enough space that she had the feeling of being by herself. She had a lot to think about. She had been horrible to Brent and was very ashamed and didn't want anyone trying to make her feel better.

This had not been the first time in her life that she had said awful things to someone who cared about her, but each time she did it, she had felt miserable afterward. He was a good man and he had his men to think of. She knew he could not let the women just walk and never expected him to. Some stipulation should be available though, for what they had been through. Special circumstances were words they had used on Earth in situations like this, but he was right. Killers were not allowed to just walk free, regardless of whether or not there were special circumstances.

A bird landed across from her, one native to Mother. It was pretty but she didn't know what it had been named. It was pecking at the ground maybe looking for worms. Sorry, guy, the stream just hasn't been here long enough for worms yet. She watched as it hopped along merrily, checking here and there for whatever sustenance it could find. It sure had a pretty song. Birds were always good for a distraction. They were very calming to watch. It gave up and flew off and she followed it until it disappeared over the wall.

"You were right," the King said from behind her, "My distaste for Blackheart has left me less than the man I should be. Less a leader and more a tyrant. I apologize for my straying and will strive to be more understanding. That being said, I hope you will accept that I will not be releasing the wilder women. Out of respect for your wisdom, I will not behead them. I will take them to the Sisterhood on the new day, and release them to their care."

She had started putting her socks and shoes on when she heard him speak and now stood and faced him. "It was wrong of me to vent on you in front of your men. You are a good King and it was evil of me to say otherwise. I hope I have not caused you discomfort. I too, am sorry. I will try not to get so enraged, and I of course will abide by your decision. Affairs of the Kingdom are not my place and I was wrong to assume so. Please forgive me."

"Consider it done," he said, "and I would appreciate it if you will me as well."

"Done." She stuck her arm in his for everyone to see and nudged him back to the camp. "I would like to sleep next to the lake tonight, if that is okay?"

"That is a decision for the Own, but I will wager not. There is a small chance of rain, and I am guessing I have lost the command tent after the strategy meeting," he smiled at her. "We can't have you catching a cold and sneezing a hole in Mother."

She laughed, and it felt good. He was right. Marie put an end to the hopes of sleeping by the lake, and she didn't feel like putting up a fight. It was feeling too good to laugh. As they were walking toward the men she noticed strain and tension leaving their faces, being replaced by mirth. She continued to hold on to him all through the camp, and he realized why she was doing it and accepted the display of her esteem.

Sup had pretty much been cleaned up and the men were beginning to leisurely set up bedrolls, and individual fires for warmth, and mingle. It was beginning to look like a massive camp out. They had walked past the outlaws, and she had wondered what would become of them, but she was not about to start that again so she squelched her curiosity. The King was heading at the wilder women and she wasn't sure if she should go with, so she began to slip her hand from his arm but he held it in place.

When they got close, the women went down again, and as prisoners, probably shouldn't be told of the news anyway, so Melanie said nothing to them, and said "Rise" instead. They wouldn't of course, and stayed down until the King also gave them leave to rise.

"Rise," he said and they began to stand, but kept their hands folded in front of them and their heads down. "The rightful Queen of Mother has convinced me not to behead you." The women all began to sob, happily for a change, but did not interrupt. "On the new day, I will be taking you to the Sisterhood at Junction City, and you may make your pleas to them about your family, and I will abide by their decision."

All four women, between sobs began thanking them and went back to their knees and began crawling toward the King and Queen, but the guards rapped their arms with their blades and they went back to the middle of the tarp. The two of them headed off toward the stream.

"I must leave you and gather my commanders and discuss the new day and what we might see when the walls come down. I hope to be finished quickly. The sun has left us and I want everyone well rested, including you. I hope to be at Junction City by mid-morning."

"Oh, my. I didn't realize we were that close."

"Three hours, maybe four." The King freed his arm and headed to where he had left Fryman and Crawford. He had them gather their lieutenants and meet him at the command tent, and he walked toward Kristen and John David.

Melanie felt a little slighted that she wasn't invited, but Marie told her that battle was not something Queens of the past had involved themselves in and since this was the first time war had ever been declared on Mother, there was no clear cut design on how a Queen should be involved. She encouraged Melanie to let the King handle things and Marie would let her know when she was needed. That didn't make her feel any better, especially since Kristen and John David went in with the King. She was jealous, for Pete's sake. This isn't high school. Get over yourself!

The New Day

Melanie sat on her horse, waiting for instructions from Marie. Marcus was beside her and the Own surrounded her. Kristen and her Riggers were at the van and all the King's forces were surrounded by John David's little six legged buddies, none of which were visible. John David himself, sat atop a horse to the right of Kristen and looked as uncomfortable as one could get. She realized she had never seen him do anything but walk. Commander Fryman had the rear guard, and her forces were directly behind Melanie. Commander Crawford sat atop his warhorse to the left of Kristen. The King's forces were in the middle. To the left of the forces were the outlaws and wilder women surrounded by more soldiers.

Kristen raised her arm, and Marie looked at the Queen and said, "Wall to the front only, Highness. When the arm goes down." Kristen's arm fell and Melanie began lowering the wall directly in front of Kristen. The Riggers were jumping and prancing in anticipation, ready to charge.

The wall was all the way down, but nobody was moving. The Riggers continued to jump around and yak, but Melanie could see nothing. The added height of the warhorses made it impossible to see over. Commander Crawford only, began down the small rise she had been asked to position there and weaved his way through the Riggers, which Kristen had begun to calm. The King and his Own, who apparently could see, began working their way forward.

When they reached Kristen, they stopped and everyone there appeared to be awaiting the return of Crawford. Melanie turned to see if Fryman was heading forward, but she was just sitting there with one leg draped over the warhorse and appeared to be filing her nails. *Really?*

The King turned in his saddle and made a couple of strange hand signals and Marie said, "The King requests you ride forward, Majesty." Marie led the way and the procession of fourteen began the move to the front. The soldiers began splitting and they rode right through the column. The column had split all the way to the front and Melanie could finally see.

Thousands upon thousands of soldiers surrounded what must have been fifty wagons. At the front wagon sat Commander Crawford talking to three sisters. He turned and led the wagons over the ruts and stones created by the wall and directed them toward the fallen. The third wagon stopped and one of the sisters stepped out and headed right at Kristen and John David. Panic surged through Melanie and, it appeared Marie as well as her horse bolted forward at a run. Melanie tried to get her's to run, but Donovan had her reins. Then it hit her. She finally understood 'Set them free'. Mother wasn't speaking of the outlaws, nor the yellow eyed wilder. Mother was speaking of the silvers, the oppressed. 'No one touches Mother, but the Queen.'

Marie got there ahead of the walking sister and positioned herself, along with the King and the commander between the sister and the allies. The sister was forced to stop her advance and despite the fact that Melanie had punched Donovan and Phillip, who were the only two she could reach, her pace had not increased in the least, and neither of them seemed to take notice of her punches. She did calm a bit when the sister stopped. The King was now dismounted and talking to her one on one. The sister was listening, but at the same time very interested in Kristen, John David and the Riggers. If she only knew about the graws.

The Queen didn't want to be led to the sister so she jerked her reins and when Donovan looked at her she asked him to let go of the reins and not embarrass her, so he did. She rode calmly and elegantly toward the sister. She looked to the left and saw the bodies being loaded in the wagons and the wilder women were having their feet wrapped and shackled by the sisters. The women were cooperating fully. Good girls. Stay smart. She looked at Marcus and saw his eyes were silver and she said only "Eyes," and he changed them.

They reached the King and the sister had been watching her approach, so the King said, "Sister Rebecca, this is Queen Melanie Thurss, the eighteenth Queen of Mother. My Queen, this is High Sister Rebecca Carey of Junction City."

"Sister Rebecca, it is nice to meet you. How do things fare at Junction City?" Melanie didn't want the first topic to be Kristen or John David.

"There is still much to do, Majesty, but the worst of the storm has passed. The City is safe enough and the Sisterhood would be honored to provide you brunch." The sister glanced again at the allies.

"That is kind of you Sister, but I have saddled the responsibility of getting me to the wilder....." she looked at the King, "...Woman to my captain, so I am at her disposal as it stands."

The sister smiled at Melanie and said, "Tell me, pray. When did we begin to seek wilders to our cause?"

"We have no wilder amongst our group," Melanie said and saw the sister's eyes return to Kristen and John David.

"Avert your eyes Sister, and instead look upon me," Melanie dismounted and walked to the sister, "Tell me, pray. When did the Queen of Mother develop the ability to fill herself while not touching

Mother?" The sister did not appear to be fond of being mimicked, but her eyes went to Melanie's shod feet.

"Marcus?" She said without looking at him. Then she filled herself and her eyes went blue as the sister was looking at them. "The Chronicles will be changed and the scribe that you assign the task will make the change this day. There are now four classifications of people that can merge with Mother. There is your Queen, there is the wilder, there is the Servant of Mother, such as John David Matthews," she pointed with her hand and John David bowed to the sister. "And the fourth are Mother's Children, such as Kristen Muller, and Marcus Landon," she pointed each of them out, and each in turn nodded to the sister.

"Mother's Children are bedtime stories," said the sister. "No one should touch Mother but the Queen."

"Yes, well, how's that been working out for us. Do you think? Your instructions stand. The Chronicles change. This day! And heed me, High Sister. Mother's Children and Servants of Mother are not available for your scrutiny. You should know as well, that His Holiness is a Servant of Mother."

The sister looked at her like she had just spoken blasphemy.

"One other note for the Chronicles. It is impossible for a wilder to have eyes of silver," Melanie put that last part in as a ploy for leniency for the wilder women that would come up after the sisters got them back to Junction. She turned and remounted her horse.

"As for the brunch, you will have to ask my captain, but I thank you for your hospitality should she decline. I understand that recent events have made you suspicious, but do not let this woman defeat us. You are the High Sister of Junction City. All look to you for leadership, not fear." She rode back to position herself amongst the Own. The High Sister turned toward the wagons and walked away.